Quetzalcoatl

D.H. LAWRENCE

Quetzalcoatl

EDITED, WITH AN INTRODUCTION,

BY LOUIS L. MARTZ

A NEW DIRECTIONS BOOK

Author photograph: Lawrence and Frieda in Chapala, 1923. Photo by Witter
Bynner, Photography Collection, Harry Ransom Humanities Research Center,
The University of Texas at Austin. Reproduced by permission of the
Witter Byner Foundation.

Manufactured in the United States of America

New Directions books are printed on acid-free paper

Published simultaneously in Canada by Penguin Books Canada

First published clothbound in 1995 by Black Swan Books. First published
paperbound in 1998 as New Directions Paperbook 864

Library of Congress Cataloging in Publication Data

Lawrence, D. H. (David Herbert), 1885–1930.
[Plumed serpent]
Quetzalcoatl / D.H. Lawrence ; edited with an introduction by
Louis L. Martz.
p.   cm.
ISBN 0-8112-1385-4
I. Martz, Louis Lohr.   II. Title.
[PR6023.A93P53   1998]
823'.912—dc21   98-14094
                                                         CIP

New Directions Books are published for James Laughlin
by New Directions Publishing Corporation
80 Eighth Avenue, New York 10011

Lawrence and Frieda in Chapala, 1923
Photo by Witter Bynner

CONTENTS

INTRODUCTION

Quetzalcoatl was the title Lawrence wanted to give to his Mexican novel, but his new publisher, Knopf, objected to the strange name of the Aztec god. "I did so want to call it 'Quetzalcoatl,'" Lawrence writes, "but they all went into a panic – and they want the translation – *The Plumed Serpent* – I suppose they'll have to have it – but sounds to me rather millinery" (*Letters,* V, 254). In presenting the early version of this novel we have returned to Lawrence's own title, since this more strongly accords with the rich native texture of the book.

When Lawrence wrote from Chapala (Mexico) to his German mother-in-law, he spoke of the work that he was writing as "*die erste volle Skizze*" – "the first complete sketch" (*Letters,* IV, 450-57). The word "sketch" is appropriate, for this revised early manuscript is truly analogous to an artist's careful and detailed drawing made as a design for a larger oil painting. Such drawings frequently have integrity and value in their own right; sometimes, through their fluency and grace of line, they come to be valued even beyond the contemplated final work. The version of the novel here presented certainly has such integrity and value. Although it is rough in places, it creates its own effect of completeness. It presents, in terms as different as crayon is from oil, a closely related, but different work, when compared with *The Plumed Serpent.*

This version is not exactly the "first rough draft" that Lawrence several times described in his letters of May and June of 1923, while he was writing the novel at Lake Chapala. It is a partially revised and corrected version of his original draft, with the equivalent of thirty pages totally revised by crossing out long passages and interlining the revision in his typically neat hand. Beyond this extensive re-writing Lawrence made hundreds of smaller, but significant revisions, ranging from a single word or phrase to passages of six or seven lines, and even to one long addition of fifteen lines at the end of chapter XVIII: the symbolic passage on the snake.

It is true that Lawrence in his letters repeats, over and over, that the work is not finished. Writing from the ranch above Taos (New Mexico), a year after he had left Chapala, he says this early version represents a novel that is only "half finished" or "two-thirds done" (*Letters*, V, 75, 128). But Lawrence does not mean that he is planning to add this much as a continuation of the early version; he is planning to expand the whole body of his complete sketch, recasting its emphasis – enlarging it in oils, we might say – thus producing a work almost twice its original size.

Some sixteen months elapsed between the writing at Lake Chapala and the re-writing in Oaxaca, where, after finishing the novel in February 1925, Lawrence suffered a grave illness and hemorrhage from the lungs that brought him close to death. Much had happened – and not only to his health – in the sixteen intervening months, to change Lawrence's attitude toward the world, and toward his wife, Frieda.

They were happy at Chapala, as photographs (see frontispiece) and letters show. "Chapala paradise. Take evening train," Lawrence had telegraphed Frieda on first arriving there (*Letters*, IV, 435). But Frieda longed for her children in England and for her mother in Germany. She kept on urging Lawrence to go back with her for a visit. Lawrence demurred, hesitated, agreed, hesitated again and again, went up by train with her to New York, with the uncertain intent of taking passage to England with her. But at the last moment he refused to go, and Frieda went off alone. Leaving the manuscript of *Quetzalcoatl* with his prospective publisher, Thomas Seltzer, to be typed, Lawrence made his way to Los Angeles, where he joined his friend, the Danish artist Kai Götzsche. Then the two of them went back to Guadalajara and Chapala, over difficult mountain ways, from the West, partly by muleback. But when Lawrence saw Chapala again, all was changed, utterly changed. The landscape and the natives were the same, but one essential element was missing: Frieda. "I went to Chapala for the day yesterday – the lake *so* beautiful," Lawrence writes. "And yet the lake I knew was gone – something gone, and it was alien to me." "I was at Chapala yesterday – It felt strange to me, not the same place" (*Letters*, IV, 519-20). But more than Frieda's absence appears to be involved here. During the two months away from Chapala, Lawrence seems to have developed a different conception of the scene: it was in his imagination no longer "the same place" in which he had written the early version.

He had been planning to finish his novel on this visit. Only a few days earlier he had written to Seltzer: "I must finish 'Quetzalcoatl.' By the way, I want you to read that MS. and tell me just what you think. Because I must go all over it again, and am open to suggestions. This winter I must finish it" (*Letters,* IV, 517). But he found himself so unhappy, so unable to concentrate upon the book, that he spent most of his free time revising the novel *The Boy in the Bush* by his Australian friend, Molly Skinner. So, in November 1923, he booked passage from Vera Cruz to England, where he caught a debilitating "cold" that lasted for weeks. Nevertheless, he and Frieda visited Paris for two weeks and Germany for another two weeks. Finally, in March 1924, they returned to New York and went from there to Taos and the ranch, where they remained for six months before going down to Mexico "in the autumn, to finish 'Quetzalcoatl.'" (*Letters,* V, 45).

During this long stay at Taos and the ranch, Lawrence found himself unable to deal with *Quetzalcoatl;* he seemed to be willing to do almost anything else. He worked hard physically, repairing the buildings on the ranch; he visited ceremonies at Indian reservations; he wrote all of the short and powerful novel *St. Mawr;* he wrote essays and short stories – some of his longest and best. But these were not really evasions: they were ways of preparing his mind to deal with the vast expansion of the Mexican novel in ways that were deeply affected by his "disheartening" winter in Europe.

Lawrence's return to England and the Continent had left him with an increased sense of the decline of the West: his letters express, again and again, his somber conviction that Western civilization, as he had known it, was doomed. Europe, he wrote, "seems to me weary and wearying" (*Letters,* IV, 597). He had felt some kind of stirring in depressed Germany, exactly what he did not know, but he saw in that stirring some embers of a new energy, to which he gave an optimistic turn (true prophets cannot live without hope). Back now in Mexico, at Oaxaca, in the fall of 1924, he was able to work steadily on his novel. But now he felt much more strongly what he had felt before coming to America: his conviction that only a new religious revival could bring life again to the Western world – a life that might arise from the native soil of America and burst through the imported crust of European modes of life and thought, to create a new era of human existence. And so, as he made his final revision, he added the long sermons of Ramón, leader of the new religious movement, prophet and "manifestation" of the Aztec fertility god, Quetzalcoatl – sermons composed in the style of the biblical prophets. He increased the number and length of the songs and hymns of Quetzalcoatl. He expanded the rituals and symbols of this religious movement. He added long conversations and disquisitions on philosophical, theological, political, and even biological themes. Through these additions, and through many paragraphs and pages of his own ruminations, Lawrence attempted to create a complete mythology for his new religion, combining the sensual and the spiritual, the sexual and the divine, the religious and the political, in a mass-movement led by an inspired, indomitable religious leader, accompanied by a powerful military figure – the "manifestation" of the Aztec war-god, Huitzilopochtli.

This is a movement that salutes its leader by raising the right arm straight up toward the sky, palm level with the ground: not quite either the Fascist or the Communist gesture, but close enough to be menacing to readers of our time. Yet Lawrence was writing in 1923–25; he knew nothing of Hitler. He knew, however, what was happening in Russia, and he knew at first hand what was happening in Italy, for he had been living there in the early 1920s, and he did not like what he saw. In his novel *St. Mawr,* written in the summer of 1924 (*between* the early and the final versions of his Mexican novel), Lawrence stops the action for three pages (78–80) in which his heroine, Lou Witt, has "a vision of evil . . . rolling in great waves over the earth":

> The evil! The mysterious potency of evil. . . . There it was in socialism and bolshevism: the same evil. But bolshevism made a mess of the outside of life, so turn it down. Try fascism. Fascism would keep the surface of life intact, and carry on the undermining business all the better. . . .
>
> And as soon as fascism makes a break – which it is bound to, because all evil works up to a break – then turn it down. With gusto, turn it down.

"What's to be done?" asks the authorial voice, and answers: "Generally speaking, nothing. The dead will have to bury their dead, while the earth stinks of corpses. The individual can but depart from the mass, and try to cleanse himself." This thought foreshadows Lou Witt's retreat to the ranch above Taos (Lawrence's own ranch), to preserve her individual soul. Such an assertion of individual integrity closely links Lou Witt with the heroine of *Quetzalcoatl.*

Why, then, did he create this mass-movement under Don Ramón? Lawrence had apparently sensed in Europe a despair that would lead to the acceptance or the welcoming of a hypnotic Leader as a last resort. His prophetic sense was to this extent true; he saw as well the potential danger in the cult of the Leader accompanied by a General, for he makes both figures express fierce anger, bitter hatred, and an urge toward violent destruction – tendencies that are held under control by the religious faith of Don Ramón, as we can see from their conversations in both versions of the novel.

But *Quetzalcoatl* provides a much more powerful questioning of this mass-movement by filtering the account of its rise through the central consciousness of the heroine, Kate Burns, Irish widow of a failed Irish patriot, a woman of strong individuality who has lost faith in political revolutions. She watches with a mixture of fascination, revulsion, and sympathy as this religious movement takes shape, but she does not agree to do the three things that she does in *The Plumed Serpent:* she does not agree to marry General Cipriano Viedma; she does not agree to become the manifestation of the rain-goddess, Malintzi (or "Malinchi," as she is called in chapter XIII of *Quetzalcoatl*); and, most important, she does not agree to stay in Mexico. In the final version, despite her many doubts and disagreements, in the end she reluctantly submits to "manhood": she marries the general, accepts the role of Malintzi, and ends the novel by pleading with the general: "You won't let me go."

* * *

The differences between the two versions of the novel become clear in two chapters dealing with the hymns of Quetzalcoatl: chapter IX of the early version and chapter XV of the later. In both versions the preceding chapter has closed with the ugly incident in which Kate attempts to rescue a helpless bird in the water from the mischievous attacks of two little "urchins" who are stoning the limp creature. Her failure to save the bird brings to a climax her feelings of revulsion against the ugly, sordid aspects of native life, to the extent that in both versions she declares that she will leave Mexico. In the final version, however, her declaration is restrained and tentative: "'But the day will come when I shall go away,' she said to herself." In *Quetzalcoatl* she speaks violently, twice: "'I've had enough of this,' she said rising. 'I'm going back to Europe.'" And again, in the last words of the chapter: "'I loathe Mexico. I loathe it. I'm going back to England.'"

In the early version the next chapter begins abruptly with a passage that shows why she becomes more sympathetic to the movement of Ramón and indeed comes seriously to consider staying in Mexico as the novel develops. The passage is a complete rendition of the first hymn of Quetzalcoatl, telling of the god's temporary departure from Mexico and his replacement by Jesus and Mary. In the early version this is the first hymn that has appeared in the novel thus far, although Kate, in an earlier scene at the Plaza (chapter V), has watched a mysterious group of men listening to an Indian "singing alone in a low voice to the sound of a mellow guitar." She does not hear the words and she has no idea what the gathering is all about, until her cousin Owen manages to discover that it has something to do with the new religion of Quetzalcoatl. As the hymn now bursts upon us, without singer or prelude, we assume that this must be something related to the singer in the Plaza, and soon we sense that this is so, for we learn that at the housekeeper's end of the house "two men were singing to one guitar." This "was the second or third night that there had been singing, and the same music, the same words." Kate moves toward the singers but does not hear the actual words. The singers are Rafael and Francisco – Rafael being one of the housekeeper Felipa's sons, and Francisco a cousin who has recently come to the house with his fourteen-and-a-half-year-old bride – an actual event during Lawrence's stay in Chapala. Lawrence needs Francisco to play the guitar and lead the singing since none of the other members of Felipa's household have such ability.

We can see Lawrence's exploratory way of writing here. He has already had Kate sit down to hear the singing, but now he writes a second setting, without removing the first. "It was Francisco who played the guitar and sang. Kate tried to persuade him to sit on her verandah and sing. But he was too shy. One night, however, when the electric light had given out," Kate hears the singing again, as "the voices of the two men rose in a queer rapid chant, Rafael, in his throaty voice, singing seconds as spasmodic as the wind in the mango trees" – "seconds" being the technical term for an accompanying (usually lower) tone. Now she is listening "alone in her open sala . . . But she didn't want to go nearer. In the morning, however, she told Felipa that she liked the singing, and asked what the songs were about: if they were love songs." Felipa says "No-o, No-o," but is reluctant to say what they are. However, she finally says that they are "the Mexican hymns . . . About the two gods." "The second evening of the singing Kate was still too shy to join the group at the far end of the house. She felt they didn't want her. But the third evening she went," and bluntly asked, "Tell me what the words are." Again, we find the reluctance to reveal the mysterious subject of Quetzalcoatl. But finally "the trumpet-like voice of Rafael" begins to recite the hymn we have just read, with prompting from the others when he breaks down. Assuming that readers know the hymn, Lawrence gives only fragments. "'And is that all?' asked Kate. 'Yes Señora. Of this hymn, this is all.'" There are more hymns, then, to be heard.

But instead of more singing Lawrence gives now a long and appealing conversation about Jesus and Mary as "gringo" and "gringuita," couched in a child-like language. The conversation includes a passage that indicates, as earlier hints have done, that Kate may be destined to become some sort of divinity in Mexico, for a rumor says "Quetzalcoatl has a wife, and they say she is a gringuita from over there." "'She will be like the Niña,' said Felipa confidently." Kate, embarrassed, turns the attention back to the hymns and asks them to sing another. "Rafael took his mouth-organ . . . and played a queer, sobbing kind of music," while "Francisco struck the same pulsing tune out of his guitar." Then the two men sing as a duet the beginnings of a second hymn of Quetzalcoatl concerning the "heavy souls" of the Mexicans. A pause prepares for the entry of a spoken voice "grave and remote," the voice of the Father, the ultimate power that guides the destinies of both Quetzalcoatl and Jesus. This trio tells the tale of angry, disordered Mexico, a land without a god, without a leader. "We could not get to heaven on the wings of love," they sing. "We are angry souls in the world." The grave voice of the Father promises to send Quetzalcoatl and tells Jesus and Mary to "come home." A painful lament by Felipa is interrupted:

> But there was a noise at the gate, and everybody started.
> "Who is it?" cried Rafael.
> "Jesús!"

It is of course Felipa's son, Jesús, who (symbolically) tends the faltering power plant of the village. Lawrence's droll humor here serves to emphasize the way in which the name of the savior is always present with these people, and they need a savior. Now they sing for Kate the short song of "the coming of Quetzalcoatl," as Jesús, son of Felipa, takes the role of Quetzalcoatl. Dead silence follows the abrupt ending of the song; everyone quietly leaves; and Kate ponders the meaning of the scene in the long passage that ends the chapter:

> Kate went down to her room, wondering. What did these people believe, and what didn't they? So queer to talk of Jesus and Mary as if they were the two most important people in the village, living in the biggest house, the church. Was it religion, or wasn't it?

For her "the world seemed to have become bigger, as if she saw through the opening of a tent a vast, unknown night outside." And the chapter closes with the words: "Life had taken on another gesture altogether." From beginning to end of this chapter, Kate is the receiver of the songs, the center of the conversation, her mind the focus of the action.

In the corresponding chapter of *The Plumed Serpent,* the situation is utterly different. The chapter heading tells it all: "The *Written* Hymns of Quetzalcoatl." The hymns here no longer create the effect of arising uncertainly and gradually from native life, accompanied by native instruments. The hymns are now being circulated on printed sheets throughout the land. Kate has already read one of them in the earlier scene at the Plaza (chapter VII), where singers render it in the circle of the men of Quetzalcoatl, after an old Indian sage has delivered a long, lyrical sermon about the coming of Quetzalcoatl. Now the little group at Kate's house is listening to the hymns as they are read by Julio (formerly Francisco), an educated newcomer who reads first the hymn that has been so slowly extracted from the group by Kate's questioning. After a shortened version of the naive conversation about Jesus and Mary (which omits the comic interruption by the entry of "Jesús"), Julio reads the "second" hymn, which now covers two-and-a-half pages. At the end of this the chapter closes with one abrupt sentence: "There was silence as the young man finished reading." Kate's long rumination over the meaning of religion among the Indians is gone: her responses are no longer at the center of the book. Ramón's presence, through the written hymns which he has composed, now dominates the scene: he speaks directly to us, without a questioning intermediary.

In *Quetzalcoatl* the atmosphere of song, arising naturally in an oral civilization, has been carefully prepared by the setting at the close of the long chapter V, mainly devoted to description of the household in Chapala and native life on the village plaza, where singing to the guitar and violin is part of daily life:

> The tall, handsome men, with sarape over one shoulder, proudly, lounged and strolled about, standing to listen to the singers, of whom there were usually two or three groups. A couple of young men, with different-sized guitars, stood facing each other like two fighting cocks, their guitars almost touching, and they strummed rapidly, intensely, singing in restrained voices the eternal ballads, not very musical, endless, intense, not very audible, and really mournful, to a degree, keeping it up for hours, till their throats were scraped! In among the food-booths would be another trio, one with a fiddle, keeping on at a high pitch and full speed, yet not very loud.

The singer of the Quetzalcoatl legend thus forms part of this tradition of "the eternal ballads."

This passage, slightly altered, appears also in *The Plumed Serpent* (113–14), as part of chapter VII, wholly devoted to "The Plaza." But here the account of village life, covering the first third of the chapter, is suddenly invaded by "a new sound, the sound of a drum, or tom-tom," toward which the peons are drifting:

> There was a rippling and a pulse-like thudding of the drum, strangely arresting on the night air, then the long note of a flute playing a sort of wild, unemotional melody, with the drum for a syncopated rhythm. Kate, who had listened to the drums and the wild singing of the Red Indians in Arizona and New Mexico, instantly felt that timeless, primeval passion of the prehistoric races, with their intense and complicated religious significance, spreading on the air. (*PS,* 117)

The ritual, then, is not native to Chapala: Ramón and Cipriano, we later learn, have imported the drums from the North, as part of Lawrence's transformation of the scene into the mythical village and lake named Sayula in *The Plumed Serpent* (the actual name of a much smaller lake in the region). Here, as the drum gives forth its "blood-rhythm," Kate notices men "giving little leaflets to the onlookers"; she receives one and finds on it "a sort of ballad, but without rhyme, in Spanish," while "at the top of the leaflet was a rough print of an eagle within the ring of a serpent that had its tail in its mouth" (*PS,* 118). Lawrence then provides the poem, Quetzalcoatl's song of his coming back to replace Jesus in Mexico. Next, as "the drum was beating a slow, regular thud, acting straight on the blood," the crowd assembles in silence to hear the long lyrical sermon of the Indian sage, telling in biblical language and cadences the full legend of the god's return. Various voices then take up the song printed in the leaflet, and finally the whole company moves into a ritual pattern, "dancing the savage bird-tread" (*PS*, 128). Kate cannot resist the invitation of an unknown man to join in the dance, and she does so, gradually losing her sense of individuality:

> She felt her sex and her womanhood caught up and identified in the slowly revolving ocean of nascent life, the dark sky of the men lowering and wheeling above. She was not herself, she was gone, and her own desires were gone in the ocean of the great desire. As the man whose fingers touched hers was gone in the ocean that is male, stooping over the face of the waters. (*PS*, 131)

Already, only a quarter of the way into *The Plumed Serpent*, it is clear that Kate will not be able to resist the spell of the men of Quetzalcoatl.

Equally important, the scene here shows that the religion of the returned god is fully developed, with its costume, symbols, ritual, sermons, and poetry. But in *Quetzalcoatl* Lawrence tells us in chapter XI, more than half-way through the novel, that the religious movement "is only just in its infancy." We watch its growth as it arises gradually from the native soil and enters into Kate's consciousness. Ramón, in the early version, seems almost like an emanation from the scene, a "dark-skinned" man of the native race (see end of chapter III) – whereas in *The Plumed Serpent* he is lighter in hue and to Kate "he feels European" (*PS*, 237).

The basic difference between the two versions is evident in the two different accounts of Kate's first visit to Ramón's hacienda, given the symbolic name Las Yemas ("the buds") in the early version, but changed to Jamiltepec in the final version, presumably for the more indigenous effect of the name. In *Quetzalcoatl* (chapter VI) Kate climbs up to a balcony, and as she turns "to look out at the water," she hears "the sound of a guitar, and a man singing in a full, rich voice, a curious music." The single voice is succeeded by "the sound of guitars and violins," while "four or five men started singing." Don Ramón, playing on his guitar, is leading his men in what he calls "the music lesson" – they are practicing a song, with laughter and high spirits. Here again, under the influence of the lake, the music of Quetzalcoatl is beginning to arise from a domestic scene with native instruments.

These are "the buds" of the movement.

In *The Plumed Serpent* no such scene occurs. Kate is ushered into the presence of Ramón's wife, Carlota, and offered a place to rest:

> As she lay resting, she heard the dulled thud-thud of the tom-tom drum, but, save the crowing of a cock in the distance, no other sound on the bright, yet curiously hollow Mexican morning. And the drum, thudding with its dulled, black insistence, made her uneasy. It sounded like something coming over the horizon. (*PS*, 163)

Carlota, it soon appears, hates the sound of the drum and all it signifies; when Kate asks, "Is Don Ramón drumming?" Carlota cries out, "No! Oh, no! He is not drumming, himself. He brought down two Indians from the north to do that" (*PS*, 164). And she proceeds to denounce bitterly her husband's effort to revive the old gods. With the focus thus shifted to Don Ramón's enterprise, the next three chapters (XI–XIII) are dominated by the words and actions of Ramón and his followers.

In chapter XI of the final version, "Lords of the Day and Night," Kate is removed from the action, as we watch Ramón praying alone in his room, then visiting the workmen on his estate, as they forge in iron the symbol of Quetzalcoatl: "The bird within the sun" (*PS*, 171). Kate and Ramón's wife briefly come upon the scene, but only to get the key to the boat which will take them away for a row upon the lake. Ramón now visits the artist who is carving his head in wood, and here, as Ramón sits for the sculptor, we are given the fully developed features of the religion of Quetzalcoatl: the prophetic leader, the ritual gestures, the transfer of power from master to disciple:

> The artist gazed with wonder, and with an appreciation touched with fear. The other man, large and intense, with big dark eyes staring with intense pride, yet prayerful, beyond the natural horizons, sent a thrill of dread and of joy through the artist. He bowed his head as he looked.
>
> Don Ramón turned to him.
>
> "Now you!" he said.
>
> The artist was afraid. He seemed to quail. But he met Ramón's eyes. And instantly, that stillness of concentration came over him, like a trance. And then suddenly, out of the trance, he shot his arm aloft, and his fat, pale face took on an expression of peace, a noble, motionless transfiguration, the blue-grey eyes calm, proud, reaching into the beyond, with prayer. (*PS*, 173)

Then Ramón visits the shed where his people are weaving a sarape that presents a more elaborate symbol of the movement: "a snake with his tail in his mouth, the black triangles on his back being the outside of the circle: and in the middle, a blue eagle standing erect, with slim wings touching the belly of the snake with their tips, and slim feet upon the snake, within the hoop" (*PS,* 174). So the way is prepared for Ramón to beat the drum, call his disciples together, and begin the service of Quetzalcoatl.

> They sat in silence for a time, only the monotonous, hypnotic sound of the drum pulsing, touching the inner air. Then the drummer began to sing, in the curious, small, inner voice, that hardly emerges from the circle, singing in the ancient falsetto of the Indians:
> "Who sleeps – shall wake! Who sleeps – shall wake! Who treads down the path of the snake shall arrive at the place; in the path of the dust shall arrive at the place and be dressed in the skin of the snake –"
> One by one the voices of the men joined in, till they were all singing in the strange, blind infallible rhythm of the ancient barbaric world. And all in the small, inward voices, as if they were singing from the oldest, darkest recess of the soul, not outwards, but inwards, the soul singing back to herself. (*PS,* 175)

In the next chapter Kate, too, feels the powerful spell of Ramón, standing and sitting there "naked to the waist," in a passage that further diminishes her individual being:

> "Ah!" she said to herself. "Let me close my eyes to him, and open only my soul. Let me close my prying, *seeing* eyes, and sit in dark stillness along with these two men. They have got more than I, they have a richness that I haven't got. They have got rid of that itching of the eye, and the desire that works through the eye. The itching, prurient, *knowing,* imagining eye, I am cursed with it, I am hampered up in it. It is my curse of curses, the curse of Eve. The curse of Eve is upon me, my eyes are like hooks, my knowledge is like a fish-hook through my gills, pulling me in spasmodic desire. Oh, who will free me from the grappling of my eyes, from the impurity of sharp sight! Daughter of Eve, of greedy vision, why don't these men save me from the sharpness of my own eyes – !" (*PS,* 184)

This is Lawrence at his least attractive – but none of this is in *Quetzalcoatl.*

In *The Plumed Serpent* Ramón, as the mythic representative of Quetzalcoatl, seems to have power even over the elements of earth and sky, for the rituals, the drumming, the songs, and the long sermon of

Ramón that follows in chapter XIII ("The First Rain") seem to evoke the thunder, lightning, and tropical downpour that ends this long central sequence of three chapters.

> Even as he spoke the wind rose, in sudden gusts, and a door could be heard slamming in the house, with a shivering of glass, and the trees gave off a tearing sound.
> "Come then, Bird of all the great sky!" Ramón called wildly. "Come! Oh Bird, settle a moment on my wrist, over my head, and give me power of the sky, and wisdom." (*PS*, 198)

Soon, after more of Ramón's sermon, the rain comes.

All this symbolizes the change that is coming over the land through the religious power of Ramón, "Lord of the Two Ways," downward and upward, uniting earth and sky and men and women in one irresistible unity, where the women are always subordinate to the rediscovered manhood of the followers of Quetzalcoatl, with their ominous celebration of the Leader.

> In low, deep, inward voices, the guard of Quetzalcoatl began to speak, in heavy unison:
> "*Oye! Oye! Oye! Oye!*"
> The small, inset door within the heavy doors of the church opened and Don Ramón stepped through. In his white clothes, wearing the Quetzalcoatl sarape, he stood at the head of his two rows of guards, until there was a silence. Then he raised his naked right arm.
> "What is God, we shall never know!" he said, in a strong voice, to all the people.
> The guard of Quetzalcoatl turned to the people, thrusting up their right arm.
> "What is God, we shall never know!" they repeated.
> Then again, in the crowd, the words were re-echoed by the guard of Huitzilopochtli.
> After which there fell a dead silence, in which Kate was aware of a forest of black eyes glistening with white fire.

"With his words," Lawrence adds, "Ramón was able to put the power of his heavy, strong will over the people. The crowd began to fuse under his influence" (*PS*, 336–37).

No one who has heard the roar of Nazi rallies or has seen the staged rituals of Hitlerism can avoid wincing here. But we know, as I have said, that Lawrence hated Fascism: Cipriano himself scorns it in *Quetzalcoatl* (chapter XV), calling Fascism a "great bully movement." *The Plumed Serpent* attempts to suggest that such mass-movements may be controlled and justified by religious belief. But in the early version of the novel, the questioning presence of Kate suggests that the European consciousness ultimately cannot accept such primitive mass-movements, although near the close, in the climactic chapter XVIII, she comes very close to accepting a role in the movement, as Ramón, in the strange initiation ritual, puts upon her all the immense pressure of his mysterious rhetoric. His long symbolical sermon here may well strike us as an abrupt and alien intrusion upon the native scene, for its terms are derived from the sort of occult theosophy that Lawrence had become familiar with in England. And indeed the appearance of this episode may be due to the accidental impact of an outside force: the arrival of the manuscript of Frederick Carter's theosophical and astrological treatise, *The Dragon of the Apocalypse,* on June 15, 1923, just as Lawrence was nearing the conclusion of his "rough draft." Lawrence at once read the treatise; his long letter to Carter on June 18 and the Introduction that he later wrote for a version of the treatise show how deeply he was impressed by it. The ending of Lawrence's letter indeed contains the essence of Ramón's sermon: "I should like to see the end of this Return. The end of the Little Creation of the Logos. A fresh start, in the first great direction, with the polarity downwards, as it was in the great pre-Greek Aeons, all Egypt and Chaldea" (*Letters,* IV, 461).

Nevertheless, the episode has its important function: it reveals the religious depths of Ramón's mission and represents the ultimate appeal of primitive symbols to Kate's sophisticated European consciousness. She very reluctantly and with intense fear drinks from the cup of wine that is pressed upon her, but she at once shudders away into the solitude of her room and renounces the implied pledge. "'I can't!' said Kate, standing rigid before the window, 'I can't! I can't! I can't!'" And she does not: she refuses to marry Cipriano and carries out her resolve to return to England. She does not promise to return to Mexico, although that possibility is left open.

Thus the entire development of the early version remains true to the principle of open-ended weaving that Cipriano explains (chapter X) to Kate in their first serious discussion of her remaining in Mexico. He explains what he has found wrong in England: that it was "all made and finished." Then he presents his central metaphor, drawn from Indian life in the north; but here the image is a blanket, not a drum:

"You know the Navajo women, the Indian women, when they weave blankets, weave their souls into them. So at the end they leave a place, some threads coming down to the edge, some loose threads where their souls can come out. And it seems to me your country has woven its soul into its fabrics and its goods and its books, and never left a place for the soul to come out. So all the soul is in the goods, in the books, and in the roads and ways of life, and the people are finished like finished sarapes, that have no faults and nothing beyond. Your women have no threads into the beyond. Their pattern is finished and they are complete."

Kate objects that she is Irish, not English, and Cipriano concedes that she may be different.

"I did not say that every English woman, or Irish woman, was finished and finished off. But they wish to be. They do not like their threads into the beyond. They quickly tie the threads and close the pattern. In your women the pattern is usually complete and closed, at twenty years."

"And in Mexico there is no pattern – it is all a tangle," said Kate.

"The pattern is very beautiful, while there are threads into the unknown, and the pattern is never finished. The Indian patterns are never *quite* complete. There is always a flaw at the end, where they break into the beyond – nothing is more beautiful to me than a pattern which is lovely and perfect, when it breaks at the end imperfectly on to the unknown –"

Kate says, "rather venomously," "Well, it may be I am old, and my pattern is finished." And he replies, "You are not old . . . and your pattern is not finished. Your true pattern has yet to be woven." The early version of this novel is the story of the weaving of Kate's pattern. In *The Plumed Serpent* this conversation about the blanket is reduced to one-fifth of its original length, and it is applied to the weaving of Mexico's soul, not Kate's (*PS*, 234).

Such an open design is quite in accord with the view that Lawrence describes in his angry letter to Carlo Linati in January 1925, just as he had nearly finished *The Plumed Serpent*. "Well well, in a world so anxious for outside tidiness, the critics will tidy me up, so I needn't bother. Myself, I don't care a button for neat works of art":

But really, Signor Linati, do you think that books should be sort of toys, nicely built up of observations and sensations, all finished and complete? – I don't. To me, even Synge, whom I admire very much indeed, is a bit too rounded off and, as it were, put on the shelf to be looked at. I can't bear art that you can walk round and admire. . . . You need not complain that I don't subject the intensity of my vision – or whatever it is – to some vast and imposing rhythm – by which you mean, isolate it on to a stage so that you can look down on it like a god who has got a ticket to the show. . . . But whoever reads me will be in the thick of the scrimmage, and if he doesn't like it – if he wants a safe seat in the audience – let him read somebody else. (*Letters*, V, 200–201)

The early version of his novel fits this description better than *The Plumed Serpent,* with Kate's reluctant acceptance of the religion of Quetzalcoatl. In the early version Kate is at first a spectator, but she plunges into the midst of the scrimmage and carries us with her throughout, until at the close she emerges with her fate not decided but open. On the last page of the early version we find her surrounded by the chattering Felipa and her children, yet "Under these trying circumstances Kate tried to get on with her packing." It is a typical Lawrentian open end. The religion of Quetzalcoatl, in this version of the novel, is a myth of the future that the world needs to create, as the soul escapes from the loose threads in the weaving.

The final chapter of the early version sums up the effect of this weaving within Kate, in a springtime scene with all the landscape coming to life after the rains, which have here come on their own, without any association with Ramón. Kate has just returned from a visit with Ramón and the new "dark" Mexican wife, Teresa, whom Ramón has so surprisingly taken. The tender relationship between the two has made Kate a bit jealous: the marriage has the effect of bringing Ramón down to earth. At the same time this episode with Teresa, coming in the next-to-last chapter, has the effect of liberating Kate from Ramón's spell: for in the concluding chapter Ramón is nowhere present. Kate stands alone looking at the springtime scene; she feels refreshed, she feels renewed strength and vision:

> The lake had come alive with the rains, the air had come to life, the sky was silver and white and grey, with distant blue. There was something soothing and, curiously enough, paradisal about it, even the pale, dove-brown water. She could not remember any longer the dry rigid pallor of the heat, like memory gone dry and sterile, hellish. A boat was coming over with its sail hollowing out like a shell, pearly white, and its sharp black canoe-beak slipping past the water. It looked like the boat of Dionysos crossing the seas and bringing the sprouting of the vine.

The mythical touch prepares the way for the brilliantly presented scene that follows as the peons urge a cow and "a huge black-and-white bull" into the interior of the boat. The bull is magnificent in his "unutterable calm and weighty poise," as the men urge him toward the boat in ritual, ballet-like movements: "with the loose pauses and the casual, soft-balanced rearrangements at every pause."

> There he stood, huge, silvery and dappled like the sky, with snake-dapples down his haunches, looming massive way above the red hatches of the roof of the canoe. How would such a great beast pass that low red roof and drop into that hole? It seemed impossible.

And then in the end he leaps down to join the cow, and the boat moves off "softly on the water, with her white sail in a whorl like the boat of Dionysos, going across the lake. There seemed a certain mystery in it. When she thought of the great dappled bull upon the waters, it seemed mystical to her."

The symbolism is clear: the men have captured, with ritual reverence, the very principle of potency. The wretched bull-fight, with its "stupid" bulls, that formed the novel's opening chapter has been redeemed by recognition of a divinity that looms within this noble creature once worshipped by the ancients. The incident is retained in the middle of the last chapter of *The Plumed Serpent*, along with details of the earlier springtime scene, but it is placed in November and surrounded by the presence of Ramón. Thus the mythological power of the symbolic bull is associated with Ramón, along with the other activities of nature.

In the springtime scene of *Quetzalcoatl*, Kate sees everywhere the signs of creative life: "A roan horse, speckled with white, was racing prancing along the shore, and neighing frantically." "A mother-ass" has just given birth to a foal, and Kate watches the foal rise on its "four loose legs."

> Then it hobbled a few steps forward, to smell at some growing green maize. It smelled and smelled and smelled, as if all the aeons of green juice of memory were striving to awake. Then it turned round, looked straight towards Kate with its bushy-velvet face, and put out a pink tongue at her. She broke into a laugh. It stood wondering, lost in wonder. Then it put out its tongue at her again. And she laughed again, delighted. It gave an awkward little new skip, and was so surprised and rickety, having done so. It ventured forward a few steps, and unexpectedly exploded into another little skip, itself most surprised of all by the event.

It seems almost the perfect image of Kate's own rebirth. She is leaving Mexico, but the "green juice" of the memory of what she has witnessed will stay with her. Her whole Mexican experience now seems like a myth of Dionysos, the fiction of a possibility. It is almost as though she had dreamed the whole experience, in answer to her need. That is why the memories of her life in England have, in the preceding chapter, come back so strongly to her. England, however "finished," is her reality, just as the enduring memory of her beloved husband remains with her until the end, helping to draw her home.

* * *

One of the most significant differences between the two versions lies in Lawrence's treatment of Kate's married life. In *Quetzalcoatl* she has one husband (the father of her two children), bearing the simple Scotch-Irish name Desmond Burns. In the final version she has two husbands, the first of whom she remembers with respect but not with love, and by this divorced husband she has had her two children. Then she marries an Irish patriot bearing the name James Joachim Leslie, a symbolic name that suggests James the apostle, as well as Joachim the father of Mary and the medieval mystic and prophet, Joachim of Flora, in whom Lawrence was deeply interested. So the second husband bears the aura of an evangelist and a prophet, whereas Desmond Burns is a beloved man – no more than man.

One of the most moving scenes in *Quetzalcoatl* is found in the third chapter when Kate, in the midst of a dinner-party, breaks down weeping before all the company at the memory of her dead husband. She never loses that link with her past: again, in the middle of chapter XII, she weeps bitterly at the memory of her husband's failure and death. The earlier incident of her weeping is retained in *The Plumed Serpent,* but here it occurs only in the presence of Cipriano and thus serves to indicate the possibility of a closer relation between the two.

To prepare for Kate's acceptance of Cipriano, Lawrence has made a drastic change in his treatment of the general. In the third chapter of *Quetzalcoatl* we hear the story of how, when he was a small boy, he saved the life of the mistress of his hacienda by sucking out the poison of a snake that had bitten her, with the result that she sent him to England to be educated. "Oh, by the way," says Owen in reporting the story, "beware he doesn't bite you, because the natives have a superstition that his bite is poisonous." This image of the snake reaches its climax in the latter part of chapter XVIII. In the initiation-ritual, as Kate is about to drink the wine, she feels Cipriano's "black, bright, strange eyes on her face, in a strange smile that seemed to hypnotise her, like a serpent gradually insinuating its folds round her."

And soon her memories of England stress the unlikelihood of her staying in Mexico and marrying the general. Near the close of this chapter, she refuses Cipriano's urgent pressure for her to stay, although she tells him that once she gets to England she may be able to choose. He offers her an old ring, possibly Aztec, with "a flat serpent with scales faintly outlined in black, and a flat green stone in its head." But Kate accepts it only with the understanding that it does not constitute a commitment.

As he rides away she sees him as "The rider on the red horse" – an ominous allusion to the sixth chapter of the Book of Revelation, where "there went out another horse that was red: and power was given to him that sat thereon to take peace from the earth, and that they should kill one another: and there was given unto him a great sword." This is quite in accord with Kate's frequently-expressed fear of Cipriano, and in accord also with the long passage that ends the chapter, where Kate watches a snake withdraw into a hole in the wall:

> The hole could not have been very large, because when it had all gone in, Kate could see the last fold still, and the flat little head resting on this fold, like the devil with his chin on his arms looking out of a loop-hole in hell. There was the little head looking out at her from that hole in the wall, with the wicked spark of an eye. Making itself invisible. Watching out of its own invisibility. Coiled wickedly on its own disappointment. It was disappointed at its failure to rise higher in creation, and its disappointment was poisonous. Kate went away, unable to forget it.

Cipriano too is disappointed at his failure to convince Kate; his bite too may be poisonous.

In *The Plumed Serpent* this association of the general with the serpent is greatly reduced, to the extent that this passage where the snake withdraws into the wall becomes at the close of chapter XXVI the image of a possible "peace"; "She felt a certain reconciliation between herself and it." This is possible because the story of Cipriano's sucking out the poison from the hacienda's mistress has been removed. Cipriano now, as a boy, was the favorite of an English bishop in Mexico, who sent him to England for his education, in the hope that he might become a priest. "So you see," Cipriano explains to Kate, "I have always been half a priest and half a soldier" (*PS*, 70). With his venom thus removed, the way is clear for Kate to marry him. By this marriage, and by her agreement to join the new movement as the representative of the goddess Malintzi, Kate denies the essence of the individual character that she has maintained throughout *Quetzalcoatl*, and throughout the earlier portion of *The Plumed Serpent*. Kate thus controls the action and the meaning of *Quetzalcoatl*, whereas in *The Plumed Serpent* Ramón and Cipriano have their way. True, she keeps a strong measure of inner resistance up to the very end of the final version, but at the close it is clear that she has decided to stay. "She had come to make a sort of submission: to say she didn't want to go away." "'You don't want me to go, do you?' she pleaded" with Cipriano. Then in the final version's closing line she continues her pleading in words that variously imply that she will and wants to stay: "'You won't let me go!' she said to him." That is to say: "Your strength is overpowering me: I can't get free." Or, "You won't let me go; this reassures me that I will stay." Or, "You won't ever let me go, will you?"

* * *

In all these ways, while making his final expansion, Lawrence has transformed *Quetzalcoatl* from a psychologically plausible narrative, focused on and through Kate, into a work that places much greater stress upon the transcendent element, in accord with the rumination in the middle of the crucial chapter VI of *The Plumed Serpent*, where Kate is overwhelmed by "the great seething light of the lake":

> So in her soul she cried aloud to the greater mystery, the higher power that hovered in the interstices of the hot air, rich and potent. It was as if she could lift her hands and clutch the silent, stormless potency that roved everywhere, waiting. "Come then!" she said, drawing a long slow breath, and addressing the silent life-breath which hung unrevealed in the atmosphere, waiting. (*PS*, 106)

And she says to herself, "There is something rich and alive in these people. They want to be able to breathe the Great Breath" – a term suggestive of current theosophical thought. Lawrence knows exactly what he is doing here: he stresses the shift in her tone:

> She was surprised at herself, suddenly using this language. But her weariness and her sense of devastation had been so complete, that the

> Other Breath in the air, and the bluish dark power in the earth had become, almost suddenly, more real to her than so-called reality. Concrete, jarring, exasperating reality had melted away, and a soft world of potency stood in its place, the velvety dark flux from the earth, the delicate yet supreme life-breath in the inner air. Behind the fierce sun the dark eyes of a deeper sun were watching, and between the bluish ribs of the mountains a powerful heart was secretly beating, the heart of the earth. (*PS*, 108–9)

So Chapala becomes Sayula, and most of the other actual names of places around the lake (which are retained in *Quetzalcoatl*) are likewise given fictitious names, where the myth of the gods' return can move beyond "concrete, jarring, exasperating reality" into the "velvety dark flux" of the earth and the "supreme life-breath of the inner air."

While the amount of material dealing with landscape and native life remains substantially the same in both versions, because of the much greater size of *The Plumed Serpent,* the native matter has proportionately less impact. In *Quetzalcoatl* the local and the mythological are closely wrought together, evenly balanced in emphasis. But in *The Plumed Serpent* the additional mythic and transcendent elements – sermons, ruminations, expanded hymns, expanded ritual – tend to dominate the landscape and local detail preserved from the early version; in the new context these exist as a thin, transient layer of temporal life, lying between two greater modes of being. *The Plumed Serpent,* as in the passage just quoted, frequently creates abrupt shifts from the local to the transcendental: a strategy appropriate to a prophetical novel designed to shock the reader into an awareness of the need for a religious awakening and renewal. But *Quetzalcoatl* works in another way, with more stress on the concrete details indicative of "spirit of place" – a way illustrated by the scene in chapter X, where Cipriano escorts Kate to her home. They come to a corner where there are "several reed huts of the natives":

> Kate was quite used to seeing the donkeys looking over the low dry-stone wall, the black sheep with the curved horns tied to a pole, the boy naked save for his shirt, darting to the corner of the wall that served as a W.C. That was the worst of these little clusters of huts, they always made a smell of human excrement.

But there is something beyond all this: "Kate was used, too, to hearing the music of guitars and fiddles from this corner not far from her house. When she asked Felipa what the music meant, Felipa said it was a dance." Now once again music is emerging from the huts, and "by the light of the moon many figures could be seen, the white clothes of the men."

> "Look!" said Kate. "They are having a baile – a dance!"
> And she stood to watch. But nobody was dancing. Someone was singing – two men. Kate recognized the hymns.
> "They are singing the hymns to Quetzalcoatl," she said to Viedma.
> "What are those?" he replied laconically.
> "The boys sing them to me at the house."
> He did not answer.

Like Felipa, the general is reluctant to speak of the hymns.

> The song ceased, and he would have moved on. But she stood persistently. Then the song started again. And this time it was different. There was a sort of refrain sung by all the men in unison, a deep, brief response of male voices, the response of the audience to the chant. It seemed very wild, very barbaric in its solemnity, and so deeply, resonantly musical that Kate felt wild tears in her heart. The strange sound of men in unanimous deep, wild resolution. As if the hot-blooded soul were speaking from many men at once.
> "That is beautiful," she said, turning to him.

And he proceeds to mythologize the song: "'It is the song of the moon,' he answered. 'The response of the men to the words of the woman with white breasts, who is the moon-mother.'"

In this way, throughout *Quetzalcoatl*, the mythological element is closely related to the native scene, with all its local detail. In *The Plumed Serpent* the musical portion of the above scene is omitted: the final version jumps from "a smell of human excrement" to "Kate and Cipriano sat on the verandah of the House of the Cuentas" (*PS*, 233). Then follows a conversation in which Cipriano attempts to persuade Kate to accept the role of "a goddess in the Mexican pantheon." For such a role the preservation of human individuality ceases to matter; what is important is to be swept away into the realms of transcendent being.

One can understand, then, why Katherine Anne Porter in her early review said that *The Plumed Serpent* "seems only incidentally a novel." While this judgment is extreme, it points the way toward a valid distinction between the two versions, or rather, the two novels.

If not a traditional novel, what is it? In its combination of prose and poetry, its mingling of narrative and description with songs and hymns, lyrical sermons and eloquent authorial ruminations, along with its frequent use of occult symbols – in all this *The Plumed Serpent* comes to resemble the mingling of such elements in the prophetic books of the Bible. Indeed *The Plumed Serpent* strives to be such a prophetic book, denouncing the evils of the day and exhorting the people to return to true belief in transcendent powers. From the standpoint of a reader who expects a traditional novel, *The Plumed Serpent* may seem to have grave flaws: we may wish that Ramón's sermons were shorter, Lawrence's own ruminations more restrained, the insistence on Kate's submission moderated, and the cult of the Leader subject to deeper questioning. But all these aspects of the book are part of its evangelical fervor, its prophetic message. Read as a novel of prophecy, with all the abrupt shifts of tone and technique that prophecy manifests, *The Plumed Serpent* may be judged a success, within its own mode of existence. For a different sort of novel, we may turn now to *Quetzalcoatl*.

Louis L. Martz

WORKS CITED

D. H. Lawrence, *The Plumed Serpent,* ed. L. D. Clark (Cambridge: Cambridge University Press, 1978). I am indebted to the Introduction and Notes to this edition, and also to the two important studies by L. D. Clark, *Dark Night of the Body* (Austin: University of Texas Press, 1964), and *The Minoan Distance* (Tucson: University of Arizona Press, 1980).

D. H. Lawrence, *St. Mawr and Other Stories,* ed. Brian Finney (Cambridge: Cambridge University Press, 1983).

D. H. Lawrence, *Apocalypse and the Writings on Revelation,* ed. Mara Kalnins (Cambridge: Cambridge University Press, 1980); includes Lawrence's Introduction to Carter's *Dragon of the Apocalypse;* for the impact of the treatise on Lawrence in 1923, see pp. 45–46.

The Letters of D. H. Lawrence, vol. IV, eds. Warren Roberts, James T. Boulton, and Elizabeth Mansfield (Cambridge: Cambridge University Press, 1987) and vol. V, eds. James T. Boulton and Lindeth Vasey (Cambridge: Cambridge University Press, 1989).

Porter, Katherine Anne, "Quetzalcoatl," *New York Herald Tribune Books,* 7 March 1926: Sect. 6, pp. 1–2.

We wish to thank the Harry Ransom Humanities Research Center of the University of Texas at Austin and the Houghton Library of Harvard University for permission to study the manuscript and typescript of *Quetzalcoatl;* and we are grateful to Mr. Gerald Pollinger of Laurence Pollinger Ltd., Executor for the Estate of Mrs. Frieda Lawrence Ravagli, for permission to publish a text based upon these sources. The editor owes a special debt to L. D. Clark for his careful reading of the Introduction and Textual Commentary, offering many helpful suggestions.

Quetzalcoatl

I *The Beginning of a Bull-Fight*

I T WAS the Sunday after Easter, and the last bull-fight of the season in Mexico City. Four special bulls had been brought over from Spain for the occasion, since Spanish bulls are more fiery than Mexican. Perhaps it is the altitude, perhaps just the spirit of the western continent which is to blame for the lack of "pep," as Owen put it, in the native animal.

Although Owen disapproved of bull-fights, yet, as he had never seen one, "We shall have to go," he said.

"Oh yes, I think we must see it," chimed in Kate, while somewhere at the back of her mind lingered the speculation as to why "never having seen one" should entail "having to go." But Owen was an American, and each nation has its own logic. And Kate was good at chiming in.

Yet the reserve at the back of her mind was substantial, and caused a slight oppression on her heart.

As none of them were very rich, and as the day was somewhat cloudy, they took tickets for the "sun." Nobody who is anything takes a seat in the sun, in the bull-ring. Of course the vast proportion of the audience always sits there. That is why, if you want to be somebody, you have to buy a much more expensive ticket and sit way up in the "shade."

Kate felt uneasy, as if she were doing something against her own nature, as she followed Owen, and Villiers followed her to the proper entrance into the vast iron-and-concrete stadium. From the outside, mostly iron framework. Along the causeways, vendors of fruits and cakes and pulque and sweets. Rather lousy.

The man who took the tickets at the entrance suddenly pawed Owen on the chest and down the front of the body, and Owen bridled like a shying horse. Then he turned with a half self-conscious, half excited smile to Kate.

"Feeling for knives and firearms!" he said brilliantly.

"Oh–" said Kate doubtfully, wondering if she was to be pawed too.

It was rather like going into the Coliseum at Rome, or the amphitheatre at Verona, modernised. And you emerged the same, suddenly in a great hollow cup. But this was flimsy concrete and iron rails, and advertisements round the arena, and there was already a lot of unpleasant people. It was towards three o'clock in the afternoon.

Having reserved seats, they were led by a lout to their places, and Kate fitted herself in, on the concrete seat, between the two iron loops: Owen on one side, Villiers on the other. She looked excitedly round.

"It's thrilling!" she said.

"Oh very!" retorted Owen in his sonorous voice, looking round very pleased and rather vague. Then thoughtfully he folded his rain-coat and made a cushion of it for her to share with him. It went along two seats.

They were placed not far above the arena itself, a big round ring of fine gravel, with a solid wooden fence around, and behind the fence, the passage into which opened the various doors for bulls and horses and fighters. Then rose the great, shut-in, flimsy-seeming concave of the stadium, filled with patches of people. Opposite sat the thickest crowd: mostly a city crew, workmen, and a very few of the big hats of the Indian natives. The crowd was shouting and jeering. Kate, whose every fibre crinkled with aversion from a mob, sat as uneasily as if the concrete beneath her were fiery hot. A great game among the opposite crowd was to snatch a hat from some victim and send it flying way up or way down the hillside of hateful humanity. Owen laughed, excited but rather nervous, as he saw the ugly men's straw hats skimming up and down over the heads of the audience, while at times the excite-ment rose high, and the mass rose and roared as seven hats at once flew like projectiles way up and way down the tiers.

"*Odi profanum vulgus,*" said Kate, with a sincerity that came from the depths of her abdomen.

"What's that?" said Owen, leaning towards her with shining, uneasy eyes.

"I *loathe* a crowd," she said. "I loathe workmen, really."

"Aren't they funny!" he said.

He was thrilled but uneasy. He wore a big straw hat himself, of native make, and he knew it was conspicuous. So, after a lot of fidgeting, he took it off and put it on his knee. But he had, alas, a very conspicuous bald spot at the crown of his head, and the crowd were already throwing things. "Bum!" came an orange, aimed at his bald spot, but hitting him on the shoulder. He glared round rather ineffectually.

"I'd keep my hat on if I were you," came the cold voice of Villiers.

"Yes, I think perhaps it's wiser," replied Owen, with assumed nonchalance.

Whereupon a banana-skin rattled on Villiers' tidy panama. He shook it off and stared round at the crowd with a cold look, and a beak like a bird that knows it can stab.

"How I detest them!" said Kate.

A diversion was created by the entrance of the military bands, carrying their shining brass and silver instruments. The largest of the bands, in fine dark grey and rose-coloured uniforms, seated themselves away up in a big bare stone tract, the region of the Authorities. The President would possibly attend. Another band, a silver band in pale buff uniforms, sat opposite: while still a third, far off on the scattered hillside of the stadium. This third was on the left hand.

The bands took their seats, but did not begin to play. Although a great number of people were already in the stadium, there were still bare patches of concrete seats, especially in the Authorities' section, and along the lower, reserved tiers. The bulk of the people sat thick, about twelve tiers up from the ground, in the unreserved seats. Kate sat only three tiers from the bottom, the mass of the people above her.

The crowd had now a new diversion. The music should start at three.

"*La música! La música!*" shouted the crowd, with the voice of mob authority. For the revolution had been their revolution, they were The People, and the bands were their bands, for their amusement. However, the bands took no notice, the shouting subsided. Then again the insolent shout of the mob, in brutal command:

"*La música! La música!*"

It was still some time before the big band struck up: very crisp, very quick, really martial.

"That's fine!" said Owen. "That's good. That's the first time I've heard them good, with some real backbone."

Kate listened for some time to the music, though her spine and her bowels were uneasy because of the mob. Then at a certain moment a signal was given and the masses above in the cheap seats poured down to take the unoccupied reserved seats below them. It was like a sudden rush of black water, humanity confusedly rushing round.

In a few moments all the lower seats were occupied, men were calling to one another and scrambling to get together. But there was no shoving and pushing, no wrangling. Two people did not dart for the same seat. It was more like water rushing quickly to its place.

Kate now sat among the crowd. Her seat, however, was on one of the pathways. People passed along in front of her, back and forth. And men began to take advantage of the ledge for the feet of those on the row where Kate sat, to squat there. Owen soon had a fellow sitting plumb between his knees.

"I hope they won't sit on my feet," said Kate anxiously.

"We won't let them," said Villiers, with fierce coldness. "Why don't you shove him off, Owen? Shove him off."

Owen laughed and flushed. The Mexicans around looked at the three.

And the next thing was a fat Mexican inserting himself insolently on Villiers' foot-space. But young Villiers was too quick for him. He quickly brought his feet together under the man's sinking posterior, the fellow subsided uncomfortably on to a pair of boots, and at the same time felt Villiers shoving him quietly on the shoulder.

"No!" said Villiers in good American. "This place is for my *feet!* Get off! – You get *off!*" And again he quietly but very decidedly pushed the Mexican's shoulder, to remove him.

The Mexican half raised himself and looked round as if he would murder Villiers. But the young American's face was calm and cold, unmoved, his eyes just coolly decided. And Kate, in the next seat, was looking down with blazing Irish contempt in her grey eyes.

The Mexican diminished in importance. He muttered an explanation in Spanish that he was only sitting there a moment till he could go to his friend in the lower tier, waving his hand in that direction. Villiers did not understand a word, but he repeated:

"I don't care what it is. This place is for my *feet,* and you don't sit there."

The Mexican, however, turned a fat black city back and again placed his posterior on Villiers' foot-rest. And again Villiers sharply shoved him by the shoulder, saying:

"Go away! Go away! You're not to *sit* there!"

The Mexican let himself be shoved, oblivious.

"Insolence!" said Kate, for all the world to hear. "Insolence!"

Villiers sat with a fixed, abstract look on his thin face. He was determined the fellow should not sit there. But how to remove him? The man solved the difficulty by rising in another moment and removing himself to another spot. Owen's parasite, however, still sat between Owen's legs, assuredly, as if Owen were a sort of chair-back.

There was an exclamation. Two horsemen in gay uniform and bearing long staffs rode suddenly into the ring and around the arena, then took their stand by the place where they had entered. Everybody waited. Then four toreadors in their tight, silver-coloured embroidered uniforms marched in a little column of four into the ring, divided, and marched round the ring, saluting the Authorities. The President had not come after all.

Yes, it was a real bull-fight. But already Kate felt a touch of disgust. There was absolutely no glamour, no splendour. The toreadors in their tight embroidered uniforms, with their rather fat posteriors and their twist of pig-tails, looked, Kate thought, vulgar, rather like eunuchs or butcher's assistants. Far more vulgar than circus riders. How in the world could such fellows be heroes? They looked like eunuchs, with their smooth faces. And common as butcher's assistants. She understood so well why the performers in Roman arenas were mere slaves, regarded as such.

But an Ah! of satisfaction. Into the ring suddenly rushed a smallish-looking, neat, dun-coloured bull with long, flourishing horns. He ran out, thinking he was free, then stopped short, seeing he was not free, but faced with strange objects. He was puzzled.

A toreador came forward and unswitched a red cloak like a fan. The bull gave a little prance, and charged mildly, of course on the cloak, which the man held at arm's length. The creature had no idea of charging on the toreador: only on the rag. The man swished the cloak over the animal's head, the bull trotted on, round the ring.

Seeing the wooden fence, that he was able to look over it, he leaped nimbly over it and into the gangway where the bull-ring servants stood. They just as nimbly vaulted away into the arena. The bull trotted along the gangway till he came to an exit, then back into the arena again.

There he trotted undecided and irritated around. The toreadors waved rags to him and he swerved on. Till he came to where one of the men stood on horseback. Kate now noticed that the horse was thickly blindfolded with a black cloth. Yes, so was the horse ridden by the other picador, thickly blindfolded with black cloth.

The bull trotted suspiciously up to the motionless horse bearing the rider with the long pole. The picador turned the horse to face the bull, slowly, and prodded the bull in the shoulder with his lance. The bull, as if in surprise, suddenly lowered his head and lifted his horns straight into the horse's abdomen. Without more ado the horse and rider rolled over, the rider scrambling from beneath the horse and running away with his lance.

The horse, a poor specimen, struggled to rise, as if dumbly wondering why on earth! The bull, with a red sore on his shoulder, stood looking around as if also wondering why on earth! He saw the horse already half on its feet just near, smelling already of blood and abdomen, rearing itself erect. So not knowing what else to do, the bull once more lowered his head and drove his long, flourishing horns into the horse's belly, working them up and down inside the horse's abdomen with a certain vague satisfaction.

Kate, watching, had never been so suddenly taken by surprise in her life. She had come with romantic notions of a gallant display. And before she knew where she was, she was watching a bull, with a red place on his shoulder, working his horns up and down in the belly of a prostrate and feebly plunging old horse.

She looked aside, almost having lost control of herself. But the greatest shock was surprise, amazement at the poor vulgarity of it. Then she smelt blood and the nauseous smell of bursten bowels.

When she looked up, it was to see the horse feebly and vaguely trotting out of the arena, led by an attendant, a great ball of its own entrails hanging and swinging reddish against the animal's legs as it automatically trotted.

And again, the shock of surprise almost made her lose her self-control. She heard the scattered Ahh! of amused satisfaction from the crowd. She looked into Owen's face.

He too was somewhat pale, with a wrinkled nose and rounded eyes behind his spectacles, half scared, somewhat disgusted, but also excited and pleased, as if to say: Now we're seeing the real thing.

"But the horse doesn't move! It doesn't do anything to save itself!" cried Kate in her horrified amazement.

"You see it's blindfolded," said he.

"But can't it *smell* the bull?" she cried.

"Apparently not. They are old wrecks that they bring to the bull-ring to finish them off," he said, with a little complacency.

She looked away from him again. It wasn't mere pity for the horse that she felt. She rather disliked the stupid thing. But she felt she had had a sudden blow, an insult to the proper fibre in her, by such a humiliating spectacle. Such a shameless spectacle! All her woman-hood and her breeding rose in anger. But the thing was going on, and she was powerless to stop it. And she was too startled to move. The thing had come on her too suddenly, too unexpectedly.

She turned to the ring again. The toreadors were playing with the bull, unfurling their flimsy cloaks at arm's length, and the animal, with the red sore on his shoulder, was running from one to the other, rather foolishly. She thought for the first time that a bull was a dull and stupid creature, in spite of his excessive maleness and flourishing horns. He never distinguished his tormentors. He never knew what to single out among the movements. He always ran blindly and stupidly for the rag, and the toreadors just skipped aside like girls showing off. It may have needed skill and courage: but it *looked* silly. Blindly and foolishly the bull ran and tripped at the fluttering rag each time, just because it fluttered, and ignored the men who were the cause of all the nasty folly. Why couldn't he look for once straight at the various objects, and see that it was just the men who were there to torment him, and quickly run them down. A lion or a tiger would have crouched and watched, and then sprung: not at a rag, either, but at the essential enemy.

It bored her. The nimbleness and feats of the toreadors bored her. The bull was too stupid.

But at least this was not horrible. – The bull really wanted to get away from the silly show. He leaped the fence again quickly, into the attendants' gangway. The attendants vaulted over into the arena. The bull trotted a little down the gangway, then sprang over again into the ring. The attendants vaulted once more into the gangway. The bull trotted round the ring, ignored the toreadors, and leaped once more into the gangway. Over vaulted the attendants. Kate was quite amused.

The bull was in the ring again, running from toreador to tor-eador. Then one of the picadors bravely put forward his old, blindfolded horse. The bull ignored it, and trotted away again, as if all the time looking for something, excitedly looking for something. He stood still and excitedly pawed the ground, as if he wanted something. A toreador advanced and swung a cloak. Up pranced the bull, his tail in the air, and with a prancing bound charged – upon the rag, of course. The toreador skipped round with a ladylike skip, then tripped to another point. Very ladylike.

But the bull, in the course of his trotting and prancing and pawing, had once more come near the bold picador. The bold picador shoved forward his ancient steed again, and prodded the bull with his lance. The bull looked up irritated: what now! He saw the horse and rider. The horse stood as calm as if it were waiting in the shafts while its master delivered milk. It must have been very much surprised when the bull gave a little bound like a dog, ducked its head, and catching the horse in the abdomen at once rolled it over, as one might push over a sewing-machine. Then the bull looked with some irritable wonder at the curious medley of a collapsed horse with rider scrambling out, a few yards from him. He was going to investigate when the toreadors drew him off, and he went caracoling at more red rags.

Meanwhile an attendant had got the horse on its feet again, and was leading it slowly and feebly into the gangway and round to the exit under the Authorities. The horse crawled slowly. The bull, running from rag to rag, and never catching anything, was getting excited, and a little impatient of the rag game. He jumped once more into the corridor and started running, alas, in the direction after the wounded horse, which was still limping its way towards the exit.

Kate knew what was coming. Before she could look away, the bull had charged on the limping horse from behind, the attendants had fled, the horse was heaved up absurdly from the rear, with one of the bull's horns between his legs and deep in his body, then he went collapsing down in front, with his rear still heaved up and the bull's horn working vigorously, pushing up and down deep inside him, while he lay on his neck, all twisted. And a heap of bowels coming out. And the nauseous stench!

This happened not far from where Kate sat, on her side of the ring. She rose to her feet. Most of the other people were on their feet, craning, looking down at the sight just below, with excitement. Kate knew if she saw any more she would go into hysterics. She was getting beside herself.

She looked swiftly at Owen.

"I'm going!" she said.

"Going!" he cried, in his full sonorous fashion, and with a look between dismay and excitement, pleasure and cowardice, on his flushed round face.

"Don't come!" she cried, and she turned and hurried along the pathway towards the mouth of the exit-tunnel.

Owen came running after her, fluttered and drawn in all directions. He caught her just as she entered the high, vaulted exit-tunnel.

"Are you really going!" he cried, in dismay, anxiety, chagrin.

"Of course," she snapped. "But don't you come. I don't want you. There are plenty of taxis here. Don't you come."

"Are you sure!" he sang. "Do you think you'll be all right?"

"Certain," she snapped.

"Then I'd better run back, or I shall lose my seat."

He couldn't run, because at that moment thunder broke and the vicious drops of rain which had been falling unnoticed thickened suddenly into a splash. People were making for the exit-tunnel, for shelter, but Owen fought his way back to his seat against them. He was as nearly in hysterics as was Kate.

That young woman found herself suddenly faced by the splashing Mexican rain, in the great archway under the stadium. Just beyond she saw the wooden gates where she had come in, and the rather shoddy soldiers pressing against the brick gateway, out of the rain. She was terrified lest they should refuse to let her out.

And anyway she couldn't go yet: the rain was falling in one thick splash. She had no covering of any sort, wore nothing but a thin green hat and a gauze dress. Twenty seconds in that rain would wet her like a mermaid, to the skin.

So there she stood hovering uneasily in the vast archway of the stadium tunnel, at the outer end, while from the inner end people from the audience surged in. Everybody was in a state of excitement. The people taking shelter were on tenterhooks lest they should lose their seats, or miss something. Kate was on tenterhooks to get away from them, and her face had the drawn, rather blank look of a woman who is on the verge of hysterics. She could not get out of her eyes the last picture of the horse lying twisted on its neck with its crupper hitched up and the horn of the bull going between its hind legs and goring slowly and rhythmically deep in its belly. The horse so absurd and utterly helplessly passive. And its bowels on the ground.

The new terror was the throng in the passage-way where she stood. They did not come very near her. They pressed near the inner mouth. But they were mostly lower bourgeois men, a type she particularly disliked, especially in Mexico. Two of the men stood making water against the wall, in the interval of their excitement. One father had kindly brought his two little boys, the elder about ten, to see the edifying spectacle. And this elder boy in his Sunday rig-out looked a pathetic pale sight. The children were oppressed by the unnaturalness of the whole affair. But there were children and a fair sprinkling of women among the audience, the women as eager as any men to see the old horses gored.

Kate stood with peaked face, in her flimsy frock, looking at the great rain, at the shabby wall and the big rickety gates of the stadium enclosure, at the shoddy, pinky-white soldiers, at the cobbled, rather sordid street outside, with its vendors taking refuge in the pulque shops. Although she had travelled in many countries, and although she knew the city, she was terrified at being alone, terrified lest the soldiers should not let her pass, terrified lest she should not be able to hail an automobile at once, terrified lest something should happen to her before she got back to the hotel. She wanted to plunge out into the rain, but remembered in time what she would look like with her thin clothing plastered to her body by rain.

It was one of her bad quarters-of-an-hour. As she stood there, an officer in uniform made his way through the crowd, slowly. She looked at him, and noticed that the crowd fell back for him, some half saluting. He was a medium-sized man in a big, pale-blue military cloak, which made him seem Italian and friendly. He came slowly towards her, and bowed, with a salute.

"Madam, did you wish to leave?" he asked, in English English.

"Yes, I want to get away," she replied.

Her knowledge at once told her he was a gentleman, gave her a sudden relief in that direction. But on his dark, rather lean, bearded face was something not merely of a gentleman.

"I am General Cipriano Viedma. Will you allow me to call an automobile for you?"

"Thank you so much." – But her face still expressed doubt.

He turned to a soldier, and gave an order. The man ran out through the rain.

"I asked him to call my car, as the man speaks English and you can be sure of him. Will you borrow my cloak for a moment? It doesn't rain so much any more, but enough to wet you."

"Oh thank you," she said flushing. "I don't think I need it."

"I am afraid you do," he said, holding it out for her.

So she perforce had to turn her shoulders and be enveloped in the big cloak of fine, pale-blue cloth.

"You didn't like the bull-fight?" he said, smiling slightly.

"Not at all. No. It was a shock more than anything."

"A shock! Yes! I could see. Naturally it was a shock. You had never been before."

"Or I shouldn't have come again."

"Naturally. – No, I dislike it myself. But in Rome one does as Rome does; until the moment comes to make a change in Rome."

She hardly heeded him. But she replied mechanically:

"Yes, I suppose things *do* change sometimes."

"When we make them," he replied.

There was the noisy sound of a car – then a big red automobile appeared beyond the gate, the wet soldier dropped off the foot-board, and came running in to the stadium, carrying an umbrella, which he handed with a salute to the General.

The General opened the umbrella, and stepped out with Kate.

"Thank you so very much," she said, handing him the cloak as she turned to enter the car.

"Won't you keep it till you are under cover, and send it back by the man?" he said.

"Thank you so much."

He closed the door, she sat expecting the car to move on. The General waited, the chauffeur waited, and she waited.

"Charles," said the General, "take the lady where she wishes to go, and come back here."

And he bowed and was retreating.

"Oh!" said Kate, starting and stammering in confusion. "Er – Er – Hotel Verona. – Oh thank you, thank you so much." And she put her hand waveringly out of the window. The General kissed her finger-tips, smiled, and looked at the chauffeur.

"Hotel Verona," said the chauffeur.

In ten minutes' time Kate found herself back in her own room in the second-class but kindly Italian hotel, with more impressions than she knew what to do with. She was too much agitated to be still. The rain had ceased, she went out again and took a taxi to Sanborn's, the tea-house, where she could have tea and feel at home without being alone.

II   *Tea-Party in Tacubaya*

O WEN CAME BACK to the hotel at about half-past six, tired, excited, a little guilty, a good deal distressed at having let Kate go alone, and, now the whole thing was over, rather dreary in spirit.

"Oh, how did you get on?" he said, the moment he saw her, looking at her rather guiltily. "I felt a most awful cad letting you go alone."

"I got on perfectly all right. Went to Sanborn's for tea."

"Oh, you did!" he cried, brightening with relief. "Oh, then you *weren't* so very overwhelmed! I'm so glad. Oh, I had such qualms after I'd let you go. Imagined you lost in Mexico – run away with by the chauffeur. – And then the rain – and the bull-fight – *and* the crowd throwing things at my bald patch. Oh, what a time I've had!"

He put his hand over his stomach and rolled his eyes.

"Aren't you drenched?" she said.

"Drenched!" he replied. "Or at least I was. I've dried off quite a lot. My rain-coat is no good – I don't know why I don't buy another. Oh what a time! The rain streaming on my bald head, and people behind throwing oranges at it. Then simply *gored* in my inside with remorse about letting you go alone. – Yet it was the *only* bull-fight I shall *ever* see. – I came then before it was over. Villiers wouldn't come. I suppose he's still there."

"Was it all as awful as it began?" she asked.

"No! No! It wasn't. The first was worst – that horse-shambles. Oh, they killed two more horses. And *five* bulls! Oh yes, a regular butchery. But there was more skill with the bulls, of course: and some very pretty feats of the toreadors: very! One toreador stood on his cloak while the bull charged him –"

"Go upstairs and change. You'll die," said Kate.

"Yes, I think I'd better. – Yes, I feel I might die any minute! – Well – I'll be down to dinner in half an hour."

Kate sat trying to sew, but her hand trembled. She could not get the bull-ring out of her vision. And she felt outraged in her soul. And she felt also a background of gratitude to that general: Cipriano; she remembered his first name, but not the other.

It was nearly seven o'clock when Villiers came in. He looked wan, peaked, but like a bird that has successfully pecked its enemy.

"Oh it was GREAT!" he said, lounging on one hip. "Great! They killed SEVEN BULLS –"

"But no calves, unfortunately," said Kate, suddenly angry again. He paused to consider the point, then laughed.

"No," he said, "no calves. – And several more horses after you'd gone –"

"I don't want to hear," she said.

He laughed, feeling perhaps somewhat heroic: like one who can look on blood without going green. The young hero! Yet there were black rings round his eyes.

"Oh, but don't you want to hear what I did after! I went to the hotel of the chief toreador, and saw him lying on his bed in his bedroom, all dressed, and smoking a fat cigar. Rather like a Venus with a fat cigar."

"Who took you there?"

"Why, a Spanish fellow who talked English, just behind us. But the toreador was great, lying on his bed in all his get-up except his shoes, and quite a crowd of men going over it all again – wa-wa-wa! Wa-wa-wa-wawa!!"

And the young man imitated the gabble of the Spanish and the fierce posturing of the men in the bedroom as they rehearsed the noble events of the ring.

"Aren't you wet?" asked Kate.

"No, not at all. I'm perfectly dry. You see I had my coat. Only my head, of course. My poor hair was streaked all down my face as if the dye had run." He wiped his thin hair across his head with a rather posing humorousness. – "Hasn't Owen come in?" he added.

"Yes, he's changing."

"Well, I'll go up. I suppose it's nearly supper-time. Oh yes, it's after!" At which discovery he brightened as if he'd received a gift. "Oh by the way, how did you get on all alone? Rather mean of us to let you go off like that, all by yourself," he added, as he poised in the half-open doorway.

"Perfectly all right," she said. "I hope I can call a taxi, at my time of life."

"Well, I don't know-w-" he said with an American drawl, as he disappeared.

Kate felt rather angry with them both. But poor Owen was really so remorseful, and rather bewildered by his confusion of emotions, that she had to relent towards him. He was really awfully kind. But also he was an American, and if he felt he was missing something, he was at once swept with the despair of having lived in vain. And the despair of having lived in vain made him pelt off to the first crowd he saw in the street, abandoning all his higher philosophic self, all his poetry, all his everything, and just craning his neck in one more frantic effort to *see*. To see all there was to be seen! Not to miss it. And then, after he'd seen something nasty, an old woman run over by a motor-car and bleeding on the floor, he'd return to Kate pale at the gills, sick, bewildered, daunted, and yet, yes, glad he'd seen it if it was there to be seen.

"Well," said Kate, "I always thank God I'm not Argus. I see quite enough horrors as it is, without opening more eyes for them."

She could not sleep in the night for thinking of the bull-ring. Neither could Owen. They were both genuinely upset.

"Oh, I never slept so well since I was in Mexico!" said Villiers, with the triumphant look of a bird that has just pecked its enemy.

"Look at the frail aesthetic youth!" mocked Owen.

"Their frailty and their aestheticism are both bad signs to me," said Kate, ominously. And she meant it.

But Villiers only smiled a cold, pleased little smile.

She had not told them a word about the General. Probably she would never meet the man again, so why talk about it. She knew practically no-one in Mexico – and she wanted to know no-one.

However, the one person she did know rang up two days later.

"Is that you, Mrs. Burns? How do you do! Yes, I've been ill, couldn't see anybody. – But look here, won't you come to tea today? What? Yes, I wish you would. What? About half-past four? Oh good, good, very good indeed! I shall be so awfully glad to see you. Goodbye!"

It was Mrs. Norris, widow of an English ambassador of the bygone days of Don Porfirio. Mrs. Norris lived on in a big, old fortress of a house beyond Tacubaya, and was famous for her collection of Aztec and Indian things.

Owen, being Kate's half-cousin, escorted her. They went in an old
Ford car, bumping out through Tacubaya. The house stood in a quiet
lane, where great cypress-trees rose dark and high above high walls,
and the dwelling itself presented a vast blind wall and a huge fortress
door to the passer-by. In the lane already was a large red motor-car,
and another shiny private car. Kate knew.

She stepped forth from the battered jitney, and Owen went to
bang the knocker on the studded doors, whose very studs were as big
as a man's two fists. Immediately there was the foolish and exagger-
ated barking of three unnatural dogs, inside the unnaturally huge and
massive doors. They waited, and Owen knocked again, and the dogs
on the other side rushed nearer. And at length a little elderly servant-
woman in neat black with white cap and strings peeped through a
chink, then said Ah! and opened the door, muttering in Spanish.

Inside was the sun-filled square patio, with red and white flowers,
silent, dead for centuries; and a glimpse beyond of garden, a handful
of sun, a splotch of rose-magenta bougainvillea, and the huge uprear-
ing of Aztec cypresses. Save for the imbecile barking of the dogs, the
square patio, or inner courtyard of the old house, with its massive,
reddened walls, its heavy red-and-yellow archways, its climbing, flow-
ery creepers and its stone basin of water, was as motionless, as poten-
tially dumb as if life had never entered it. Kate was always impressed
with the dead dumbness, each time she came. Like some unbroken,
still-inhabited Pompeii. A tomb. A red-washed, red-and-yellow tomb
of dead Conquistadores, the massive old house. With the Aztec
cypresses rearing dark and enormous above it, and casting the dumb
weight of Aztec silence down on it.

However, Kate climbed the slippery, black stone stairs to the
upper terrace, and went through the leather door. Mrs. Norris came
out of the dark sitting room, and took Kate's hand in both her own.

"I'm so glad to see you. I've been so ill with my heart. The doctor
said there was nothing for it but a lower altitude, but I said to him,
'You've *got* to cure me here. It's ridiculous, this rushing up and down
from one altitude to another.' So he tried one treatment, and that was
no good. Then he tried another, and that was quite successful. Yes,
thank you, I am quite well now. And how are you – ?"

Mrs. Norris was an elderly woman, still rather like a conqueror
herself, in her black silk dress, and her little black shoulder-shawl of
silk cashmere, with its short fringe, and a rather fine ornament of black

enamel and gold, round her neck. Her face had gone slightly blackened, her nose was sharp, her voice well-bred but hammered until it
had gone hard. Her face reminded Kate always of one of the Aztec
masks carved in black-grey lava, with a sharp nose and slightly prominent eyes and a look of tomb-like mockery. She had lived so many
years in Mexico, and rooted among Aztec remains so long.

"But come in, do come in," she said, after keeping her two visitors
out on the terrace where rather dusty Aztec carvings and dusty native
baskets adorned the wall, like a museum.

Three men were in the sitting room that opened on to the
terrace – all three in civilian dress, Kate saw at a glance. Major Harper,
the very correct but watchful young man who was American military
attaché at the moment; General Cipriano Viedma, and Señor Ramón
Carrasco. Kate saw the American Major look quickly at her dress –
which had no relation to the fashions, being of a dull-blue silk, the top
made something like a Russian shirt, with brilliant red silk Persian
embroidery on the shoulders and down the front – to see whether she
was real "society" or not. When he'd looked he didn't know. But he
knew, in Owen, at once, his fellow-countryman, saw in him a high-
brow, only a moderate income, crank of some sort, probably bolshevist. As a matter of fact, Owen was a bolshevist by conviction but a
capitalist by practice. He lived on his income but sympathised fiercely
with communism. He sent out waves of hatred, at sight, to the
military attaché.

General Viedma shook hands in silence. Señor Carrasco, a big,
handsome, dark man, was also silent and quite impassive, though his
silence was perfectly courteous. When he sat down, Kate noticed the
beautiful poise of his head, and the handsomeness of his thighs:
something almost god-like, in an Indian, sensuous, statuesque way.

"Well, and how are you getting on in Mexico? Do you still like it?"
asked Mrs. Norris.

"Yes," said Kate. "Sometimes I'm a bit scared of it. But it has a
fascination. I like it much, much better than the United States."

"Why," said Mrs. Norris, with a deprecating declension in her
voice, for the sake of the attaché who sat next to her; "of course this is
older, it has an older background, that we haven't altogether explored
yet, which makes it perhaps more interesting."

"Yes," said Kate. "And of course I have seen so little of the United
States, I really ought not to talk."

"One jumps at one's first impressions," said Mrs. Norris, smiling.

"So childishly," laughed Kate.

"But how refreshing to have somebody who *can* jump," said Owen, rather vicious.

The American Major, who was watching Kate as if she were an unknown fish, and Owen as if he were a fishy fish, also laughed. Then he rose and excused himself, saying he really must go.

"But won't you stay to tea?" said Mrs. Norris, who was evidently glad to get rid of his immaculate, correct, but uneasy presence. – No, he had to etc. etc. And he was gone.

Everybody seemed to have slightly muted lips: so Kate felt it.

"Now tell me what you have been doing," said Mrs. Norris.

"We went to a bull-fight – and it was loathsome," said Kate.

"Yes, one goes once, but never again. I went, oh many years ago, in Madrid. . . ." And Mrs. Norris was off on a reminiscence.

"When they say that such shows purify the passions – that one lets off one's low lusts by looking at them," said Kate; "it isn't true, is it? One doesn't naturally have lusts of that sort, does one? And they take little children and try to make them have such lusts. I call it *bad*."

Mrs. Norris gathered her little shawl at the breast, uneasily. Owen therefore put in, smiling to himself and turning to the Mexicans:

"But perhaps you don't disapprove quite so strongly as we do?"

"Oh yes, we disapprove," said the General, smiling easily.

"Where there are so many things to disapprove of, however –" added Mrs. Norris, rising. "But come, let us go and have tea."

She led through a little sombre antechamber on to a little terrace, where creepers and flowers bloomed thick on the low walls. There was a bell-flower, red and velvety, like blood that is drying: and clusters of white rose: and tufts of bougainvillea, a glow of pure magenta colour.

"How lovely it is here!" said Kate. "Having the great dark trees beyond."

"Yes, it *is* beautiful," admitted Mrs. Norris, with the pride of a possessor. "I have such a time trying to keep these two apart," she added, going across in her little black shawl to where bougainvillea and the rust-scarlet bell-creeper were just separated by the flowering white rose. She pushed the rose-magenta, papery masses of bougainvillea one way, and the dry-blood cups of the scarlet creeper the other, and stroked the white roses, to encourage them to intervene.

"I think the two reds are rather amusing together," said Owen.

"Do you!" retorted Mrs. Norris dryly.

The two Mexican gentlemen stood in the background. The sky blue overhead, but on the lower horizons in the distance a thick, pearly haze.

"One never sees Popocatepetl or Iztaccihuatl these days," said Kate, disappointed.

"No, there is too much mist. But there – in the other direction, look, you see Ajusco: between the trees," said Mrs. Norris.

"Ajusco!" echoed Kate.

On the low parapet of the terrace were various stone Aztec things, carved, grimacing heads, obsidian knives, and a queer thickish stone stick, like a thick stick to hit somebody with, but of blackish stone. Kate took it up.

"Ah!" she said wondering. "A stone stick to hit with! Not very heavy! But heavy enough to hurt – ugh!"

Owen rubbed his bald patch, ruefully.

"The very sight of it makes me know what a split skull feels like," he said.

But he too picked it up, fascinated. And he fingered the little idols and faces of grey-black, porous stone, fascinated.

For the first time Kate turned to the General.

"Aztec things make me feel oppressed," she said to him.

His black eyes watched her. He stroked his short, black beard.

"So they do me," he said. "Or they used to, till Ramón – Señor Carrasco – gave me hope about them."

"Hope?" she said, wondering, and looking at the other man. Then for the first time she met his eyes also. And they too were black, and seemed to be looking at her from a great distance. And at the centre was a strange, living soul that looked at her. Her heart gave a quick thud. She was a little afraid of him.

"Did you say you always feel oppressed by the Aztec spirit?" he asked, in slow, foreign, but correct English, smiling at her.

"Yes," said Kate. "I always thought it had no hope – no hope."

"No hope," he reiterated. "No, perhaps it has no hope. Yet why should you think that?"

"It always makes my heart sink. So do the eyes of the natives – those that I call peons. – Their eyes have no middle to them. That frightens me. Under their great big hats, they don't seem to be really there, the men. And they are often so good-looking too. But when

you look again, they aren't really there. Their eyes have no middle to
them."

Ramón was watching her from his curious distance. His face
seemed to smile, yet he wasn't smiling. She felt there was something
withheld, mysterious, about him. For the first time in her life, she
seemed not to be able to see, not to be able to grasp what was before
her. Suddenly her grip on the world seemed to be leaving her.

"They aren't really there!" repeated Ramón, in his quiet, yet rich
voice, as if it came from magnificent depths in him. And again Kate
realised she heard these splendid, yet subtle voices fairly often among
the Indian men, porters and laborers. And that they startled her.

"What does it mean, *not really there?*" he said again, in his slow
English, turning to the General.

The two Mexicans talked for a moment or two in Spanish. Then
Ramón bowed to Kate.

"It is true as you say – *not really there!* No-one has wished them to
be there."

"Señor Carrasco is a great philosopher," said Mrs. Norris, in a
high voice. "Far beyond my grasp. – But come to tea." – And she led
the way along the terraces, while Ramón Carrasco replied to her,
rather teasingly, in Spanish. And she answered again in Spanish, in a
high voice, marching ahead in her black shawl and grey, neat hair, like
one of the Conquistadores followed by a quiet, mocking Indian chief.

It was a round tea-table, with shiny silver tea-service, and silver
kettle with a little flame, and pink and white oleanders, and cakes, and
a parlour-maid in black and white: exactly like England. Mrs. Norris
cut the cakes with a heavy hand, and sent them round, pouring tea also
with a heavy motion.

"Nobody lives without hope," she said; "if it's only the hope of
getting a *real* to buy a litre of pulque."

"Ah Señora," said Ramón, in his voice that was so beautiful, but
which yet made one uneasy; "if the pulque is the last blessing we
know!"

"Then a peso will buy all the hope in the world," she retorted.

He made a slightly exasperated gesture, and Cipriano Viedma
smiled. Kate looked across at him. There was something contained in
him, which suggested great energy. His eyes were very dark and full,
and not quite fathomable. He too seemed to see something in the
universe which she did not see. When he looked at her he made her
heart go hot inside her breast.

"But nobody has to *ask* people to be there, do they?" she said. "Either they *are* there, or they never can be."

Cipriano's full dark eyes seemed to be playing on her, as if he heeded her words very little, as if he only heeded *her*.

"*Como dice la Señora?*" murmured Ramón. "*Qué nadie –* ?"

Mrs. Norris translated for him, in a rather high, schoolmistress voice, and even then she broke down.

"How was it you put it – Nobody has to *ask* people to be there. They have to come of their own accord – or by –"

"No," said Kate, feeling rather foolish. "They have to *be* there, under their big hats, all those peons. If the Lord hasn't made them be there, they never will be there."

"Ah!" exclaimed Mrs. Norris, washing her hands of it. "You make me feel I don't know where *I* am. – And my dear, there *are* no peons in Mexico any more. They are all Nature's noblemen. Isn't that so, Don Ramón?"

"As you say," he smiled, bowing.

But still he looked at Cipriano for an interpretation of Kate, which Cipriano gave, keeping his full black eyes on Kate's face quite unconsciously all the time. When he looked away, she felt as if a strong *black* light had suddenly gone out.

"No," said Don Ramón, with sudden fierce energy and fluent English. "It all consists of a call and an answer. The answer can not come before the call."

Kate watched him half fascinated. Was he a fanatic of some sort, with his noble bearing and his sensuous, statuesque repose?

"You mean you can call the peons into being?" she asked, half timidly, half ironically.

He nodded quickly and with energy.

"Call them into being, yes. That is how I mean."

And the far-off center of his eye seemed to catch her and almost overpower her. She turned to Cipriano quickly. His black, full, keen eyes seemed to support her and to seek her at once. She made a slight, unconscious gesture of appeal to him, and a glow of warm light seemed to mount over his face.

"Won't you try these little native cakes with the sesame seeds on them?" said Mrs. Norris. "Teresa makes them, and is so pleased when the guests like them."

"What, *Open Sesame!*" cried Owen, "Oh do let's have one!"

At that moment the muted, elderly maid mutely announced somebody, and there entered a smallish old man in a morning coat and with white hair and beard, followed by a woman in black crêpe-de-chine with the hat that was almost fated for her sort, black silk shape turned up on three sides till it became almost a toque, and with black ospreys in it: underneath the hat of bourgeois destiny, a faded baby face with round eyes and grey hair, and the inevitable middle-west accent.

"Oh, how nice to see you, Judge – how nice to see you, Mrs. Ball!" And the hostess gave a conventional kiss at the other woman's cheek. There was a bit of conventional exchange, an exchange of introductions, and the newcomers sat down at table. Owen, being next to Kate, seeing there was really only polite space for six at table, said:

"If I may, I will take my cup to the low chair, it looks so inviting."

He couldn't for his life sit elbow to elbow with that Judge.

The Judge, for his part, was one of those white people whom Mexico drives into a state of perpetual bad temper. He could hardly hold up his head, he was so furious at finding other people at table, particularly, perhaps, the two Mexicans. Having yapped a question to Owen as to how long he had been in Mexico, and if he'd been to the club, he turned again to the table.

"No," said Owen, "I haven't been at the club yet: though Garfield Witt gave me a letter of introduction."

"Garfield Witt! Garfield Witt! That fellow! Why he's nothing but a rank bolshevist. Why the fellow even went to Russia. Did no end of harm down here, with his talk. Letters from a man like that shouldn't be recognised."

Up came Owen's gorge.

"He may be in sympathy with the socialists," he retorted; "as I am myself. But he's a very fine man, and the Americans in Mexico ought to think themselves lucky to get such a man to come down to them."

"A very fine man! That what you call a very fine man? Comes down here puffing the ignorant people up and doing all he can against his own country? We don't want any more of that sort. We've got enough as it is. Why –" and the little man with his white little beard and lame-dog face turned his spectacles round the company in a spasm of extreme irritability "– the town's full of malcontents and *sinver-guenzas* from New York. And they welcome them. The government welcomes them. Place is a hot-bed of bolshevistic aliens. All of them doing their best against their own country."

Mrs. Norris quietly handed the cakes to Kate, to pass to the Judge.

"Won't you have a cake?" said Kate, holding the plate.

"Don't want any," snapped the Judge, looking the other way as if he had been handed a plate of bolshevists.

A little surprised, Kate looked for somewhere to put the plate down. Poor Mrs. Norris, who really did like to preserve a bit of the old English tea-time suavity at her table, adjusted her *pince-nez*. The General relieved Kate of the plate, and offered it to Mrs. Judge, who was sitting bolt upright under her inevitable hat, her faded baby face looking, trying to look, a little superior too.

"Did you read that article by Willis Rice Hope in the *Excelsior,* Mrs. Norris?" said the Judge, leaning forward on the table. He wanted, evidently, to get into Mrs. Norris' good graces.

"I did," said Mrs. Norris, with easy emphasis.

"You did! And what did you think of it?"

"I thought it was the *only* sensible thing I had read on these Agrarian Laws."

"Sensible! I should think it was. Why Rice Hope came to me for a few points, and I put him up to some of the things. But his article's got *everything,* doesn't miss an item that's of any importance. Why it's marvellous how the fellow's got it."

"Excellent!" said Mrs. Norris.

"What was the article about?" asked Owen from the background.

"Do you read enough Spanish to make it out?" yapped the Judge.

"With difficulty," said Owen.

"Then get yesterday's *Excelsior* and read it for yourself."

"It is an article written by an American journalist who has been here a fortnight," said the General, "for his paper, the *New York Times,* and translated into the *Excelsior*. It says, that because of the *Ley Agrarista,* the Land Law, the land is all falling into uncultivation, that the State of Morelos produces no more sugar, and that the Mexican people are already feeling the first pinch of famine, and that soon the whole country will be without bread – like Russia in her famine; unless the government repeals the law, which as you know says that the land belongs in the first place to the nation and the people."

Owen made round eyes behind his glasses.

"Why," he said, "I've travelled a good deal, and the country is everywhere full of corn, marvellously under cultivation, more prosperous than I could possibly have imagined, from all the stuff one reads in America. And I understand that the land belongs almost less to the people now, than it did under Diaz."

"There are always two sides," said the General.

The Judge turned round like a lame dog harassed by a cat.

"How long have you been in the country, Mr. – What did you say your name was?"

"I've been in the country more than a *fortnight,* at least – and as far as I'm aware I didn't say my name was anything."

"How have you been, for walking, Judge?" said Mrs. Norris. "You heard of the time I had with my ankle?"

"Of course we have!" said Mrs. Judge. "I've been trying *so* hard to get out and see you. How *did* it happen? We were *so* grieved for you."

"Why I slipped on a piece of orange-peel in town – just there at the corner of San Juan de Latran and Madero. Oh yes, I fell right down. And the first thing I did when I got up was to push the orange-peel into the gutter. And what do you think, the Mexicans standing there at the corner laughed at me for doing it, thought it an excellent joke."

"Of course they would," said the Judge. "They were waiting for the next person to come and fall on it."

"One does have to be careful!" said Kate.

"Careful!" snapped the Judge. "I nearly lost my life on a banana-skin. Slipped in the street on a banana-skin, and lay in a darkened room for days, between life and death, and am lame from it for my life."

"How awful!" said Kate. "What did you do when you fell?"

"What did I do? Just smashed my hip."

"How dreadful!" said Kate.

"There's a good deal more danger in a banana-skin than in all the anarchist bombs," said the Judge, momentarily mollified.

Owen, of course, was paving the city with large, juicy banana-skins, in his happy fancy.

Kate thought she was never going to escape from that table. But Mrs. Judge having said: "I'm sure your garden's looking wonderful, Mrs. Norris," Mrs. Norris actually responded, rising at the same time:

"Shall we go and look at it?"

The happy party trooped out, the Judge hobbling rather behind, near Kate.

"Isn't that strange stuff," said Kate, picking up one of the Aztec obsidian knives that lay on the terrace parapet. "Is it jade?"

"Jade!" snarled the Judge. "Jade is green, not black. That's obsidian."

"But I've got a lovely little tortoise of black jade, from China," persisted Kate.

"You can't have. Jade's green."

"And I'm sure there's white jade," she insisted.

The Judge ignored her as if she was a fool.

"What's that?" cried Owen, hearing the word "jade" and being a Chinese enthusiast.

"Surely there's more jade than green jade!" appealed Kate.

"What!" cried Owen. "More! Why there's jade of every imaginable tint. White jade, rose jade, lavender jade – *beautiful!* Why, you should see the jade ornaments I collected in China! Exquisite work, and beautiful, beautiful colours. Only green jade! Ha-ha-ha!!"

They had come to the black, polished stairs. The Judge and Ramón Carrasco were last.

"I'll catch hold of your arm down here," said the Judge. "This stair-case is a death-trap."

Ramón silently gave his arm, and the white-haired little man hobbled down. Mrs. Norris pretended not to hear.

Evening was falling. In the garden roses and carnations were in bloom, and some beautiful scarlet hibiscus. But the flowers were not in the gorgeous profusion of South Italy.

The party broke into two parts. Mrs. Judge was being rather fadedly effusive with Mrs. Norris. The Judge was hobbling mid-way. Owen was hanging back with the General, and bridling, saying awkwardly:

"Really, one is almost driven to apologise for one's fellow countrymen."

"You can't be responsible for all the United States," replied Cipriano.

Kate was last, with Ramón Carrasco, trying to keep several flower-beds between herself and the Judge.

"Ah!" she sighed. "It is lovely to be out of doors again."

"Yes," he laughed. "That the vegetable kingdom has no tongue."

"I used to think I liked tea-time. I only know now how much I dislike it," she said.

"It is part of the game of life," he replied.

"I'm a little tired of the game of life. It's awful to be forced to take part in a game all the time."

"If the game is not worth to be played."

"And it really isn't, is it?" she said.

"This game – no – not as I find it. There might be other games."

"No," she said. "I am rather afraid of the game of life any more. It can be *so* meaningless: and *so* overbearing, so endlessly cruel in a small way. I wish there were some other game."

"There may be," he said.

Owen and Cipriano Viedma were waiting by a flowering arch. Dusk was really falling, under the big trees, and a firefly sparked now and then.

"General Viedma was asking if we'd go to dinner on Thursday," said Owen to Kate. "I said for my part I should like nothing better."

Kate looked at the smallish, silent man opposite, and felt his black eyes on her, half commanding her, half wanting something of her, waiting for her. And she wavered. She truly was weary of any more contacts.

"Thursday?" she said slowly. "Thursday?"

"Or another day if you wish," said the General, rather curtly.

"No, Thursday is as good as any other day," she replied, wearily.

"Thank you very much," said the General; while Owen once more brightened up wonderfully, thinking he had a new experience ahead.

They drifted through the archways into the patio, and there waited in silence for their hostess. The General had very little to say: he was too concise and direct for a conversationalist. While Ramón seemed voluntarily to withdraw from speech.

Up came the hostess with the Judge family, Mrs. Judge saying:

"When will you come and have lunch with us? I don't mean come out to our house. – Anywhere you like, in town –"

And Mrs. Norris was putting her off.

The two Mexicans took the opportunity to leave. And in another minute Kate found herself outside the great doors with Mrs. Judge asking her:

"How are you going back? There wasn't an automobile to be found when we wanted to come, and we were late, so we took a tram-car. Which means, I suppose, we shall have to go back by tram."

"We came in an old Ford," said Owen. "But where is he? He seems to have disappeared. General Viedma asked me if he could give us a seat in his car, but I said, No! We have a car. – Apparently, however, the man's gone! – What a curious thing!" And Owen disappeared into the night.

"Which way do you go?" asked Mrs. Judge.

"To the Zócalo," said Kate.

"Where are you staying?" asked Mrs. Judge.

"At a little Italian hotel, the Verona."

"We have to take a tram the opposite way, to San Angel," said Mrs. Judge.

"You vulgar little woman," thought Kate. "You are actually afraid lest I should want to claim acquaintance with you."

But aloud she said nothing; she didn't care.

The Judge was hobbling on the side-walk at a corner where two roads met, like a cat on hot bricks. Across the road stood a gang of natives in their big hats and white clothes, a little the worse for pulque. A second gang stood rather nearer: workmen.

"There you have 'em," said the Judge savagely. "The two lots of 'em."

"What two lots?" asked Kate.

"The country laborers and the town workmen, all more or less drunk, both the lots of them." And the Judge turned his back on Kate.

At that moment a tram-car with brilliant lights came rushing up out of the night.

"Here's our car," said the Judge, beginning to scramble for it already.

"You go the other way," said Mrs. Judge, also fluttering forward as if taking a perilous swim in the dark.

The couple clambered into the brightly lighted car and were whizzed away, without proffering the least "Good-night."

"Well," said Kate to herself. "I think you're the most ill-bred couple I *ever* met."

However, they were gone, she let them go. She was rather afraid, standing there at the corner by herself in the night, with those two gangs of men not quite sober. And yet, somehow, the tipsy laborers in their little cotton blouses and huge straw hats were more sympathetic, more pleasant to be near, than the people who had just gone.

Yet she was glad when the Ford came bumping up.

"I found the man in a pulquería," said Owen.

More terrors! Would he drive straight on that tiresome road back to Mexico City?

III   *Dinner with the General*

K ATE READ a little paragraph on the English page of the *Excelsior* that made her wonder.

"Considerable stir was made in Chapala, Jalisco, yesterday morning. Women who had spread their washing on the beach to dry, suddenly noticed a man wading out of the lake towards them, without any bathing-suit or covering. They withdrew to the promenade, but the man advanced among the washing, and picked up a pair of workman's cotton pants, which he proceeded to don. He was then looking round for a shirt, when the women ran down to defend their laundry. The man said he had come out of the lake, where he had been speaking with the God Quetzalcoatl. A crowd gathered, and the stranger, in his newly appropriated outfit, said that he came naked from the home of the god of the Indians, who lived under the lake. He was allowed to keep the clothing, and he disappeared into the town. The police are searching for him, suspecting one of the bandits from Ajijic. Considerable excitement prevails among the natives."

The chief effect this item of news had on Kate Burns was to make her wish to go to Chapala. She was tired of Mexico City. It was May, the end of the dry season, and dryness unbearable. The thought of water drew her at once. And so did the thought of a place where anybody, whether bandit or lunatic, could announce that he had spoken with the God Quetzalcoatl. She had always loved the name Quetzalcoatl. Altogether the Aztec and original Indian names fascinated her. She liked to think of a return of the God.

So at once she looked up Quetzalcoatl again in the guide book. He was god of the air and light, half bird, half serpent. He had ascended into the air from the top of the volcano of Orizaba, in the form of a peacock, or a bird of paradise, and had given a promise to return. It seemed queer that he should choose to rise from the bottom of a lake.

Kate also went to the museum, to look at the stone idol of

Quetzalcoatl. She came away feeling depressed, and hoping that none of those gloomy, gruesome Aztec things would ever come back. Life seemed all snakes and writhing things and malevolent birds like serpents, in that museum.

Nevertheless she said to Villiers:

"I should like to go to Chapala."

"Where's Chapala?"

"A little resort on a big lake not far from Guadalajara."

"A lake! Oh let's go!" said Villiers. "Why not?"

There was no reason why not. Nothing kept them in Mexico City. They were all three straying rather aimlessly round.

Kate had gone to the United States for a visit. She was the widow of an Irish rebel, or patriot, have it as you will, who had been killed in the late revolution in Ireland. She herself was of Irish blood, but her family had gone to live in England. She had two children, a boy and a girl, of fifteen and seventeen years old. They were at school in England. Their home was with her mother. Kate felt she couldn't live in England any more.

From the United States she had drifted with her cousin Owen, who lived in New Mexico, down to Old Mexico. Owen was a poet when he was anything: that is, he wrote poems and criticised them. Villiers was his friend, secretary, or disciple – any or all of these.

"Did I tell you how General Viedma rescued me at the bull-fight?" she said at luncheon, to Owen.

"Rescued you! Why no! What was that?"

She told him.

"Why how very nice of him! So much nicer than *we* were –" and Owen flushed with a little shame still. "Wasn't that courteous and nice! A bit of the real Mexican courtesy one hears of but so rarely meets. – But why did you keep it so dark!" – And Owen laughed uncomfortably.

"I don't know," said Kate.

"Perhaps so as not to make us feel ashamed. Ha-ha!" said Owen, lapsing into a muse, rolling back his eyes to think it over.

"That makes it heaps more romantic," said Villiers.

"Why yes!" said Owen. "And no doubt it was *he* who arranged the tea-party at Mrs. Norris'. I'm sure she'd never have asked *me* again, for the sake of seeing me. She asked you because the General wanted her to. Hm-hm! Quite interesting!"

"Oh I'm dying to meet him!" cried Villiers.

"Yes, he's quite interesting. I hear he's quite the power behind the throne – or behind the Presidential Chair – in Mexico. They say he has an extraordinary power over the men in the army, and that he's scheming to be President, or to make Ramón Carrasco President, next election. The radicals here don't like him at *all* – suspect another Diaz in him. They think he wants to become Tyrant of Mexico, as Diaz was. But apparently he never states his aims. – Anyhow it's awfully interesting that he engineered Mrs. Norris into that tea-party. – Ha-ha! – The Knight of the Cloak. A second Walter Raleigh. – Better: Walter Raleigh didn't have an automobile at hand for the lady – who was it – yes, Queen Elizabeth. Ha-ha-ha!"

And Owen ended on his uncomfortable laugh.

Kate saw that he was rather jealous. Men are so unreasonable. Owen was a confirmed bachelor, a bachelor by conviction and by practice. If he had thought he had to marry his cousin Kate he would have fled to the ends of the earth, not with her, but away from her. No, what made it so nice was that she didn't want to marry him any more than he wanted to marry her. She neither wanted to flirt nor be emotional in any way. Only she was a very sympathetic presence, and a perfect travelling companion. As for sex, she had got over it. Certainly between her and Owen there was nothing but good-natured friendship, with a touch of kinship.

He enjoyed her company immensely. But if she had wanted any closer contact he would have left her in a minute. Luckily she wanted closer contact as little as he did: probably less. Even Owen's amiable company was often a weariness to her. But she liked him.

What then could be more unreasonable than his spurt of jealousy against the General? Kate was not in love with Cipriano Viedma. She was in love with nobody, and she wanted to be in love with nobody. In the younger days she had loved her husband. Now he was dead. And with him was dead for her all that in-love business. She was a woman of thirty-eight. She wanted to be left in peace, not forced into close contact with anything or anybody.

The inside of her soul had gone remote from contact. Even her children were a weariness to her, when they were about. She felt, somehow, that her life wasn't in accord with their lives. They belonged to England, to their grandmother, to tennis and cricket matches and summer at the seaside, and school. And she was glad. But it all wearied her. Her destiny had been to marry Desmond Burns. And he

had taken all that away from her. In the end he had taken away even
the desire for love. He had made the world lose all its value for her, he
had made her almost as remote as himself. And she could not go back
on it. He was dead, but somehow he did not seem dead. She never felt
he was dead. His spirit lived so strongly in her. She never felt for a
moment she was a widow. It was as if he had placed their marriage
outside the world and outside of events. She was always married to
him, he was always married to her. Death, somehow, didn't make it
different. He left his influence upon her for ever.

So she didn't fret, or grieve. She wasn't unhappy at all. Only she
avoided the thing she had known as the world. On the whole, she
avoided it: England, her mother, her children, Ireland – she just kept
out of range, out of reach. She felt it had to be so. It was her nature,
now.

And in the same way she avoided any further close contacts. She
did not want them. Something was accomplished in her, she sought
for nothing further. As for her wandering, that was really negative.
She did not wander seeking. She wandered to avoid a home, a group, a
family, a circle of friends, an "interest." She wanted to avoid all that.

In a way, Owen was the same. His very rushing to every little
commotion was really an avoiding of the fixed world. He too was very
sensitive to contacts. But he was American, he unconsciously believed
that the man who lived out of contact with the world missed life
altogether. So, as a compromise, he rushed for all the little contacts.

In spite of all these facts, he was at once jealous of General
Viedma. It was as if he had had a slight smack in the face, himself. He
thought about it, swallowed a little wine, and thought again.

"The idea of your keeping the cloak incident dark from us –
absolutely cloaking the General from our sight. I suppose if we hadn't
met him again at Mrs. Norris' – that is, if *he* hadn't brought it about –
we should never have heard of him from you at all. General Cipriano
Viedma! Or was it Viemda! I'm getting mixed."

"Oh I think Cipriano is such a gorgeous name!" cried Villiers.
"Cipriano! That's Cyprian in English, isn't it? Gorgeous! I'm dying to
meet him."

"You *shall* meet him, you American child," said Owen.

"But when? Can't I go to dinner with you on Thursday? I suppose
not, if he didn't ask me."

"We'll give him a dinner back again," said Owen soothingly.

And after luncheon he immediately set out to glean more information about his new rival.

After dinner, sipping a gin-and-vermouth cocktail, he said:

"Oh, by the way –"

When Owen said By-the-way, Kate always knew it wasn't by the way at all, but something Owen had had long on his mind.

"By the way, I heard several quite interesting things about General Cipriano Viemda – Viedda – *Viedma!* Viedma! That's it, isn't it? I can never get that Vied-*ma*."

"Well go *on*," said Villiers. "Let's hear it."

"Oh, it's most romantic. Apparently he is a child of the people – pure Indian – son of a peon on a big coffee hacienda somewhere near Jalapa, belonging to English people. There was a story that he had been inoculated against snake-bites – or something like that. The mistress of the hacienda, an Englishwoman, happened to be bitten on the ankle by a snake, in her bath-room, when little Cipriano was a boy about the house. Apparently he was the first to hear her scream. He ran in to the lady's bath-room – we are not told the state of her déshabille – and seized her ankle and sucked out the poison. As a result, she was slightly ill only, and he too was slightly ill. After that she took an interest in him, which seemed to develop as he grew older. Anyhow she sent him to school in England, and then to Oxford. While he was at Oxford she died, without leaving him a penny. He made his way back to Mexico, and Diaz gave him a commission in the army. – Oh, by the way, beware he doesn't bite you, because the natives have a superstition that his bite is poisonous. Apparently they have a considerable fear of him, in the snaky line, which no doubt accounts for his power over them. The radicals, as I told you, fear him more as a schemer for power. They think he wants to be a second Diaz. However, he has pledged himself to be faithful to the present government. It is at election time they fear him. Apparently he hates the bolshevists – or they think he does. And at the same time the property-owning people and the business people hate him, because they say he is more bolshevist than the bolshevists. In fact he seems to be one of the best-hated, and feared, men in Mexico, by the so-called 'upper' classes. Apparently the lower classes look upon him as their real representative: all, that is to say, except the factory-workers, who are rampant bolshevists every one of them.

"Now isn't that romantic! And isn't it amusing to think of his effect on our friend Judge Ball! Almost worse than a banana-skin. Mrs. Norris apparently is a shrewd old lady, with an eye for the exceptional anyhow. She has friends in all camps; and doesn't always succeed in keeping them apart – like last Sunday. Ha-ha! Wasn't it amusing? – She doesn't like the Americans, really, although she tries to keep up appearances. You see there's quite a large anti-bolshevist party, the hacendados and business people, who want to get into power and then join Mexico to the United States in a sort of federal union: the first step to annexation by us. The people with property look on annexation as the only hope – for their property, of course. I don't suppose it will ever come to pass. I don't think the United States altogether wants to take the Mexican serpent to its bosom. Ha-ha-ha! Especially with the I.W.W. growing more troublesome at home, and England in such a state.

"But isn't it fun! Isn't it fun down here! You feel just *anything* might happen: bolshevism, or annexation by the U.S., or a new Napoleon. Of course, in spite of all my communist sympathies, the last is what I would like best. *Never again,* the radicals declare, 'Never again will Mexico fight for a *man.* That at last is finished. Mexico has her eyes opened. In the future she will fight only for an *idea,* for a principle.' Well, that's all right. Only a man is rather more fun.

"But I haven't told you the whole of the story. The god in the Viedma machine is apparently Don Ramón. He, apparently, is of a good family, and supposed to be one of the cleverest men in Mexico. But he won't have anything at all to do with politics. They suspect him of trying to found a new religion. This man among the washing, at Chapala, is apparently being used by Don Ramón to influence the people to a sort of new religious revival. I don't know how much truth there is in the story. Some people look on Carrasco as a crank, a sort of latent lunatic, and some think he is really a remarkable person. I say, why not both? Anyhow he is fairly rich, and the government doesn't get in his way. He and Cipriano, apparently, are inseparable: a David and Jonathan couple without any love. The august Ramón apparently considers himself beyond and above all love. But he has allied himself very closely with General Cipriano, who seems to have a fixed belief in him.

"And between them, apparently, they ignore all Mexican and foreign 'society.' Since the last revolution, Don Ramón says there is no Mexican society, there are only Mexican parasites. It seems to me he's about right there. So he just blandly ignores all the people with houses and motor-cars. Mrs. Norris is one of his *very* few friends: or acquaintances, perhaps, is better. The rest he just won't know. They call him Don Augusto Misterio. That's rather nice: Augusto Misterio! Ha-ha-ha!"

"What does it mean?" snapped Villiers.

"Don Augustus Mystery," said Owen.

Villiers gave a little snirt of laughter.

"Oh what fun!" he said. "I must meet Don Augusto. I suppose he'll annihilate me with a look!"

"There!" exclaimed Owen. "Didn't I find out a great deal! And how well I remember it all! It surprises me. But don't you think we've run up against the two most interesting figures in Mexico?"

"You'd make a good private detective," said Kate. "A mixture of private detective and old maid."

Owen glanced at her quickly, with round, rolling eyes, at once feeling her contempt and preparing for some later revenge.

"But aren't you glad to *know* it all?" he said.

"Why should one know about people!" she replied. "It only prejudices one, and makes a false approach."

"Oh, in that case, if I've spoiled your approach to Don Cipriano, I'm sorry. Why didn't you stop me sooner?"

"I didn't say you'd spoiled my approach to Don Cipriano," she replied. "But I don't care for finding out about people. I'd rather get to know them direct."

"Why can't you do both? Will what I've told you about Cyprian prevent your knowing him for yourself?"

"I don't care about knowing him. But if I've got to know him, I'd rather not start by knowing things about him."

"Not even the snake-poison myth?"

"No, not even that."

"Well there I differ from you. It seems to me I get a much fuller picture of the man when I know these important facts."

They were to dine at General Cipriano's house in Coyoacan. Owen was anxious, wondering whether or not to put on a dinner-coat.

"No," said Kate. "You say you feel humiliated to the earth every time you put on a dress-suit. You say you feel it is a ridiculous and humiliating sight, a man in evening dress. So why should you think about it? Especially as nobody has sent you a card with *dress essential* on it."

"Oh, very well," he said, "then I suppose I won't."

But his nose was a bit out of joint for all that.

Especially when he came down and found Kate looking very handsome in a simple gown of black velvet and glimmering, velvety-brocaded chiffon, and a long string of jade and crystal. His face fell terribly as he squared his shoulders.

"Why you're dressed up to the eyes!" he cried. "Bare shoulders notwithstanding!"

"I made it myself!" she said.

"And that lovely chain!"

"Judge Ball's green jade."

"Exactly! You're all of a green jade yourself, tonight."

The General lived in a smallish modern house, with a garden enclosed in high walls, out at Coyoacan. They went up a path under orange-trees, in the darkness heavy with the scent of southern honeysuckle. But already the night air was chill, though May was well in, so Kate drew her yellow shawl around her.

They found the General in a white regimental dinner-jacket, and Don Ramón also in white. Owen was really chagrined.

The house, and the meal, were very simple.

"Is Chapala nice? I want to go to Chapala," said Kate.

"Chapala is a little place by the lake, with several hotels that will now be empty, and a little sandy beach where Guadalajara people come and bathe. But they go home in their motor-cars, or in the camions, as a rule before dark, being afraid of highwaymen," replied the General.

"But do you think we should like to stay the summer there?" asked Kate. "My cousin and Mr. Villiers and myself."

"It depends on what you want. Why do you think of Chapala?"

"Because there is water. And when I read of the man who said he had seen Quetzalcoatl, suddenly I wanted to go."

"To see Quetzalcoatl?" smiled the General.

"No, for the water."

"Yes, I think you would like Chapala. – Then you don't think of going back soon to England?"

"No. No. I think of going. I am always thinking of going. I nearly bought my ticket last week. And now, instead, I want to go to Chapala."

"My cousin would go to England if she *could*," said Owen. "But the moment she makes a move to set off, she recoils, and retreats farther back from it than ever."

"That is curious," smiled the General. "Yet you have children in England, I am told."

"Yes. But really I belonged to Ireland, with my husband, if I belonged anywhere. And my children are so happy at school and with their grandmother in England, I only disturb them. I know I only disturb them. And why should I!"

"You think they should not be disturbed?" he smiled.

"No! No! Some people it is good for them to be disturbed. It isn't good for my children. They belong to their grandmother's world, curiously enough."

She said it, however, sadly, as if disappointed. As if something were lost to her.

"It may easily be so," he said.

The General had full, dark Indian eyes, without the Indian vagueness or sadness. His look was bright, almost imperious. And yet, as his eyes rested on Kate's face, she knew he wanted something of her. The bright, Indian imperiousness was rather fascinating, at a distance. That he wanted something of her also – and she knew by instinct that he did – wearied her. She did not wish to make any great effort any more, as long as she lived. She wanted to be left in peace.

"So you wish to stay a long time in Mexico?" asked Don Ramón.

"No. I am half my time anxious to go away. I get moments of terrible depression – oppression it seems like – here. The country oppresses me sometimes – or something does – terribly."

"What it is that oppresses, or depresses you?" asked the General.

"I don't know. It may be inside myself. But it seems to me something is trying to drag me down, down, down all the time."

"Down to where?"

"Down to earth absolutely. Right down. And never get up again."

"But why should one not come down to earth?" smiled the General.

"I know. I always wanted to. But not like a deer dragged down by wolves. Or a tree chopped down. Not to be *dragged* down."

"Do you know what drags you down?"

"I don't know. The spirit of the place. Democracy. There seems to be such a heavy, heavy democracy here – like a snake pulling one down. And I don't want to stand up on any class distinction or anything false. But surely, in myself, I do stand a little higher than the mass of people. My husband made me believe I did, and I still believe it. And people seem to want to pull one right down."

"But all people?" said the General, laughing a little.

"Yes," she cried, "all people. Even Owen does. The bourgeois people all just insult one, because one is by nature something better than they are. Knowing them is one continual insult."

"That is true," said the General. "But they are still a minority."

"No," she said. "Because working-people are the same. Oh I *don't* like workmen. I used to like them so much, to think they were right. And now I don't. I *don't* like them. They only want to pull everything down, even the *natural* things. They want to pull one's *natural* soul down, and make it something mechanical and vulgar. Oh, I don't like them. And I don't believe in liberty. I don't believe in socialism. I don't believe in liberty. And I *don't* like workmen who work for wages and think about politics. I've been insulted, insulted, insulted all the way. That's the last word my husband said to me: 'Kate, perhaps I've been wrong. We should have kept away from it all. We shouldn't have given ourselves to them. It's been a wrong done to the best in us. I'm so sorry, Kate. But I'll try and look after you better in death than I did in life.' – And so he died –"

Her face became the mask of anguish that is almost mortal. Bitter tears came down her cheeks, and she hid her face in her serviette as she sat there at table. There was a dead silence. Owen of course was crying. The General had gone pale, his black eyes gleamed with a fierce, almost demonish look, and at the same time seemed to envelop the woman with a sheltering pity. Kate, with the napkin pressed to her face, showing her spread hands, with the wedding ring and one big emerald ring engraved with her family crest, for a seal, was just a bit absurd, as Owen saw her through his tears. But she had been vulnerable, and the hurt was mortal in her.

Owen coughed, and dared not take off his spectacles to wipe them.

The two Mexicans did not see the absurdity. To them, convention was a shallow, if stiff thing. Don Ramón watched the woman and her hidden face with a strong, roused gaze. There was a profound, dark passion in his soul, the passion of an unexpressed belief. A passionate belief in gods half known to him.

He waited for a while, then he said, in his subtle, resonant voice:

"And native people – the country laborers – the campesinos, or peónes, the men in the big hats – do they also pull you down?"

Kate did not answer, but remained behind her napkin. Then she wiped her tears, and her face was all red and spoiled with tears and the moment's anguish. Then she took a mouthful of wine.

"I'm sorry!" she said, with a blurt of a laugh.

Then she turned towards Don Ramón with eyes that glittered still unseeing in her scalded face.

"What did you say?" she asked. And her face was breaking again with bitter emotion.

"The world has made a mistake," he said, in his slow, measured English and his hypnotic voice, that had a throaty quality above a startling deep resonance: something like a violoncello. The sound of his voice distracted Kate from her emotion, drew her elsewhere.

"The world is mistaken. There is no liberty, only the will of some God. The will of our own gods is liberty to us, nothing else. Nothing else is liberty. And for men to have free will is the worst and cruelest of slavery. They are slaves to every formula. – Now tell me," he added, "what you think of our men with big hats and our women with shawls, the peons, as you say. Do they drag you down?"

Kate still did not hear what he was saying. Only the words: "There is no liberty! – there is no liberty!" re-echoed in her consciousness.

"My husband worked so hard for liberty," she said.

"It was his destiny," replied Don Ramón.

And for some reason that soothed her.

"I always knew, at the bottom," she said, "it was a mistake. I always knew, at the bottom, that there is no such thing as liberty. I always knew. Yet my children don't seem to know. It seems real to them."

"Perhaps they are weak," said Don Ramón. "Liberty is the delusion of weak people. When life is strong it wishes to act. But liberty is a sick soul that cannot get well."

"But why should my children have sick souls? – I don't say they have –"

"I do not know that they have. Yet they are the children of your liberty delusion."

"But my husband wasn't a sick soul —" she pondered.

"Perhaps he was deluded by all the sick ones crying around him."

There was a long pause.

"Terrible," said Kate slowly, "to live so long in a mistake."

"We are only men," said Don Ramón. "We live to find out our mistakes."

"But we have to realise the mistake in the end," said Kate.

"That is manhood."

There was silence again, while the man-servant brought the plates for dessert.

"Still," said Kate, "it is bitter."

"But it is good to realise the mistake, and kill it."

"My husband didn't have a chance to kill it," she said, thinking of her children.

"The soul is immortal, of all brave people," said Don Ramón.

He assumed a quiet authority, sitting there at the table peeling a sticky mango. He was handsome too; and well-bred. But he did not care much whom he talked to.

"But tell me," he said to her. "Return to the conversation before you became sad." And he smiled at her curiously, but with fascinating delicacy. "Tell me, do the peons, the men with the big hats, and their women with shawls, rebozos, do they also pull you down?"

She tried to collect herself sufficiently to answer. She thought of the peons, driving their strings of asses along the country roads, in the dust of Mexico's infinite dryness, past broken walls, broken houses, broken haciendas, along the endless desolation left by revolutions; past vast stretches of the maguey, the huge cactus with its magnificent upstarting rosette of iron-pointed leaves, that covers miles and miles of ground in the Valley of Mexico, cultivated for the intoxicating drink of the natives, pulque; past the wonderful fields of wheat and maize, sloping towards the lower land; past tall, bright-green sugar-cane: the eternal peon of Mexico, in his huge straw hat, and his white cotton clothes, with wide, flopping trousers, and with his inevitable sarape, the blanket which is his cloak, his bed, his shelter of every description. She thought of the tall, erect peons of the north, of the more uncertain men of the Mexico Valley, with their heads through the middle of their ponchos; of the rather short, Asiatic-looking Indian in the Vera Cruz State; of the handsome men in the west, with their great scarlet sarapes, real blankets now, hung splendidly over one shoulder. They had all of them something in common, whether they wore blue overalls for Mexico City, or the tight, skin-tight trousers on their handsome legs, as in the east, or the wide, floppy white cotton as in the fields westward. They had almost all the same erect, somewhat prancing walk, stepping out from the base of the spine; the same jaunty way of balancing the huge hat, as if it were a crest; the same stiff shoulders, slightly swinging; and the same swagger of the sarape. Many of them were handsome, with their dark, bronze-dark skin, finely poised heads, and their thick, fine, black hair. They had a splendid proud look. Till you met their black eyes fully. And then their eyes had no centre to them. As Kate said, the essential man wasn't there.

A fair proportion, too, of smaller, sometimes insignificant-looking dark men, who had often a cat-like antagonism in their look, which made her feel afraid. Devoid of human sympathy, poisonous, thin, stiff little men, cold and unliving like scorpions, and as dangerous.

And then the awful, pulque-brutish faces of some of the Indians in the city, with a slightly swollen look, and black, dimmed, awful eyes full of an inchoate, evil misery. She tried not to see these faces. Yet they had gone deep into her consciousness.

Yet, withal, she felt a natural, true compassion for them, such as she never felt for white men. They were not cowed. These men were not cowed, even if they were not quite created. Almost deeper than her consciousness, the bowels of her compassion stirred and bled. And at the same time, she feared the presence of the Indians. They would pull her down, pull her down.

The same with the women, in their full, long skirts and bare feet, and with the big, dark-blue, wide scarf over their womanly round heads and enfolding their shoulders. Many women kneeling in a dim church, all hooded in their dark-blue rebozos, the pallor of their skirts on the floor, head and shoulders wrapped close and dark in the scarf, and swaying with devotion: the devotion of fear. A churchful of dark-wrapped women kneeling like dark toadstools on the ground, and silent in a devotion of fear. The crouching of people not quite created, fearful for themselves.

Their soft, untidy black hair; the round-eyed baby joggling like a pumpkin slung in the shawl over the woman's back; the never-washed feet and ankles under the long, flounced, soiled cotton skirt; and then, once more, the dark eyes of the women, soft, appealing, and, it seemed to Kate, untrustworthy. Something lurking in their eyes, where the womanly centre should have been. Fear – and the companion of fear, mistrust – and inevitable result of mistrust, a lurking insolence.

It was the same, really, in the eyes of the men: the void in the blackness, the fear, the mistrust, and the lurking, waiting insolence. But then the men were more reckless than the women. They would risk themselves with a certain generosity. But they would perhaps never trust. And in the end, maybe the insolence would be the last thing left.

Kate was much too Irish to have any respect for blind belief between human beings. No, if belief was to have any value, it must be slow, and wary. But it must be possible.

After the death of her husband, she had been driven to believe that she must trust nobody, nobody, nothing any more. But since she was in America, where no one *does* trust anybody any more: where no man or woman ever seems to have a final, resting trust in anything, man or woman or god, but where everybody depends on the social code of behaviour, which everybody supports in order to make life possible at all; since she had been a year in America, she felt a craving for human trust, for belief.

She felt life could not go on any further. There was no faith left.

What was she doing herself? Drifting there in Mexico, with her cousin Owen, and with young Villiers. Why? Why? What had she come for?

She looked at the two Mexicans, and her soul seemed empty.

What had she come for? Just to fool her time away. No more. She wanted just to fool the rest of her life away, for her life was over. Like Owen. He too had no life. Perhaps his life had never even begun. So wearily he played around. The Playboy of the Western World.

Oh he had been in business. He had been successful too, and had made money. The business men could take no rise out of him. But business had been the weariest of all his games, the dreariest of all his Main Street pastimes. He had even thrown it up, in contempt, and been satisfied with a moderate income.

Better play, simply and purely play at playing, than keep up the heavy hand at whist, which was the business game. Better fool about in Mexico taking kodak pictures and exclaiming over peculiarities of the natives. For after all, if one had a life to live, better not make the farce too heavy. The light hand, the light hand! And business was played with an absurdly solemn, heavy hand.

Playboys of the Western World. Owen, snapping kodak pictures and carefully putting together bits of poetry, or reviewing little dramas in the solemnity of his hotel bedroom! Owen, exploring the Thieves' Market in Mexico for odds and ends, with all the eagerness of another Humboldt. Owen darting to the Literary Club to get communistic and angry with some capitalist. Owen being thrilled by the natives, and hoping that at last they had got a real representative government!

And Owen not caring, inside him, one single straw about any of these activities. Just forcing himself to be a playboy, by strength of will. Almost a martyr to his own amusement. And inside, hopelessly, helplessly indifferent to everything. A playboy with a hopeless void of indifference and dreariness at the middle of him. A void growing slowly wider and more gaping. The gap where his soul should be.

Young Villiers almost worse. He hadn't even the rags of liberalism and idealism to flutter. He didn't even care vastly about amusing himself. He hadn't done anything and he hadn't loved anybody. He wanted to be a playboy of the western world also, but he was frightfully difficult to amuse. He was almost all gap, with a fine hard-stone self around it. Like a finely-cut stone hammer with a hollow core, only pleased when he was giving little destructive taps at something.

Villiers was absolutely cold about love: as cold as an obsidian hammer. But he always dressed himself with meticulous care. Why, Kate never knew. Unless the hollow at the middle of him was haunted by the self-admiring ghost of himself. Poor Villiers, so young, yet with absolutely nothing ahead except tapping against everything he came across, to knock a chip or two off it. He never wanted to break anything. Just knock a chip or two off everything, and he was delighted with a bird-like delight.

At the centre of his eye, all the same, the strange, arching void that sometimes seemed to dilate with horror, but which usually basked like a snake asleep. There was in his eyes the curious basking apathy of a snake asleep. But sometimes, again, the apathy uncoiled in a sort of frenzy.

The gap. The awful gap at the middle of people. In Owen, it was a slow, soft caving-in. With Villiers it was a hard, finely-wrought rim around an everlasting void: like some sort of jewel with a blackish centre. With the Mexican natives it was an unutterably dark pit in the midst of a strong, soft-flaming life.

The pit! The bottomless pit of hollowness where the soul should be, in a man and in a woman. The white soul just caving in, like Owen. Everything in the white world going with a slow, soft slide over the edge of the bottomless pit that has opened like a fissure in the white man's soul. Down which all the world will slide, since the white man's soul has been the centre of the world for many years now. And now it has caved in upon an inner emptiness.

And the dark man's soul not ready yet. She was, in some way, afraid of these natives, afraid of their gleaming black eyes with no centre to them. She felt they might explode like gunpowder in some horrible passion, a passion with nothing to control it. A terrible black potentiality, without any soul to assume responsibility. Without any soul to hold control over the dark life-potentialities.

They fascinated her, these people. She felt they had never had a soul, and lost it. They had never been cowed. Owen had been cowed. Villiers looked as if he were always trying to bear up against some hateful menace. Almost all white men she knew were cowed, their souls were cowed inside them, though they had amazing courage of self-sacrifice still. But the strange soft flame of life-courage had gone out of them, leaving that hateful gap, which so often becomes me-chanical and demonish, like a reversed pivot. That reversed look! The look which is in the very middle of the eyes of so many white people. As if life were running in the reverse direction.

But in the eyes of the natives, the strange soft flame of life-courage. Only it was not knit to a centre, that centre which is the soul in a man. The soft, full flame of life in dark eyes. But centreless, the eyes centreless and helpless, sometimes demonish, diabolical.

The white men have not been able to fuse the soul of the dark men into being. Instead, in his attempt to overwhelm and convert the dark man to the white way of life, the white man has lost his own soul, collapsed upon himself.

Kate thought of Mexico, the great, precipitous, dry, savage coun-try, with a handsome church in every landscape, rising as it were out of nowhere. A revolution-broken landscape. But everlasting tall, hand-some churches. Magnificent patriarchal haciendas often in ruins. But churches, great gorgeous churches standing still above everything, above the straw and adobe huts of the natives, above trees and ruins and deserts. And meaningless. No meaning in all these fine churches. No reason why they should be there.

The cities of Mexico, great and small, Spanish cities with their strong square houses of stone, their fountains, their plazas or public squares with trees and side-walks and water, their cobbled streets, their gorgeous, rather overdone churches. The Spaniards planted them all, created them all, as it were, out of nothingness. And all, except perhaps Mexico City, are nothing: standing waiting to fall down. The churches all feel alike: as if standing waiting to fall down. Waiting for the earthquake that will shake off Spain again, from America. Shake off England and all white influence. The men go to church still – not so much; the women still go much. But it is fear that takes them. Fear of the revenge of a dangerous omnipotence, should they fail in worship. Fear of a dangerous authority.

It has not been the fate of Spain, and it has not been the fate of Christianity, to bring the Indians of the west into their own being. The Amerindian has not come into his own soul during the Christian occupation. Perhaps he has been held back. And he is waiting still. Waiting for his own fulfilment of his own destiny.

And there, Kate felt, was the difference between Owen's vacuum and the Indian void. Owen's was the loss of his own old soul: the other was the failure, so far, of a race of men to possess their own souls. The one was a negative, deathly thing: the other the painful slow process of creation.

For this reason she felt a throb of compassion for the Indian. He was still vulnerable, still in the process of suffering for his own incompleteness. Owen was invulnerable, save on the surface. He would wince from hurt or insult, and then the hurt, the insult would pass on into the vacuum, where of course it turned into nothingness. Whatever penetrated deeply in Owen passed straight into the void of nothingness. Only the surface was sentient. Below the surface he just negated everything. Since nothing really mattered. Living was but a superficial fuss.

But the Indian, the Mexican native was still a hot flux of life, like lava. Only uncontrolled, uncentred, and therefore horrible. And wanting to pull down the white man from his white centrality. – That definitely.

But the white man's authority and religion have given the Indian a certain breathing space, a certain relief from his own blind, blood-stained self.

The religion and the authority are now both broken. The Indian once more knows he is thrown on himself. The white man is mechanically exploiting him, now. For the heroism of the first manly conquerors, and the beauty of the first Christian padres has disappeared into the automatism of capitalism and exploitation. What is there now to honour in the white man's world!

So that, naturally, in one sense the Indian is the white man's enemy. Naturally he wants, in his slow, silent persistence, to pull down the white man and the white man's world. Good and bad alike, perhaps, since he has not come to the point of fine discrimination.

"Yes," said Kate, in answer to Don Ramón's question. "I feel that the peons do want to pull me down, too. But not so much personally, out of a desire to destroy me, personally, as white people do. They don't seem to me *mean,* as white people are.

"Only, they do seem to me on a lower level than myself. And they do want to bring me down from my level. Even they want to love me at their own level – like the old woman-servant who is so awfully nice. But they never want to come up to my level. They won't even *look* up to it. They don't look up to it. They just solidly expect me to come down to them. As if they were the magnetic earth which everything must come down to."

"But maybe," said Owen, "you are mistaken in considering their level as lower than your own. It may only be different."

"No," said Kate. "They are lower. Their sort of heaviness, and their unfreeness, as if a stone lay on their souls. No, I think it would be wrong of me to disown my own higher self."

"But maybe," persisted Owen, "the magnetic earth *is* the greatest reality: much greater than any human loftiness."

"No," said Kate. "The human soul is more than the magnetic earth. I *know* I mustn't let myself be pulled *right* down."

"It seems to me," said Owen, "that we can only get back to reality by coming right back to earth."

"I used to think that," said Kate. "I used to want to live in a cave. Now I know that a cave isn't any more real than a villa. The Indians in their straw huts aren't any more real than I am in a flat in London. Perhaps less. They are even less fulfilled. They seem so hopeless in their straw huts."

"Do you think so?" cried Owen.

"They are less fulfilled, they feel less real than I do. They never feel quite real to themselves. That's how they seem to me. And that is where I am higher. Don't you think so?" she asked, turning to the General.

He was watching her with uneasy black eyes.

"I think it is as you say," he replied. "But is it necessary, pardon me, for a woman to know so much?"

"What else should I do!" she replied.

"Ah Señora!" he exclaimed, with a faint smile and a deprecating wave of the hands, dropping his head as if it made him feel impatient and a little hopeless.

"Nobody can live my life for me, can they?" she said.

"I think," he replied, "that some-one might think all these things for you, so that you need not have the trouble of thinking them. I am sure Don Ramón will think it all for you – and even for me, since he is a better thinker than I, and I believe what he says."

His eyes, as he watched her, were mocking, and baffled with pity, and at the same time pleading for something.

"Can Don Ramón think my thoughts for me?" she said.

"Such big, heavy, serious thoughts," he replied, smiling.

She looked across at Don Ramón. He looked so large and portentous.

"I shall *always* think my own thoughts," she said. "You cannot prevent it, without beheading me."

"*Bueno, Señora, bueno! Muy bueno!*" deprecated the General. "But we also think. We also have thoughts. Yes, we also!"

"Ah!" she said distrustfully. "Men can't think for women."

"No?" said the General, sceptical.

"With my husband, I always had to think for myself. He had his ideas, and his ideals, and his enthusiasm. And it all broke down in the end. And I was left with nothing but the things I had learnt for myself, looking at things with my own eyes."

"Ah, Señora, your husband! A white man! They never come to earth, as you say. They are like the aeroplanes the world is so proud of, always in the air. That, they say, is higher." And the General smiled sardonically.

Kate flushed, and bethought herself.

"I know it," she said. "That is why I must think for myself."

"We are not all white men. There are other men in the world except white men," said the General, perhaps sarcastically.

She looked at him in doubt and mistrust.

"I should always have to think my own thoughts," she said.

"*Bueno, Señora, muy bueno!* They need not always be such thoughts."

And he smiled soothingly.

Her face hardened a little as she considered this.

"Señora," said Don Ramón, shifting a little from his statuesque motionlessness, and smiling that strange, fascinating smile which always made her heart contract with fear. "We come back to earth to have roots in the earth. Life is still a tree, it is not a loose leaf in the air, or an aeroplane. Come back to earth to have deep roots, deep in the earth." He made a gesture downwards, and the look of his black eyes, so determined on something to her unknown and unspeakable, made her blood stand still. Then, with a return of the slowly unfolding smile, that had such a dark gleam at the centre of it, he said: "But from the roots we grow up, up, as far as the sap will carry us." And he made the gesture with his dark, suave hands, whose palms were a little paler and more naked-seeming than the backs. "We grow up, up as far as the sap will take us. Like a tree: a very great tree." And he spread his fingers in the air, then looked at her with that point of light in the middle of his black eyes. "Now the Indians in America are lying low. They are sending up no shoots of life. Not yet. But their roots are deep, their roots are very deep, and when they start to grow upwards, it will be like an earthquake to the white man's world of factories and machines. Life is still a tree, Señora, it is not a collection of aeroplanes or a swarm of insects."

His words sounded like a threat, to her.

"I shall be very glad," she said, meeting his eyes, "when life *is* a tree again, with roots. No one will be more glad."

"It will rise from the roots only. It will not descend from above, out of words or aeroplanes," said Don Ramón, "or thin air."

"But what exactly *are* the roots?" asked Owen, rather petulant.

"The roots are the human blood. That which rises up out of the blood, like a tree with its roots in the dark water which is below the earth, that is manhood. The human blood sends up the tree of life. The human mind is only a flowering on the tree, which passes and comes again. – And only those that have power of blood will live, when the blood begins to send up the new tree from the darkness under the world."

Owen felt oppressed, but not convinced of anything. For him the blood was a red fluid whose laws and properties are known. This rather portentous prognosticating, as he felt it, annoyed him. Yet he felt oppressed and annulled.

Kate also battled against Don Ramón. But she believed what he said, in her heart of hearts. And it made her go dumb.

And so it ended in a silence of the two white people, against the two dark-skinned men.

IV   *The Lake*

O WEN WENT ON AHEAD to Lake Chapala to scout round. Kate felt so weary of aimless travel. She wanted Owen to find a house where she could settle down for a month or two. Owen sent word that the Orilla Hotel, near Ixtlahuacan, was perfect, that they were to bring the luggage and leave it at the station, and come on straight to the hotel.

Kate sent a telegram to Owen, and she and Villiers set off in the night train from Mexico, westward. The Pullman was almost full, people going to Guadalajara and Colima, mostly bourgeois Mexicans, three military officers, one deeply craped widow, two country farmers in tight trousers. It was a Pullman, looking clean and fresh, with hot green plush seats, exactly as in the United States. But the atmosphere so different. So much more silent, more guarded. And so much more casual. The farmers had beautiful sarapes, folded on the seats. The military officers seemed shy, as if they were new inside their clothes. Nobody spoke except in low tones.

Villiers looked round with bright eyes, pleased to be setting off again.

"My how different from a crowd in an American Pullman!" he said.

It was a grey evening, with a sudden wind and whirling dust, and a few spots of rain. The train drew out into the scattered, hopeless fringe of the town, and stopped after a few minutes in the main street of a suburb village, where dust was whirling. It was a grey evening, and men stood in groups sheltering their faces with their sarapes, while donkey-drivers ran frantically, uttering short cries, to prevent their donkeys from wandering in between the cars of the train, on the lines. Silent dogs trotted in and out from under the carriages, women, their faces wrapped in their blue rebozos, because of the dust, watched the passengers in the Pullman, or came to offer tortillas, flat, round, dry pancakes of maize, wrapped in a cloth to keep them warm, or pulque, in an earthern mug, or pieces of chicken smothered in oily red sauce, or oranges, or pitahayas. It was about six o'clock, and the earth was absolutely dry and stale. Everybody was in the street, the men balancing their huge hats against the wind. Men on quick, fine little horses, guns slung behind them, trotted up, lingered, then trotted away again with the wind.

Villiers got down to look, and stood watching a little girl kindle the careless charcoal fire in the street, to cook the evening meal. He wandered down the train. It had two Pullmans, and two other coaches, the third-class coach at the end crowded with peasants camping with their food and bundles of all sorts. One peasant woman was travelling with a fine peacock under her arm, putting it down sometimes and trying in vain to suppress it under her skirts. But she always had to take it up again. Melons, pumpkins, jars, baskets, bundles, guns, soldiers, and a great medley of people. In the van at the end, more soldiers with loaded guns, little fellows in dirty whitish uniforms, looking more dangerous than the bandits they were there to guard against. A great confusion of life. But all subdued, hushed, without the clamour and stridency of Europe.

It was falling dusk when the train moved at length out into the country of the Valley of Mexico, the flat plain, the mountains invisible save just near at hand. There were some green trees and green, irrigated fields. But for the most part, bare, dry land with broken masonry, sometimes a broken hacienda, a row of broken adobe huts. Partly it was revolution, partly the natural collapse of the grey-black adobe, the mournful adobe made of volcanic mud. The flat, desolate-seeming stretches of the Valley, with occasional vivid sections of cultivation. And everywhere dark-seeming.

There came a heavy shower. The train was passing through a pulque hacienda, the lines of the giant maguey stretched away bristling and menacing in the gloom. Then the lights came on in the Pullman, and the attendant passed along the car, quickly fastening down the blinds, to shut out the night, and prevent as far as possible anybody's shooting at the passengers from the darkness outside. The train's evening had begun.

Kate ordered a little food, at an exorbitant price, from the buffet of the Pullman: such tiny little portions, at such large charge. And nobody complained. It was the Pullman, it wasn't the natural earth.

And at eight o'clock the attendant was already beginning to prepare for the night, pulling down the beds from above. He was an elderly Mexican with an Irish, pug-dog face. His assistant was a young Mexican pitted with small-pox. There was no gainsaying them. They were determined to make the beds at once. The passengers were driven unprotesting from their seats, while the operation was performed. Kate *almost* protested. But her Spanish wasn't good enough. And the other passengers had submitted so dumbly. So when the old Irish-face came up and muttered "*Permite,*" she rose and cleared out to the women's toilet room. They were a dumb, stricken crowd in the grip of those two short-legged monkeys of attendants.

At half-past eight there was nothing to do but go to bed. The Mexican passengers were silently and intensely discreet, immured behind the green curtains, in their berths. Kate loathed a Pullman. She loathed the horrible nearness of all the other people, like so many larvæ in so many sections, behind green serge curtains. She loathed struggling to undress inside the oven of her berth. Her elbow would hit the curtain and no doubt reveal a flash of white arm, for there was a man's body outside, the attendant buttoning up the green curtain. And her elbow, as she struggled with her hair, would butt him in the stomach through that odious curtain.

But thank goodness, once she was in bed she could put up the window-blind and open the window a little, her light being shut out. She wouldn't have put up her window-blind for anything, till her light was out. Her respect for the guns of bandits or low thieves was considerable.

There was a rather cold wind, after the rain, up there on the high plateau. The moon had risen. She saw rocks, and tall organ cactus. Then more acres of maguey. Then the train had stopped at a dark little station on a crest, where men swathed in sarapes held dusky, ruddy lanterns. Why did the train stay so long?

At last it was going again, and she saw a pale downslope before her, in the moonlight, and away below the lights of a little town. She lay watching the land go by, rocks, cactus, maguey, rocks, as the train wound its way down. And soon she dozed. To wake at a station where, in the dim, dusky light, women in rebozos were running along the train with tortillas, and dishes of meat or chicken or tamales, and fruit. It was only about nine o'clock. The women's faces came near the dark wire-screen of Kate's window. She lowered her window, in a kind of fear. The Pullman was all dark. But at the back of the train, outside, Kate could see the light from the open coaches of the first class, and the third class. She almost wished she was there, in the first-class coach, looking out of the window and buying an orange, or a little box of Celaya sweetmeat. *La de Celaya!* she heard a man calling.

But she was shut up with the comfortable passengers in the Pullman, there was nothing to do but to listen to an occasional cough behind the green curtains, and go to sleep.

She woke at a bright station: probably Quarétaro. If Owen had been there, he would have wanted to get up in his pyjamas, to see if anyone was selling Mexican opals. Owen was a passionate buyer of trifles. She wished she could really look out. The green trees looked pretty and theatrical in the electric light.

The moment the train moved on, she dozed. It was a poor sleep, in a Pullman, so shaken. Yet sleep it was. She was very dimly aware of stations: then, deep in the night, aware of being awakened from a pure, sound sleep. The train had been standing in the station of Irapuato, the junction. It was moving west.

She would arrive at Ixtlahuacan at twenty-past-six in the morning, and was mortally afraid of over-sleeping. But the man awoke her. It was light, the sun had not risen. Dry country, and green wheat alternating with bearded, ripe wheat, and men already cutting the ripe wheat with sickles, in short little handfuls. Then bare country with ragged stumps of maize-stubble. Then a man on horseback driving a mingled flock of cows, sheep, bulls, goats, lambs, from a forlorn-looking hacienda. Then a sort of canal choked with leaves, and mauve-coloured waterlilies poking out. The sun was just lifting up, red. In a few minutes the strong golden sunshine of real morning.

She was dressed and all ready, sitting facing Villiers, when they came to Ixtlahuacan. The attendant came to tell her, and take her bag. And the train drew up casually near a wayside station, a desert as usual. Villiers craned his neck for some sign of Owen. Nothing. They got down. A barn of a station, some standing vans, an expanse of cobbled approach with grass growing between the cobble-stones, an ancient horsetram standing like a monument, one or two forlorn men swathed in big scarlet, or brown, sarapes, going across the open space, two porters asking about luggage, and no more.

"What now!" said Villiers.

"Orilla Hotel?" said Kate to the porter, on a note of query.

"*Sí, Señora –*" and a long string of Spanish, pointing to the tram-car.

"He means we go in the tram," said Villiers.

Kate went back to see all the masses of heavy luggage taken out of the van. It was all there. The porter was as eager for it as if it had been a juicy beef-steak. Kate decided the only thing to do was to leave it where it was.

"*Mas tarde,*" said Kate, using that invaluable phrase. "Later on."

The porter broke into speech, showed her the brass plate of his number, and she set off to the tram. Villiers had found out from the guide book that you could take the tram to the town and then the motorboat of the hotel would carry you across the corner of the lake.

At last the driver whipped up his mules, and they rolled slowly down stony, cobbled roads, between walls, and between houses. A desert. Occasional men in huge hats and scarlet sarapes passed like concrete ghosts, morning-silent. An occasional man on horseback. A boy on a high mule delivering milk from red jars slung on either side the mule. And still another stone-uneven, sterile street. All seeming absolutely dead, the whole place an inhabited deadness.

At length they came to an end, in a plaza with broken pavements and rather broken-down arcade, with fountain-basins where low water bubbled up, milky-dim, and brilliant trees blossomed in masses of pure scarlet, one in lavender flowers.

"What next?"

They got down from the tram, and a boy appeared.

"Hotel Orilla!" said Kate.

"Orilla!" said the boy, looking rather vaguely ahead, up the street.

"*Sí! Un bote! Una barca!*"

The word *barca* did it. The boy pointed vigorously ahead. So off they set, along the incredibly uneven, painful street, following the boy who was trotting the Indian trot, with the bags.

They came in a while to an old, dusty bridge, a broken wall, a wide, pale brown stream down below, and a cluster of men. The men were boatmen, and wanted her to take a boat. She announced she wanted the motorboat from the Hotel Orilla. They said there was no boat from the hotel. She didn't believe it. Then a dark-faced fellow with his black hair down his forehead and a certain intensity in his face, said, Yes, the hotel had a boat, but it was broken. In an hour and a half he would row her there. "In how long?" asked Kate. "An hour and a half!"

"And I am so hungry!" cried Kate.

"What does he say?" came the inevitable question from Villiers.

"For how much?" asked Kate.

"Two pesos, Señorita." And he held up two fingers.

So Kate said yes, the boatman ran, and then she noticed he was a cripple, with inturned feet. Yet how quick and strong!

She clambered with Villiers down the broken bank to the river, and in a moment was seated in the boat. There were pale green willow trees. The river was not very wide, and of a pale fawn colour, flowing between deep earthern banks. There was a funny, high kind of barge with rows of chairs. The boatman said it went up the river; and he waved his arm to show the direction. So they passed under the bridge, and almost at once the river became lonely. Kate wondered if she ought to feel frightened. She decided not. The crippled boatman was energetic and handsome, in his tense way, and when she smiled because she did not understand his Spanish, the answer of his smile was so quick, and so real, and rather pathetic. But the smile of a man with real, sensitive manliness. She knew he was trustworthy.

Morning was still young, on the silent buff-coloured river between earthern banks. There was a blue dimness in the lower air, and black water-fowl ran happily, unconcernedly back and forth from the river's edge, on the dry, baked banks, feeling the blueness and moistness of the dissolved night still about them. The boatman rowed hard upon the flimsy, soft, sperm-like water, only pausing at moments swiftly to smear the sweat from his face with an old rag that he kept on the bench beside him. He rowed so earnestly that the sweat ran from his brown-bronze skin like water.

"There is no hurry," said Kate, smiling to him.

"What does the señorita say?"

"There is no hurry."

He smiled back again, and only rowed the harder.

The river was fairly wide, and all of a soft, flowing buff colour. On the banks were some willow trees, and some pepper trees of delicate spring green. For the rest, the land was dry and lonely. Big hills rose up to high, blunt points, buff-coloured, baked like dry loaves. Across the flat near the river a peon, sitting perched on the rump of his donkey, was slowly driving five luxurious cows to the river to drink. The big black-and-white cows stepped slowly, luxuriously to the water, the dun cows followed. There was no sound in the air: the water, the land, the life was all soft and silent. Only in the blue above, the ragged-edged buzzards were already circling, as they always circle over life in Mexico.

"There is no hurry!" repeated Kate to the boatman, who was again mopping his face as if his life depended on it. "You can go slowly."

The man smiled deprecatingly, and with a wave of his hand, said:

"If the señorita will sit at the back, we can go to please her."

Kate did not understand at first. The boatman rested his oars, took off his hat and put it in the bottom of the boat, and at last wiped his face *quite* dry. He had the thick, beautiful black hair of the Indians. Then he repeated his request. And Kate looked round at the stern of the boat.

As she did so a ruddy-skinned, black-headed man rose naked from the water, bending, stretching out his arm and seizing the stern of the boat. The boat swerved. The man in the river stumbled and recovered his footing, then stood holding the boat, which had only a very mild pull in the stream. The water flowed almost up to his waist. He was young, and had full, handsome flesh, ruddy-brown.

Villiers and Kate both gave a slight exclamation of fear, the boatman, sitting watchful at the further end, almost without motion, gripped his oar as if it were a weapon. There was a moment of paralysis.

The man in the stream laughed as the water ran off him.

"Where are you going?" he asked unconcernedly.

He was a young man, with the handsome shoulders and hot, metallic flesh of the Indians.

"What do you want, you?" asked the boatman, in a muted voice.

"I want to salute you as you pass by," said the man, nonchalant. He spoke educated Spanish, with a certain effrontery. His naked arm held the boat fast.

The boatman cast cautious eyes to either bank, and waited dumbly.

"I salute you, Señorita and Señor, in the name of the God of the lake. Do you know the God Quetzalcoatl?"

"The God Quetzalcoatl – !" repeated Kate, agitated and not quite understanding.

"Ah! Yes! Did you know he has come back to Lake Chapala?"

"Oh!" exclaimed Kate, understanding this. "Is it really true?"

She spoke for the sake of answering. But the man in the water was insistent.

"Yes. Yes. You can believe it. He has come back now. He has been looking for a wife in the watery countries, and he has come back with her. I don't know if it's true about the wife. But he has come. You can believe it, I assure you." He was watching her all the time closely, with his staring black eyes. She had to try not to see his naked breast. It was so near.

"Yes," said Kate, dimly understanding and made more uneasy by the man's bold black eyes, that were full of fire, and by his voice, which she seemed to understand apart from words.

"Look!" – and the man held out his other hand, in which were two little pots, encrusted from lying under the water. "These are the ollicitas of the wife of Quetzalcoatl. They come from under the water. Take them, Señorita."

Kate very hesitatingly took the two little vases. They were really two tiny rough cooking pots, one a tripod and the other with two long ears, made apparently of soft black stone, and crusted with lime from the water. Each was about as big as a thimble.

"They are pretty. They are very pretty. Thank you so much," she said nervously, determined, as far as possible, to humour the intruder.

"Ollicitas of the wife of Quetzalcoatl," said the man. "I found them in the shallow water." He was watching her searchingly, to see the effect on her. His earnest, eager watching, that had at the same time something domineering, reminded her of the General.

"Thank you so much," she said, stiffening slightly.

"*Adiós Señorita! Adiós Señor! Adiós hombre!* We are those of the God Quetzalcoatl."

He announced his goodbye in a different, more insolent voice, and at the same time gave the boat a little push, which sent it downstream, while he waded away as if he would ignore them now. Kate turned to look again at the dark, glowing face, that seemed almost to contain fire, and at the searching black eyes. He was all the time watching, as if something were important to him. – But he had retreated, was wading out of the water, the sunlight flashing on his wet, strong back.

"Who is he?" asked Kate of the boatman, who was rowing again as if for dear life. The boatman merely shook his head.

Then, when the boat had travelled some distance, and he had seen the naked man disappear into the green of the pepper-trees a way off, he said in a rather cautious voice:

"They are those of the God Quetzalcoatl, Señorita."

"But what are they?" she asked.

The man gave a shrug of his shoulders as he rowed. He was already sweating again profusely. He rowed hard so as not to be questioned. – She saw this.

"Let me go to the back now," said Kate.

The man rested his oars, and she carefully climbed back to the little seat in the angle of the stern.

"What is all this about?" asked Villiers, making round eyes.

Kate told him. She was examining her little pots. They undoubtedly came from under the water. They were made, she thought, of black clay.

"They really come from under the lake?" she asked.

"Yes, Señorita. They find them at San José. They used to find many, now they only find few. On the shore by the water."

"Ollicitas of the wife of Quetzalcoatl?"

"Yes, Señorita. So they call them." Again the man did not want to answer.

"I read in the newspaper about a man that came out of the lake," said Kate.

"Yes, Señorita."

"Is that the man who is Quetzalcoatl?"

"No, Señorita. He is a man from I don't know where. The god would be different." And now the boatman's black eyes were watching her furtively.

"But you think he has really come back, Quetzalcoatl?"

"*Quien sabe!* Who knows!" – And with a vague gesture, the man wiped his face. He did not look at her any more, but pulled the oars.

"I am glad if Quetzalcoatl has come back," she said. "He is your own God."

"Yes, Señorita." He flashed a slight, bright smile, which died at once again in his face. Then, his face a mask of the commonplace, he rowed his hardest.

"Now we are going well!" he said, seeming to want to avoid the God Quetzalcoatl for the future. And his face, like dusky, semitransparent stone set motionless. But his black eyes were stirring like water.

Ahead, the banks were growing lower, and wilder: reeds, and willow trees, and seeming marshy places. Above the low willow trees in the distance a square white sail was standing, apparently not moving.

"Is the lake near?" asked Kate, pointing.

"Yes, Señorita. The sailing boats are waiting for the wind, to come into the river. We, Señorita, we will take the canal, and in a little while we are there."

The canal proved to be a narrower, twisting outlet of the river, to the left. Many water-fowl were flying. The banks were buff-coloured mud, and there was a flat place with pale-green willow trees. For some reason it reminded Kate of the River Anapo: perhaps because of some slight mysterious quality in the atmosphere, a barbaric sacredness. The boatman, with creases half of sadness and half of secret exultation in his bronze face, was rowing from side to side of the winding stream, and Villiers was guiding him with a slight, nonchalant motion first of the right hand, then of the left, as the boat ran into shallow water. This was just about the amount of effort that suited Villiers. None of them spoke.

And in a moment they were slipping past the loose edges of the land, through an uneasy ripple, out to the wide surface of the lake. A breeze was coming from the east, out of the completed morning, and the surface of the flimsy, dun-coloured water was already in motion. Out to sea some square white sails were moving, and away across the pale, buff-coloured expanse rose the blue sharp hills of the other side, a pure, pale blue.

"There!" said the boatman, pointing to a little eminence across a sort of bay. "That is the Hotel Orilla."

And he pulled rhythmically through the rippling, sperm-like water, across the corner of the lake. In one place the water was breaking. The boatman drew away from the shallow bank, and pointed across, to where a native sailing-boat was lying at an angle. She had run aground some days before. Another boat was approaching, and the natives in their loose white drawers, brown chests, and huge hats, were poling her past the shallows. She carried a huge cargo of leaf mats, high above her black, stiffly-hollowed sides.

The hotel was near, a long low building on a bank above the water, behind pale-green trees. On the broken-down landing place stood a man in white flannel trousers. It was not Owen. Ducks and black water-fowl were bobbing about like corks. The man in white trousers turned back to the hotel. The boat drifted up to the broken masonry beside the boat-house.

"I don't want to break my little pots of the wife of Quetzalcoatl," said Kate, eyeing the slippery stones on to which she must clamber.

"Give them to me," said the boatman quickly. He took them in his hand, and looked at them. Then he lifted his black eyes to Kate, and said, with a touch of mockery:

"They don't eat much rice, the Gods." Then, turning the little pot upside down, "Look!" he said.

Kate saw that it was the head of an animal, with wide ears and a snout. Rather like a cat.

"A black cat!" she said.

"Yes, or a coyote."

"And the other one?"

He held up the other pot. It too had a resemblance to some queer head of an animal. Both pots were perforated through each projection.

The man gave her back her ollicitas, when she stood on land, smiling a queer, almost sententious smile at her as he did so.

"*Adiós! Vaya con Quetzalcoatl!* Go with Quetzalcoatl," she said, when she had paid him.

"*Adiós!* Yes, Señorita, I am going," he replied, simply, with the same sardonic touch.

One thing she noticed, how the name of the Indian God seemed to give the man a secret satisfaction, as if he had something that she had not; even a touch of watchful arrogance. She was interested – and rather piqued.

She walked with Villiers up the path between tattered banana trees, most of which were bearing green fruit, to the hotel. No Owen. Three men at a corner table of the glass-fronted dining-room; obviously Germans. Then another man, obviously German: the manager. He was about forty, young-looking, erect, but with his blue eyes going opaque and stony behind his spectacles, though their centre was keen. It was the look of a European who has been many years in Mexico.

Owen was still in bed. He hadn't had their telegram. He was full of protestations, in his red-blobbed dressing-gown. But Kate, after washing her hands, went down again for breakfast, for she was hungry. Before the long verandah of the hotel the green pepper-trees drooped like green light, and small scarlet birds with brown wings and blazing impertinent heads flashed brightly among the pepper-buds. A train of geese passed in automatic march down to the lake, in the bright sun, towards the eternal tremble of the pale, earth-coloured water.

It was a beautiful place – queer and different. It wasn't even really beautiful. But it had that same touch of mystery, of barbaric sacredness which lingers in some spots of the earth. Nevertheless she was glad when the thin Mexican in shirt-sleeves and patched trousers brought her her eggs and coffee. Villiers, with his determined imperviousness to Spanish, asked for two Tiberius eggs. "Tiberios, tiberios!" he exclaimed firmly. But the muted waiter understood, and brought him his eggs boiled.

The whole place seemed muted. Nobody seemed able to open their lips more than a hair's breadth, and everybody seemed to be glancing uneasily behind all the time, as if there lurked an assassin with a knife.

"I'm not so sure," said Owen, when he did at last appear, "that I like the place as much as I thought I did. It's uncanny. Only last year the Indians broke in one evening as the manager and the proprietor's son were sitting in that little room there, and they killed the proprietor's son and threw a machete at the manager, but he managed to get out and behind those bushes. They shot at him, but he got to the hills. – Fancy being murdered by an Indian's hatchet these days! Of course they *say* it's safe enough *now*, but a man sleeps on the stairs with a loaded gun."

Owen was rolling his eyes in one of his nervous fits. Kate knew he would not stay.

She went up to her room. Behind the hotel, the land rose utterly dry, pale and dessicated, in savage little round hills baked as if in a kiln. Yet the dark green chunks of the organ cactus stuck up in the dryness, supposed to look like clusters of organ-pipes, certainly looking like nothing else on earth. And grey ground-squirrels like rats were slithering about. In front, below her window, among bricks and fallen rubble a large white turkey-cock strutted with his bronze hens. And alternately he stretched out his pink wattles and gave vent to fierce and powerful turkey-yelps, like some strong dog yelping, or he ruffled all his feathers like a great, soiled white peony and chuffed hissing here and there, raging his stiff feathers. Beyond, the eternal tremble of pale, earth-coloured water, and stiff mountains losing their pristine blue.

In the dry air the distances were distinct and yet frail, dim-seeming, everything pale and half real.

When she had taken a bath in the sperm-like water, Kate sat in the shade of the boat-house, above a heap of collapsed masonry. Some small white ducks bobbed about, raising clouds of dust in the thin shallows of the water. A canoe came paddling in, a lean fellow with sinewy brown legs. He answered Kate's salute with the promptness of an Indian, made fast his canoe inside the boat-house, and was gone, stepping silent and bare-foot over the green stones.

No sound in the morning save a faint touching of water, and the occasional powerful, startling yelping of the turkey-cock. For the rest, silence, a muted silence. Ringing to the white turkey-cock. And the strange lymphatic expanse of water, trembling, trembling, with the hills beyond in substantial nothingness. Near at hand, banana trees, bare hills with cactus. A hacienda with peons' square mud boxes of houses. Occasional farmers in tight trousers, on horseback, or men in floppy white cotton, seated over the rump of asses. The big hats, the sun, the silence!

And the morning passing all of a piece, without issue, empty of issue. It was a land empty of issue, around the long, pale, unreal lake. A land so dry as to have a quality of invisibility, and of water that seemed hardly water at all. The ghost of water. Or the milk of black fishes, as Owen said. Between the ghosts of utterly dry, parched, pale-earth mountains.

V

O F COURSE OWEN had learned everything about everything. The
hotel had been built in the good old days of Don Porfirio –
meaning Diaz. In those days, when a foreigner and a gentleman *could*
make money in Mexico, an American hotel company had built this
Orilla Hotel, and the place was destined to be the Riviera of Mexico.
But nowhere are the knees of the gods so slippery as in this same
Mexico. In the course of the various revolutions the hotel company
went bankrupt: the Orilla was started again: but the Indians broke in
and killed the proprietor's son and looted the place, and it was closed
once more. Two months before Owen's arrival it had been opened
afresh.

"But there is doom written all over it," said Owen, wrinkling his
eyebrows nervously. "And over everybody. It's as if the hotel were a
violation here, and couldn't continue. And the German manager the
same. He's quite intelligent, and quite nice. But the country has
beaten him. He's been on rubber plantations in Tabasco, and sugar
plantations in Vera Cruz State, then for some years here on the lake on
a big hacienda growing wheat and maize and some oranges. As
manager, of course. But nothing doing. He says, with the peons
demanding such high wages, and wheat so cheap, and the attitude of
the government towards land so unsatisfactory, nothing can be done.
And on the top of that, mind you, I found out from a boy of sixteen
working on the hacienda here, that he gets fifty centavos a day, and his
midday meal. That is less than twenty-five American cents a day. And
he works from six in the morning till six at night, and *wants* to work.
They offered him thirty-five cents a day, but he said it wasn't enough. I
suppose he is an example of the peon demanding high wages. Ha-ha!
The regular working wage for a man is a peso a day: half a dollar. And
that is the high wages.

"Of course, if a peon has to sow the wheat with a *hoe,* and reap it
with a sickle, six stalks at a time, of course the cost of production will

be high. Think what it would be under the same circumstances in the United States! Why we should be wearing necklaces of grains of wheat, like jewels. – No, all it amounts to is that the hacienda owners *won't* spend a little capital to buy machinery. That's all it is. – And as for losing their land, why there was a big fat hacendado here the other day in a motor-car: he was lamenting the days of Porfirio Diaz, as they all do. He owns a huge hacienda between here and Guadalajara, and he said that in Diaz' time it supported five thousand head of cattle. He had five thousand head of cattle then – and now he has nothing, nothing. The government had divided up some of his land for the peons, the workmen wanted so much wages, you could do nothing, now, nothing. I asked him what he meant, exactly, by nothing. And he waved his hand so contemptuously: nothing, a mere nothing. But when I pinned him down to it, he had to confess that he's got three thousand head of cattle now, instead of five. Think of it, nothing! I said it seemed to me considerable. But he still insisted it was nothing.

"That's how they are. As a matter of fact it turns out that the government does not confiscate any land from these huge estates, except the land that is unworked. They divide up the land that is not being worked: just a small portion. Of course the peons want more, and better land. But they don't get it. – Apparently the peons are rather worse off now than they were under Diaz. And that's why they are beginning to realise that there is nothing in revolutions. The Generals of the army seize what spoil there is to seize, and the peasants are a little worse off, every time.

"And the owners of the haciendas! Oh, the hacendados! They are so indignant. They go so far now as to say they *actually want* the United States to intervene, and take over their country. They all sing the same song: the country will never be safe, it will never be any good till the United States takes it over. It will never be a civilised country till it is in the hands of the United States. I ask them if any of them were ever in Pittsburgh. But imagine it! And from what I can gather, there is quite a large plot among the foreigners here, and among the hacendados and business people, to get the United States to intervene. Work up another mild upheaval and then petition the United States, in the name of all peace-loving Mexicans, to take over Mexico. Just imagine it!"

"In the name of all *money-loving* Mexicans, of course," said Kate. "And money-loving foreigners. Of course money-lovers will want the

United States government, because it's the one government that exists simply and solely to protect money. – And Mexico, of course, has always been a place for men to fill their pockets without hindrance. Everybody comes here for money – money, money, money! Cortés came for gold, and it's gone on ever since. In one way, it's the dreariest country I've ever been in. Everybody you meet is here for money. One never meets a soul except just money-getters. Besides the peons, and those one doesn't meet. Socially, it's the dreariest, vulgarest country in the world. Because those who've *got* money go somewhere else to be people of leisure. And there's nothing left but the great class of the greedy ones. – If I were the Mexican poor, I'd hate the foreigners."

"But they don't," said Owen. "Not in most cases."

"No, that's because they're nice," said Kate.

In her soul she was rather weary of this political sort of talk. She had suffered so much from it. She had imagined Mexico a pure pastoral patriarchal land. For she wanted, oh so much, to get back to the human simplicity of the non-political life. But no such luck. The liberals said the peasants wanted land, the hacendados said the peasants didn't. No doubt both were right. It is no fun, anyhow, being the farmer of a few weary acres of land.

"By the way," she said, "have you met the God Quetzalcoatl yet?"

"The God Quetzalcoatl!" exclaimed Owen, a little puzzled. "Oh, you mean the man who came out among the washing, that we read of in the *Excelsior*. No, I've not dived into Quetzalcoatl's patio yet."

Then Kate told him of the incident that had happened as they rowed along.

"Now isn't that extraordinary!" said Owen. "What do you imagine it means?"

"There must be more people who have seen Quetzalcoatl, besides the man among the washing. But I must show you the two little cooking pots of the Goddess."

"What can *her* name be, I wonder!" said Owen.

"Yes, I wonder!" said Kate.

"What!" exclaimed the manager of the hotel, eyeing the three friends sharply when they came to ask him about the Indian God. "Quetzalcoatl! The Children of Quetzalcoatl! It's another put-up job of the bolshevists." And he watched the three most suspiciously.

"The bolshevists!" exclaimed Owen with a laugh. "Ha-ha! isn't that funny, now! The God Quetzalcoatl and the bolshevists! What an odd assortment! However are the two things associated? What is the connection? – Why I shall soon think, if a cow moos it is saying something bolshevistic. I'm sure your turkey is."

And he laughed heartily at the hotel manager, who, however, brittlely stood his ground.

"A put-up job of the bolshevists," he asserted again, dryly. "They thought bolshevism needed a God, so they got him out of Lake Chapala."

"How very interesting!" said Owen. "I feel far more interested in Quetzalcoatl than I ever did before. What is the idea, though? I don't quite get it."

"The idea," said the German, "is to catch the peons. The peon is ignorant, so they want to catch him through his ignorance. They've only to tell him the God Quetzalcoatl has come back, and that he says this thing and the other, and the peon will believe it. So they form their new society of Sons of Quetzalcoatl, bolshevists, nothing else."

"And where? Where do they form the society of the Sons of Quetzalcoatl?" cried Owen.

"In Chapala. And all along the lake. They pretend to keep it a secret. But where you see a bunch of men talking together, that's what they're talking about. They've got songs about it too."

"Oh let's go to Chapala!" cried Owen.

"You've no need," said the manager quickly, "to go to Chapala. There's just as much of it here in Ixtlahuacan. But they won't tell *you* anything about it. You're a gringo, you're all gringuitos, and this is for pure Mexicans, for Indians."

"But I *must* know more about it," said Owen.

Then Kate told the manager of her experience, and showed him the ollicitas.

"Oh there are plenty of these things about," said the man, holding the two little jars in the palm of his hand and eyeing them as if they were dragon's eggs. "There's nothing in *them*. You can pick them up in the mud at San Juan. Just playthings, or charms, that the Indians used to throw into the lake in times gone by, when they wanted more fish, I suppose. – San Juan is the Midsummer Night village. These ollicitas have got nothing to do with this new Quetzalcoatl business."

Kate, however, was quite ready to accept Owen's suggestion that they should go on to Chapala, which was some thirty miles further along the lake. Not because she was so very much interested in the

God Quetzalcoatl, but because she had been told that at Chapala she would easily find a furnished house that she could rent for a month or two. And she dearly wanted a house of her own.

Because she felt tired, weary in body and soul. She had been wandering about and staying in hotels so long. And she had been on the very point of going back to England. Her mother wanted her to come. And Kate was still attached to her mother. But since she was in America the real yearning she had always felt for her children had snapped, and with it, a great deal more had broken in her. She had always really hoped that one day, when they grew up, they would come to her. She had, rather bitterly, granted them their conventionalism for the time being, believing that in the future they would come to her and be the children of her spirit. But her husband had never mentioned them, when he was dying. And at last, in America and Mexico, the bond of her mother-yearning and mother-hope had snapped. They were the children of her idea, they had nothing to do with her deepest blood, or her soul. And now they were nearly grown up, the bond of the mere physical connection was weak, and there was no other connection. They were not, and never would be the children of her deepest desire. They were not her descendants of the soul. They inherited none of her onward-striving spirit. They had slipped back into the conventional, meaningless mass.

Her love for them seemed to slacken as her hope in them weakened. The two things were so closely associated in her. And now she would have no more children. She did not want any more. So that her great womanly connection with the future was gone. This left her feeling a great loss, and a sort of barrenness inside her. Which was very bitter. For she had always been filled with such a strong sense of futurity and hope. And now, as a female woman, she felt cut off, somewhat meaningless.

For this reason, because of the sense of loss of connection, she could not go back to England. The vital connection seemed to have broken. She felt she *could* not go back. So she had drifted further west in Mexico. For there was something in Mexico, something in America that sustained her, made her feel her loss less disastrously. In this country it did not seem a disaster to be cut off as she was cut off. It seemed inevitable. Something strengthened her, something unknown and rather grim, here in the western continent.

But she felt really tired, and incapable of any further effort, either emotional or physical. But especially emotional. She hated the thought of any more emotional burden. And she was tired too of Owen. The barren bachelor that he was, with all the sterility of an old maid's egotism. It was not just egotism in Owen, but simply the fact that he had never really suffered and known his own limitations and his own confirmation at the hands of a woman. He knew the world, and he knew life, for he was a good deal of an artist. He was both sensitive and shrewd, and not easily beaten. But it was as if his adolescent mould had never been broken, smelted down, and re-cast into full manhood, through marriage. All his cleverness and sensitiveness was in a sort of adolescent mould.

And in the long run this wearied Kate's soul. She was weary of the two men. But she had no-one else, nothing else. She could not dispense with them entirely.

What she wanted was a house of her own, with a Mexican woman-servant, to be alone for a time. Owen and Villiers could stay in the hotel. And she, Kate, could be alone to nurse her wounds and her weariness, and wait for a new relief to enter into her life. She believed that here in Mexico a new relief would enter. She was aware for example that General Viedma was to some extent attracted by her: how much, and how little she did not really know. But her spirit refused to take count of it. She didn't want it. She wanted to be left alone.

To be left alone, and for nobody, nothing to touch her: that was the one and only thing she wanted at present. To be left alone, not to be touched by anything or anybody. Not to have to feel anything at all, or know anything at all. To hide, and be hidden, and never really be spoken to.

That was why she liked the old Spanish houses, with their inner courtyards or patios, shady, with an arched gallery around, and in the centre, water, and a few growing flowers. The shade, the enclosure, the few bright flowers, or the oranges, growing within the enclosure. Life turned inwards, instead of outwards. Not to have to look out and see a wide, aching world. Not to look out any more. To turn inwards, to sit quietly in the shadow of the patio and be still, without effort of any sort.

That was what she wanted. And that was why she hankered after a Spanish house with a patio. For that, and nothing else. To turn away, and be alone, inside her own patio. Without thinking, or feeling, or straining in any way. This she wanted, nothing else. If she couldn't have this, she almost wanted to die.

But she knew she could have this. And she felt sure she could have it in Chapala. So she made Owen hire a motor-boat to go down the lake with her. And when she saw the two white, ornate obelisk-towers of Chapala church rising above green willow trees, and the dry, tall mound of a hill with dry bushes beyond, with corrugated mountains back of that, she believed in Chapala. It looked peaceful, almost Japanese. And when she came abreast with the little lake-side resort with its small jetty and fishing nets hung up to dry, and little promenade behind feathery green trees, and a few villas with palm-trees and trees blazing with scarlet blossom, gay with pink trees of oleander, scarlet spots of hibiscus, and magenta clumps of bougainvillea; also the little green bathing house, and the white boats on a little sandy beach, and the boatmen lying under the shade on the sand, and the few women with parasols, she felt sure she would find a place for herself. This was not too wild, not too savage. Even she didn't mind the advertisement for motor-tyres, painted along the jetty in huge letters. It seemed human.

Walking down the short street from the lake to the plaza, the first thing she saw, on a green slate in smeary chalk letters: *Se renta una casa amueblada*. She at once asked about it, and in ten minutes' time was looking at the low one-storey house that formed a letter L, the other two sides of the square being filled in by the next orchard of thick, tall mango-trees. So she had her patio, except that two sides were dark trees instead of house. And in the middle, flowers, big white oleanders, dark red oleanders, hibiscus, an orange tree or two, all growing from their rings of water in a green lawn. Then round the two sides, a deep verandah, all shade, with large pots of geranium and other flowers.

It was an old house with a tiled roof and a jutting-out dining room in front of which the queer, smooth, snake-like trunks of cropped mango-trees rose at flexible angles. Right at the far end of the building was a tropical-tattered cluster of banana trees and a little hen house, then two savage rooms where lived a Mexican Felipa and her two girls. Felipa, with her untidy black hair and centreless black eyes, was a woman of forty or more, rather short, with a dark, full face and a limping way of walking. She looked as if she could be aggressive: but honest. Too much of the old barbaric indifference towards things, to be a thief. She didn't have any hankerings and finger-itchings: in her own earthy way, she was too proud. She might drink the whisky. That was a different matter.

In another hour Kate had taken the house, and Felipa along with it. Then she wandered through her domain: the sala, with its two circles of cane-bottomed chairs, suggesting ghastly Mexican visits in front of the cane-bottomed sofa: the four bedrooms, one after the other: the dining-room projecting in a bow: the kitchen with its charcoal fires and no oven: then the well, which was nearly dry: the toilet, whose water didn't run any more; and Felipa's den under the banana trees. There was no bath, but then the house was only a minute from the lake.

Kate liked her new place – the space of red-tiled floors, the rooms opening one after the other on to the verandah: the deep verandah with its pairs of heavy, square white pillars, and its defence of big flower-pots: the groups of leather chairs: the flowers in the sunshine, the wild birds, the tall papaya tree, the green, healthy palm, all in the strong light; and at the end the yellow and green disorder of bananas and black shadows, by the chicken pen, inside which walked Felipa's three scrappy white chickens.

Making a considerable effort, for it cost her an effort to do things in Mexico, Kate banished one suite of chairs from her sala, banished pictures and pieces of carpet, had beds removed from the double-bedded rooms, put down her own rugs and sarapes, and settled in.

And the second day came the warning that it was not safe for her to sleep alone in the house, with only Felipa at the end. The village was having one of its periodical scares. Bandits were out – eight of them on horseback: and unknown thieves were committing depredations in Chapala itself. She must go to sleep in an hotel: or have people to protect her.

She thought of Owen and Villiers: but they were more nervous than she was. And yet the second night was rather terrible. She was locked and sealed fast inside the pitch-dark house: the electric light being cut off at ten-thirty. She was sure she heard naked footsteps at the doors. And then, in the pitch dark, she must lie and listen. Five doors opened on to the verandah, and any of these might be broken in at any moment. And two large windows opened on to the road, and three small windows opened on to the field behind. She knew quite well that Mexican robbers, when they are in force, do not hesitate to smash in a door. So, through the black night, she lay and listened.

She had had nervous nights before. But not until now did she realise the thick terror of a Mexican night. At long intervals she would hear the police patrol riding by on horseback, giving the short shrill whistle that is their night-cry. Then the abject silence, the rising wind from the lake, the strange noise in trees, the shaking of many doors: and above all, the sense of fear and of devilment thick in the air.

Her fears were not just nonsense. The whole village was in that state of curious, reptile apprehension which comes over dark people. Four robbers were captured and put in prison. But the scare continued. Felipa's inky eyes became more blob-like and inky, and the old, weary, monkey look of subjection to fear settled on her bronze face. The look of the races subject to fear, unable to shake it off.

And still Kate would not discuss the terror with Felipa or with Owen. She didn't believe in giving way. But the thing got worse. It was usual for the natives all to throng in the plaza, sitting under the trees on the benches in the cool of the dark night, while some young men thrummed and sang eternal monodies to guitars, and the booths where men ate their evening meal kept the charcoal fires going till late, and a man went round with ice-cream, saying *Nieve! Nieve!* – Snow! Snow! – and the plaza was dense with people, men in big hats with sarape over one shoulder, women in their long skirts and their dark rebozos, boys running barefoot, and groups with babies sitting on the pavements. All the stalls lit by tin torches that flared in the wind.

But this night, by nine o'clock the plaza was empty, and Kate got home and locked herself in, her heart beating thick. It is not easy to withstand the atmosphere of fear that rises when dark people fall into panic. Kate had heard various grim stories during her stay in Mexico. She remembered the eyes of some of the low-class men: the queer, evil light lurking in a blackness. It was strange. Even Humboldt, she remembered, said that few people had such a gentle smile, and at the same time, such fierce eyes, as these Indians. It was true their smile was wonderfully gentle. And their eyes were not exactly fierce: but black, with a strange dagger of light in them: as if they themselves were not sure of their own unquenched blood, as if they never knew what their own sudden dark blood might do with them. Any spark might kindle it to deeds they had never thought of. And when men are like that, the very fear of themselves makes them more dangerous, makes fear more frightful. Because, she had decided, their essential nature was gentle.

But there was in them the black gulf of uncertainty, and that liability to utter, diabolic rage, which knows no outlet but the stroke of a knife.

Everything seemed fair enough in the daytime. But in the middle of the night there was fear like curdled blood. It was a dark, heavy-souled people, with a fathomless resentment at the bottom of the soul. The heavy, passionate resentment of men who have never been able to free themselves from the chaos of the dark, uncreate world. Men who have never succeeded in coming to completeness, but are swayed to hot ferocity by a too-strong sun, or stunned by the heavy electricity of the Mexican air, made sulphureous by the boiling volcanoes below ground. Clogged and tangled in the elements, and never able to come into their own self-possession. And hence subject to an ever-recurring, fathomless hatred of everything, a black demonish hatred of life, a desire for cruelty, a lust for murder. Better the heavy thud and thrust of a stabbing knife than even the keenest thrust of sexual gratification. Better the fingers strangling a live throat, than the touch of the most desirable woman. Man in his incompleteness, unable to come into complete being, turning into a dread thing. Liable to fall under the hideous spell of money, mere money, and to murder and murder again for the sake of a handful of silver. A brutal lust in the murder, the lust started by the thought of a handful of silver pesos, or a little heap of gold.

In this night she felt again the heavy horror of Mexico, the same that the Conquistadores felt when they smelt the stench of human blood darkening the air round the pyramids of Huitzilopochtli and Quetzalcoatl. A black-blooded, volcanic, uncertain people. As Bernal Diaz says, the hearts of men are changeable but particularly the hearts of the Indians. Men never able to balance themselves amid the elements, to gain a responsible centre to themselves. Swayed from extreme love to diabolism, never knowing when the reaction will set in.

Kate lay and thought hard, at the same time listening intensely, with her heart, beyond her control, getting into a knot inside her throat. Her heart seemed wrenched out of place, and actually did hurt her. She was physically afraid, blood-afraid, as she had never been before. And it made her feel her heart wrenched, her spirit humiliated.

In England, in Ireland, during the war and the rebellions, she had known cold *moral* fear: the worst thing she had ever known. Absolute cold, cold torture of fear of the *government,* of society in its ghastly mob-cruelty, trying to kill the spirit. That was what her husband had said during the war: "They are trying to kill the *spirit* in the individual, in all individual men and women. Because once they have killed the spirit they can handle everybody." And during the war this pseudo-civilised lust to stamp out the individual spirit in human beings reached a demoniacal pitch, a pitch of cold, demoniacal horror. The more horrible because it was the cold, collective lust of millions of people, against each solitary outstanding individual.

In those days Kate had known the agony of cold social fear, as if a nation were a huge, huge cold centipede with poison in every foot, that wanted to spread itself over the individual solitary man and woman. That had been her worst agony of fear. And she had survived.

Now for the first time she knew the real heart-wrench of blood-fear. Her heart seemed pulled out of place, in a stretched pain.

And just as she dozed, came flares of white light through all the window cracks, and the crash of thunder as if great cannon-balls were falling on her heart. She had been near to hysterics in the bull-ring in Mexico. She was even nearer now.

At last, morning came. But she felt a wreck.

"How have you passed the night?" asked Felipa, the conventional phrase.

"Badly!" said Kate. "I can't sleep shut up in the dark. And the thunder and all. I shall either have to go to the hotel, or I shall have to leave my door open."

"No, no," said Felipa. "You can't leave your door open, Niña. There is danger, much danger. I too can't sleep for thinking of you poor innocent lying there alone. And what if I got up in the morning to find you lying there murdered, and the house robbed. A lonely innocent! No no, Niña, you can't continue like this. Either you must have Rafael to sleep outside your door with a pistol, and he will shoot anybody who comes near – *brum! brumm!!*" – Felipa levelled an imaginary pistol at an imaginary robber – "or else you will have to go to the hotel, Niña."

Kate never ceased to be amused by the Mexican woman-servant's way of calling her mistress "Niña," "Child." If the mistress is eighty, and the servant eighteen, the mistress still is "Child!" to the serving-lass.

But for the moment Rafael was the point. Felipa had two sons, Jesús and Rafael. Jesús, the elder, ran the little motor which made the electric light for the village. Rafael, the younger, a black-eyed lad of eighteen, worked in the fields, but slept with Jesús in the planta, as the little hole was called where they made the electricity.

When Kate had seen Rafael, with his black, bright eyes that had the dagger of light in them, and heard his resonant, breaking voice, and after he had told her, with his gleaming eyes and handsome smile: "The pistol has five shots. If you open the door in the night, you must say a word to me first. Because if I see anything move I shall fire five shots, Pst! Pst!!"

And she saw by his black eyes that not only would he fire the five shots, but he would fire them with eagerness, and with a complete desire to hit. He was not in the least afraid, having that pistol.

So Rafael slept on a straw mat outside her door, with the pistol, and she could leave the upper shutter open, for the good night air. The first night she was once more kept awake by his fierce snoring. Never, never had she heard such a resonance! What a chest the boy must have! What magnificent organs of respiration! What a savage noise it was! He must have got into a weird position. But even though it kept her awake, there was something in the snoring that she liked: something so unbrokenly strong and fearless, and even generous. She felt more safe, thank heaven. But even then, in the thick of the next horrific night, what soothed her most was her determination to believe that what these people wanted most of all was good. They wanted the wholeness and the good of life, at last. But they were helpless. Their Christian religion could never save them from themselves. They wanted even to be trustworthy, but their natures erupted like volcanoes, beyond their control. Jesus could not save them, finally, Christ could not hold them together. They needed a stronger, darker god, a god who knew the dark sacred depths of man's sensual being. Otherwise it was no good. These dark people could never become spiritual. They were heavy souled, with a deep, true sensuality for their well of life. They could never deny it. Always they were driven back to it. They would never offer themselves up on the Christian cross. They would never understand love, in the Christian sense, and self-sacrifice. Their blood was their whole being. How could they sacrifice it? – But their blood was not evil. It was deep and rich. But helpless. If only it could come into its own!

Soon Kate was fond of her limping, untidy Felipa, and of the fierce young Juana, who was fourteen, and of the queer, gentle Pedra, who was only twelve. There was a basic, sardonic recklessness about them all. They lived from day to day with a stubborn, dark, silent carelessness, careless about the future, careless about anything. They were pinned down on nothing, not even a desire for money. They had no aim, no purpose, but lived absolutely *à terre,* down on the dark, volcanic earth. They were not animals, because men can't be animals. In their dark eyes was fear, and wonder, and a certain misery. The misery of human beings who have never been able to come into their own being, and wait, and wait, and wait, as it were forever outside their own unaccomplished selves. To Kate, there was a great pathos in this. Also a great untrustworthiness. And a slight repulsiveness.

Yet Felipa and her children were honest, with a native, barbaric honesty. And always, since they liked their Niña, ready to serve, as the fertile earth is ready to serve. Careless, with a basic indifference to everything, they yet were glad that Kate cared. They were glad that Kate wanted the house nice and tidy. Their own rooms were just caves. But they watched with wonder while Kate arranged her surroundings and made them pleasant. They watched her and wondered over her, with insatiable curiosity. She was always a source of wonder, half-amused wonder to them. In a way they saw in her a wonder-being, a sort of god. But never a social superior. They never saw her as a social superior. They never thought her blood and birth were better than theirs. These things meant nothing to them. They didn't realise that she was a social being on whom they must not intrude. No! She was their Niña, an amusing sort of god-being different from themselves, who was there to make life for them and to be served. They were willing to serve for ever. But she must not withdraw herself and hold herself apart. She must not hold her soul apart from them, in the white social manner, or they would jeer at her, and pull her down. Her position as Niña, she soon discovered, was no sinecure.

It was a queer family life. Felipa considered herself as belonging entirely to Kate. She established herself in the kitchen, and kept her daughters off as much as possible. Juana was left in possession of the little, smoky, doorless hole which was Felipa's own kitchen, not Kate's. And here, her head peering all the time through the square aperture that served as window, Juana would stand for hours making tortillas: the flat maize pancakes, or girdle cakes, cooked without fat. For hours at a time Kate would hear the clap-clap-clap, as Juana slapped each cake time after time from one palm to the other, that being the correct way of making tortillas light. It was part of the sunny

morning, like the wind fluttering the rags of the banana trees, and the
stark sun on the flowers, the birds swiftly coming and going, the
white-clothed Indians passing in the dark mango trees, like ghosts.

At one o'clock, the girls would be eating the warm tortillas one by
one as Juana picked them off the earthern plate upon the slow wood
fire. The youngsters just lived on tortillas. In the afternoon they would
go to bathe in the lake. Sometimes, when they felt like it, they went to
school. Both girls could read a little. But neither Jesús, who was
twenty-two, nor the eighteen-year-old Rafael, could read or write.

Jesús, a very dark fellow, ate at the house of his master, for whom
he worked all day, running the planta at night. The Mexican law is that
every workman and every servant shall have one whole day free each
week. But Jesús worked seven days out of seven, till half-past-ten at
night, and earned twenty-two pesos a month. Which is eleven American dollars. Of course he had his keep.

The boys were never at home. Rafael appeared with his proud
walk and his sarape over his shoulder, at about six o'clock in the
evening, marched to Juana's fire-hole, sat on the floor, and rapidly
folded and ate one tortilla after another. In five minutes he was gone
again. Sometimes he ate tamales or another Mexican, fiery dish with
pork in it, bought at a booth in the market. Many of the Mexican
women cooked nothing at all, except tortillas. The Mexican food at
the stalls was just as cheap as cooking at home, so the men had their
tasty dish bought ready-made, or they ate there in public in the plaza,
by the flare of the little floating oil-wicks. It always amused Kate, the
lordly way Rafael assumed command of his sisters, during the brief
five minutes when he was at home, sitting on the floor eating his food.

For a Catholic country, the woman was as little of a Madonna, a
mother with a son, as could be imagined. Felipa saw as little of her two
sons as she did of any boys in the village. She didn't speak twenty
words a day to them. Juana washed them their shirt and cotton
trousers once a week. And Felipa was there if they wanted anything,
ready to get it them. But the family was almost like an animal family,
so careless and detached, without the strain of love or hate. They had
no personal intimacy, and therefore no quarrels. Juana teased Pedra,
tormented her, and Pedra wept a few tears. It was always the same:
this endless, not very serious tormenting. All the boys were the same:
they tormented one another. And the tormented one always cried. But
neither torment nor tears seemed to matter at all: until, as didn't often

happen, ferocity entered in. Usually it was an endless teasing torment. Always throwing stones at one another. Always aiming with savage ferocity, just to miss. Always so strangely careful not to hurt. And if one did happen to be hurt, he always collapsed at once, in tears on the floor. And the others moved away embarrassed.

The people were a great puzzle to Kate. Because she realised that Felipa and her children were all strongly attached to one another. It was a silent, careless, and yet enduring connection, impersonal and unthinking: very different from the effusive affection and personal feeling in white families. Felipa took from the boys a bit at a time the necessary money for food. And everything was spent, with the same casual indifference. When Rafael was pining for a new sarape with little flowers in it – florecitas – then Felipa did all she could to get it for him. When she needed a new rebozo, the boys sarcastically helped her to it. But her rebozo was only of black cotton, with black cotton fringe.

The detachment and the callous indifference to the future, and to gain, were a curious relief to Kate, who had suffered from the strain of English families and the anxiety of people "getting on." Neither Rafael nor Jesús cared about "getting on." They were what they were. They worked without effort, they lived without meaning. The life of the plaza was a life to the men, and when they worked, that was casual life to them also.

Yet no one could call them dead. In the black eyes of Rafael at least there was a splendid free flame of life. He liked to work, he said, but he wanted to work in the fields, not in personal service or in a planta. And not for the sake of making money. Just to live.

He was a handsome, strong, erect youth, full of life. Only he had none of that white men's *aspiration,* which had sent all white men scrambling to get at the stars, and made the world a heaven and a hell. Rafael had his stars in his own eyes, inside himself. His pride was effortless, just natural in his blood. Kate often found herself wondering at the stars of queer light in the boy's black eyes. So curious that he did not strive for his completion outside himself. He strove for nothing, just asserted his own presence in the universe, as if that took all his time. "I am here!" And beyond that, nothing, save perhaps a certain resistance.

They had their own pride, a pride also of resistance. Felipa did not want to feed her children at Kate's expense. She didn't want to support her family from Kate's table. She just didn't have any desire to *get* things. She took from the household supplies what she wanted for her own needs, as naturally as if everything were her own, and as coolly, and as frugally. And beyond that, she paid for her family with her own money.

True, she had a reputation for honesty, which is a good thing to live up to. But the main-spring was a resistance to everything, even to the desire for possessions, or even for food. She refused to care. The family feeling was clannish, a defence against the world. For the rest, they refused to care for anything. Like Rafael, when he just lay down on the garden path, to sleep. When he might have had a mattress. He resisted even his own comfort. Almost he resisted eating.

Nevertheless, they had their grudge. Felipa and her sons had known a fair amount of mean treatment at the hands of richer people. As when Rafael worked for two months, when he was fifteen, just to get a sarape. And at the end of the two months the sly, avaricious master said he would pay later, always later. So the boy was never paid, and didn't get his sarape. This gave another reason for locking the backbone in resistance.

There was a pathos about the family. They, with their sardonic, careless honour, how could they fail to be cheated and insulted at the hands of people "on the make?" The sense of insult and of dishonourable return was fairly deep in Felipa. – But Jesús' master at the planta, though stingy, was not bad to him and her. – And Kate of course was a godsend. So the good and the bad fairly well balanced. Though sometimes Kate felt they really preferred the bad. It satisfied their passion for resistance. She knew the same thing very well, in the Irish. They reminded her a good deal of the Irish.

Still she didn't very much resent having the family about. It was like birds or animals coming and going. There was something natural, if a trifle sordid about it. Very much like curious dark, quiet animals slipping about. If they wouldn't get too fond of her, and try to prey on her life. This was what she always dreaded, about people of this sort. They had not enough life of their own, they enjoyed preying on other people's life. But meanwhile they went their own way. Clap-clap-clap she could hear the tortillas going from the flat of one of Juana's hands to the other, back and forth. And a queer crunching as Felipa crushed the chili and tomato-pulp on the lava stone in the kitchen. And the noise of the bucket in the well. Jesús had come to water the garden.

To all of them, the work was just a game. It was a sort of fun, no matter how many times they did it. And if there was work that was *not* fun, then they could hardly bring themselves to perform it. They just couldn't work if it wasn't fun. Consequently everything was rather careless as to detail, a natural confusion and untidiness. But it was a *living* confusion, not a dead, dreary thing. What you call discipline, method, strict order, they had none. They would do the same thing differently every day. They couldn't do anything twice in precisely the same way. That made Kate feel a bit muddled. But she just left it to them, and everything was done in time, and done well enough. And it was so nice for once to feel that no wheels were working, that things were just casually evolving of themselves, and evolving satisfactorily. It was nice, when you got used to it, to take your breakfast at one corner of the verandah, to find yourself moved to the middle for lunch, served in the dining-room for supper, and the next morning posed under a tree on the grass. Just as it took Felipa's fancy.

Sometimes she liked them so much: the absence of fuss, the absence of wheels, their real childishness. They really looked on life either as a pastime, or as something to fear and to resist. They had no morals, no standards: careless as the animals. And yet not animals. Never animals. Something dark and cognisant in their souls all the time. They worked in bits, in fits and starts. And they lazed in fits and starts. They were quite merry by fits and starts. But underlying all was a dark gloom of resistance. They resisted even their own merriment, seemed to recoil on to a sinister silence. They resisted whatever work they undertook, – throwing down the tool suddenly. They loved with a sinister abandon, for a time. Then they fell into as sinister, or more sinister a resistance of the very love they felt. Always the same underlying resistance, even to life itself. And sometimes Kate was glad of it, for she herself was driven to hate the shape of life now. And often she resented it terribly, felt their heavy weight on her intolerable.

The servants about the house were her clue to the rest of the people. But she watched them all. She watched them passing down the lane to the lake, she watched them in the plaza. Always the men together, erect, handsome, balancing their great hats on the top of their heads. And the women together separately, watchful, wrapped in their dark rebozos, and separate. The men and the women seemed to be turning their backs on one another, as if they didn't want to see one another. No flirting, no courting. Only occasionally a quick, dark look, the signal of a weapon-like desire. And the women seemed, on the whole, determined to go their own way: to change men if they wished. And the men seemed not to care very profoundly. The native women, with their long black hair streaming, bathed from one end of the beach. The men took absolutely no notice. They didn't even look the other way. It just wasn't their affair, it was the women. They avoided the place as if it were a vacuum. And the women sat in the shallow lake-edge, pouring water over themselves with a gourd scoop, isolated in themselves like the black mud-hens.

Always the separate streams of life, the men by far the most in evidence. The women seemed squat and insignificant, in their rebozos, or sitting in the water with their black hair streaming, or passing with a red water-jar on one shoulder, or sitting on the doorsteps lousing one another. It was a permanent occupation of the women, catching the lice in each other's dark, abundant hair. Kate's servants liked to perch as much in evidence as possible, to perform this pleasant task. Especially when the Niña had visitors. This was their delicate way of providing entertainment for the guests. And they looked very sheepish and sardonic when Kate, with blazing eyes, told them they must catch their lice in private. Afterwards, however, they always did so, for she saw them no more lousing.

The men were the handsome, prominent feature. They rarely touched one another. And often a single silent man in a sarape would stand motionless like a statue for hours at a street-corner, curiously spectral. Or one would lie alone on the beach, like jetsam. But usually they were in loose groups together. And, Kate said to herself, the highest thing this country had produced would be the faithful, complete attachment of one man to some hero-friend, a life-and-death fidelity. Not marriage. Marriage seemed to count little. Except the men loved their little children, and carried them about. But that was the tenderness of protection, the gentleness of protecting their own, in a dark and sinister life. The unison of the family for mutual protection. But as far as intimacy went, the men seemed to care for one another. And sex was a half-sinister thing powerful but hidden in the dark caverns of human consciousness.

There they were, the Indians in their straw huts, little holes built of straw, dark inside, with half-naked children and a rather lousy woman-squalor around, and the sharp smell of human excrement. And a man standing a little way from the hole of a door, silent, erect, handsome very often.

It was curious to contrast the peons with the city people who came down to the lake in motor-cars, for the day. Elegant young men, called Fifis, languidly hanging on to the arms of shrill, self-conscious girls in organdie frocks; the girls often very pretty, but hopelessly unattractive in their new, metallic emancipation; then young couples dancing in the plaza on the pavement of the café, the fellow stalking his legs between the girl's thin frock, hunching up his shoulders over her and sticking out his elbows, and looking like some huge, repulsive insect in the act of copulation. Ugh, what a sight! And the tall, erect, elderly peons in their big hats standing inscrutably watching. And then the flow of youths of the peon class surging on across the pavement which the bourgeois had tried to clear for their dancing, the lower, Indian class almost deliberately swamping out the jazzers and fox-trotters. So, the slow current of Indian life circulating, and the dance put out.

Kate had heard the bitter complaint from the western cities, how the life was ruined. Once the peons were not allowed in the walks of the plaza, under trees. And then it was a sight to see all the elegant women in silks and high heels and high combs, parading in the fashionable evening hour, and fanning themselves and their perfume. Alas, all over. The peons have got possession of the plazas, the eleganza can parade no more. Now, the elegance is all shut up in motor-cars and driven slowly, at walking pace, round a circle of a few central streets, in a slow, funereal, mechanical procession, most lugubrious to look on. This is the "quality" taking the traditional evening stroll. But a dismal sight, even in Mexico City.

The peons have taken possession of the Alamedas and the plazas. Kate could not but be amused, watching it in Chapala. The Fifis, young elegants, and the flappers in organdie, trying to dance on the pavement of the café, to the music of the four musicians. And the young peons in their huge hats and little white jackets, with a big scarlet sarape over one shoulder, slowly, indifferently, irresistibly passing through the dance, ignoring it utterly, and extinguishing it. The mysterious faculty of the Indians, as they sit there so quiet and dense, for killing off any pretentious life, bringing it down to earth again, to nothingness. The poor organdie butterflies of flappers, unable to live up against the silent ignoring and resistance of those passive devils of peons.

After three or four days the bandit scare passed, evaporated completely. The people were as cheerful as if they had never known fear. At night the plaza was thronged, the whole village lived there, after sundown. It was like evening in a big camp. The booths that sold food and tequila were busy till towards ten o'clock, men, women, youths sitting on the benches with their elbows on the board. One of the vendors was a large, stout, imperturbable woman with a cigarette on her lip, and danger in her lowering black eye. No one offended her. The sweetmeat man stood patiently by his board, and sold sweets at one centavo each. The tall, handsome men with sarape over one shoulder, proudly, lounged and strolled about, standing to listen to the singers, of whom there were usually two or three groups. A couple of young men, with different-sized guitars, stood facing each other like two fighting cocks, their guitars almost touching, and they strummed rapidly, intensely, singing in restrained voices the eternal ballads, not very musical, endless, intense, not very audible, and really mournful, to a degree, keeping it up for hours, till their throats were scraped! In among the food-booths would be another trio, one with a fiddle, keeping on at a high pitch and full speed, yet not very loud. Even the singing, public as it was, seemed half secretive, and the singers invariably faced one another and pressed close on one another as their instruments would permit, as if to keep the sound to themselves. The natives in the square listened casually, without paying much attention. Sometimes a listener gave a centavo. The men stood about in groups, or sat on the pavements or on the benches, not drinking, not even talking, just being there. And the tin torches flared their small flames, low down over a dozen mangoes or a few cents-worth of nauseous red tropical plums.

Kate liked to go with Villiers and Owen and watch them and be with them. On weekdays there were few outsiders. Then she would wrap herself in her yellow silk shawl and sit on a bench in the half dark, and really belong. Once she went in her heavily embroidered Spanish shawl. But that seemed to attract attention and cause the wrong feeling. It excited them to thoughts of robbery and violence, she felt, by accentuating the *difference* between them and her. Whereas in her yellow silk shawl they didn't heed her. She passed as one among the rest. It seemed to matter so little what one wore. The only thing to do was to avoid making an impression. Because the only impression one could make, with fine clothes, was a bad one. The natives hated the dressed-up women: didn't envy them, only hated them. Hated dressed-up men the same. Any attempt at being smart, above the level, at drawing attention to oneself, roused a curious smoke-like hatred in the plaza full of Indians. And this silent hatred was powerful. It darkly and silently seemed to shove the offender out. Kate therefore abandoned all idea of *chic,* left that to the bourgeois trippers from the city.

Sometimes a definite circle would form in a dark corner of the square: an Indian, in a white poncho, wearing it with his head through the middle, was singing alone in a low voice to the sound of a mellow guitar. He was invariably surrounded by a thick circle of men, so thickly pressed, so solid, and so silent, standing there, that it was impossible to break through. Owen of course was at once piqued. He stood on the outside of the ring, pressed up against the solid backs of the men, craning his neck to look over their shoulders. And there he saw the Indian in the beautiful white sarape with brilliant coloured borders and, most unusual, a brilliantly coloured fringe. Also the man wore no shirt under the blanket, the dark arm that held the guitar was naked, and lifted showed his dark side. But he wore the wide white cotton pants of the peons, and the red sash. So much Owen could see.

He was a middle-aged man, with a sparse Indian beard at the end of his chin, and that unseeing, almost sightless look of some of the natives. He played rapidly, brilliantly, and sang in a high-pitched voice, but not at all loud. There was something intense and inhuman in the sound. Owen strained his ears, and made Kate come and strain hers, but they could not catch a word. The ring of men stood solid, and absolutely silent, as if spellbound. When the singer finished, and he did not sing long, many of the men followed him as he quickly, silently went away. Owen noticed that he wore the trousers fastened close round the ankles with red and blue cords, and that his sandals, guaraches of woven leather, were dyed red and blue.

Altogether there was something a little mysterious and exciting about it, which made Owen wildly curious. He questioned the people of the hotel, but they could tell him nothing. He got guests, English-speaking Mexicans, to enquire. All they found out was that the man was a singer, that he sang songs about the Indians before the white men came, and not love songs at all, and that he used such a strong local vernacular that they could hardly understand anything. But, they suggested, he was part of the new Indian movement which took the name of the god Quetzalcoatl for a sort of mystic inspiration.

"These, then," exclaimed Owen, "are the new Children of Quetzalcoatl. Oh, I wish I could find out more! If only I spoke fluent Spanish! What a wonderful article one could write for *The Nation!*"

Kate was the one who *did* find out. When they were leaving Mexico, Don Ramón had told her that he owned a house on the lake, a small hacienda that produced wheat and maize and tequila, which he would probably be visiting in a short time, and he hoped, if Kate really stayed by the lake, he might meet her again there. She gathered, from his exclusive mention of herself, that he did not want very badly to see Owen. When, therefore, an Indian brought her a note one morning, she was not surprised to see that it was from Don Ramón, asking if he might call and bring his wife.

Doña Carlota was a thin, gentle, wide-eyed woman with a slightly startled expression, and with soft, brownish hair. She came from Chihuahua, and was quite different from the usual stout Mexican matron. Her thin, eager figure had something English about it, but the strange, wide, brown eyes were not English. She spoke only Spanish, but in such a distinct, slightly plaintive sing-song, very musical and a good deal like the Indian women, that Kate understood her easily, much, much more easily than Don Ramón.

The two women were at once in sympathy, but a little nervous of one another. Doña Carlota was delicate and sensitive like a Chihuahua dog, with the same slightly prominent eyes. Kate thought she had never seen a human being with such doglike finesse of gentleness. Don Ramón, large, swarthy, handsome, with his beautifully poised head, seemed remote and in another world. Almost menacing. And as if his words would never come across. It was evident that Doña Carlota had never for an instant criticised him. He was one of her absolutes, like God.

Kate gathered that Señora Carrasco was a pure Catholic. She had two boys, one ten years old, one about fourteen, whom she loved intensely. But also she had a work of her own. She was the director of a Cuna, a foundlings home, in Mexico City. The waste, unwanted babies were left at her door. The undesiring mother had only to knock and hand in the living little bundle. Doña Carlota even found this bundle a name. It was accepted out of nowhere. And as soon as possible some decent Indian woman was paid a modest sum to take the child to her home. Then every month she must come with the little one, to the Home, to receive her wage. In former days, Doña Carlota said, nearly all the well-born ladies of Mexico would adopt one of these children, and bring it up in her family. There was this loose, patriarchal generosity natural in the bosom of the Mexicans. But now, not many children were adopted. Instead they were taught to be carpenters or gardeners, if they were boys, or dress-makers or very often school-teachers, if they were girls.

Kate listened with interest, really touched. Although in her own heart the desire for charity, to take part in charitable works, no longer existed, still she felt that if she had been Mexican, a native of this half-wild disorderly country whose people still wrung her heart, she might have been happy doing as Doña Carlota did. And yet, even so, Doña Carlota had just a bit the look of a victim: a sensitive, gentle, slightly-startled victim. And there was something remotely suggestive of cruelty in Don Ramón's poise. An impassive cruelty, somewhat god-like, and yet none the less resented, instinctively, by Kate Burns.

She had a few words with him, and he told her that General Viedma was for the time being in Guadalajara, in military command there: and that he came frequently to the lake. He had heard that Kate was in Chapala, and sent his respects.

"Will you do me the pleasure of coming to see me?" smiled Doña Carlota, rather wavering and tentative. She was a wee bit afraid of Kate. "I have my two boys here – they do so love to be by the lake, so they came with me for a short vacation."

Kate stammered her acceptance in bad Spanish.

VI *Ramón at Home*

THE HOUSE was only a league or so from Chapala, but the road was very bad. Kate went on foot, escorted by Felipa. They passed large and handsome villas, built in Porfirio Diaz' day, now most of them empty, some of them becoming rather dilapidated, with broken walls and smashed windows. Only the flowers bloomed in masses above the rubble. And they passed many houses of the natives, flimsy straw huts carefully thatched with reed, dark-grey adobe huts with a few tiles, all scattered haphazard, as if the wind had blown them where they were. No careful selection, no little garden – just a haphazard little rubbish-place, where people lived like fowls. And in front of these huts the women would sit, their magnificent hair flowing, lousing one another, the children would run about naked or half-naked, the man would stride home proudly, his sarape over his shoulder. In many places they were busily thatching, in readiness for the rainy season, which was at hand. And the land was being clumsily ploughed, by two oxen and a mere lump of pointed wood. No plough at all, but the best thing for this stony land.

Kate and Felipa walked on through the dust, past the last of the broken villas, on under the shade of the big trees with queer, curling beans. On the left the pale, dove-coloured lake was lapping on the pale fawn stones. At the water-hole of a stream, on the beach, a cluster of women were washing clothes, and in the lake itself two women sat bathing, their brown shoulders heavy and womanly and of a fine orange-brown colour, their splendid hair hanging in wet masses. From the lake came a fresh breeze, but the dust underfoot was hot. On the right the hill rose precipitous, yellowish, giving back the sun from its dryness like a vast high wall, and exhaling the subtle, dry smell of Mexico. Endless strings of donkeys trotted laden through the dust, their drivers stalking erect and rapid behind, watching with eyes like black holes, but always answering Kate's salute with a kindly, respectful *Adiós!* To which Felipa responded rather stiffly. She disapproved terribly of the Niña's walking. Even riding a donkey would have been permissible, if humble. But to go on foot!

They turned the corner of the promontory into real country, the road with thorn fences and a few green trees, naked grey fields lying flat between the lake and the bluff of yellowish rock which rose suddenly inland. And in a little while they saw the hacienda. First it was a bunch of huts made of black adobe bricks and tiled with darkish red tiles – huts where children were playing, and women were carrying water, and fowls and pigs lay about. Then beyond, under trees, a big barn and stable place, with a litter of straw and a strange sour smell of tequila. Then the road, with trees, led to the high white wall of the hacienda house. The solid doors of the outer court-yard stood open, a man was sawing poles to repair a roof, and two other men were just unloading red roof-tiles from three donkeys. Two huge black dogs rushed up barking. A more important peon ran out to call them off, then he ushered Kate and Felipa into the smaller inner courtyard of the house itself, and pointed to the stone staircase.

Kate climbed to the upper balcony. Doors stood open, but she did not quite know where to go. On the upper floor the terrace was open in wide arches, to the lake. She turned in that direction, to look out at the water. As she did so there rose the sound of a guitar, and a man singing in a full, rich voice, a curious music. She walked along towards the sound, which came from the lake side of the house. Then the singing stopped.

"I will stay here, Niña," called Felipa, in an anxious voice, waiting at the top of the staircase.

At the same moment came the sound of guitars and violins, and four or five men started singing. Kate, who was always attracted by people singing, went forward excitedly. She came to the end of the corridor, and there opened an arched terrace, in arches open towards the lake and the trees. On the stone bench of the lake-ward wall of the terrace sat four men with guitars and violins, naked to the waist, one foot crossed over the knee of the other leg, their white cotton pantaloons bound at the ankle with blue-and-red cords, singing; while alone on the bench of the opposite wall sat Don Ramón, in exactly the same dress, except that his sash was of a brilliant blue, instead of red. He was sitting with his handsome black head bent, leading the singing, and did not notice her. But the other four noticed her.

They took no notice, however, keeping up the rapid, high, plangent singing, that had somehow the effect of a messenger delivering a message, Don Ramón leading, in his rich voice, of which he seemed only to be using part. Kate stood in amazement, a good deal embarrassed, and somewhat entranced. The black eyes of the men watched her as she stood motionless, and she in her turn watched their dark, abstracted faces, the barbaric showing of their white teeth. She was a little afraid.

But when Don Ramón raised his head and saw her, the greeting in his eyes was quite frank and cordial. He bowed his head to her, with a slight smile, but kept up the rapid playing of the guitar and the rapid singing until the song came to an end. Then he at once put aside his big, golden-coloured instrument, that was shaped something like a huge gourd with a flattened surface, and rose laughing. The four other men were laughing too, and one of them called to him something in a teasing voice, of which she caught no word except *Don Ramón*.

"You find us making music," he said, shaking hands. "Pardon that we do not look as gentlemen should, but this is the music lesson. Let me put on my sarape, and I will take you to my wife."

He picked up the fine white sarape, and quickly dropped it over his head. Then he laughed, saying he was in his native costume.

"It is a beautiful costume," she said. "And a lovely sarape."

"Miguel made it," said he, pointing to one of the musicians, who laughed rather shyly.

It was a beautiful sarape, of natural white wool, washed white, soft and finely woven, with an exquisite inwoven pattern of earth-brown and blue at the neck, very becoming on the handsome Indian shoulders, and an intricate coloured border of the same, and a fringe of blue and brown and white wool. The blanket hung halfway down his thighs, in front, and showed the golden bronze of his naked sides, when he turned to pick up his beautifully-woven, white and earth-brown sandals. When he stood erect, his naked feet in the sandals, he had a real nobility of appearance, and at the same time, a naïve, vulnerable look, that again touched Kate's heart. She was always struck by the vulnerable naïveté of these handsome men. They were living, naked men under their sarapes, not unassailable, cloth-bound automata.

Doña Carlota, in a simple white muslin dress, cried out because Kate had found no servant to announce her. "Ayee! Ayee!" exclaimed the hostess, making the queerest little sound of distress. "But we are in the country, you must forgive everything, even my husband's sarape."

"The sarape is beautiful. And your husband in the sarape is very beautiful."

"Yes, yes, it is true. But whether beautiful things are wise things, I don't know. So much I don't know, Señora. Ah, so much! And you, do you know what is wise?"

"I!" said Kate. "No. I used to think I did."

"Ah! – And do you think Ramón is wise, in his sarape?"

"Oh very! It must be wise, to be so beautiful. And men in their clothes usually look so ugly –" Kate had lapsed into English, and Doña Carlota watched her with intelligent, half-scared eyes, divining what she said.

"Ah yes – ah yes – *muy feo!*" she murmured.

The house was not very large, and scantily, even miserably furnished, the rooms almost empty. But Kate knew it was usually so on haciendas liable to be attacked from time to time and pillaged by revolutionaries or bandits. The two boys came in from the lake, the elder big and nearly as dark as his father, the younger with his mother's soft brown hair. They were handsome, healthy school-boys, in white cotton shirts and white, short breeches.

"You don't wear sarapes, like your father?" said Kate.

"No, a shirt is more comfortable," said Francisco, the elder.

"No shirt is more comfortable still," laughed Don Ramón.

"No. No. That's not true," replied Francisco quickly. "Because with no shirt we are ashamed to be seen, and that is not comfortable."

"You know the donkey who was ashamed to look at the wild ass that had no saddle on," teased Don Ramón. "It looked so naked."

"Papa, a shirt is not the same as a saddle."

"And a boy is not the same as a tame donkey."

"No, Papa, because a boy is the arriero, he's the driver of the donkey."

"And the man in the sarape is the donkey?"

"No, because he's only got two legs."

"Otherwise yes," laughed Don Ramón.

But the boy had run to his mother.

"If I went into the plaza in these calzones," said Don Ramón, glancing at the peon's loose cotton trousers, crossed in front and held in a blue sash, which he wore, "the authorities would arrest me: if they dared."

"What for?" cried Kate.

Don Ramón spread his small, brown hands in a gesture of helplessness.

"That is the law. If the campesinos go into the plaza in their own wide pants, they are arrested. They must wear the ready-made city trousers. They pull them over their field pants."

"But how absurd!" cried Kate. "Why? Why? It seems to me the wide floppy peon's trousers are quite as decent as shop trousers, and so amusing in this hot country. Sometimes in the distance they look like skirts – when they haven't rolled them at the ankle. Why should they be forbidden?"

"Who knows – except that the authorities wish to give an air of *tono*, of tone do you say? to the plaza. Or unless, of course, some-one had a large supply of workmen's pants to sell."

"Who would have expected such nonsense in Chapala!" said Kate.

"Oh, the Mexican is very delicate. He has no skin except on his face, and his lady has none even there: only talcum powder. I speak, of course, of the refined classes."

"They don't *seem* to me so terribly refined."

"That is the old order of refinement. It is dying out. It is a curious thing, to me, that here in Mexico, and in the United States, where the Indians went naturally in their live skin, as we say, and at times a blanket, that the white people should be so much afraid of even a tiny bit of uncovered man. Have you ever been at the seaside in California, or in Florida?"

"Only nearer to New York."

"Isn't it a curious, disagreeable sight? The people so excited because they are flesh, under so much bathing-gown?"

"Very ugly," said Kate. "Oh very ugly."

"As you say, very ugly. It seems to me that the white man doesn't belong to this continent. He is a fish without water, as you say. All the little white Christian fishes crowding in the small bit of Christian water they brought with them from Europe. And soon that will be dried up."

"There are very many millions of white fishes in America, any-how," said Kate. "All swimming very fast, and all dressed very fast in their clothes."

"All swimming very fast, and all dressed very fast in their clothes," he reiterated. "But soon they will be high and dry. Isn't that the word? The dry Flood!"

He smiled at her quickly. He was very handsome, but he made her blood run cold. At the back of his black eyes the devil was smiling fiendishly.

"I'm afraid you will never get the white man out of America again," said Kate.

"Who knows the future?" said Don Ramón, with a sardonic reserve.

"You don't think you will ever get America back, for the Mexicans and the Indians, do you?" asked Kate.

"Why not?" he said.

"Because it seems impossible."

"Seems impossible, yes," he replied.

Kate thought of the Indians of the northern pueblos. They believe with such devilish certainty that the wheel of fate will bring the end of the white man's day, that the white men will perish from the earth, and the Red Men will be the world's lord.

Kate and Ramón were sitting alone on the terrace. As soon as Don Ramón started to speak English in a certain tone, Doña Carlota excused herself and fled. Yet she hovered from room to room, never very far away, like a conscience hovering outside her husband's body.

"Tell me then," said Kate, "why they don't arrest the man who was singing here with you, one of the four, and who sings in the plaza."

"Because," laughed Don Ramón, "they don't dare." And his eyes seemed to contract dangerously.

"Why not?"

"I will tell you," said Don Ramón. "I would not, pardon me if I say it, tell the same to your American cousin, or to any other inquirer."

"Oh, I'm sorry," said Kate. "I am always so rude, asking why."

She felt she had had a slap in the face.

"No no, no no! I wish to tell you. In my philosophy there are exceptions to all generalities. You will pardon me when I say that I regard you as an exception."

"To what," said Kate, slightly offended.

"To the ordinary white people, with white blood and white minds."

Kate flushed a little. She saw, in the faint satiric smile on Don Ramón's face, how deep went his hatred. Profound, unchanging hatred. Even of her. She felt again he hated her, generically, not specifically. She had become again just an object to him, that he talked at.

"But Mexicans are white people?" she said.

"Many of them are powdered very white."

Kate laughed, and was uncomfortable. She was not getting on well with Don Ramón. Yet he had seemed so handsome, and with a certain demonish geniality, when he was singing. Now he seemed to be wanting to hurt her all the time, wanting to be cruel, all round cruel.

"Don't you think of yourself as a white man?" she asked, timidly.

"No, my skin allows me no place among the elect. And I do not wish to pray, with the negro, 'Lord, Lord, sure the heart of this nigger am more white than a white man's skin?' – My heart is no whiter than my hair."

Kate laughed, and was silent for a time.

"You don't like speaking English," she said. "I am sorry my Spanish is so bad."

Instead of answering he rose from his chair suddenly, with a violent motion.

"The afternoon is very hot," he said. "With your permission I will remove my sarape."

"Certainly," she replied.

He lifted his sarape over his head and threw it over the balustrade of the terrace. Then, naked to the waist, his black, splendid hair all ruffled, he stood with his back to Kate, looking out to the lake. She saw the soft, cream-brown skin of his back, of a smooth pure sensuality that made her shudder. And the broad, square, rather high shoulders, with the neck and head rising steep, proudly. It was handsome, but with a certain insentience, fixed and, to her, stupid. She could not help imagining a knife stuck between those pure, male shoulders.

The evening breeze was blowing very faintly. Two sailing boats were advancing through the pearly atmosphere far off, the sun above had a golden quality. The opposite shore, twenty miles away, was distinct, and yet there seemed an opalescent, sperm-like haze in the air, the same quality as in the filmy water. Kate could see the white specks of the far-off towers of Tizapán.

Just below her, in the garden below the house, was a thick grove of mango-trees, through which the path went down to a little shingle bay, with a small breakwater. There the boys were throwing a big, fine round net to catch the little silvery fish, called charales, which flicked out of the brownish water sometimes like splinters of glass. Among the dark and reddish leaves of the mango-trees, scarlet little birds were bickering, and pairs of birds, yellow underneath as yellow butterflies, went skimming past. The yellow birds were quite grey on top. In this country the birds had their colour all below, their colourless sheath above.

Don Ramón still stood looking out to the lake, turning his naked back on Kate. She knew now why the full cotton pants were forbidden in the plaza. The living flesh seemed to emanate through them. He was handsome, horribly handsome, with his black head poised splendidly, rising above a brown, smooth neck of pure sensuality. Nothing impure. But hostile. There, with the blue sash round his waist, the cotton pants falling thin against his hips and thighs, so that the flesh seemed to speak through, he seemed to emanate a fascination like a narcotic, the male asserting his pure, fine sensuality against her. There was a strange aura about him, that seemed to deny her existence, so pure in its hostility. He seemed to wish to annul her existence, as a white woman born of Christianity. And he emitted an effluence so powerful, that it deprived her of movement, for the time being.

Doña Carlota appeared by instinct on the balcony, looked at her husband, looked at Kate sitting there in the chair in silence, and hovered uneasily. Then she came near.

"Shall we take tea? Yes?" she asked uncertainly.

"Yes," said Kate to her. "I would like that."

"Good! Good!" And the little woman was turning away, pleased and relieved.

"Send a tray here, Carlota," said Don Ramón, in a gentler voice.

His wife stopped as if some hand had suddenly grasped her.

"Good! Good!" she repeated abstractedly. Then she hurried again on her way.

"In this country birds have all their colour underneath, and are colourless on top," said Kate, making this observation out of polite determination.

Don Ramón turned and stood in front of her, above her, with his naked breast, looking down on her with inscrutable black eyes.

"They say the word Mexico means *Below this,*" he said, with that faint Indian smile which she hated.

She puzzled a moment.

"Below what?" she asked. She was ready to fight now.

He broke into a sudden laugh, and threw himself into a chair beside her, reaching out his naked arm to her.

"*Bueno! Bueno!*" he said in Spanish. – "We are friends." And he took her hand in a sudden subtle grasp. "You know that General Viedma wishes to be your friend?" he added, a little more stiffly, in English, at the same time letting his hand slide away again. His touch was so strange and soft, beautiful, yet a little bit horrible to her.

"No, not particularly," she said. "At least I didn't know definitely."

"But indefinitely, eh? – Yes, he wishes to be your friend. And you?"

"I?" said Kate, and she didn't know how to go on. She felt she was being overcome, she had to force herself to answer. "I – I don't mind being *friends* – with anybody whom I like. But – I don't know that I shall ever want to be *more* than friends."

"You have sworn to remain a widow, eh?"

"No! I haven't sworn. Why should I? But I feel that I have *had* that part of my life – that one doesn't have it twice," she added fixedly.

"*Bueno! Bueno!*" he said very softly. "*Muy bueno!*" And he pressed her hand again, suddenly, then withdrew his hand, and sat for some time silent.

"You know," he began in his foreign English, relapsing into a sort of abstraction, "each man has two spirits inside him. The one is like the early morning in the rainy season, very gentle and sweet, with the mocking-bird singing. – And the other is like the steady, dry hot light of the day in the dry season, which seems everlasting and without end."

"There is certainly more of it," said Kate sarcastically.

"Of the dry season!" he replied, with a slow, dark smile. "That is true. – In the first period, the earth seems full of flowers, and a man feels his own body like the stem of a flower that is just opening. Oh, desire is then like a perfume. – But this passes. The sun begins to glare, and the breast of a man is like a steel mirror. Then he is all dark inside, and a serpent coils and uncoils in the darkness behind him, below his sash. – You know that the symbol of Mexico is an eagle holding a snake in its [claws]?"

"Yes," said Kate. "And I've wondered so often which is more

awful, the eagle or the snake."

"One may wonder," he laughed. "But sometimes the eagle holds the snake, and sometimes the snake holds the eagle. Neither can escape, so therefore both are usually angry. Only in the early morning of a man's life they both seem free. But the morning passes, and the eagle pounces on the snake, in the glare of the day, and in the shadow the serpent winds round the feet of the eagle, heavier than iron. There are the two. That is the soul of man in America, in Mexico. The snake tormented between the claws of the eagle, and the eagle tortured by the snake that coils round his legs and bites him."

"But it needn't be," protested Kate.

"Doña Carlota says, let us give our breasts like doves, for the snake to bite. But at the same time she tries to peck the eyes out of the snake's head. She thinks if she could make him blind, it would be peace. – Why must there be peace? Why do all Christians and white people insist that there is only peace?"

"There *should* be peace," said Kate. "One *should* have a centre of peace inside one."

"Look, you insist the same! And how will you get this peace inside you? Do you have it? Do white people have it? Does Carlota have it, for all her good deeds and her piety? See her, what an uneasy bird! Secretly trying to peck out the eyes of the snake, thinking that when he is blind he can bite no more. – Yes, he will bite, he will bite. She will never be able to let him go."

He smiled with his black, gleaming eyes into Kate's eyes.

"But one *can* have a centre of peace inside oneself," persisted Kate. "One *must* have it."

"How do you get it? By killing the snake and swallowing him? Or by letting him swallow you?"

"I am neither a snake nor an eagle," said Kate. "I am myself."

"Why sure! You have swallowed the snake, the snake that bites the genitals of the bull Mithras. This must be peace, to have him dead with all his poison, inside you. To be a tomb, this must be peace. Even the tomb of the snake. – In Mexico, the eagle still has not swallowed her adversary. We are not yet a tomb. Our sepulchres are not yet whited."

"Why do you hate me so?" asked Kate in dismay.

"Because you think you have swallowed the snake. But you can never digest him. And Viedma desires you so greatly, because you appear to have swallowed the snake. You may have swallowed him, but you can never digest him. You will sink down to the grave with the dead weight of him inside you."

Kate was silent. It seemed useless to answer. She believed that Ramón hated her because Cipriano loved her. He was jealous of his friend.

"I don't understand snakes and eagles and mysticism. I am myself," she answered.

"Like Doña Carlota –" he continued – And at that moment Doña Carlota appeared, with her wide, pathetic brown eyes, and her nervous hands. Behind her came a mozo, a man-servant with a small round table. She was carrying an embroidered tablecloth.

"Carlota," said Don Ramón to her, "I want you to go yourself and gather me a few hibiscus flowers."

"Good!" she said, vaguely, as if distracted.

And Kate realised how jealous poor Doña Carlota was: how the poor woman knew that her husband was dismissing her for a few minutes longer: but how it was her creed to obey. For a moment it flitted through Kate's mind, whether she ought to rise and accompany the wife to the garden. Don Ramón was stupidly male and cruel. He was all snake and eagle himself: sometimes all physical and fascinating like a serpent, sometimes mystical and high-flying like a menacing eagle. But he was the enemy, she must hear him out.

"Doña Carlota," resumed Don Ramón, "believes in peace. But I, I know I have no peace. If I have no peace, why should I lie to myself, that I have peace?"

"But you could have peace if you wanted it," persisted Kate.

"Is that so? What kind of peace could I have?"

"The peace of your own soul," she said.

"Is that so? Is that so?" he replied, leaning forward to her with his black eyes smiling devilishly and his cream-brown flesh like opium. He spread his hand on his naked, rather full breast. "Here," he said, "is the Mexican eagle, staring at the Mexican sun and unable to escape from the heavy serpent below. And here –" he pressed his fist in his side, in his groin, "is the heavy Mexican serpent, pierced by the claws of the eagle and biting up at her. Where is the peace between them?"

"You are a man," she said. "You can control the two halves of your nature."

"I am a man," he said venomously. – "I am a man, and therefore I

will not be like the whited sepulchres of the pale-faces. Not even if a
pale-face squaw wishes it of me. I will not be the tomb of my serpent. I
will not be a pale-face machine that adds up money. No. Nor shall they
turn my people into adding-up machines. Reckoning machines, that
are at a standstill when there is no more money to add, and call that
peace. That they call peace. – My people shall never know such
peace."

"I don't call it peace," she said.

"You! You have sufficient money, which someone else is always
adding up. And you are like Doña Carlota. You take the money when
it is added up. And you talk about love and peace and possessing your
own soul. All the time that the adding-machines are talking louder
than thunder. You say let them talk, let them talk? So all the world,
even I, must fall to adding up, and reckoning money. True, there is no
more snake in the adding-machine."

She looked, with her gold-gleaming eyes, into the black rage of
his bottomless eyes. It was a war. She herself had her own anger, but it
was set hard and static at the depths of her. She wanted no break in
this. While she lived she would be gentle and kindly towards life. Her
will was fixed for this. But the bedrock of her soul was anger, anger,
unappeased and unreleased, static like a rock. She would rather die
than have this anger broached, have the static rock broken, for the
boiling lava to flow forth. But there it was. And there she would keep
it, as a bedrock. Whilst she preserved a gentleness towards life.

With her eyes, she defied Ramón to break open the rock of her
anger.

"And what would *you* do?" she asked coldly.

He was leaning forward towards her, and she felt the massive
weight of his psyche, like heavy iron. And oh, how she hated this
Mexican heaviness. She wanted a certain carelessness. The bosses of
his naked, golden breast seemed to thrust forward, full of a strange,
half-divine power. But he was bullying her. So she put it to herself. In
the depths of his wonderful black eyes, he was watching her as an
enemy, and his naked breast was like a naked war against her. She
found it, also, much harder to withstand the naked smoothness of his
arms, in their quick gestures, than if they had been covered in coat-
sleeves. He was taking a dreadful advantage of her, in his physical
nakedness.

"What would I do? I will bring back the Mexican gods with all

their anger. The snake that the white men have killed I will set up
again. And he shall bite them. Oh, he shall bite their genitals, as he bit
the bull of Mithras. I will set up the snake again. I will bring back the
Mexican gods, and deliver the snake from the claws of the eagle. And
the snake shall bite the genitals of the white men, till they are bitten to
death. And then I will lift up my eagle and let him fly to the sun. And I
will take the serpent softly in my left hand, and let him glide away to
the bowels of the earth. And I shall be the man on earth, I shall be the
man of the world, I, the Mexican. When the white men who are all
sepulchres and adding-machines are dead, and the white women, who
are all sepulchres and charity institutions, are dead too. When all the
flowers are not set on tombs —" he concluded bitterly, as Doña Carlota
came hurriedly forward and set a bowl of rose-scarlet hibiscus on the
finely worked cloth.

"*Bonitas, bonitas, Cosita,*" he said with a smile, touching the
flowers with the tips of his brown fingers. "*Qué bonitas!*"

"And then, Ramón," she said, with a little air of righteous authority, handing him a white garment, "you will wear this, yes?"

"Good! Good!" he said, rising and thrusting his arms into the
short, man's shirt or blouse, such as the peons wear, a white blouse
with a narrow yoke and three flat pleats down the back, and a small
open collar like a shirt. The naked man had gone again. But he was not
gone very far, inside that short peasants' blouse.

None the less, Kate felt more comfortable, seeing him covered.
Her face lost its bright, sharpened look, the look of a bright dagger-
point, as she turned very amiably to Doña Carlota. Doña Carlota at
once recognized an ally.

"I hope I came at the right time," said Kate. "I didn't know exactly
when you wanted me, so I came about teatime."

"Good, very good!" sang Doña Carlota in her bird-like, attractive
voice. "Any time is good. I expected you all the day. And now you will
stay the night, yes? I think General Viedma will come, but he and
Ramón are so busy with their schemes. They have told you? Yes? That
they want other gods? Yes?"

Don Ramón laughed and went away.

"And you are very much interested in their schemes?" asked Doña
Carlota, smiling her gentle bright smile, and speaking in her gentle,
light voice like a bird chirruping. Underneath all her gentleness,
however, was an infinite passive resistance, a great fear, and an ob-
stinacy even greater than fear.

"Not very much," said Kate, in broken Spanish. "I have known so many."

"So many – ?" queried Doña Carlota delicately.

"Schemes – pronunciamientos – revolutions. So much liberty. So much work for the good of the people, and it never does any good. Only does harm."

"Only does harm," repeated Doña Carlota, with gentle conviction. "Yes. Yes. It does only harm. The people were happiest when they had their faith, when they lived in the belief in the Church, and the Church took them to God. Ah yes –" said Doña Carlota hurriedly, "Don Ramón is a philosopher, but his philosophy cannot give me the Purest Virgin, and prayer. And it cannot give the people peace. No, if we love the people, we should give them the Church, and the Virgin, and good, kind, *strong* masters. Yes. That is the only way."

"Yes," said Kate, though without conviction.

"I have tried, I have tried to follow Don Ramón," said Doña Carlota, fluttering. "But I cannot give up the Most Pure Virgin, I cannot. I can much more easily die."

There was a pause.

"So now," continued Doña Carlota, looking at her teaspoon as if gazing into Hell: "Now I am here in my husband's house, while he intends to teach false gods to the people." There was strange vindictiveness in her words.

"Surely," said Kate, "we don't want any *more* Gods."

"More Gods, Señora," said Doña Carlota, shocked. "How is it possible! Don Ramón is in mortal sin: in mortal sin."

"And General Viedma?" asked Kate.

"The same. The same. But it was Don Ramón who proposed this mockery he calls Quetzalcoatl. Quetzalcoatl, Señora! What buffoonery, if it were not horrible sin! What buffoons, for two clever and well-educated men. The sin of pride, Señora, men wise in their own conceit."

"Men always are," said Kate.

She left shortly afterwards, wanting to be home by nightfall. Doña Carlota ordered a man to row the two visitors back to the village. It was sunset, with a big level cloud like fur overhead, but the sides of the horizon fairly clear. The sun was not visible. It had gone down in a thick rose-red fume behind the wavy ridge of the distant mountains. Now the hills stood up bluish, all the air was a salmon-red flush, the fawn water had pinkish ripples. Boys and men, bathing in the shallow lakeside, were the colour of deep flame.

The boatman looked at the sky.

"A storm is coming?" asked Felipa, swathed in her black rebozo like a swarthy madonna, and carrying a bunch of gaudy flowers.

"I believe so," said the boatman.

"Soon?" said Kate.

"Not *very* soon, Señora."

"No, no," exclaimed Felipa. "In the night."

But the man pulled hard. The air was thick and hot, there was a slow, thick breeze.

"How nice it is," exclaimed Felipa, "to row in a boat. Also a motor-boat is nice, you go quickly – ssh! – But Don Ramón hasn't got a motor-launch?"

"No, he hasn't got one," replied the boatman. "He has two sailing-canoes."

"Yet it would be a good thing for him to have one," said Felipa. "What a nice soul is Doña Carlota! What a good woman! If she sees a man on the road who is poor, she sends him a shirt and a peso. How nice she is! And if anyone has children and they find themselves poor, they go to Doña Carlota. So good! so good!"

"And Don Ramón?" asked Kate.

"Oh yes! Yes! Also! But he is different. Very learned, Don Ramón. He knows many things that we don't know. – Look, how pretty Chapala. How nice Chapala is!"

The green trees on the low shore were very green, in the pinkish light. The hills rose behind abruptly, like steep mounds, dry and pinkish. Down the shore, among green trees, shone the two graceful white towers of Chapala Church, obelisk-shaped. And villas peeped out from trees. The strand was in shadow, but still one could see the white scattering of many people, and sailing ships with their masts lying up on the beach, and the pleasure boats side by side on the water's edge. The lights flickered on as Kate's boat drew near. It was half-past-six. Boatmen were busily pulling their boats high and dry, expecting a storm.

Kate decided she would speak to Owen before she went home, so she crossed the beach and entered the big, careless dining-room of his hotel: a rough, happy-go-lucky place. She wandered up the broken stone steps to the great dilapidated square place upstairs, on to which opened the bedroom doors. The panes of glass in Owen's door were half of them smashed, so he kept the shutters closed. She tapped.

"Hello!" came his voice from within.

"Only me."

"Oh!" – and quickly he opened the door. "You!" he exclaimed. "Come in and have a cocktail. Or would you rather wait till I put a shirt on."

Owen too was naked to the waist, in belted trousers and sandals.

"I go like this for coolness," he said, "and because of my shoulders. They are quite painful! Look!" – And he bowed his shining, sun-scorched bald head before her like a Chinese bonze making an obeisance. On the tops of his shoulders the sunburn was a scarlet inflammation, and in two round spots the skin had gone, showing two purple, angry places.

"Why," she said, "that is serious. You must be careful."

"I know I must. I had hardly a wink of sleep last night."

He had been lying out on the beach in his bathing drawers in order to get brown. His arms, indeed, and his breast were already almost as brown as Don Ramón's, but of a more smoky colour. His head and shoulders were angry red.

"But you are absurd," said Kate, "to stay in the sun till you are in that state."

"No," said he, "it's not the sun, it is letting the little boys stand on my shoulders to dive into the water." He broke into a laugh. "It was quite the game. They climb up my back and stand with their naked feet on my shoulders, to jump into the water. But it has taken the skin off." – He looked down ruefully.

"You've had to pay for your oh-so-friendliness this time," she said.

"Yes, I have. But they're awfully nice kiddies. – Let me make you a cocktail. – What have you been doing all day?"

"I should love a cocktail," said Kate, sitting down by the window.

On the bed was a spread of letters written, envelopes addressed, loose poems, and piles of the Chicago *Tribune*. Owen, stooping forward his reddened shoulders, was putting letters in their appropriate envelopes and licking the flaps. Each letter had its long brown stamp on. Each, as it was done, he dropped in a little squadron on the counterpane. Dozens of letters as usual.

"You don't mind if I just finish these," said Owen, "then they're done."

Kate looked at the American newspaper, but she could only half understand its jargon, and somehow its tone made her feel sick. Owen was rushing through his letters and hastening to clear them away. Kate went over to his dressing-table. It was a litter of papers and books, and things he had bought, little earthern plates, little curios, a peon's sash.

"Oh, and look!" he said, holding out his foot. He had bought a pair of handsome plaited sandals. "Three pesos and a half," he added. "The man wanted four and a half, but he took three and a half."

Kate was sniffing at the guavas in Owen's big bowl of fruit.

"Take them if you care for them," he said.

"I think I like the smell better than the taste," said she.

"Yes," he laughed. "One does. But these have a rather strong, coarse scent. – Oh, and look!" – He hastened to his cupboard and switched out something white. In an instant he had dived into a pair of the great white cotton pants, had crossed the flaps over the front and tied the ends behind.

"There!" he said.

Kate laughed, he was so pleased, standing there in his big-rimmed spectacles, with his red-burned round face and naked chest. Owen too was tall and well-built. But his physique was somehow meaningless, and in the floppy white drawers he looked just absurd. But he was a dear.

"I had a wonderful time getting these made," he said. "One of my little boys took me to the dress-makers – three young ladies. Imagine my attempt to explain what I wanted. But with a great deal of gesticulating and the help of the boy – such a bright little fellow – I managed it. Then she had to measure me to see how much material I should want. Oh embarrassing moment! She most gingerly held the tape about six inches away from me, and reached down to the floor, measuring my *aura* rather than me. Then she said I wanted two metres and a half. Oh it was great. They were all as solemn and elegant as if they were in church. But I turned as I went out and saw, to my relief, that they were just going off into fits of laughter. It was great – Then my little boy whisked me off to the dry-goods store."

Owen had now got into a well-fitting blue shirt of fine crape, and tied his tie and settled his neck.

"I suppose just a shirt doesn't hurt your shoulders?" she said.

"No. Not just a shirt. But a coat is agony."

He was squeezing orange-juice into a glass.

"Spud!" he called, to the next room, whose door of communication was open.

"Yes!" replied Villiers' thin voice.

"Get a couple of small glasses, will you."

"Where from?" came the thin voice.

"*Where from!*" reiterated Owen, with a burst of laughter. "Why just go and ask your mother for them."

Villiers' mother being in California, this was sarcasm.

In a few moments Villiers appeared, very neat and spruce in a delicate shirt of apricot colour and neat-fitting trousers, carrying two tumblers.

"Oh, you brought tumblers!" said Owen.

"Well, there's nothing else in this hotel, except the little glasses with the toothpicks in," expostulated Villiers.

"All right, we'll use tumblers," said Owen, absorbed now in squeezing the juice of a sweet lemon into the orange juice.

"These lemons we got in the market at three centavos are quite wonderful," he said.

"Oh, wonderful, they make the most beautiful cocktails!" chimed Villiers.

"So smooth!" said Owen. "Just the right consistency."

"I like them awfully," said Villiers.

"And the juice of one of these eight-centavo oranges practically fills a whole glass."

The business of the cocktails proceeded. Owen poured in the gin judiciously, then changed the mixed juices from tumbler to tumbler.

"I find," he said, "that by adding a little water I get them cooler."

Kate pronounced her drink delicious. She sat by the big open window watching the mountains dark in front of the still rosy smoky-looking sky, and the lake still pale.

Owen pressed her to stay to supper, and they were quite gay, laughing and making jokes all the time. Owen was famous for being lively company, and he always inspired Kate to jokes. He called to the people at the next table, a mother, a girl of sixteen, and a long-legged young girl of eleven, called Patchy.

"Oh," he said, "listen to Patchy's latest description of Spud. She sat looking at him for a long time, then she suddenly said: 'Your eyes are sad, and your mouth is sad, and your chin is sad. And your nose *would* be gay if the rest of you weren't so sad.' – Isn't that great?" And he went off into a whoop of laughter.

Villiers, hearing this description of himself once more, put his napkin to his mouth and laughed, self-consciously pleased.

"I say," called the elder girl from the next table, "are we going to finish the tournament?"

The tournament referred to a little dining-room game, like bagatelles, where you knocked a ball with a cue, up a little sloping table, and it either fell or didn't fall into a numbered hole.

"Mother," said Patchy, swinging her plait of hair, "I thought a tournament meant burying somebody."

Of course Owen's quick ear caught this, and he went off into a shriek of laughter. He was always going into a loud shriek of laughter, then apologising quite humbly to Kate.

As soon as supper was over Patchy ran clinging to Villiers, to drag him to the board of the unknown game. The first gusts of wind had slammed the great doors of the room, coming from the lake. The waiter ran to fasten them. There was enough broken glass in the house.

Kate also declared she must run. The night, the lake was quite black now, and distant lightning was playing among the far-off circling hills. Sudden gusts of wind raised the dust. Kate and Owen hurried along. It was only three or four minutes to her house. But already the wind was tearing like torn silk in the mango-trees.

"I'll just fly back," said Owen. "Goodnight!"

"Goodnight!" said Kate. "Thank you so much. It was so nice."

He laughed, and ran into the black wind.

"Ah Niña!" cried Felipa, seeing Kate appear. "Good that you have come. Good that you are here. The water is coming."

She meant the rain. And she was no false prophet. The wind suddenly blew with enormous violence, with a strange ripping sound in the mango-trees. The oleanders with their white flowers leaned over quite flat in the garden, the palm-tree bent and spread its leaves on the ground. Lightning flashed and ran down the sky like some blazing writing. Kate wondered what the message was. And the soft, velvety thunder broke inwardly, strangely.

"Good that we are at home, Niña," said Felipa, as she and the children stood beside Kate on the terrace, waiting for the storm.

Kate wandered uneasily from room to room, in her house. Then she sat in a big cane rocking-chair under the light in the sala, rocking herself.

"Ah! Ah Niña, the water! the water!" cried Felipa. And once more Kate went out to the terrace. The first great drops were flying darkly at the flowers.

In another minute down came the rain with a crash, waters breaking downwards. And all the time, from every part of the sky, very blue lightning fell and lit up the garden in a blue, breathless moment, while the thunder dropped and exploded. Kate watched the masses of water. Already the garden and the walks were a pond with little waves. She strayed round her rooms, looking if the scorpions were coming out: and called to Felipa to come and kill a small one that was just scuttling across her bedroom floor.

Then she sat in her sala and rocked and rocked, smelling the good wetness, and breathing the good chill air. She had already forgotten what really chill air was like. She rose and fetched herself a little velvet coat.

"Ah yes, yes! You feel the cold!" cried Felipa. "Sometimes, in the time of water, it is so cold at night, that I lie and shake. But you have plenty of sarapes, plenty of covers. Yes! Yes!"

She and the girls were wrapped tight in their rebozos, watching the night. At half past nine the rain began to abate, and Felipa began putting pails and kerosene-cans under a spout, to get water. There was no water in the house. The water-man carried all the wash-water from the lake, and for drinking and cooking brought two square kerosene-cans full of the warm water from the hot springs at the other end of the village: a pole over his shoulder, and a heavy pail hanging from either end. The aguador! He wouldn't earn so much tomorrow. He was paid six centavos for each trip to the lake, and twelve for each trip to the hot spring. Kate listened to the water pouring into the can.

At about ten o'clock Rafael came running in from the planta. Then they locked the house, and Felipa carried out the mattress for the boy, and laid it outside Kate's door. Rafael brought his sarape, and his old, ivory-handled pistol. The rain came on again, breaking downwards. The house went to its uneasy sleep.

VII   *Conversion*

D ON RAMÓN'S HACIENDA by the lake was called Las Yemas. It was not a large property, and yielded him not much return. Indeed, by himself he was a poor man. The money was his wife's, and it came from silver.

He had been brought up at Las Yemas, by a father who was twice banished from Mexico, once for being too liberal, once for not being liberal enough. As a boy, Ramón had seen the uselessness of politics. He had had, however, a passionate interest in philosophy and literature. His father had sent him to school in Europe. There, for a time, he overflowed with romantic enthusiasm. And then he went cold again. He wanted to go back to America. He believed that the only hope lay in America.

This was in the prosperous days of Don Porfirio. Ramón's father, though a liberal at heart, was weary and disillusioned with Liberty, and supported Diaz for many years, even holding office as governor of Jalisco for a term. But later, he saw Mexico gradually passing into the power of foreign exploitation, and he retired into solitude at Las Yemas. Diaz however had been several times a visitor at Las Yemas, had taken a fancy to Chapala, and decided to build himself a villa by the lake. This was too much for Don Octavio. He departed with Ramón to the United States.

Ramón was in his first twenties. He attended lectures in history and philosophy at Harvard, and travelled the United States to study the conditions. After two years, he was thoroughly depressed. The great democracy of the north depressed him and made him feel hopeless. He went back alone to Mexico City, leaving his father in San Diego, California. In San Diego Don Octavio died. Ramón stayed in Mexico through all the miserable times following the shameful flight of Diaz, but he took no part in the disturbances, revolutions and anti-revolutions and colossal swindlery. He had married a gentle wife whose gentleness he found beautiful, a kind of sanctuary in the

howling greediness of Mexico's great men. At heart, like his father, he
too was a liberal, even a socialist. He was a friend both of Madero and
of Carranza, and had many talks with Zapata. Through all the chaos of
Mexico from 1911 to 1921 he stayed in the city and watched. He
occupied himself writing a history of his country from the year 1800
to the present day. But his real occupation was to watch.

And during the ten long years he came to many conclusions,
conclusions which slowly formed in his heart before he accepted them
in his head. And the first conclusion was, that liberty is an illusion.
There is no such thing. Man is never at liberty to do anything except
obey some dictate, some dictate from his own soul, or some dictate
from without. The mass of men can never know the dictates of their
own soul. It needs a greater man than the ordinary, a man more
sensitive and more pure, to be able to listen to the unknown of his own
innermost soul. The mass of people, let them listen ever so hard to
their own soul, with ever so much sincerity, hear nothing but the
confused roaring of old ideas, old phrases, old injunctions, old habits.
Then they invent new tricks out of old habits, to convince themselves
they are moving on. New automatic tricks. These satisfy for ten
minutes, then they invent another trick.

This was what Ramón gradually realised in his wife. She was
really good. She was really gentle. But, after years of loving her, he
came gradually to feel that she was hostile to life. Her spirit was too
much afraid, and too egoistic, to listen to her own inmost soul. Every
prompting of her urgent soul she recognised only as a command of the
old law: Be good. Be kind. Be unworldly. Try to help your fellow-
men. Love God and love what is good in men. Above all, love and be
loved. And she *was* good, she *was* merciful, she *was* unworldly, she *was*
lovable. And more than this, she was a whimsical, sometimes elfish
creature for whom he had a great affection.

But as time went on she seemed to wear out that whimsical, elfish
nature of hers, with an insistence on amiability, with a *will* to have
things lovely. He felt she cheated him. She was his wife, and he was
struggling with all his soul to come to some new understanding. And
as the glimmering of new understanding came to him, she foiled him
and entangled him in the nets of old emotion, to keep him in the old
ways of love and action. She didn't want him to change, or to bring
about any change. If he could have made the world good and gentle
and loving, she would have idolised him. But gradually he knew that

the world was not and never could be gentle and loving, it was something much more. He himself was not really gentle and loving: he was something else. Life was not a *safe* thing. The formula of love would never make it safe. He must struggle to liberate the thing he actually was, rather than struggle to obey old commandments which had really nothing to do with him. He must struggle to liberate the thing he actually was, and in that way liberate his people. Oh, he was a liberator. But he realised with chagrin that Liberty was a very dreary prison for him and for his people. Oh, to liberate himself and his people from this mechanical Liberty which white men had invented, and which imprisoned the Mexican soul in the narrow circle of its conception. This Liberty which is a safe chrysalis-case inside which we all die like larvae. To break out, like the great dark, dark-eyed moths of the Mexican night!

Now Doña Carlota loved him with all her soul: but inside the chrysalis-case. She loved him always, silently and pathetically, but obstinately and devilishly, to keep him, as she said, true to himself. She loved him desperately. But she loved love most. And particularly she loved her own love for him. That was her own form of deadly egotism.

She fairly soon succeeded in drawing the young life of her boys all towards herself. Ramón was too proud to appeal for love, especially to his own children. He smiled ironically and let her have them.

"Remember," he said to her, with the logic of southern people, "I don't like the benevolent tyranny of love any longer. I don't like your love for your god. I don't like your love for me. I don't like your love for your children. I dislike your way of love. I dislike intensely your insistence on love, I dislike the monopoly of one feeling, I disapprove of the whole trend of your life. You are weakening and vitiating the boys. One day they will hate you for it. – Remember I have said this to you."

Doña Carlota trembled in every fibre of her body, with shock at this. But she went away to the chapel of the Annunciation Convent, to pray for his soul, and praying she seemed to gain a victory over him. She succeeded in purifying her spirit of all baser emotion, was able to pray for him in singleness of heart, and came home in exquisite triumph, like a pale flower that has bloomed out of a cannon's mouth.

But Don Ramón now watched her in her beautiful, rather fluttering gentleness as he watched his closest enemy.

"You, Carlota," he said to her laughing, "are the Mexican eagle of the sky, and I am the Mexican serpent of lower earth, and though you have me in your beak, I have my tail tight round your neck, and the question is whether I strangle you before you bite me in two."

"No, Ramón," she said, "you know none of that is true."

"You wish me always well, don't you?" he laughed.

She gave him a strange look from her hazel-brown eyes, and went away.

"Ha, how demonish her gentle bird-spirit is!" he said to himself. "She is capable of biting me in two."

Perhaps her opposition only determined him the more in his own direction. The single way of love was to him a falsehood and disaster. The commandment of self-sacrificing love was monstrous in itself. Particularly for a dark, barbaric people like his own, who could never understand except in terms of give and take. The whole proposition was just a perversion, for the Indians. He looked at the patriots, from Hidalgo and Juarez to Madero. He looked at the tyrants, from Santa Ana to Diaz and Huerta. The principle of love and self-obliteration fighting the principle of tyrannical power. And the two things equally fatal. The sickening oscillation of the half-savage country between the two half-savage impulses. For self-sacrifice seemed to him as barbaric as blood-sacrifice. The fiasco of both sides. The gradual sinking of the country into mechanism and commercialism, betrayed in its own nature; the gradual sapping of real life. Soviets even more ugly and more killing to the soul than a dead Catholicism and a spurious autocracy. The ghastly theorism of communism against the vile mechanism of industrialism. The peons being gradually betrayed into Labor Unions and the communistic dreariness. The great material anti-life mechanism triumphing everywhere. His half-barbaric people betrayed into politics! To drag the peon into political consciousness was to destroy him in his own self. And the peons were being gradually dragged into political consciousness. And into industrial, mechanical servitude.

What then? There was nothing else. All the energetic men Ramón knew sent their vitality down one or the other channel of political passion. Liberty, or money for the many; conservatism, or money for the few. The rest were dully interested in commerce. Only the really unlightened peons remained for a brief time yet unbroken, blind but dangerous instruments of political and commercial scheming. One party was in a frenzy, to exploit the peon. The other party was in a frenzy, to prevent his being exploited. Between the two, he was nothing: no more than a bone between two dogs.

So Ramón came back to his old conclusion. There is no liberty. Man is only free to obey either the dictate of his own soul, or the dictate from without. Only the genius and the purely great man can know the new dictates of the soul. The rest of the people are helpless. They hear only the old dictates, they act only according to old habits. The most novel tricks of Liberty are only variations of a dead, weary gesture. With the best will in the world, men are helpless to escape from their own automatism. Round and round they go, inside the corral of the old Idea. They invent endless new tricks, inside the corral. And it seems to them, all heaven and earth and hell is inside the corral. There *is* no outside. Till a great man makes a break in the thick thorn fence. Then there is panic.

Animals inside a corral. Turn where he would in the world, Ramón saw nothing but this: free humanity inventing new automatic tricks to amuse itself, mankind in a frenzy of greed for money, and in an even greater frenzy of sheer cowardly terror for its own self-preservation. The cowardice of self-preservation being the greatest of all human principles, followed hard by the greed for money, which should provide the means of self-preservation. And apart from this, the tricks of Liberty. The chief inspiration of all modern liberals, communists, bolshevists, radicals, all the lot, a biting, acid grudge against all people possessing money. And conservatism nothing but a slavish terror of those who possess money, lest they should lose this self-same money. The "liberal" government of the moment was just wavering helplessly between the Scylla of bolshevism and the Charybdis of industrialism and exploitation, and inclined to choose the latter as the slightly lesser evil, at least for the time being.

The peons of Mexico were gradually being inspired with the great grudge of the poor against all people who have money, a grudge that eats up the soul. Life was to be nothing but a collision between have and have-not, between envy and the lust of possession. Freedom being in a frenzy of envious grudging, and authority being in a frenzy of panic-stricken lust of possession, what was to become of the living man? A mere bone between two rabid dogs.

Don Ramón saw this with gloom. Of all the people in the world, the Mexican peons have perhaps the greatest reason for bearing rich people a grudge. Mexico, the treasure-house of the world, and the peons used as nothing more than spades to dig the treasure out, for four centuries. Counted not even as animals, as mere shovels and spades. And the impoverished "world" in a greater frenzy now to get the peons once more firmly gripped by the neck, to dig out more treasure with them, quickly, in order to stop the hole in a leaking system.

And yet, Don Ramón knew, as soon as the Grudge fixed itself in the hearts of the Indians, they were dead men. For the grudge of the have-nots, like the lust of possession in the haves, is a kind of cancer of the soul. In spite of all the centuries of misusage, the Mexican Indians were only here and there consciously infected with the grudge. This Ramón believed. But it is an infection that spreads with strange rapidity, and then goodbye to life.

Was a man to sit by and see it grow? Supposing all the world passed into communism, what was the good, seeing that the victorious communists became dead-alive men in the process? Automata, with theories. Busy, hideous, automatic communists!

And yet the further spread of the capitalistic exploitation could not be submitted to, not at any price.

A Scylla and a Charybdis, with a vengeance. Men all doomed to lose their manhood, one way or the other. Two bottomless pits, down which all real manhood pours. The swirling grudge that is called Liberty, and the vortex of greed of possession. And the tiniest thread of a way out, between the two.

Man is not man for nothing. He does not possess his manhood without the means to preserve it. Nor is he doomed unless he chooses.

So, thought Ramón to himself, if I myself keep myself out of the cesspool of greed for money, and if I don't split my head hating the people who *are* greedy for money – though I hate them sufficiently; and if, though I mean to escape both the rock and the whirlpool, I am still out in the stream, and not tremulously picnicking on the muddy banks, like the cowardly self-preservers who all play at being happy: if then I am none of these things, neither a haver nor a grudger nor a picnicking self-preserver; and I reassure myself that I am not: what then am I?

As the years went by, Ramón felt himself driven into a further and further loneliness. His wife was picnicking with a love-and-charity basket. He had no inward friends, not one: not an approach to one. Inwardly he was quite alone. And he was not sure whether he didn't prefer to be quite alone.

But being alone, more and more deeply alone, he was driven to ask himself if this was to be all his life, this standing aside from life and trying simply to realise. Letting the great drift go by, and trying to discern its direction.

And he knew something surging at the bottom of his soul like the depths of a black volcano. Over and over again came up in him a desire for revenge, for revenge on all humanity, this mass of automata inside a corral which they call infinite. The idiotic sheepfold of the Infinite. And the rank, self-satisfied sheep inside it.

A black wave would surge up in him, a desire for revenge, revenge, unending revenge on this foul humanity which refuses life and will not let life be. Invents more tricks of machines and sentimentality, and calls these tricks *Life*, so as not to let any real life be.

Oh for revenge, for revenge! Oh his terrible hatred of men, his hate of the hearts of men. Oh to be able to strike out their hearts and hold them smoking to the sun, as his ancestors had done in the blood-stinking temples of Huichilobos. To take revenge on men for the vast unmanliness of men. To have revenge, a colossal blood-revenge. Revenge is for the gods. But men are executors for the gods. To serve the gods of revenge. Only that! Only that! To take an unspeakable revenge on mankind, because of the utter unmanliness of mankind.

Mankind! Mankind! Who is mankind? he asked himself. Are all men mankind?

All men, except his own people. All men, except the dark-eyed peons. The dark-eyed men of his own Mexico. He did not idealise them. They were men as yet unmade. They were false, they were indifferent, callous, brutal, monstrous. Above all, undependable. Rather undependable than treacherous or false. They did not set out for treachery. Something changed inside them. Sometimes he hated his own people as much as everybody else. They would be firm and true to nothing on earth. They would never stand up for their own manhood. You could never look at one of them and say, in Napoleon's words, *Voilà un homme!* No, you could only say: There is a brave creature! There is a handsome creature! There is a devilish creature! Always a creature. Never quite a man. None of them had achieved their own manhood.

Had he himself achieved his own manhood? He asked himself the question often, vaguely, with struggle and bitterness. And he re-echoed to himself: Alone I cannot complete my manhood, my being. If I die alone, I shall die with the same uncompleted manhood, like all my people, like all the rest.

And then would come over him a great compassion for his own people. They had waited so many centuries outside the gates of their own being, and never had the gates been opened. Men can never come into being save some heroic man cleaves the way for them. As Jesus had cleaved a way, with his cross, for the Europeans, and Mohammet with his curved-moon sword had cut a way for Arabs and many nations. But no man had broken the invisible walls that shut the Indians of America from their own. They had no hero.

And the Cross was not the key of life for the Mexicans. Ramón knew that. He respected Christianity as a great religion. But it was the religion of aliens. It would never bring the awakening to the souls of the native Mexicans, the Amerindian. Alas that it was so! But so it was. Man does not make himself, in the first issue. God makes him. And it is the inscrutable God that makes these mysterious differences between the great races of mankind. Each race needs its own religion. What is the good of proselytising? A European Christian may be a man true to his own blood, whole in his own spirit. But an Indian Christian, or a Chinese Christian, is just a man deflected from his own nature, waiting pathetically for the day when the great God will give him back to himself.

This Ramón believed. And hence his agony of struggle inside himself, and his agony of compassion for his own people. The black eyes, the gentle smile, the erect bearing, the lurking devilishness of the peon. The eyes like black holes, going down, down to nothingness. And in the depths, below all the tranquillity, the gentleness, the passivity, there was a deep misery, the misery of a man who has never been able to come into himself, never able to accomplish his own manhood, never been able to complete himself. The profound disappointment of an unaccomplished race, waiting for its own accomplishment.

This Ramón realised in himself, and hence he realised it in his race. Hence the passionate fury of frustration crying for blood-revenge. Hence also the great heave of compassion, much deeper than love. Compassion for his own people, who were not quite men. Creatures, brave human creatures holding out for their own destiny, never quite able to become men. They had thought the white men, the white gods, Jesus, Mary, the unknown white gods, would bring them fulfilment. But alas, it was not so, Jesus with all his beautiful and liberating words could not quicken the Indian blood to the last bright flame. Jesus could soothe this blood to a certain passivity, a relief from the torture of the old frenzy. But he could never give the complete sacrament, he could never put the final bread of Indian manhood between Indian lips. After a certain period, Christianity only put off the day of the Indian's fulfilment, postponed it indefinitely. And meanwhile Christianity itself was collapsing, the great Anti-christ of mechanism and materialism was ruling. And the natives of America, who had never yielded their final hope of fulfilment, through all the centuries, now saw the last letter of their doom looped in iron letters across their country. Christ would never destroy them. But the Anti-christ of industrialism, commerce, mechanisation, and fathomless greed, this would destroy them. The white Christ would never be their death. But the white Anti-christ would certainly be death to them.

Was it to be borne? Was it to take place? Would the Great God who is Father of all gods, Father of all the gods and of all the multifarious races of men, would He allow it? Would He allow this one race of men, the dark-eyed men of America, to be eaten up without their ever having come into their own?

He would, unless they saved themselves. Ramón knew this. Jesus, after all, was a man. And if the Man Jesus had never gone forth in ultimate heroism, the Old World would slowly have destroyed itself. Men must save themselves. A race must produce its own heroes, its own god-men. Men, some men, some man must take the heroic step into his own godhead, in the sight of all his people: or there *is* no godhead for this people. The Christian padres were pure and beautiful heroes, in Mexico. But they only provided for the interval, not for the great entry.

"I must act! I must act!" said Ramón to himself. "Soon it will be too late. If only I could call one man to myself: only one man."

The answer came first in the person of Cipriano Viedma. The two had known each other for some years. They were almost of an age, Viedma being a year or two younger than Carrasco. But they had never been really intimate. They had kept aloof, as it were suspicious of one another, although all the time they knew there was some secret bond between them. A bond which must one day assert itself. So one day Viedma suddenly said, looking at the other man with a flame in his eyes:

"Carrasco, I think I should like to be dictator of Mexico."

Ramón smiled slowly.

"To what end?" he asked. "To elope at last to Paris, carrying off thirty million dollars in cash, like President Porfirio Diaz, his great excellency?"

"No, not that. Couldn't I leave a better mark on Mexico?"

"Isn't Mexico badly enough marked?"

"No, but what I mean, isn't my will a better thing than any of the other wills in the country, whether will of the people or any other bunkum? I can see no clean thing in the country but my own will."

"And what is your will?"

"I don't know. To be really Mexican. To see if Mexico can't become himself. – It is good that Mexico is 'he,' and not 'she,' don't you think? It pleases me Mexico is masculine."

"So it does me," said Ramón. "But what are you going to do about foreign property here? What are you going to do about oil? What are you going to do about silver? How are you going to settle the ownership of land? What, above all, are you going to do with the United States and the United States capital that is already in the country and that is waiting for another favorable moment to come into the country?"

"I would find a way," said Cipriano, his eyes clouding.

Ramón shook his head.

"There is no military road to a real Mexico," he said. "While the United States is solid and all-wealthy, there is no military road to Mexican Mexico. There is no road to Mexican Mexico at all. The pressure of foreign capital means our exploitation, and that means Labour Unions and organised strikes, and goodbye Mexico. The only thing is to equivocate and postpone the evil day, in the hope that the great white industrial world may collapse before it absorbs us. – But there is small hope of that."

Cipriano glowered with black, dangerous irritation.

"There's a devil in Mexico that makes a man thirst for personal power – blind personal power," said Ramón. "And there's an even stronger devil in the people that makes them destroy all power or any power, even the power of God, after a certain time of enduring it."

"But what about the devil that is outside Mexico, and just wants to coin her dead body into silver, and squeeze it into oil? What about the devil in the outsiders?"

"It usually takes possession of the ruling Mexican, in the end."

"It should never take possession of me."

"The people would turn against you and shoot you, after a time."

"Why can't the devils be faithful," cried Cipriano, "if I control them for their own and their children's sake, not for my own?"

"*How* would you control them for their own sake? *How* would you treat foreign capital? *How* would you answer the United States about oil, and silver, and Lower California, and all the other things she is waiting for an answer about?"

"One couldn't do more than let Hell loose, if things became impossible."

"One couldn't do less."

Cipriano bit his moustache with black irritation.

"I could get the presidency, I could make myself Dictator," he said, moodily.

"I know," said Ramón. "And what then?"

Cipriano was silent for a time, looking down sideways. Then he flung himself into a chair.

"I know too," he muttered. "But I'd rather smash Mexico to bits, and spill every drop of blood in the country, than let him become like New Mexico or Arizona or worst of all, like California."

"And have the United States, England, and France intervene for the peace of the country," said Ramón, "and Mexico finally planted out like California, oh, in a very short time; most of the Mexicans dead, and the remainder day-laboring for the Yankee money-makers, and all hating your memory. You've seen the United States. The United States is ideal, in Yankee eyes. They only wait to clean us up the same. Mexico needs cleaning up. You would provide the excuse. They only want to clean up Mexico: for our own good. They truly see it like that. And from their point of view, it is truly the best that could happen to us."

"At least," said Cipriano, "I'd be dead before they began."

"What would be the good even of being dead," said Ramón.

"What is the good of being alive, at this rate?"

They faced each other in the silence of helplessness, knowing they were cornered by the great world of industrial mankind. And in the silence that was almost despair, the moment of dark suspense, their hearts swung into final unison. They looked into each other's eyes. Ramón's eyes were obscure, black and pondering: Cipriano's were flashing with impatient anger.

"We must do something," said Ramón, with a faint smile.

"It is what I say," replied Cipriano quickly, waiting on the other man.

Ramón turned away and flung himself into a chair, putting together the tips of his fingers.

"But we've got to start far off."

"*Vamos!*" said Cipriano. "I'm your man."

"We don't have to think of today," said Ramón, "and we don't have to think of tomorrow. We have to get away from events, and from this Mexico. We have to sink away from the surface of events, like a swimmer that shuts his eyes and sinks under the water and dies."

"How! How!" said Cipriano.

Then Ramón put it to Cipriano, that you can do nothing in real achievement till you get down to the religious level. And though Cipriano was sick of the cowardly sentimentalism that passes as religion today, or the political scheming that makes use of this sentimentalism, he still did not shy at the word.

"So long as it is a religion of *men,* not of monks and women," he replied.

"Now listen, Cipriano. Our strength, our manhood, doesn't come to us just from the dinner we eat, or the air we breathe, or the fine thoughts we think. Nor from the books we read, nor the good deeds we do. Nor from any work performed. – Where do you get your manhood, do you consider?"

"It is in me. I don't get it."

"But think about it. Your manhood. It is not like money in a safe. It is something that flows and ebbs, and sometimes it almost leaves you, and sometimes it is very strong. Isn't it so with you? It is with me."

Cipriano watched Ramón for some time. Then he burst into a laugh.

"It is so with me," he said.

"We are not self-made," said Ramón. "Something controls the flow of my manhood, something greater than I. Sometimes people seem to bleed all my manhood away from me. Then I have to turn away, and I have to try to get back to the place where my manhood flows again. Do you know?"

Cipriano's eyes had gone dark, his face stern and gloomy, and he clenched his fists.

"Yes, I know," he said.

"And I have to be continually fighting for my manhood – against everything and everybody. And that puts the devil into me. Because all the rest seems like the devil to me, wanting to eat my manhood out of me as a devil might eat my liver."

The General, who was in uniform, took a turn round the room, clashing his spurs in a defiant manner.

"I feel my devil is stronger than theirs," he said, smiling in his black beard.

"So is mine, once he's roused. But till they've roused my devil, they bleed me of my manhood. And once they've roused my devil, I'm nothing but devil for them all."

"Keep your devil roused," said Cipriano, smiling grimly.

"I do," smiled Ramón. "I pray to my devil, to keep his tail lively."

"Good," said Cipriano, lowering his eyelids curiously.

"The point is, though," said Ramón, "shall I be nothing but devil?"

"The devil is a gentleman," said Cipriano, "and there are few enough in the world."

"It would be good to be a pure devil, Cipriano, and to shake hands on it," said Ramón, lifting his black eyes and watching the other man with a curious glisten, almost like a smile.

Cipriano stood still, his legs apart, his spurs glittering, gazing at a perfectly blank place in the white wall. Then he turned again with his half-wicked laugh, and put out his hand.

"Ramón, friend," he said, "here is my hand."

"Wait a bit," said Ramón, "before I take it."

Again the fixed, mask-like look had come on his face, a look of blank repose. And *in* this repose his black eyes seemed to have gone abstract like the eyes of a passive serpent.

Cipriano stood very still, very definite in his military uniform. His face had a hard, fine, military look, as if cut in semi-transparent stone. Then he turned his hard black eyes down to Ramón, who sat with his arms spread on a table, looking vacantly before him. Ramón wore a little white jacket, from which his dark wrists thrust out. And his feet were naked in slight sandals. – The two men looked each other in the eyes for some moments in a kind of war.

"Ramón," said Cipriano, "wouldn't it be good to be a serpent, and be big enough to wrap one's folds round the globe of the world, and crush it like an egg? I almost feel in myself the strength to do it."

"The dragon of the universe," said Ramón vaguely, slowly gathering himself together and rising from his chair to take a few strides about the room.

"To be the power that could exterminate the universe in its folds, and live on afterwards in the dark. Wouldn't that be good!" said Cipriano, a slow smile curling his black-bearded mouth.

Again the black eyes of the two men met, and a spark seemed to flash across. Then Ramón stood perfectly still, as if in a dream, in a strange blank suspension.

"Have we no choice?" he asked, in a queer small voice, out of his blank.

"Choice of what?" said Cipriano nervously.

"The demon in us – or –" Ramón said slowly, his face averted.

Cipriano started abruptly, and walked about the room, clashing his spurs as he turned.

"Who knows!" he said mechanically.

Ramón stood perfectly still and blank, suspended in the middle of the room, an abstract expression on his face, irritating and beautiful. He seemed unspeakably, irritatingly far away and negative. Cipriano suddenly seized him violently by the arm, demanding:

"Man! Where are you?"

"Wait! Wait!" said Ramón, still unaroused, still in the sleep voice. "Whether we have any choice between the demon in us, and the –" Again his voice faded out unfinished.

Cipriano came to rest, standing in front of him with feet apart. There was a moment's silence.

"What?" said Cipriano, in a low voice. "What?" There seemed to be pain in his voice.

A faint, uneasy smile came on Ramón's face, and he lifted his hand blindly.

"Between the demon in us, and – the good –" his voice was strange and small, not his own voice. He stood with his hand still blindly lifted.

And now Cipriano had become perfectly still, with averted face. Then again he turned to Ramón, his lips flickering curiously.

"Thou canst kill me," he said. "I have nothing but my demon."

Ramón slowly lowered his hand. And as he did so, Cipriano suddenly caught it and pressed it over his eyes. Standing thus, with the other man's hand pressed over his eyes, Cipriano's blind mouth said:

"I will obey you. I will obey you."

"General!" said Ramón queerly. "What are you saying?"

"I don't want to see any more," said Cipriano, still from behind the blindfolding hand.

"Nor I," said Ramón: and suddenly he sighed and covered his eyes with his wrist. There was a silence and a darkness like a swoon, as the men stood with their faces covered.

Then they seemed to melt apart again. Ramón went back to his chair at the writing table, and sat down, covering his face with his hands. Cipriano also sat down at the big table, threw his arms upon it, and buried his face in his arms. For a long time neither moved.

Then at length came the muffled, tentative voice of Cipriano, saying once more:

"I will obey you, Ramón. I will obey."

And still Ramón did not answer. After a while Cipriano raised his face a little from between his arms, looking from under his brows at the other man. Ramón sat bent in his chair, the lower part of his hands pressed into the sockets of his eyes. He looked like a man whose soul has gone out of him.

"Answer me," said Cipriano.

"*Bueno!*" said the passive lips of the other.

Cipriano lowered his head between his arms again, and slept.

When Ramón looked out again, he saw Cipriano's head down on the table, the handsome brown nape of the neck drooping out of the military collar, the thick black hair ruffled. Cipriano was asleep. There was a certain weariness on Ramón's face. In his eyes was the question: "Must I take this responsibility? Must I?" He felt his soul break with weariness, and sat on in his chair immobile, semi-conscious.

Suddenly Cipriano awoke, and looked up alert.

"Well then," he said, exactly as if he had never slept, "the good then between us."

He was his own decided, military self again.

"*Bueno!*" said Ramón, with a faint smile.

"There will always be plenty of enemies," said Cipriano.

Ramón smiled more deeply.

"*Bonis mala spina sum, malis bona spina,*" he said.

"What is that?" said Cipriano.

"The motto of the Malespinas – Carlota claims their crest."

"To the good I am a bad thorn, to the bad I am a good thorn," said Cipriano, translating to himself. *"Bonis mala spina sum, malis bona spina.* – You shall be the Malespina, and I will be the Buonespina. I will be a good thorn in their flesh, at your command, master." And he laughed wickedly.

"I believe it, command or no command," smiled Ramón.

"No!" said Cipriano. "You must command me. My nature is demonish, and demonish it will remain. But you have sworn me over to the good. I will swear you fealty. Take my oath." Cipriano went over and pulled round the chair in which Ramón sat. Then he kneeled down at Ramón's feet, and bowed his head.

Ramón sat erect in his chair, with a steady, impassive face.

"What do you swear?" he asked coldly.

"I swear to be your man, in the fight. Do you take my oath?"

Ramón put his hand on Cipriano's bent head.

"I take your oath," he said. "But listen. Swear to me further. If I fail to lead you, swear to kill me."

Cipriano lifted his head suddenly, and looked into Ramón's eyes.

"If you fail to lead me?" he repeated.

Ramón nodded.

"Shall I know?" he asked.

Again Ramón nodded.

"If I fail to lead you. If I am not a leader. Swear to kill me," said Ramón.

"Must I judge you?" asked Cipriano.

Ramón nodded.

"Always judge me. Swear that too. Say this: *I swear that I will always judge you.*"

"Must I say that?" asked Cipriano.

"Yes. And when you have sworn, you must keep your oath. Always to judge me."

"I swear I will always judge you," said Cipriano, looking into Ramón's eyes.

"Good. Now swear upon your manhood not to misjudge me."

"How can I swear?"

"Swear. You have it in your power to keep the oath."

"I swear upon my manhood not to misjudge you."

"Now swear this. *If I judge that you fail to lead, I will kill you.*"

"I refuse to swear that," said Cipriano rising. "I have sworn to be your man. I have sworn always to judge you. And I have sworn on my manhood not to misjudge you. I will swear no more."

"Good!" said Ramón. "Now listen. I swear myself to the Unknown God and the gods. – Bear witness to my oath."

"I bear it witness," said Cipriano. "I judge that you will keep your oath. I judge I shall know the Unknown God and the gods through you. I am content. Is it good?"

"It is good," said Ramón. "Now there is much to do."

"Tell me."

"I am going to bring back our own gods."

"Which are our own gods?"

"Quetzalcoatl – he is my god. Huitzilopochtli – he is your god. Then we will see."

Cipriano saluted with a slow military salute and a queer little smile.

"I swear to be your man," he said. "Though I don't understand."

"Yes, you understand. We need our own gods. Jesus is the white man's god: he is not the god of our people. Neither Jesus, nor Jehovah, nor Mary. We need our own gods, we need Quetzalcoatl and Huitzilopochtli and Malintzi and Tlaloc."

"Are they any more than names?" asked Cipriano.

"If they are only names! Even so, which calls an answer in your blood, the name of Jesus, or the name of Quetzalcoatl?"

Cipriano thought about it.

"My blood gives no response to the name of Jesus," he said seriously. "But – yes – my heart stirs just a little to the word Quetzalcoatl. Quetzalcoatl! Quetzalcoatl!" He repeated it several times to himself, smiling. "Curious!" he said. "But yet, Ramón, need we revive old gods? Isn't it an antiquarian thing to do? – Do you know what Padre Ignacio once said to me, about you? 'Ramón Carrasco's future is the past of humanity.' – That always stuck in my mind. Can you find the future in the past?"

"It is only the spiral of evolution, if you care to see it that way. We must make a great swerve, and gather up the past, before we can have any future. As it is, we are futureless."

"I really believe you beforehand," said Cipriano. "It would never have occurred to me that we need the old gods. But the moment you say it, I believe it. That is curious."

"You are a whole race of men in yourself," laughed Ramón. "People may talk as they like, friend, but the future lies in the dark of the blood of men. And out of the dark of the blood of men the future will arise. Not out of the whiteness of the mind and the spirit. And in the dark of our blood live the unfinished, unadmitted gods of our race. I cover my eyes, Cipriano, and my mind and my spirit humble themselves before the gods in the dark of my blood."

"Give me your blessing, then!" said Cipriano, lifting his face to Ramón.

Ramón pressed one of his hands over Cipriano's eyes, and the other round the back of Cipriano's head, saying:

"In the name of the unspeakable gods!"

In the darkness and the warm pressure a great relaxation passed over Cipriano's brain, and from the depths of him a dark fountain of life seemed to rise up. He felt this dark fountain rising strong, till it seemed to cover his vision. And then he felt whole again. It seemed to him the world had passed, fallen from his vision like a hard white shell, and his vision was dark and fluent again. He dropped on his knee and kissed the bare feet of the other man.

"I never want to see the world again," he said. "You have given me my life back."

Ramón felt the kisses on his feet, and his heart stood still. But he knew he must accept them and be responsible for them.

"And that is life to me," he answered.

"We will not be afraid to live," he said, when Cipriano had risen.

Cipriano shook his head.

"My demons are gods," he said.

"We have got black souls," said Ramón. "It isn't the pulque which is demoniacal, it is our souls. The devil is in us, the pulque only finds him there. – Yet once we accept our own souls, our demons are gods."

"My demons are gods," repeated Cipriano. "My demons are gods. Beware everybody. All the demon in me thanks you, Ramón, will always thank you."

Ramón laughed.

"Your god is Quetzalcoatl," said Cipriano. "Which did you say was mine?"

"Huitzilopochtli – the god of war."

"The one that ate all the hearts? – Very well, let it be so. My god is Huitzilopochtli."

"The resurrected Huitzilopochtli," said Ramón. "He has learned a great deal in his four centuries of oblivion. The lesson of death and oblivion. Even Jesus never learned oblivion. You've got to remember your death and oblivion all the time."

"It's the hardest thing," laughed Cipriano. "Because we love to let ourselves go. – Ramón, there is a white woman I want."

"An American?"

"An Irish woman. She is a widow."

"Here in Mexico?"

"At the Hotel Verona. I saw her at the bull-fight."

"And why do you want her?"

"Who knows."

"And does she want you?"

"Who knows what she may want, in the future."

"You'll have to play the white man, if you marry her."

"No, she can come into this death and oblivion. That's what I want."

"Would you rather our gods came back, or would you rather have this woman?"

"I would rather our gods came back and took this woman. I want our gods and this woman."

"And if you have to choose between our gods and this woman?"

"No no. I don't choose. I have never wanted a woman before, of whom I could say: she is here. Now I want this woman, as I want my own gods. I want my own again, in the world."

"But a white woman – an English woman – ?"

"An Irish woman – So it is – I did not invent my fate. It is my fate."

"But do you want her in a terrible hurry?"

"No, or I shouldn't get her. I shall get her as the gods come back to me. Only as the gods come back to me. I know it. It is my fate. When I feel my fate about me I can be patient as a pelican."

"Tell me about her."

"No no, there is nothing to tell. She is a woman, that is all. She is not a child nor a fool. All I know is, she is a woman with a face that I shall never really see, but a woman whose presence almost enters me. When I really enter into her presence, I shall be perfect for you. When I really enter into her. – Ask me no more."

"Very good. Your own gods will get you the woman. If you dare everything for them, you will get the woman thrown in. You have said it."

"I know it," said Cipriano. "I am nearly forty years of age. But I am neither old nor young. The time has come, since I know there is the woman, and I feel the gods rousing to come back. No, I have that timeless feeling which comes to me when my fate and I are at one again. Tell me, what shall we do?"

VIII

K ATE WASN'T VERY HAPPY in her house, after all. She felt the same as in the United States, as if her life were refused, and pressed back on her. But here it was a dark opposition, and complete, there was none of the social nervous excitement of the United States to keep her going. And here, too, she had no relief as a woman. In the United States she felt a curious triumph in being a modern woman, an elation part suffragette and part Bacchic, like the Bacchae. She recognised it as a destructive excitement, but still it was something.

Here in Mexico this destructive female elation even was denied her, and her life was thrust back upon her. She felt that in America altogether the spirit of place, the very trees and air seemed hostile to man, hostile to his living. Every minute was a fight. Every breath was something snatched from the enemy. But this fight stiffened one's backbone and purified one's soul of the great nausea of European sentimentality. If one was sentimental in America, it was without self-delusion. She saw the people turning on their sentimentality as they turned on the hot water in the bath, and turning it off again the minute the bath was getting too hot. This deliberate, self-controlled sentimentality of America seemed to her like a game. Sentimentality was just a cynical emotional game. Nobody, at least among the people she met, went overhead in the slush. Everybody played the game of sentiment with at least one cynical eye open. And this, though it is really an Irish trick too, was so coldly done that it rejoiced her. It seemed to her like a triumph over the great mush of false emotionalism which has swamped England.

Nevertheless, after a time the game becomes sterile, the soul feels barren and life seems nothing but a matter of stupid, obstinate will and struggle for self-preservation. The struggle for self-preservation is very real. Even if one has a sufficient income to spare one's thinking of the morrow, financially, still the struggle for self-preservation is there. It is deeper than meat and drink. Deeper even than money.

Each returning day Kate felt she had to fight the morning, for her life. As if the dawn didn't wish her to have her existence under another day, and she must fight to carry on. And when the night came, the moon was like a devil in the sky, trying to shove her out of the night, and she had to fight even in her sleep, to remain living and maintain her place.

And what was true of the elements was true of the people also. The people seemed to be silently annihilating one another all the time. Openly, they were kind. They helped her in difficulties and would take trouble for her. But silently, unconsciously, they seemed to be doing her in all the time. Unless she was all the time on her guard, on the rapid defensive, inwardly, she was prostrate and felt her life going. Then the spirit of battle rose in her, and she swept, also silently, but with a mocking smile and a brief hint of awareness and of contempt, upon her deadly friends, and the atmosphere cleared for a time. Till one or the other went off guard again, and she felt a knife at her scalp suddenly.

So it was, in America. You pretended the utmost democratic amiability. But secretly, you were armed to the teeth, and you never, never ceased to watch your friend, lest she should gently insinuate her knife among your hair and suddenly rip at your scalp. You watched your male friend the same, but he was clumsier.

At first Kate had been rather horrified, when she woke up to the first attacks. She had been somewhat accustomed to the same game in Ireland. But there it was much more sentimental, and you had certain very definite group defences. Here in America, money or no money, class or no class, every man, and particularly every woman seemed like a naked savage with a knife hidden in his breech-cloth, a suave smile in one eye, and an anxious look darting behind him to see if anyone was getting behind his defences, in the other eye.

That was life. They didn't try to steal your money. But your very best friend was *always* trying to make a fool of you, and to get the better of you, spiritually. That was just life, in America: a collecting of spiritual scalps. Subtly taking the life of your best friend: who would then continue your best friend in the hope of getting your life, more vitally, later on.

Kate had to admit that there was something in the game that she really liked. It kept one on the alert, it braced one's spiritual backbone, it had a certain excitement in it. So long as you didn't really let them get you under. Particularly so long as you never let them *see* that you were got under.

But it was an endless game, like an endless staircase that went a little faster than anybody could climb. When it threw you down on the bottom step you died or went into a nursing home. The grimmest old climbers kept on for eighty or ninety years, grim old hacked weapons by that time.

And Kate decided it wasn't good enough. Her stomach had absolutely turned from the *toujours perdrix* of Europe. But she wasn't sure that she didn't find the American diet of perpetual tough cat harder to digest. Anyhow, after about a year it left her feeling appalled and rather sick. So she went to Mexico.

She went with her cousin Owen because he wasn't altogether a tough cat. He had some of the soft niceness of the partridge. Or rather his round, startled eyes were somewhat the eyes of a hare which feels the breath of a cat at the back of his neck, and will turn round and make a fight for it. Owen, like an unyielding hare, had given fight to many a cat, and had never been quite beaten. For he could lash out with a hare's mad ferocity on occasion, and then he would bolt like the wind.

So she and he had got on very well. They were both Celts by blood. The difference was that Owen had fought more and at one time or another had lost more of his fur, whereas Kate had *lived* more, she had had deeper and more vital, if sometimes more tragic human relationships. And that was why, sometimes, Owen wearied her. He had dodged, like a canny, unbeaten old hare, out of so many tight places on the face of the globe, he had stood up to so many grinning cats, and driven them off. But he had never united with anything in all his life. He was a tough lone rabbit in a Tarascon of cats.

Any lone animal, however, is limited by his own outlines. And that was Owen. For him the world was outlined by Owen. In spite of all his cleverness and Celtic femininity of perceptions, the outline of Owen was never anything but Owen. And inside this a great hollow unbelief in anything but Owen; and at the very centre, a hollow little unbelief even in the reality of the Owen.

Kate realised this, and Owen at once paid her back. He was still perfectly courteous and sufficiently attentive. But at Chapala the real American came out in him. Without doing anything at all against her directly, he made a fool of her.

In Chapala he had found a nice soft milieu. In the hotel was no-one but himself and Villiers, and an American mother with two young daughters. Immediately he rose to the opportunity. He became absolutely American, showing off to the top of his bent, and duly impressing the American mother and the two daughters. He said *Yep* instead of *Yes,* he let it be seen how many famous people he knew, he was most awfully nice to the mother and daughters, he played the bagatelle game and squealed with laughter and told anecdotes rather like a professor bosom to bosom with his class. Frightfully familiar, he was. Yet always on a sort of rostrum upper-level. Putting it over that mother and those daughters in a thoroughly American fashion. Saying "Bless you!" when the mother gave him a pot of honey. "Bless you!"

Oh, Owen was enjoying himself.

And then the bathing. He lay for hours on the sands cooking like a beefsteak and surrounded by a swarm of little boys, the boot-black boys and the regular urchins of the place, spanking their little posteriors and being spanked back by them, letting them climb over him and dive from his shoulder when he was in the water, letting one of them sit on his naked chest as he lay on the sand. And all the time, in the most grotesque way, learning Spanish from them.

Kate went twice to bathe from the hotel: to find herself, when she came out of the water, sharing the bath of half a dozen *gamins,* and when she sat on the beach, surrounded by louts and street arabs poking insolent questions at her, and pulling at her sandals, since she was one of Owen's suite, while Owen and Villiers, like real democrats, pawed and were pawed by the swarming crew, and giggled and crowed as if they were having the time of their lives. Owen with his bald head!

Kate was very angry. She felt so insulted. Whenever she happened to go down the pavement under the trees, there she saw Owen lying in his bathing suit or his dressing gown, a heap of little boys around him, and he like a Chinese bonze of a school-teacher with his pupils all swarming promiscuously over him. And seeing Kate, he would wave to her *Hello!,* with a certain insolence, as if to let her see how much more important and *alive* his little boys were than she, and would not trouble to come across the sand.

No, he had found life, LIFE, in a gang of Mexican *gamins,* and was learning Spanish from them *so fast*. Kate, who understood Spanish much better than he, heard the Spanish they were teaching him, and heard the insolence of some of the louts. Some of the boys were really nice little fellows. But some of the louts were vermin.

Owen was really in a wild state of excitement about his boys and youths. He photographed them in all imaginable poses, took nude photographs of those that would let him, on the beach, told them things about America, like a good school-teacher, and let them correct him and jeer at him, like a humble pupil. *"I'm out to learn,"* he said.

And he walked the streets of the little town with his chest out and his eyes glistening behind his spectacles, boys running round him asking him their impertinent questions in Spanish. If he chanced to be walking with Kate, it was "Hello! Hello Son!" every moment, and then to Kate "Excuse me just a moment." – And there she stood in the plaza waiting, while he, a little distance off, stood stooping over a couple of boot-blacks in a delighted but usually vain attempt to make out their Spanish. Then he would at last rejoin Kate, all flushed and his eyes glistening, clearing his throat:

"Hm! Hm! *I* don't know what they say. *Aren't* they funny little youngsters?" – Then he would laugh to himself.

After this, Kate thought there was something in the English idea of a man's keeping his dignity: if he'd got any to keep, which few Englishmen had, whom she had known.

She would walk alone a little way by the lake. You couldn't walk far – only just along the lake front as far as the houses went. It was not safe to go outside the village, for her alone, not half a mile.

She liked the lake with its queer pale-brown water and the few very green trees. She liked the women washing clothes in the lake's edge, and the endless come and go of animals driven down to the water: men on horseback, in Mexican saddles and huge hats, driving slow cows: a man leading a huge bull: a woman enticing two hairy pigs, one of them spotted black and grey like a hyaena, one of them a hairy rust colour: a calf, three goats, a black, long-legged sheep with a lamb, and a little biscuit-coloured dog, driven by three tattered little girls in scarlet frocks and blue rebozos: six asses with empty saddles, braying and kicking one another. An endless come-and-go of animals to the pale, unreal water, while the mountains stood across stiff and pale and unreal too.

But the animals did not seem happy – there was no glisten or glitter of animation in the scene: so unlike the Mediterranean in that. Even on Sundays, when the sailing boats came over the lake in the dawn, with loads of wood, or charcoal, or great hats, or bricks, or tiles, or broad reed mats, and strings of donkeys were trailing over the beach, and groups of men stood in their white clothes and great hats and brilliant scarlet blankets hanging over one shoulder, or dark blankets, or magenta, and cargadores in blue trousers were trotting under huge loads, in the strong morning sunshine, still there was no real animation. It was all silent, with a silence like an echo of an old, old gloom. There was no glitter of life. A movement of tiny people and many insignificant-looking animals on the edge of the wide pale water, up to the fleecy trees and the church and the red house, women in full white skirts and dark rebozos going down to the boats, agua-dores trotting with two heavy cans of water hanging from the ends of a pole, piles of timber, of black sacks of charcoal, big baskets, of reddish tiles standing beyond the stagnant water this side the broken breakwater wall, on the untidy beach. It had a great charm, a great remoteness. But that curious *feeling* of dumbness in the air and earth, the curious smallness of the human life, as if it had no meaning, no soul, the incomprehensible absence of life. As if all the human beings, and even the animals, dwindled inside a dark and coffin-like, transparent aura. No life came through the dead auras that enveloped all the live things. Only there seemed a mystic life in the birds that flew in short files, black, their necks stretched out as if eager for the place they were making for, away low above the surface of the water.

But it was all remote and unreal in a vague sense. The strange groups of animals trailing down the irregular, dirty beach to the water somehow reminded Kate of her old visions of Israelites in deserts, and Abraham seeking water: remote pictures having an inward Jewish dreariness, which remained to her from the Old Testament. Life seeming dumb and as if bruised. The very animals the same, so slow and indifferent. And the big hairy pigs, hairy as unclean dogs, also seemed like the Bible, with their long, upscooping snouts and their stiff, slow walk. A sow would lie on the sand with her hairy, hyaena-spotted brood heaped on her, and it didn't really seem they belonged to life as Kate knew life. They were not pigs as Morland painted pigs. They had none even of the pink indecency of English farm-yard sows. A long-haired, utterly foul ugliness.

"Look!" said Kate to Owen. "It's a sign of degeneracy when creatures want to heap and huddle together. A wholesome animal keeps a space round itself. People and pigs like to heap on top of one another."

The rains came, and the trees that were in bud flamed with tropical scarlet and with rose red and with lavender. But these flowers were not real flowers to Kate. They seemed soulless, and even, strangely enough, invisible. It was as if they were hardly noticeable: they had no presence as flowers. Again, like the animals, they gave off no life-radiance. They ended where they were, like paper. Nothing came across the air from them.

Kate thought of the thorn-trees in bloom, in Ireland, and of the lovely glow of a group of tall fox-gloves, and tufts of ling and heather, and the fugitive harebells. And sometimes she felt she must go back at once, just for the beauty of the air and the leaves and the wind and the rain.

For the wind, in Mexico, was only a hard draught, the rain was only a sluice of water, to be avoided. There was no lovely fusion in the air, between water and sun. Either the sky was black, full of lightning, and sending down masses of heavy, breaking water. Or the sun was shining persistently and stiffly over a dry, unreal land of unliving mountains, that reminded her of the awful dry abstraction and ugliness of Mount Sinai, as you see it from a ship in the Red Sea. The sun did not melt into the rain, the rain did not melt into the sun, and between them they did not produce the nodding, lovely flowers and fruits of Europe, cowslips and apples and raspberries. – She cared no more for the fruits than for the flowers. Mangoes, custard-apples, mameyes, guavas, pitahayas, bananas, limes, pineapples, zapotes, papayas, and a dozen other tropical fruits, she never really cared for them. They had a slight ghastliness, she always imagined a slight taste of blood, as if their roots were watered by blood. The only things she truly liked were the oranges.

And the smell of rain was not the smell of rain she had known, the sweet good earth. Here the rain smelt cold, and a little uncanny. And the beach, the roads were all so dirty, covered with refuse and the droppings of animals and the ordure of man. She could hardly sit under any tree, at her own end of the beach. In the lonelier places it almost everywhere smelt of human excrement, worse after rain. And particularly under the trees, where one might sit for shade, the natives urinated or crouched down to evacuate. This, and the litter, the old rags and old bones and many remains of old huge hats, spoiled everywhere except just the beach in front of the hotel and the villas, where a man cleaned up.

The depression and gloom of it came over Kate when she had been in her house a month. She had been fond of Felipa and the two wild girls. And it resulted, as usual, in insolence, the strange insolence of the American Continent, not impertinence, but a sort of underneath jeering. Felipa did her work, in her haphazard way, conscientiously enough: chiefly, perhaps, because Kate herself tidied whatever was untidy, and cleaned whatever was unclean, and kept the place in hand. And Felipa also was honest still, she wanted Kate to have the things she liked. There was no flouncing or impudence. No.

But the strange jeering. Even in the very caress of the cry *Niña, Niña,* there came a certain mockery. Felipa would pile the dinner on the little table on the verandah, then sit herself down at a little distance to talk in her rapid Spanish, or dialect, while Kate took her meal. And all the time Felipa talked, in her rapid mouthfuls of words with long, musical endings, she watched her Niña, and in the black, unseeing eyes with the spark of slow light on them would lie the peculiar slow, malevolent insolence of the Indian, jeering her Niña out of existence. Kate was not rich in money, but of course Felipa considered her rich. And in Mexico more than anywhere Kate felt that it was a crime to be rich, to be superior. Or not so much a crime, as a freak. It was like having two heads, or three eyes. The antagonism was not really envy. It was the slow, powerful, corrosive mockery of the volcanic Indian nature, for anything which strove to be above the bed rock of human necessity.

"Is it true, Niña, that your country is through there?" And Felipa jabbed her finger downwards, pointing to the earth's center.

"No," said Kate, "not quite. My country is *that* way –" and she slanted her finger at the earth's surface.

"Ah!" said Felipa. "That way! Ah!" – And she looked at Kate as if to say only potatoes or camotes could come from that way.

"And is it true that over there, there are people with only one eye, here!" Felipa punched herself in the middle of the forehead.

"No," said Kate, "that isn't true. That's a story."

"Ah!" said Felipa. "It isn't true. Do you know it isn't true? Have you been in all the countries?"

"Yes," said Kate, a little amply.

"Ah, you've been there! And it isn't true? There are none of them?"

"No," said Kate. "There are none."

"Ah! There are none! – And in your country are they all gringos?"

"Yes," said Kate.

"Like you?"

"Yes."

"And they talk like you?"

"Yes."

The two girls inevitably came up during such a discourse. The little one, Pedra, with her black wide eyes and thin arms pitted with small-pox, she was the soft, adoring savage nature, while Juana, the strapping girl of fourteen, with her masses of black hair, was the savage termagant. Juana was always teasing Pedra, calling her names, pinching her, jeering at her mercilessly, in real savage torment. And Pedra was always lapsing into a few wild unmeaning tears. Felipa was as absolutely indifferent as if they were two rabbits, and they very rarely took any notice of their mother.

Yet Pedra was utterly, vacantly lost if Juana were not there. As for Juana, she spent some of her hours slapping tortillas from one hand to the other, and peering like a young demon out of the window-hole at the far end of the house, near the banana-trees. If Kate came near, she called out to her some rough, half-intelligible question, gazing at her Niña as if the same Niña were some slightly comical beast from a menagerie.

Kate would go in to the cave of a kitchen-place and watch Juana slapping the thin tortillas on to a thin earthern-ware baking-plate, which rested on the burning faggots, slapping them over as they were cooked, then slapping them aside on to the dirty bricks of the top of the fireplace, or slapping them down her own throat. She did not have to do more than slap and bake the tortillas, because the maize-dough they bought in ready lumps, from the plaza.

"Do you eat tortillas?" shouted the wild and towsled-haired Juana.

"Sometimes," said Kate.

"Eh?" shouted the young savage.

"Sometimes."

"Here. Eat one now." And Juana thrust a dirty brown hand holding a dingy-looking tortilla, at Kate.

Now Kate really disliked the indigestible things.

"Not now," she said.

"Don't you want it? Don't you eat it?" – And with a savage, impudent laugh Juana flung the tortilla on to the little heap.

So that at dinner-time, when Felipa had piled all the food on the table, soup, rice cooked with grease and tomato, bits of boiled meat and vegetables, and the little fried fishes called charales, all in one mass at the same time on the table in front of the Niña, together with bread, thin butter, honey, and a heap of mangoes, pitahayas, bananas and so forth; then had seated herself in one of the chairs and opened the strange, blind flux of words; while the sun poured in the green square of the garden, the palm spread its great fans green-lucent at the light, the hibiscus dangled great double red flowers from its very green tree, and the dark green oranges looked as if they were sweating; then, hearing Felipa's voice upraised, from the far end of the house's shadow would emerge Pedra, barefoot, black-haired, in a limp, torn red frock, and after her the wild and towsled Juana in a dirty white frock. And Pedra, the loving one, would come and stand by Felipa and stealthily touch Kate's white arm, stealthily touch her again, and, not being rebuked, stealthily lay her arm on Kate's shoulder, with the softest, lightest cling imaginable, and her strange, wide black eyes would gleam with a ghostly black beatitude, very curious, her whole face slightly imbecile with a black, arch, beatitudinous look. Then Kate would quietly remove the thin, dark, pock-marked arm, and the child would withdraw half a yard, the beatitudinous look foiled, but her very wide black eyes still shining absorbedly, like some young snake rapt in love. While Juana would break into some jeering remark which Kate would not understand, extraordinarily brutal and savage, and would have to go up to the glotzing Pedra, to poke her. Whereupon Pedra with her hand wiping a meaningless tear away, Juana breaking into a loud, brutal, mocking laugh, like some violent bird, and Felipa halting in the black and gluey flow of her words to glance at her elder daughter and throw some ineffectual remark at her. And all the time, Felipa, Juana, and Pedra were absolutely indifferent to everything. The children were even indifferent to the cake Kate gave them. They only on the surface stirred their black souls into a show of interest.

The two girls could both read a little, so Kate would sit in the sala in a rocking-chair, in the hot mornings, and the girls would stand by her, reading slowly from a school-reader or from a ballad-sheet. This went very well for a time. Pedra was the gentle and insidious serpent of adoration, Juana was the violent serpent of mockery, but both were rather defiantly proud of being able to read. The boys couldn't read at all.

Then Kate found herself in for trouble. The two girls followed her into her bedroom, Pedra subtly stroking the Niña and insidiously clinging to her body, Juana watching with a savage's alert eyes, and shouting a rude question now and then. They filled the rooms with their wild hair and their savage, slightly repulsive presence.

Kate closed the doors to keep them out. Then, when she went on to the verandah, there they sat near her door, Pedra carefully picking the lice out of Juana's black, abundant hair.

The girls were not dirty, because they bathed in the lake. But Kate did not care for the proximity. She sent them away to their own end of the house, and, barefoot, untidy, off they went, jeering and laughing. And outside the kitchen door, or under the trees of the garden, they would sit while their mother loused them, or they loused each other, or one of them loused their mother. – Kate hardly noticed it, it was so common. The village beauties sat in their doorways with their splendid locks flowing, spending a chatty afternoon hunting in the forests of one another's heads. – But even this was not so bad as Ceylon, where the men louse each other in the public street.

The two young hussies went to school when they thought they would. Kate tried to send them off.

"No," shouted Juana. "We're late now, and when we're late she pulls our ears –" she being the teacher. So they stayed at home. – A fair number of girls went to school, but few boys. And the attendance was as casual and as intermittent as any youngster chose to make it. Some of Owen's little friends had never been to school at all: some had attended two or three times, and found it a bad joke. Hardly any could read.

Juana would set off with a handful of washing, to the lake. She would return at nightfall, her masses of wet hair hanging, for a bathe was the end of the washing, a handful of wet clothes in her hands, having lost one of the stockings from her mother's only pair.

Then a very mild uproar – and a sort of half hope that Kate would give another pair of stockings.

Next day another lament – Juana had *gone* to school, and lost the fifty-cent piece with which she was to buy grease and maize-dough. Volumes of words like bats out of a cave. And the hope that Kate would make the money good. Kate didn't. So at evening Felipa asked for the advance of a peso on her wages.

"I have no memory, no memory!" said Felipa.

"Yah, you'll forget the money you've had from the Niña," jeered
Juana.

"Then I'll remember it," said Kate.

And the two girls went off into a laugh of derision.

They none of them really cared about anything. But this curious,
absolute uncaring carried with it an insolent, veiled attack on anything
that was to be cared for. Kate felt this – felt the steady, derisive attack
on her self, from all of them, from everybody, from the whole atmosphere of the natives.

It ended one morning when the two gawky, unkempt, barefoot
girls came pulling one another and shoving one another into Kate's
bedroom, giggling and talking their jargon. Kate was glum. At length,
after fidgetting about – for they knew at once how Kate was feeling –
Juana barked a rude question.

"What did you say?" asked Kate. She never understood Juana.

Then the young mild Pedra lifted her face and murmured, ending
on a nigger simper:

"If you've got lice in your head?"

Kate felt they wanted to examine her hair.

"Out!" she said. "Out of my room. Ugly girls, ugly girls, go to
school. Go to school! Out! You ugly girls!"

And instantly, like something that melts or evaporates, they
disappeared, all the jeering and laughing ceased, only two tangled
black things scuttling. They might have been lice themselves, running,
thought Kate angrily at that moment.

She was angry for many days after this. Everything changed. The
girls seemed to have gone to live somewhere else. Heaven knows
where they were. Felipa was subdued. And the hopeless, helpless
Indian melancholy settled over the house, a dead weight of gloom.

That's how it was. They were sensitive at once to a feeling. They
knew at once when Kate was detesting them, wishing to be back in
Ireland, finding them all a bit repulsive. They knew at once. And a
gloom, with a slight touch of dangerous resentment settled down on
them all. They knew Kate found them slightly repulsive. And a heavy,
almost reptile depression came over them, with a reptile resentment.

It was no easy life. So empty – empty of flow.

In the morning, out of disgust with her household, Kate went and
sat under a fleecy willow-tree on the sand. The lake was still, some
women in the near distance were kneeling in their wet slips on the

edge of the lake, and Kate was reading a Pio Baroja novel that was almost as out-of-temper as she was herself. On her left, where the beach ended and the cultivated lands of the Indians stretched almost to the water's edge, were three little hovels of reed and straw, inconspicuous under the trees. Kate knew these people by sight.

She glanced up and saw a little urchin, son of one of the straw houses, marching to the water's edge, and dangling from his tiny outstretched arm a bird, held by the toe, head down and feebly flapping its outspread wings. It was a black waterfowl with a white bar across the inner side of the wing: one of the many mud-chicks that were bobbing about on the lake.

The urchin she knew quite well. He was a tiny brat, seemed not three years old, yet as independent as a young animal on the warpath. He wore a tattered rag of a red shirt, and weird rags of white trousers. Kate knew his little round head, his stiff, sturdy Indian walk, his round eyes, and his swift, scuttling run, like a bolting animal.

"Now what's the little demon doing?" she said, as she watched him stiffly march to the water, dangling the mud-chick, which seemed huge as an eagle suspended upside down from the tiny hand. Another urchin came pelting down. The two little figures paddled a yard into the lapping water, and gravely stooping, set the mud-chick on the lake. It seemed to paddle hardly at all. The lift of the ripples moved it. Then the urchins dragged it in. They had got it by the leg on a string.

"Ah the little wretch!" thought Kate. "Yet he seemed such a nice boy."

She pondered within herself, whether she should go and release the bird. "But," she said to herself, "if a mite like that caught it, and if it can't get away from him, really – !" – So rather unhappily she returned to her book, casting an uneasy eye at the water now and then.

She heard a splash of a stone, and looked up. The two diminutive brats were throwing stones at the unhappy bird. It, apparently, was fast by the leg, the string fastened to a stone. There it lay, a couple of yards out on the water. And there were those two little fiends, with their tiny, sober manliness and cold ferocity, stooping, picking up big stones, and throwing them down on the bird, which fluttered feebly.

"You demon incarnate!" said Kate to herself, seeing the warrior-like attitude of the mite, as he stood with his arm upraised. "And he seemed such a nice child!" was her afterthought.

In another second she was darting down the beach.

"Ugly boys! Ugly children! Go! Go! Ugly children! Ugly boys!"
she cried in one breath.

The round-headed dot gave her one glance from his manly eyes,
then the two of them scuttled like a rat that disappears. Kate marched
into the water and lifted out the bird. It was all wet, and warm, and it
feebly tried to bite her hand. The bit of coarse hempen string hung
from its limp, greenish, water-fowl's ankle.

She rapidly stepped out of the water and unfastened the string,
holding the wet bird, that was about as big as a pigeon, softly against
her. It nested in her hand, the hot, wet, soft thing, without stirring,
and her heart gave a cry of distress again.

So she stooped and pulled off her shoes and her stockings. She
looked round. In the dark shadow of the trees, the reed huts showed
no sign of life. But she knew those brats were watching. She lifted her
skirts to her knees and staggered out over the cruel stones, in the
shallow water. The stones hurt her feet so that she almost fell. The
water was quite hot at the edge of the lake, and blood-warm as she
waded further in. Staggering, she went on quite a long way in the
shallow, shallow lake-side, whose water never seemed to get any
deeper, till she was up to her knees. Then gently she launched the
greeny-black bird, and gave it a little push towards the expanse of
water.

It lay there wet and draggled on the pale sperm of the water, like a
buoyant rag.

"Swim then! Swim!" she said, trying to urge it into the lake.

But it didn't. Perhaps it couldn't. Who knows?

Anyhow it was well beyond the reach of little boys. Kate struggled back to the shore, back to her tree, to the shade. The sun was
fierce. The world was still. Full of slow anger, she resumed her book,
glancing up from time to time at the floating bird, and sideways at the
reed huts in shadow.

Yes, the bird was dipping its beak in the water and shaking it – it
seemed to be coming to life. But it would not paddle. It let itself be
lifted, lifted on the ripples, and the ripples would gradually drift it
ashore.

"Fool of a thing!" said Kate exasperatedly.

Two more black dots with white specks of faces were coming out
of the pale glare of the lake. Two mud-chicks swam busily forward.
The first one went and poked its beak at the inert bird, as if to say:

"Hullo! What's up with you?" And immediately it turned away in complete oblivion and paddled to the shore. The second bird did the same.

Kate watched her bit of feathered misery anxiously. Surely it would rouse itself now. But no. There it lay slowly, inertly drifting on the ripples, only sometimes shaking its head.

The other two alert and busy birds waded confidently among the stones.

"Anyhow," thought Kate, "it will surely follow them."

So she read a bit more.

When she looked again, she couldn't see her bird. But the other two were walking among the stones, jauntily.

So she read a bit more.

The next thing she saw was a youth of eighteen or so, in pale, faded blue trousers, running with big strides down to the shore, and the stiff little mop-stick of a brat pelting after him with scuttling determined bare feet. Her heart stood still.

The two wild mud-chicks rose in flight and went low across the water in the blare of light. Gone! The youth in washed-out blue trousers and big hat, and those stiff, swinging Indian shoulders that she hated so much sometimes, was peering among the stones. She made sure her bird had gone.

But no! The stiff-shouldered lout stooped and picked up the damp thing. He turned, dangling it like a rag from the end of one wing, and handed it to the stiff-backed little brat. Then he stalked up the shore.

Ugh! and at that moment how Kate detested these people, lock, stock and barrel! How she detested their broad stiff shoulders and high chests, and above all, their walk, their stiff, prancing walk, as if they were driven by a hard motor at the bottom of their back. So their legs seemed to prance out, as if some motor-engine at the base of the back drove them. Stooping rather forward and looking at the ground so that he should not look her way, the youth pranced back to the huts in shadow. And in diminutive, the dot of a child marched stiffly, speedily after him, dangling the wretched bird, that stirred very feebly, downwards from the tip of one wing, and from time to time turning his round, childish face to gaze at Kate, in terror lest she should swoop down on him again, and a kind of passive male defiance.

Kate glared back from under her tree. "Yes, my young man," she said to herself, "if looks will annihilate you I'll annihilate you." And she glared as if all the devils were in her. The boy turned his face like a bit of clockwork at her from time to time, as he strutted palpitating on towards the gap in the reed fence where the youth had disappeared.

"Is it any good rescuing the miserable thing any more?" thought Kate. "It isn't. It is beyond helping itself. It will die soon. It's no good. Why didn't it have the spirit to escape, or the spirit to preserve its freedom? Now let it suffer to the end, the miserable thing."

And she detested the flabby bird. Likewise she detested that brat of a boy, with his dark moon-face looking at her in apprehension.

"I've had enough of this," she said rising. "I'm going back to Europe."

She looked westward at the receding lake, the lousy shore, the lumps of women at the water's edge: the dilapidated-looking villas and the mockery of a white church with its two fingers to heaven: the scarlet flame-tree, the dark mangoes. And she smelt the smell of Mexico, excrement, human and animal, dried in the sun on a dry, dry earth: and mango leaves: and clean air with refuse and a little wood-smoke in it. And she said again:

"I loathe Mexico. I loathe it. I'm going back to England."

IX

I AM QUETZALCOATL with the dark face, who lived in Mexico in other days. Till there came a man with a white skin, and holes in his hands and feet, who said in a strange speech:

My name is Jesus, whom men crucified on a cross till he died. Now I have come from heaven, to live in Mexico, as my Father tells me.

Quetzalcoatl said: *You alone?*

Jesus said: *My mother is here. She shed many tears for me. She will take the tears of the women from Mexico to my Father, and he will taste the tears, and for the good tears he will send back smiles to the people in Mexico.*

Quetzalcoatl said: *Brother with the name Jesus, what will you do in Mexico?*

I will put love in the hearts of the people, and peace on their lips, and clothing upon their nakedness, and gifts in their hands.

Quetzalcoatl said: *I will go. Farewell, son of my Father. Farewell, woman called Mary. It is good for the people of Mexico.*

So Quetzalcoatl embraced the god Jesus, and he embraced Mary the Mother of Jesus, and turned away. And soon the temples of Mexico were on fire. But Quetzalcoatl went slowly up the mountain, and past the snow of the volcano. As he went, behind him rose a cry of people dying, and a flame of places burning. But Quetzalcoatl said to himself: *Surely those are Mexicans crying! And yet I must not hear, for Jesus is in the land, and his Mother will gather the tears.*

He also said: *Surely that is Mexico burning! But I must not look, for Mary is bringing back smiles to the people, and Jesus is teaching them love.*

So Quetzalcoatl reached the top of the mountain, and looked up into the blue house of heaven. And he saw the Lord standing on heaven's edge. Quetzalcoatl looked up to the Great-God, his Father. Then fire rose out of the volcano around Quetzalcoatl, and towards the fire fell streaming wings and streaming, brilliant feathers. So Quetzalcoatl flew across the space between the mountain-top and the steps of heaven like a bird, and as he flew, the night fell. So men in the world saw only a star travelling back into the sky, and entering heaven.

Then men said in Mexico: *Quetzalcoatl has gone. He is a star in heaven. Jesus is the God in Mexico, let us learn his speech.*

And men in Mexico learned the speech of Jesus from the white priests. And they became Christians.

Down at Felipa's end of the house two men were singing to one guitar. A little oil wick gave a small light in the dark, and showed figures of men with dark sarape over one shoulder, standing behind the singers, and inside the little cave of Felipa's room the women, faintly discernible. This was the second or third night that there had been singing, and the same music, the same words.

Kate went slowly across the garden patio and sat on the pavement of her house, behind the singers. The group were all talking now, eagerly. Only Felipa, who was in the open little room, saw her Niña and rose.

"Will you also come, Niña?" she said in her musical voice.

"Yes. I want to hear," said Kate.

"Fetch a chair for the Niña, Juana. Quick!"

"No," said Kate, "let me sit here."

She was rather shy, with the dark faces of the men under their big hats turned silently to her. But they were not hostile.

The singers were Rafael and Francisco. Francisco was Felipa's cousin. Suddenly one morning Kate had noticed two new figures at the far end of her house: a girl with a full, oval, Madonna face, a clean dress, and a necklace, and a tall, straight young man with a dark face and a slightly pressed-in nose, and black, proudly arched eyes. He had a curious face.

"Who are the two others?" Kate asked.

"They are my cousins," said Felipa. "They are bride and bride-groom."

"Bride and bridegroom?" said Kate.

"Yes. Carmen is fourteen-and-a-half years old. She was married six days ago to Francisco, in Tizapán."

"And how old is he?"

"As old as my Jesús. Twenty-two."

"And are they paying a visit?"

"Yes, paying a visit."

Kate said Oh!, and wished them well. For they were a handsome couple, clean and modest, and Francisco seemed very proud.

Night came, and they were still here.

"Are the cousins sleeping here?" asked Kate.

"Yes, poor things. They have no house in Chapala. She is from Tizapán."

"They can have one of the spare bedrooms," said Kate.

There was a bedroom with two beds. She put out two blankets. That, she knew, was all the bedding the bride and bridegroom would need.

And henceforth Francisco and Carmen also lived at Kate's house, the house of the Cuenta, so called from the big cuenta tree at the gate, which shed down round little balls. These little balls enclosed, in a yellow skin, perfect little black marbles, and these black marbles, or big beads were used for the big beads in rosaries, by the Indians. So Kate's house was the house of the Cuenta, of the Bead.

The bride and bridegroom stayed a week, a fortnight, and showed no signs of retreat. However, they were very quiet, and their presence was pleasant, so Kate did not trouble. Her house was rather like a camp.

It was Francisco who played the guitar and sang. Kate tried to persuade him to sit on her verandah and sing. But he was too shy. One night, however, when the electric light had given out – and it gave out several nights a week, so Kate sat by a candle fluttering in the wind half her evenings, with the jungle of the darkness pressing round – the figures gathered away at the far end of the house, where the oil wick made a queer spot of light in the window-hole of Juana's kitchen. Then the voices of the two men rose in a queer rapid chant, Rafael, in his throaty voice, singing seconds as spasmodic as the wind in the mango trees, while blue lightning appeared and went in unnatural gleams in the garden.

To Kate it seemed just a little unnatural. Yet she listened with pleasure, alone in her open sala, while the lightning from time to time stood like an apparition in the patio. But she didn't want to go nearer.

In the morning, however, she told Felipa that she liked the singing, and asked what the songs were about: if they were love songs.

"No-o," came Felipa's long, crooning negative. "No-o, Niña, they are not love songs."

"What then?"

Felipa laughed her odd, childlike little laugh.

"They are the Mexican hymns," she said, rather unwillingly.

"What Mexican hymns? About fighting?"

"No-o. No-o. About the two gods."

And she didn't want to say any more.

The second evening of the singing Kate was still too shy to join the group at the far end of the house. She felt they didn't want her. But the third evening she went.

"Tell me what the words are," she said, when the song was over.

This was received in silence.

"Tell the Niña what the words are," commanded Felipa from the dark hole of a room, which seemed like a cave full of obscure animals.

And suddenly Rafael's half-broken voice came defiantly:

"It says," he announced – But he could get no farther.

"It says –" he started again. And Juana broke into a whoop of a laugh.

"You, quiet your mouth," said Felipa ineffectually, into the dark.

Francisco gently rattled the strings of the guitar. Then again came the trumpet-like voice of Rafael:

"I am Quetzalcoatl with the dark face, who lived in Mexico . . ." He kept breaking down, and one or another from the invisible audience would prompt him. Even Felipa went on with the phrase about Mary.

"Ah!" said Kate. "Felipa knows it too!"

"No-o, Niña! I've got no memory. I've got no memory. I only remember: *My mother is here. She has shed many tears for me.*"

Juana yelled out the phrase about flying across the space to the steps of heaven, and then ducked down behind her mother in savage embarrassment.

"And is that all?" asked Kate, when she had understood to the end.

"Yes Señora. Of this hymn, this is all."

"Señora!" yelled Juana. "Is it true that heaven is up there, and you come down steps to the edge of the sky, like the steps from the mole into the lake? Is it true that El Señor comes to the steps and looks down like we look down into the lake to see the charales?"

Juana shoved her fierce swarthy face into the feeble light, and glared at Kate, waiting for an answer.

"I don't know," said Kate. "I don't know everything."

"You don't know?"

"How should I? I haven't even been to the top of the volcano."

"But you don't believe it?"

"Yes, I believe it."

"She believes it," said Juana, turning up her face to her mother.

"Is it true," said Felipa, "that the Holy Maria is a gringuita, like you? – Look!" she turned to the crowd. "Look at the feet of the señora. Aren't they like the feet of the Santísima! Look!"

Kate was wearing sandals from India, that left her soft white feet quite bare, save for a leather band over the instep. She pulled her skirts down and laughed self-consciously.

"Look!" repeated Felipa, while Pedra crept forward and touched the white feet with a dark forefinger, stealthily. "They are the feet of the Santísima. Isn't it true that the Holy Mary was a gringuita?"

"Yes," said Kate. "She came, like me, from over the sea."

"Ah!" exclaimed Felipa. "Ah! It is true."

And her voice was soft with astonishment and a slight dismay.

"And Jesus as well. He was a gringo?" blurted Rafael. "He came from over there!"

There was a touch of fear in his defiant question.

"Yes," said Kate.

"Ah! Ah!" sang Felipa softly. "He was a gringo!"

And she seemed half relieved, half horrified to realise it.

"And how was he? Was he like you? What are you?"

"English," said Kate. "No, he wasn't English."

"Ah! No? But he came from over there, over the same sea, not far from you?" persisted Felipa.

"Yes, not very far from me!"

"Ah! Look, he came from not far from the Niña's country. Look!"

"And it wasn't the Mexicans who killed him?" shouted Juana.

"No, it was not the Mexicans."

"It was the gringos?"

"Yes, the gringos."

"But he was a gringo too?"

"Yes, he was a gringo."

"Look!" said Felipa. "He was a gringo, and the gringos killed him."

"Now he has left Mexico?" barked the young, powerful voice of Rafael, always with a defiance.

"I think so," said Kate.

There was a murmur among the audience.

"And the Santísima as well?" asked Felipa in a hushed voice.

"Yes," said Kate recklessly.

"Ah, as well!" echoed Felipa, on a forlorn note.

"But," blurted Rafael, "it is because Quetzalcoatl has come back, so Our Lord has to leave. He was only here for a time. They say that Quetzalcoatl was wounded in the chest, and had to go to heaven to God the Father, to be cured. He is stronger than any of the gods now, so he has come back to Mexico, and Jesus Christ has gone home."

"Do they say that?" said Kate.

"Yes, Señora."

"And is it true?" came the plaintive reiteration of Felipa.

"Yes, it is true," cried Rafael.

"You see I don't know," said Kate.

"It is true," asserted Rafael.

"And the Holiest Mary has left us?" repeated Felipa mournfully.

"Yes. But Quetzalcoatl has a wife, and they say she is a gringuita from over there. They say she is a very nice goddess, very good wife of Quetzalcoatl. They say."

"Do they say that?" said Kate.

"She will be like the Niña," said Felipa confidently. "*Muy bonita*, but not sad. But without the sorrows. Yes, she will be like that. Like the Niña."

"No no," said Kate.

"How no? Do you know her?"

"No! No!" exclaimed Kate.

"Ah, you don't know her! Yet they say she is in Mexico."

"Are there any more hymns about Quetzalcoatl and Jesus?" asked Kate.

"Yes, Señora. Many."

"Won't you sing me another?"

"We don't know many. We only know the first one, all of it. But Francisco knows the second."

"Won't you sing it?" Kate repeated.

"We don't know it well," said Rafael.

There was a pause. Then Rafael took his mouth-organ, the only instrument he had been able to buy as yet, and played a queer, sobbing kind of music. It was remarkable how much music he could get out of a mouth-organ. Francisco struck the same pulsing tune out of his guitar. Then he began to sing.

"Maria, Maria, mother, dost thou know the Mexican people?"

To which Rafael answered, in a queer high yell:

"Ay-ee! Ay-ee! My Son! I know them well."

"Maria! Maria! Mother! How do they wear the wings of love?"

"Ay-ee! Ay-ee! My Son! The souls of the Mexican people are heavy for the wings of love."

"Maria! Maria! Mother! How do they get to heaven?"

"Ay-ee! My Son! They flutter like weak young birds. Ay-ee, they fall back! Ay-ee! Ay-ee! They fly only half way, and fall back. Few, few arrive!"

"Maria! Maria! Mother! Is it that the wings of love are weak?"

"Ay-ee! My Son! My Son! That Mexican souls are so heavy!"

"Maria! Mother! My Father, the Lord Almighty, has given the Mexicans heavy souls. What shall we do?"

"Let us go and ask him, my Son, what we shall do."

The song ended for a moment. Then Francisco muttered to the men with him, and after a rapid little talk, began to strike the strings again. Francisco took the lead, still as Jesus, and Rafael sang a queer seconds along with him, striking in at unexpected moments, towards the end of the phrase.

"Oh Father, Father Omnipotent, I am Jesus calling to Thee" – "Mary calling to Thee," yelled Rafael, as the guitar struck quick notes.

"I am listening, I." Another voice *spoke* these words, awkwardly but gravely.

"Father, you sent me here to be patrón of Mexico –" – "*Patrona de Mejico*" came the high addition of Rafael's seconds.

"It is true," said a voice, grave and remote.

"To give the souls of the Mexicans wings of love when they die –" – "Of love when they die." – "*To bring them to the Gloria.*" Both voices sang this phrase. "But Father, the Mexican souls are heavy for the wings of love" – "for the wings of love." – "And many fall back from mid-way, and cannot get across" – "Ay-ee! Ay-ee! Get across!" – "And they walk about the land in anger, and burn the churches, and are bandits, saying *We could not get to heaven on the wings of love. We are angry souls in the world.*" Both voices sang the speech of the souls fallen back to earth, in the queerest lost yell. "Father, heaven is far off, and Mexican souls are heavy. Give me sharper feathers like knives for the ends of the wings of love, give me longer, sharper feathers, tempered like knives." – "Longer, sharper feathers, tempered like knives for the wings of love" – "To cut through the black air of the night." – So the two voices ended in unison.

"I can't do it! I can't do it!" spoke the voice of the unknown man.

"Oh Father, Father, make the souls of the Mexicans light."

"I can't do it."

"Oh Father, Father, make the way to heaven less steep."

"I can't do it."

"Oh Father, Father, let the night not fall while Mexican souls are flying."

"They must fly for a night and a day."

"Oh Father, Father, command the fallen, angry souls to be peaceful in Mexico's land."

"I cannot command them. I gave them to you to command."

"Father, they will not listen. They are many, they rob my churches and steal my strength, my churches are beginning to break. We are gringos in the land, and the bandits are attacking us. Father, help!"

"Come home to the *Gloria,* my Son. Come with your Mother Mary."

"I cannot leave the men of Mexico without a master." – "I cannot leave the women of Mexico without a *patrona,*" wailed the two voices to the guitar.

"I will send Quetzalcoatl. Then come home."

The song died, and there was silence.

"Ah! Ah! It is true!" said Felipa, in a hushed voice. "*They rob my churches and steal my strength.* Isn't it true, Señora, that the soldiers robbed the cathedral of Guadalajara, and put their horses in the choir, and dug up the bodies of the buried saints, the bishops, and took all the jewels? And they stood the mummies of the bishops against the walls, and pushed a cigar in the mouth of the dead saints. Ah! Ah! Ah! – And the Lord has not done anything to them. He didn't kill them. They went to Mexico and became presidents and excellencies. Ah! The Lord couldn't do anything to them. That is to say the Lord isn't strong, and they are the angry souls, bandits and thieves. They can come and kill us all in the night, and the Lord can't help us. Ay! Ay! What a horror!"

"You be quiet, Mother, and don't let anybody hear you," commanded Rafael.

"They can't do anything to me," said Felipa, with sly defiance.

But there was a noise at the gate, and everybody started.

"Who is it?" cried Rafael.

"Jesús!"

"Ah, Jesúsn!" said Pedra, who added an "n" to the end of most words. "He is coming from the planta."

Jesús, the eldest son, came up in his black shirt and cotton trousers, silently. He lifted his hat to Kate. Then the men talked in low voices among themselves.

"Señora," said Rafael. "We will sing you the coming of Quetzalcoatl. It is very short."

Jesús began, in a deep, very sweet voice.

"I salute ye, Jesus, my brother, and Mary, my Aunt."

"We salute thee, Quetzalcoatl," sang the two voices of Francisco and Rafael. "Where dost thou come from, into Mexico's land?"

"I left the realms of heaven by the farthest gate, and came up out of the darkness under the world, having taken the long way round."

"What dost thou come for, into Mexico's land?"

"For my own."

"Thou art the feathered serpent. Thou art the snake-blooded bird. The Mexican people are asking for none of thee."

"The serpent sleeps in my bowels, the knower of the under-earth. And the eagle sleeps in my heart, the strength of the skies. But I, who am Quetzalcoatl, am man and am more than both. I am lord of two ways."

"How wilt thou bring the heavy souls of Mexicans into heaven?"

"The way I came. The serpent will carry them down through the night of the west. And from the cave at the other end of the dark, the eagle will fly with them out, across the space of daylight to the steps of heaven."

"Ay! Ay! Is that the way?"

"That is the way."

"But what will the women of Mexico do for thee, womanless Quetzalcoatl?"

"When my house is ready I shall bring my bride."

"Ay, ay, and must we go, must we leave this land where our churches are?"

"It is time."

"Give us a little while yet, Quetzalcoatl, to say farewell. Leave us a little while, in the land we love. Do not drive us out like orphans, like refugees."

"In a little while you must go."

"Ay! Ay! A little while. Already the land is no longer ours. Leave us a little time to shed our tears of farewell."

"Do not shed too many tears over Mexico."

"Ay! Ay! We shed our tears."

The song ended abruptly, in a dead silence. Then the strangers who were present muttered among themselves and turned to go, silently, saying only *Adiós,* and lifting their hats to Kate. Nobody said any more.

Kate also rose from the pavement.

"I like the songs of Quetzalcoatl very much," she said.

"Yes!" they answered. And then dumbly, they began to move to go to bed.

Kate went down to her room, wondering. What did these people believe, and what didn't they? So queer to talk of Jesus and Mary as if they were the two most important people in the village, living in the biggest house, the church. Was it religion, or wasn't it? There was none of the exaltation and yearning, or ecstasy, that she was used to associate with religion. There was no definite pull in any particular direction. And yet the world seemed to have become bigger, as if she saw through the opening of a tent a vast, unknown night outside. She didn't know whether to look on her servants at the end of the house with an affectionate pity, as if they were dark male children and female children with powerful passions; or whether to pause and ask herself if their lives were not really deeper than her own. So she went to sleep dissatisfied with herself, and irritated. A sense of the superficiality of her life, even of her love and her tragedy, exasperated her. Why did she feel that love and tragedy and happiness were really only superficial things? So long as you remained on the surface, they seemed all-important. They seemed to embrace the whole of life.

But the surface on which they were built could break, and underneath was a vast obscure world where the ruins of love and tragedy and happiness remained only as curiosities. Life had taken on another gesture altogether.

X

ON SATURDAY AFTERNOONS the big black canoes with their large square sails came slowly approaching out of the thin haze across the lake, from the west from Jocotepec with hats and pots, from Ocotlán and Jamay and La Palma with mats and timber and charcoal and oranges, from Tuxcueco and Tizapán and San Luis with boat-loads of dark-green globes of water-melons, and tomatoes, boat-loads of bricks and tiles, and then more charcoal, more wood, from the wild dry hills across the lake. Kate nearly always went out about five o'clock to see the boats drift up to the shallow shore, and begin to unload in the gold of evening. It pleased her to see them carry out the hundreds of great, dark-green globes of water-melons, dark-green with a pale place where the heavy fruit had lain on the ground, up on the hillside across the lake. And to see the scarlet tomatoes all poured into a shallow place of the lake, bobbing about there while the women and youths washed them, then loaded them into baskets. Then long, heavy bricks were piled in heaps by the scrap of a breakwater wall, and little gangs of donkeys came trotting to be laden. The cargadores became all smutty from the sacks of charcoal. One man asked her if she needed charcoal at her house.

"At how much?" she asked.

"At twenty-five reales the two sacks," he said.

"No," she replied. "I buy them at twenty reales."

"At twenty reales then, Señorita. But you give me twenty centavos for carrying them."

"The owner pays for the transport," said Kate. "But I will give you the twenty centavos."

And away went the man, trotting bare-legged with the two great sacks of charcoal on his shoulders. When she had arrived in Chapala, he had trotted all the way from the station to her house with two massive iron trunks on his back. An ordinary porter could barely lift one trunk from the ground, much less carry it. But these cargadores had spines of solid iron. The iron spine of the unbroken Indian.

Baskets of guavas, baskets of green, sweet lemons, baskets of orange-red and greenish mangoes, baskets of pineapples. Oranges, carrots, cactus-fruit in great abundance, a few potatoes, huge pink radishes, flat, pure-white onions, little calabacitas, and middle-sized speckled calabashes, camotes cooked and raw: she liked to see what was coming to market.

Then, rather late as a rule, big red pots, bulging red water jars, earthernware cooking pots, red earthernware mugs with cream and black scratches of majolica pattern: big plates with weird dogs and a maze of scratches: bowls, jars with handles: a great deal of crockery, all red earthernware. On the west beach, men running up the shore wearing twelve great hats at once, huge heavy towers of hats, trotting quickly to the plaza. Men carrying a few pairs of beautifully woven sandals, guaraches, and some ordinary strip-sandals. A man with a bunch of new dark sarapes with gaudy patterns.

By the time the church-bells clanged for sundown the market had already begun. On all the pavements round the plaza squatted the Indians with their wares, arrays of red earthernware, globes of melons, hats in piles, guaraches in pairs side by side, much fruit, little stands of sweets. And people still coming in from the country with laden asses.

Yet never a shout, hardly a voice to be heard. Never the animation and excitement of market. Never any thrill. When dark fell, all the vendors lighted their tin torch-lamps, and the flames wavered and streamed, and the dark-faced men in their white clothes and big hats squatted silent on the ground, waiting. They never asked you to buy. They never showed you their wares. They didn't even look at you. It was as if they didn't want to sell their things: didn't care.

The food-stalls were brilliantly lit up, men sat at the plank board in rows, drinking soup and eating hot food with their fingers. The milkman rode in on horseback, his two big cans of milk slung before him, and advanced slowly to the food-stalls. There he delivered milk, and, sitting on his horse unmoved, ate his bowl of soup, his plate of tamales or minced, fiery meat and mush, while the peons slowly drifted round, and music was playing, and sometimes a big motor-car would shove its way through, choked with girls and people, excursionists from Guadalajara. And the foreign-looking soldiers with their knives and pistols and looped hats, and their curious northern speech, would stand in couples, more alien even than Kate herself.

All this life and flare of torches low down upon the ground. All

the throng of white-clad, big-hatted men, and women in dark rebozos, circulating slowly. And the dark trees overhead, and the bright-
lit doorway of the hotel at one corner of the square, and girls in
organdie frocks from the city. So little noise, so little animation, and
groups of singers singing as if secretly. The dark life of the peons
thronging thick, and absolutely ignoring the city people. The dead,
black power of obliviousness in the peons. They seemed, in some way,
to be able to extinguish the presence of the girls in organdie frocks and
the men in correct suits. It was really pitiful, the pretty girls from
Guadalajara, in their gauze of red and white and rose and lavender,
how they went arm in arm round the plaza, and the native people,
particularly the men, did not so much as glance at them. The peons
seemed to emit a dark negative will-power, all the time, making the
plaza seem dark in spite of all the light.

Suddenly there was a shot. The market-place was on its feet in a
moment, scattering. Another shot. Kate, from where she stood, saw
across the emptying plaza a man sitting back on one of the benches,
firing a pistol up into the air. He was a rough from the city, half drunk.
The people realised what it was. Yet they crowded away into the side
streets. Two more shots, rapidly, still into the air, and at the same time
a little man in uniform darted out of the dark street where the hats
were, and before you could take a breath, slapped the pistol-firer
across the face with a slap that sounded like a pistol-shot itself, then
again, *Slap!* Two of the strange soldiers also rushed up, seized the
man's arm and wrested the pistol from him. The crowd instantly,
silently began to return. Kate, her heart beating heavily, sat down on a
bench. A little while later she saw the culprit led away between two
soldiers; his cheek was already swollen and discolored, and streaks of
blood were running down it. The little man in uniform, who was the
chief of police, must have had knuckle-dusters.

The market went on as usual. Kate rose to go home. Felipa, who
was keeping her guard, suddenly said softly, pulling her arm:

"Ah! *El General.*"

A man in a dark suit was saluting her. General Viedma!

"Oh!" she said. "Is it you?"

"That drunken fool startled you?" he asked.

"Oh, not much," she answered. "I didn't *feel* anything sinister."

"No, just a drunken prank. But it is never wise to have firearms
going off in this country."

"I suppose it isn't."

"I hear you think of leaving Mexico soon," he said.

"How did you hear?" she replied.

"It is easy, in Chapala – or in all the Republic, for that matter."

"Have you been in Chapala before?"

"Yes, several times. Several times I have seen you here – listening to the singers or sitting at one of the tables with your cousin."

"Why didn't you speak to me, then?"

"How should I know that you wished it?"

She was silent, uncertain whether she *had* wished it. Only certain that she didn't like the thought of his having watched her without her knowing.

"Even now," he said to her, laughing, "you do not say you wished me to speak to you."

"Yes," she replied. "I would rather."

They had drifted down the little road past the pots, to the church.

"You were going to your house?" he said. "Allow me to escort you."

"Why, don't trouble unless you wish," said Kate.

"It will be a pleasure."

So they went through the sand towards Kate's house. There was a moon above the lake, the air was coming fresh, but not too strong, from the west. The wind from the Pacific Ocean. Little lights were burning ruddy by the boats at the water's edge: some lights inside, under the wooden roof-tilt of the boat, some outside. Women were cooking a little food.

"The night is lovely!" said Kate. She was still feeling sore at Mexico.

"With the moon a little clipped on one side," said he.

She glanced behind. Felipa was following close, and further behind, two soldiers.

"Do soldiers escort you?" she said.

He laughed without answering.

"But the moon isn't lovely here as it is in England or in Italy," she said.

"It is the same planet," he laughed.

"But the moonshine isn't the same," she persisted. "It doesn't make one feel thrilled and happy, as it does in Europe."

"How then?"

"It's a hostile moon here, that would like to hurt one."

He did not answer for some moments. Then he said:

"It may be you bring with you something from Europe that hurts our Mexican moon. It may be something in you that is hostile to us."

"But I come here in perfectly good faith."

"The faith of Europe. Not the good faith of Indian Mexico."

Now she was silent. Then she broke into a rough little laugh.

"Fancy your moon's objecting to me!" she said sarcastically.

"Why not?" he answered.

They came near the corner of Kate's road. At the corner, just beyond the tall Villa Aurora, was a group of trees, and under these trees in the corner were several reed huts of the natives. Kate was quite used to seeing the donkeys looking over the low dry-stone wall, the black sheep with the curved horns tied to a pole, the boy naked save for his shirt, darting to the corner of the wall that served as a W.C. That was the worst of these little clusters of huts, they always made a smell of human excrement.

Kate was used, too, to hearing the music of guitars and fiddles from this corner not far from her house. When she asked Felipa what the music meant, Felipa said it was a dance.

"But why should she?" persisted Kate, referring to the Mexican moon's having an objection to her.

"You object to our moon, why shouldn't our moon object to you?"

"Why? Because I don't *do* anything to her. My will is good. And a good will is the same, whether it's on the moon or in Mexico or in Europe."

"Perhaps that is not *quite* true. The good-will that Mexico needs may be somewhat different from the European good-will."

"No," said Kate. "We are all people with two eyes and one nose. Our feelings aren't so very different. Hate is hate all the world over, and love is love.

He did not answer. – They were opposite the corner under the trees, where the huts were, and the music. By the light of the moon many figures could be seen, the white clothes of the men.

"Look!" said Kate. "They are having a baile – a dance!"

And she stood to watch. But nobody was dancing. Someone was singing – two men. Kate recognised the hymns.

"They are singing the hymns to Quetzalcoatl," she said to Viedma.

"What are those?" he replied laconically.

"The boys sing them to me at the house."

He did not answer. They both stood looking over the wall. It was not very easy to see. – The song ceased, and he would have moved on. But she stood persistently. Then the song started again. And this time it was different. There was a sort of refrain sung by all the men in unison, a deep, brief response of male voices, the response of the audience to the chant. It seemed very wild, very barbaric in its solemnity, and so deeply, resonantly musical that Kate felt wild tears in her heart. The strange sound of men in unanimous deep, wild resolution. As if the hot-blooded soul were speaking from many men at once.

"That is beautiful," she said, turning to him.

"It is the song of the moon," he answered. "The response of the men to the words of the woman with white breasts, who is the moon-mother."

She wanted to ask him more. But she could not. She stood there in a kind of spell. Till this music ended too, and the group of men broke up. A woman was coming holding aloft a piece of flaming wood, to see who the strangers were, looking over the wall.

"Shall we go?" he said, and she turned away.

"How beautiful!" she said.

They reached the green gates under the cuenta tree.

"Will you come and see my house?" she said.

They sat on the verandah looking at the garden, where the intermittent fire-flies made continuous sparks of green light, in the air, among the leaves. The night was fairly still again, save for the far-off braying of an ass, and the continuous faint pip-pip-pip-pip! of the motor which made the electric light in the little planta that Jesús managed, just up the road. Then a cock from beyond the banana grove crowed hoarsely.

"But how absurd!" said Kate. "Cocks don't crow at this hour in other countries."

"He thinks the moon is dawn," laughed Viedma, ironically.

And the cock crowed again and again.

"No," said Kate, "it is too absurd. He must stop."

Felipa was bringing glasses, and tepache, the only drink in the house.

"Listen to that cockerel," said Kate indignantly.

"It will be the cock of Saint Peter," said Felipa.

COLLECTED WORKS

Store hours:
Mon - Sat 9 AM to 9 PM
Sundays 10 AM to 6 PM

71256 Reg 1 1:42 pm 06/05/06

S QUETZALCOATL	1 @	14.95	14.95
S ALBURQUERQUE REIS	1 @	14.95	14.95
SUBTOTAL			29.90
SALES TAX - 7.625%			2.28
TOTAL			32.18
VISA PAYMENT			32.18

Thank you for shopping at
Collected Works Bookstore
Returns for Store Credit Only
with Receipt & within 30 days of sale
Sorry, NO cash refunds...

"So you do not feel happy in Mexico, you want to go away?" said Viedma.

"I'm not a bit happy," said Kate.

"Why not?"

"I can't *do* anything here. Felipa won't let me do anything in the house. And it's mostly too hot to walk, and anyhow it isn't safe to walk outside the village. So here I sit and rock in a rocking-chair, and that's all the life I have. Felipa won't let me cook – she just doesn't intend me to. And I can't do anything with her and all the rest of them. I can't come near to them, they are such savages. And they don't understand unless I *do* come near to them, and insist and force myself into their consciousness. I can't do that. So I just sit in a rocking-chair and rock myself through the days."

"You read?" he said, looking at the books and magazines lying around.

"Oh, and it all seems to me so stupid, so stupid, so stupid. I never knew the world was *so* stupid!" she cried. "The books and papers are beyond words stupid."

"Perhaps they aren't. – Perhaps that is only Mexico too," he laughed, "makes them seem so."

"Oh, and I long for England, with a house and a lawn and a garden, and the sea not far, and a bit of peace in my life."

"When do you think you will leave?" he asked.

"In three weeks, when I have arranged the money and everything."

He was silent. And he made her uncomfortable. He too seemed to take away her freedom, to have the paralysing effect of Mexico upon her, as if her soul were paralysed.

"I had hoped you would choose to live in Mexico," he said, in the quiet, secretive-seeming voice of the Indians.

"Not for the world!" she declared, panic-stricken and defiant.

"But when you get to England," he said, "perhaps you may wish to be in Mexico again."

"Well," she said. "One never knows what madness may come over one, and so I suppose even that is possible."

He was silent, and the Indian gloom came out of him, like a black mist.

"When I was in England," he said slowly, "I stayed all the time to find out what was the secret of it. But all the time my spirit was in

Mexico, and only my mind was in England, learning things. My spirit was in Mexico. It seemed to me only Mexico was life. The rest was lifeless."

"And did you find out the secret of England?"

"No," he said. "I found out the chief secret, that there was not much life, only many habits and conventions and ways of life, and ideas. All, all the intricate ways of life, so many, like the pavements of a city. Even your country, very beautiful, your woods and fields and hills, but like a beautiful park around a city. All made. All made and finished. And your women so made and finished, as if they too were the excellent goods of your country. Your country makes such excellent goods, fabrics. And the people are like excellent fabrics, some more expensive, some less. But all made and finished off – finished off. – You know the Navajo women, the Indian women, when they weave blankets, weave their souls into them. So at the end they leave a place, some threads coming down to the edge, some loose threads where their souls can come out. And it seems to me your country has woven its soul into its fabrics and its goods and its books, and never left a place for the soul to come out. So all the soul is in the goods, in the books, and in the roads and ways of life, and the people are finished like finished sarapes, that have no faults and nothing beyond. Your women have no threads into the beyond. Their pattern is finished and they are complete."

"But I am Irish," said Kate.

"Nearly all English people," he said smiling, "are Irish or Scotch or Welsh or Cornish, or they had a French grandmother. *Qui s'excuse s'accuse.*"

"No, I don't excuse myself," she said. "I only state a fact."

He made a slight mocking gesture with his hand.

"And you don't like English women," she said. "And I don't like – I don't like Mexico. You don't like England because it seems finished, and I don't like Mexico because it feels like a black bog where one has no foothold."

He was silent for some moments before he replied:

"I did not say that every English woman, or Irish woman, was finished and finished off. But they wish to be. They do not like their threads into the beyond. They quickly tie the threads and close the pattern. In your women the pattern is usually complete and closed, at twenty years."

"And in Mexico there is no pattern – it is all a tangle," said Kate.

"The pattern is very beautiful, while there are threads into the unknown, and the pattern is never finished. The Indian patterns are never *quite* complete. There is always a flaw at the end, where they break into the beyond – nothing is more beautiful to me than a pattern which is lovely and perfect, when it breaks at the end imperfectly on to the unknown –"

There was passion in his voice. Kate sat embarrassed and afraid.

"But when the pattern is closed and finished off," he added in a low tone, "I hate it."

Kate felt that his hatred of a finished pattern was more vivid than his love for the unfinished. – She remained silent as he was. Till she said at last:

"Well, it may be I am old, and my pattern is finished. – I wish it to be finished, as far as Mexico goes," she added, rather venomously.

He crossed his legs and looked sharply the other way, in anger. Then he looked at her with the frightening Indian anger in his eyes. She felt he would like to kill her there and then.

"You are not old," he said. "And your pattern is not finished. Your true pattern has yet to be woven. But if the white man's cowardice and the white man's egotism have got hold of you, then you are finished and you are dead. You are dead as you leave Mexico."

"*Ça reste à voir,*" she replied in French.

She saw that his anger had almost overcome him, the strange, black, overwhelming anger of these people. When they are angry they do not care if they kill or are killed. Life ceases to have any value for them. They are black volcanoes of anger. Until, of course, they are *acobardado,* as they say in Spanish: until they are encowarded. And most of the bourgeois Mexicans, like the bourgeois the world over, are just *acobardado,* cowed. Society needs people to be cowed.

But Viedma, and the mass of the Mexican Indians, are not cowed. They may appear so for the moment, the peons. But they are watching their opportunity.

Viedma was not cowed. Perhaps not sufficiently so. And Kate saw it. And although she always halted before any naked, real passion, of anger as well as of love: and though she always loved any man or woman who could reveal a naked passion: still, she wished to preserve herself. She shrank from the black volcanic nature of these people, men and women alike. They seemed sulphureous, like craters of volcanic life. Not sufficiently mingled into humanness.

So Cipriano. She shrank from him, though a dark, soft flame seemed to envelop her soul for a moment as he turned his black, angry eyes on her. She felt a sort of reverence for the passion in him, and a womanly tenderness for the nakedness of the passion, but she wished to preserve herself. It made her afraid, too. And she could never submit to fear.

Viedma still watched her with his black eyes, in which anger and arrogance and hate seemed to struggle with a great desire and yearning. She was distinctly afraid of him: even a little afraid lest he should have some hold over her, through her fear.

"You see," she said more gently, "one must remain where one belongs. I don't believe one can change one's nature. And if my nature is British —"

"Ah!" he said impatiently. "You might as well say your nature is Cockney or Birmingham, whichever city you come from."

"I don't come from any city, least of all London or Birmingham."

"Village then. It is the same. The human soul is greater than any circumstance, of nationality or even race. That is the unfinished end of the pattern."

"But you are so *very* Mexican," she retorted.

"My soul cries out for Mexico. I *want* Mexico. My soul wants Mexico. But your soul no longer wants England, or wants Ireland. There the pattern breaks."

"But I belong to my own people, my own country."

"No, the pattern is broken for you. Your soul can weave your life no longer in the English or Irish pattern. That pattern is finished. And the loose ends lead into the beyond. Lead into the unwoven pattern of Mexico and America. The loose ends of your life lead into the Mexican pattern — the pattern of unwoven America."

"I must go home," she said.

"You have no home," he cried passionately. "The past is a grave to sleep in. Home is where you tie the new threads of your life, to weave a new pattern. That is home, even if you are houseless. And that is here — here —"

He had almost said: "With me." And Kate heard the words as distinctly as if he had uttered them. But thank God he had *not* uttered them.

"I can't tie any more new threads," she said. "That part of my life is finished. I have woven all there is of me to weave. Now I want to rest. I do. I want to have peace, and grow slowly old. I do."

"Let me tell you," he said, "you will die. The peace you want will poison you. Such peace is worse than bad suffering. Cancer is better than such peace."

"But you don't know, since it isn't your peace. Besides, death does not seem to me such a disaster," smiled Kate. She saw that he *wanted* her to be poisoned by such peace.

"*Acobardado!*" he said, smiling angrily. "*Acobardado!*"

Kate blenched at the word. Her husband had always said: The most hateful thing on earth is a life-coward. She would never admit herself cowed, encowarded: particularly by life.

"It may seem to you, *acobardado,*" she retorted. "That is because it is *my* life, and not yours. You are not European, and I am."

"*Acobardado!*" he repeated.

Then he lapsed into a hostile silence. After which he rose, and putting a smile on his face, bowed, saluted her, and left her.

She, absolutely exhausted, asked Felipa to lock up, and went to bed. She was asleep almost as soon as her head touched the pillow.

In the night she woke up startled, not knowing where she was. She could not recognise her bedroom, she did not know which was the door, where was the way out. "Is it my bedroom in New York?" she asked herself, and she looked for the signs.

It took her some time to find the door, open on to the verandah, and the chair in the doorway, and a faint light of moonlight outside, and the sound of Rafael muttering in his sleep, on the mattress outside the door. But at last, in a panic, she had deciphered it all.

And there came to her, in a shock that woke her completely: General Viedma wants to marry me. He wants to *force* me to marry him.

The fear of the Mexican night was as great as it had ever been. She wanted to run, to run away. Oh, she wanted to go. She felt as if some huge beast had almost caught her, some horrible beast. She thought of Viedma almost with horror. The thought of his dominating her through fear came on her like a madness. She must get out, get out at once. She thought of the train, of the journey to Mexico and Vera Cruz. Or of the journey to Irapuato and El Paso. Or of the flight west, not so far, to Colima and Manzanillo. Whatever else she did, she must escape out of this country. For she felt they would try to detain her, try not to let her get out.

As she lay in her bed looking at the chair-blocked open door she figured out all the best ways of escape. And for some reason she thought she would flee west. It was not far from Guadalajara to Colima, and then Manzanillo and the sea were near. A steamer would take her up to Los Angeles.

Then she thought of her heavy trunks: having them carried by the cargador to the station: booking them to Guadalajara: then again to Manzanillo. And what the steamers would cost. And if she had enough money to get to Los Angeles. And what she should say to Owen? – She would not have to speak of her flight to Owen. Not to anybody. She would leave, without any luggage, and get Owen to bring her things to the United States. He would hate all the bother, but he would do it.

The thought of the United States was like heaven to her. A great escape. Owen seemed almost like an angel: he left her so free. And Villiers was the perfection of niceness, so attentive and unobtrusive. And the white men's countries were the only places where she could breathe.

This was in the middle of the night, with a pallor of moon outside, beyond the balcony, the occasional antiphony of night-hoarse cocks, and the occasional little apparition of greenish light in the air of her room, like someone striking a match, from the intermittent firefly. And she herself prostrate in her bed, quite *acobardado*.

Curiously enough, she woke in the morning with a new feeling of strength. It was only six o'clock, yet she felt the life rising up in her. Rafael had gone, had rolled up his mattress. The hibiscus trees were hung with big scarlet blossoms, there was a faint scent of roses, the sun was a soft flood of light. The big, dense mango-trees always seemed most sumptuous in the early morning, when their hard green fruits dropped like testes from the bronze new leaves, absolutely still, yet strangely potent. Outside her window along the road slow cows were marching down to the lake, with a little calf, big-eyed and adventurous, trotting to peep through her gate at the grass and flowers. The peon lifted his two arms to send it on, without making a sound. Only the noise of the feet of the cows. – Then two boys trying vainly to urge a young bull-calf down towards the lake. It suddenly jerked up its rump and gave dry little kicks, or butted them with its blunt young head. They were terrified, and took to the inevitable recourse of the Indians, of throwing stones at the creature.

"No," shouted Kate from her window, in English. "You're not to throw stones at it. Treat it sensibly."

The boys dropped their stones, all their ferocity disappearing from them. They seemed to dwindle and make themselves almost invisible. Two women were coming along, with a red water-jar on one shoulder, going down to the lake for water. They always put one arm over their head and held the jar on the other shoulder. This had a slightly contorted look, so different from the proud way women carried water in Sicily.

When Kate was dressed she walked to the shore. It was hardly beyond her gate. The lake was pale blue in the morning light, the opposite mountains dry and ribbed like mountains in the desert. Only a darkness of trees at the water's edge, and white specks of Tuxcueco. Five cows stood with their noses in the water, drinking. Women were kneeling filling their red jars. On the frail fishing-nets hung up on sticks a red bird perched facing the sun, red as a drop of new blood. And from the straw huts under the trees her urchin of the mud-chick came pelting towards her, to offer her little ollitas, tiny little jars which he held out to her on the palm of his tiny hand, telling her they were chiquitas, and asking her, in his brisk, warrior-like way, if she wanted them. But she hadn't got a penny with her, so she told him no.

"*Mañana?*" he said, like a little pistol shot. "Tomorrow?"

"Yes, tomorrow," she replied.

Her scrap of an enemy had evidently forgiven her, but she hadn't quite forgiven him yet.

Somebody was singing, beautifully in tune. They seemed not so much to produce the sound, as to let it issue from them.

And yet, in spite of all, the morning seemed neither fair nor young. There was still an old cruelty somewhere. And the shore was so strewn with rubbish. And the red bird was like an angular drop of blood twittering about on the almost invisible fishing nets. And the black birds that flew in fours, with their necks pushed out, along the surface of the lake, they were all angles, and their flight was the flight of a jagged weapon. A boy with a sling was prowling, trying to hit birds.

The Sunday passed indefinite, the sun shining straight down and everything going vague as it always did in this blankness of sunshine. In the afternoon the air was thick with electricity, Kate could feel it pressing on the back of her head. It stupefied her almost like morphine. The clouds gathered in the evening, lightning was flapping. But still it did not rain.

She walked along the shore in the dark with Villiers, watching the sailing boats depart. The wind was from the west, so several of the boats sailing east had gone. The boats for Jocotepec could not leave. There was a big one that had carried many people, and the people were now going on board again. They clustered in a group at the edge of the flapping water. The big, wide, flat-bottomed canoe with her wooden awning and her one straight mast lay black, a few yards out, in the night. A lamp was burning under the wooden hatches, you could look in. Then a short man came to carry the passengers on board. The men stood with their backs to him, their legs apart. He ducked his head between their legs, straightened himself, and there they were riding on his shoulders, his head between the fork of their legs. So he waded out to the black boat, and heaved them on to the side, like heaving a pig. For a woman, he crouched down and she seated herself on one shoulder. Then he rose, clasping her legs while she held his head to balance her. And so he waded through the water. The strength of these men's spines seemed almost unnatural.

Soon the boat was almost full of people. There they sat, on the floor along the sides, baskets hanging from the hatch roof, swaying as the boat swayed to the water. Another little woman came running across the sand. She had forgotten something. The men inside the boat spread their sarapes and lay down to sleep. They would leave when the wind changed, after midnight.

And almost for the first time, Kate wished to be with them. Not actually with them, sleeping on the floor of that canoe like so many cattle. But in some way participating in their lives. She wanted in some way to participate.

Owen was leaving at the end of June, going back to the United States. And she must make up her mind whether to go or not. She was determined to go. Yet when the very moment came to give up her house, she equivocated. "Perhaps," she said to her landlord, "I shall go at the end of this month."

She had never in her life been so indefinite. Usually, when she wanted to do a thing, she just did it. Now she wanted to go away, to go back to Europe. And instead of doing it, she hung neutral. It was as if she couldn't gather herself into decision or into energy. That was Mexico. It acted like morphine on her, and didn't let her do anything, not even go away.

Scarlet birds like drops of blood, in very green willow-trees. So she often saw them in the mornings by the lake. And she felt she was hypnotised. A film was over her, a film over all her will and her feeling. She would never be free till she was back again in Europe, or in the United States.

An aguador trotting towards her house with a pole over one shoulder and two heavy square cans of water hanging, one from each end of the pole. Barefoot, bare-legged, his dark, handsome face bent in shadow under the big hat, the young man trotted softly, softly, with a rhythm that was pure hypnotism.

Dark heads on the water in little groups, like black water-fowl folded up and bobbing. Were they birds? Were they heads? Was this human life, or something intermediate?

XI

Y OU MAY have to do without her," said Ramón to Cipriano. Cipriano slowly shook his head.

"No," he said.

"But if the woman chooses to go, you can't detain her."

"She will not go."

"You mean you won't let her? Will you kidnap her, like the bandits?"

"If necessary. But it is my will that she shall not go. It is the will of the gods in me that she shall not go."

Ramón watched the general carefully.

"In that case," he said slowly, "her proper destiny is to stay. But you know that when a man, or a woman, chooses to be perverse, she can defy her proper destiny and have her own empty will. So she loses her destiny."

"Then," said Cipriano, "I will act. It is my destiny too. She shall not make my destiny empty also."

"Is that one woman essential to your destiny?"

"Yes."

"If you don't have her, your life will be all empty?"

"Yes. Essentially."

"I can hardly believe that. You would fulfil your life, whether you had her or not. You're not a boy, to be desperate with love. You're a man almost forty. You've finished with love affairs."

"That is true. I don't love her. She is indispensable to my life, to my natural destiny. That is all. She knows it too. I want her for my destiny."

"No no! She doesn't know it. She isn't as we are. She doesn't know these things. Her education doesn't include the understanding of a natural destiny. She thinks she can go her way according to her lights."

"Ah well. Then her lights must be put out."

"It is much better, of course, that she should realise and choose for herself."

"If she doesn't, I will choose for her."

"And prevent her leaving?"

"Yes."

"Detain her here?"

"Yes."

"Where?"

Cipriano spread his hands.

"If you feel it must be so, it must," said Ramón. "But it would be much better if she realised and chose for herself."

"I know it perfectly. But if she *won't* realise, if she *can't* choose! If the habit of an old life is too strong – !"

"Then have your way, if you feel it necessary."

"You agree?"

"If you have an inward necessity, I agree, even if it comes to shutting the woman up as a prisoner. One must obey one's gods first, come what will."

"Then you are with me?"

"Yes."

"Good."

The two men suddenly embraced, breast to breast, Mexican fashion.

"If it were not for you, Ramón, the gods in me would turn into devils."

"Keep your eye on *me,* Cipriano. It's my danger too," said Ramón.

The two men looked at one another and laughed shortly. Then a new calm came over their hearts. They were silent for a time.

"The priest is coming this morning," said Ramón.

"Yes?"

"Shall I see him alone?"

Cipriano looked into the black eyes of Ramón. Ramón was grave and remote, with again some of that immobile, statuesque, god-like look which was so impressive. It was now Cipriano's turn to hesitate a moment.

"No," he said. "I will be there."

They were sitting in the library of General Viedma's quarters in Guadalajara. As military commander of the State, and as a general with extraordinary hold over the mass of the soldiers, Cipriano was perhaps the strongest man in the country. Yet he had always kept very quiet, he had avoided as much as possible the military and political leaders of Mexico. It was his instinct to be a man by himself. Only he was attached to Ramón. So far, however, he had never publicly identified himself with Ramón's effort to change the religion of the country. The movement was only just in its infancy. No one could foresee the future. Cipriano felt it would be unbecoming in him to compromise the government by appearing as a new sort of agitator. Also it would do the new cause no good, to have a general in the fore-front. It would be like another political trick.

Now, however, the priests in the parish churches had begun, by order of the bishop, to preach against these Hymns of Quetzalcoatl. For the Hymns were spreading rapidly from one end of the Republic to the other. But the State of Jalisco was the place where they had started, and where they already had great vogue. Hardly a village or a hacienda in the west where the men had not learned the first and second of the hymns, at least, and where the people were not arguing, in their blind way, about Jesus and Mary being gringos, and about their departure again into heaven, and about the mystic virtues of Quetzalcoatl. It seemed as if some passionate, positive mystic chord had been touched in the Indian's soul, something active and almost violent. It put their passive worship of Jesus to flight almost in a breath. Their natures kindled like straw. They were ready, more than ready for their own gods. Somewhere, their slumbering volcanic souls were aching for a passionate release, for passionate, active gods to serve.

The government in Mexico City, of course, was anti-Catholic, leaning towards communism, hating the priests. It was not at all hostile, then, to this rise of a new, national religious impulse, seeing in it a wonderful instrument against the Catholic Church. "You can only dislodge an old superstition with a new superstition," said the President, who was a general, and an unselfish man with a real desire to serve the people of his country, but who was almost powerless to act, surrounded as he was by bullying generals at home, and by the various Mammons of the foreign powers, all of them waiting to seize the bone of Mexico. He was a politician and a general, so he had not much belief in religion, new or old. Its chief use, he saw, was as a political instrument in handling the masses of the people. But as a sincere liberal he disliked intensely the underhand methods of religion in politics. Still, he kept his eye on Ramón Carrasco and General

Viedma, when the stress of answering all the requests from the great financial powers left him a moment to turn his eyes aside.

The Church, too, had of course watched the growth of the new legend closely. The Bishop of Guadalajara was a Mexican who had lived many early years in Rome, but who had preserved a good deal of his native freshness. He was by nature easy and good-tempered. If he had to choose between Rome and his native country, he would probably choose the latter. It was nearer home to him than his creed. But he had no intention of choosing. Why choose between blessings? Why not keep both?

So he ignored Ramón Carrasco and the Hymns as long as possible: till his orders from the Archbishop, who was a fierce Churchman, made him take steps. The first step was an interview with Carrasco. They met at the house of a common friend, outside the city.

"It is you, Señor, is it not," asked the Bishop frankly, "who have started these so-called Hymns of Quetzalcoatl among the peons?"

"Not exactly," said Ramón. "The very first account of the man who came out of the lake saying he had seen Quetzalcoatl, I read in the newspaper."

"Ah Señor," said the Bishop, spreading his hands. "But this man is not right in his mind."

"Perhaps a divine madness, Bishop," smiled Ramón.

"If it were *madness,* Don Ramón! But when it is only silliness —"

The Bishop smiled an amiable, amused smile. Then, rather unwillingly, he straightened his face and looked grave.

"Tell me though, if you will be so kind," he said. "What is your idea, in these hymns? What is it you wish to effect?"

"It is fairly obvious," said Don Ramón. "I want to release the natural religious passion which is in us Mexicans, particularly if we are Indians, the religious energy native to our own blood."

"But isn't that already released? Do you think you can improve on the Church, dear Don Ramón?"

"No, I really don't. I have the profoundest admiration for the Church, as a historical institution. But it is no growth of our soil. It isn't ours."

"My dear Don Ramón! Surely the Church is universal. Surely the Church is as universal as your world-socialism?"

"I haven't any world-socialism, dear Bishop. Only I think we poor devils of Mexicans have always been swamped in universals invented by foreigners from Europe. Now I would like it if we could get to heaven by our own visions."

"Which is what the Church helps us to do."

"Nay, as you say, the Church is universal. I want something particular. – If we are to talk theology, Señor, then by your leave I will admit that I believe with you in the One Great God. But the Mediator is not one and exclusive. He is many. There is One Great God with an Unutterable Name. But that is not altogether the point. The point, for us men, is how are we going to come into connection with the invisible God."

"Through the Church of Christ Jesus, Señor."

"No, it doesn't help any more."

"Don Ramón, how can you say it doesn't help? If you choose yourself to resist the Holy Church in her administrations, how can you assert that the Church fails in her mission to the people of our country, who still are faithful? You must not blame the Church for your own want of faith, Señor."

"I must. Because I would believe if I could."

"So you must take upon yourself to try to start another heresy?"

"Yes, I must do that. Whatever I am, I am not a protestant, Bishop. I don't believe that men can come in one leap to the Almighty God. There must be mediation, human and divine. The Son of God, who is Himself a God. And the Daughter of God, a Goddess Herself. These must intercede between men and women and the Most High God. But the Most High has other divine Sons than Jesus, Bishop; even divine Daughters. Each race of people may be compared to the Virgin which bears divine sons and divine daughters to the Most High. And the divine Son and the divine Daughters are forever born anew, while a race remains Virgin to the Most High God."

"This is strange theology, Don Ramón," said the Bishop, smiling easily and not trying to understand.

"Not so, Bishop. – And now I wish Quetzalcoatl to be born anew of the Mexican people and the Most High God."

"And of Don Ramón Carrasco. Don't deny your child, Don Ramón. Don't leave the parenthood to the Holy Spirit, like so many fathers," smiled the Bishop.

"I would rather call myself, as a fragment of the Mexican people, a fragment of the Virgin Mother."

"Well, Don Ramón, I hear you have a blue mantle."

"Only blue stripes, Bishop."

There was a pause.

"So you feel you must take up a new weapon against the Church, Señor?" asked the Bishop rather coldly, angry that he could no longer remain amiable.

"I do not feel any active resentment against the Church, Bishop. The Church has done what she could. She has a great history. But now I want to see a new Church in Mexico. If you will become bishop of the Church of Quetzalcoatl in Mexico, Padre," Ramón added, smiling teasingly, "I shall beg you to hear my confession."

"I hope that soon I may hear your penitent confession in my church in Guadalajara, Don Ramón."

"Who knows?" said Don Ramón.

The conference, like most other human conferences, ended without any result. The Bishop even didn't wish to bother. He felt no animosity towards Ramón Carrasco. He had no liking for his thin-jawed, domineering, jesuitical Archbishop. He had a great, but indolent affection for his country and his people, and a certain inner dislike of Rome, Spain, Europe. Like every other honest American, he hated being ruled or commanded from Europe. And he had no illusions about Rome itself. He was really more a Mexican than a Churchman, and therefore not in very high favour with his Archbishop. But he didn't care. He had only one life to live. And he calculated that by dodging when the revolutionaries came too near, and obeying at least the *letter* of commands sent from his superiors in the Church, and by being amiable with his people, he might continue comfortable in his see for the rest of his days.

Ramón understood the Bishop fairly well. The two men had both more Indian than Spanish blood in their veins, and in both the bias was distinctly Indian. They felt the same indifference for European or ecclesiastical niceties, the indifference towards the white man's so-called Education. To Ramón, this was almost a test of a man's true inclination: did he believe in Education, or not. If he believed in Education, he belonged to the white man's world. If not, to the still mute world of the Indian.

Also the Bishop and Don Ramón felt towards one another that curious easy sympathy which belongs to men of the same race, when they are under an alien influence. They might be ever so hostile in act and fact. But in their bowels the hostility was all factitious, they had the same plumb, indifferent sympathy with one another. Since neither of them was greedy for money. The moment the Bishop had showed signs of money-greed, Ramón would have plotted his destruction. And vice-versa. But neither man cared about possessions, one way or another.

Yet when the Bishop received orders to counteract the new and foolish heresy started by Don Ramón among the Indians, he obeyed at once, without taking any notice of Carrasco. He sent the order to every priest in his diocese, to preach against the so-called hymns, to forbid the singing of the so-called hymns, and to refuse to confess any man or woman who persisted in singing or in any way communicating to others these so-called hymns.

This order was given after the famous Fourth Hymn had begun to spread over the country.

Then over the land of Mexico a weariness came. For men had shed blood through many years, to bring the Kingdom of Christ to their land. And whenever Mexican blood was shed, men from all countries came, appeared out of nowhere, eager to find something. And the greedy ones found silver, much silver, and carried it away. And the greedy ones found the oil of the earth, much oil, very much oil, and blackened the land to get this oil into ships. And the greedy ones said: Let us get sugar out of the earth, from the tall tubes of the cane. And among the cane-fields smoke of factories rose, and in the fields the peons of Mexico sweated, to bring the sugar from the living earth into the trains and ships of the greedy ones, who carried it away.

So more blood was shed, and the Mexicans said: Let us shed our blood, to have brotherhood and the ways of the Lord in Mexico. For Jesus says: *Give all thou hast to the poor.* Let us shed our blood, and let all be given to the poor.

So more blood was shed, and many houses were broken. And many, many greedy ones ran away out of Mexico, taking with them all they could take.

Then the Mexicans, being weary, said: Let us shed no more blood. We are poor. Let each poor man work in his garden, for maize and milk. For all is given to the poor.

But the greedy ones from afar, seeing that quiet had returned into the bodies of the Mexicans, came stealing back, stealing back. In trains they came, in many automobiles, and in ships. All over

Mexico was a noise of trains, and a dust of motor-cars. So the peon in his hot garden said: Where is the camion going? Why does it hurry?

Then the greedy ones, and the educated ones said: It goes far, to better places. It goes to great cities where men are rich, where they do not sweat in the fields, where are heaps of all fruits and food, and many things to see.

So the peons said: Let us go and see.

But the man in the camion, and the man in the train, and the man in the automobile said: Pay your money.

The peons said: Where should we get money?

And they answered: Go and work. Go and work for money.

In this way the greedy ones came quietly in again, saying: We will give you money if you will work, and you shall ride in camions and wear trousers of fine cloth.

The peons wanted to ride in camions and wear trousers of fine cloth, and they wanted to see the strange sights and to know the strange things the educated ones told about.

How nice! they said, to go rushing in the great train.

How nice! they said, to sit in the camion going quickly across great distances.

How nice! they said, to be among many, many people in the city, and not to work.

How nice to see the Cine, where the world passes before your eyes.

How nice it would be to have much, much money, and never to work, but to see all things in this world.

Then the greedy ones came again, saying: We will give much money for your land. We will pay much money for your work. We will bring you more camions and more cinematographs, and much fine cotton cloth for the women, and much fine wool for the men. We will bring you many good things, and give you money to buy them with. If you will work a short time each day for us, and let us take away the oil and the sugar and the silver and the corn and the copper you do not want.

So again the peons found themselves working for money and for the greedy ones. And all the time the greedy ones said: Make haste, Make haste! Get us the oil and the silver, the sugar and corn and copper quickly, weave us the cotton rapidly, we want a great deal, we want a very great deal of everything. We want much, much, much. Make haste, and we will give you money, even a little more money.

Then the souls of the people were weary. And they said: Why is this? Every time we wish to give all to the poor, the greedy ones are before us, and everything is theirs. Why is this? We are surely a helpless people. Why does *El Señor* forsake us in the hour when we are ready to win, why does he put us again in the power of the greedy ones?

So men arose, saying: Jesus is weak. Jesus is not strong enough for the greedy ones. Jesus hides in the church like a patrón when the campesinos are angry, hides in his house and dare not go out. Jesus is too weak, he hides in his church and is afraid. He can't help us any more. The greedy ones are too many for him.

Then the people went into the churches and looked at Jesus. And they saw him on the Cross, caked with blood. And they saw him standing in a corner, in robes. And they saw him dead. And they saw him alive. But dead or alive his face was feeble, they knew in their bowels he could not help them.

So they said: He has betrayed us. Take him away. He is a gringo too.

For the hour had come for Jesus to leave Mexico.

This hymn spread quicker than the others. Even in the cities, in Mexico itself, the workmen learnt it. It gave them a strange satisfaction.

So it happened that in several churches in the city the images of Jesus disappeared, and in their places were found grotesque Judas figures, such as are seen everywhere at Easter time. Easter in Mexico being really the great week of Judas. In the city all the time men hawk numbers of grotesque figures made of *papier maché* and brilliantly painted, like great dolls. And they are all grotesque men-dolls, some very big, more than half life-size, some not very large. These men-dolls are distorted in all ways. But mostly they represent a fat Mexican with a sticking-out stomach and tight trousers and turned-up moustaches: the old-fashioned sort of property-owner, the patrón. Many represent white men, like Punch. But they never represent the dark-faced peon. Judas always has a rosy complexion, and a stiff, ridiculously haughty expression.

Men, well-dressed men, buy these enormous figures in the street, walk home with them in their arms, like great children with great dolls, laughing. On Saturday, Easter Saturday, Judas is hung from the balcony and burned. Often he has a loud cracker in the middle of him, and ends with a bang. All the town is popping with Judases.

Great, then, was the scandal when three of these Mexican Judases were found occupying the place of the Statue of the Saviour, in three city churches. A thrill of horror and excitement went over the country. Secretly, the government was pleased. But the Catholics were beside themselves. If they could but have put forward a leader, they might at this moment have captured the country. The Knights of Columbus, with their ferocious oaths behind them, ought to have accomplished something. But they didn't.

"Bah!" said Cipriano. "If a soldier was violating their wife on the bed, they'd be under the bed hiding, not drawing a breath. No such cowards in the world."

Ramón was afraid everything would take a wrong turn now. He regretted the Judas incident sincerely. That was not what he wanted. He had to move at once. For this reason he had asked for another interview with the Bishop.

The Bishop arrived, in a simple black cassock with purple buttons. Cipriano was in uniform, Ramón in black city clothes. The three men saluted one another courteously, and the Bishop sat slowly and amply in a chair by the window. It was evident he was annoyed. A ray of sun fell on his creamy-brown hand with the huge amethyst. He moved his hand irritably.

"I have come at your order, Señores," he said irritably.

"We would have waited on you in any place you chose, Bishop," said Ramón. "You know that."

"I suppose I chose a lesser evil, coming here. – What is it you want, Señores?"

The Bishop's plump, smooth, creamy-brown face looked petulant, as if he might cry. At the same time, angry, very angry.

"You understand I regret the incident of the Judas figures in the City, Bishop," said Ramón, faintly ironic.

"It pleases you to regret it?" said the Bishop sarcastically.

"Why surely."

"For my part," said Cipriano, "I think it a stroke of Mexican genius."

The Bishop bowed in his direction, sarcastically, adding:

"It is well understood, General Viedma."

There was a pause. On Ramón's face flickered a look of amusement, but he was pale, and very much perturbed. His lips were pale with emotion, his bearing statuesque and immobile, because he suffered a good deal. He said:

"I should wish to see the image of Jesus carried reverently out of the churches, and burned in the last ritual of Christianity."

The Bishop quivered in his chair as if a paralysis would overtake him, turning aside his face as if from something deathly.

"You don't propose such a thing?" he said in a small voice.

"Yes," said Don Ramón, also deathly pale under his brown skin. "It is what I propose to do at Chapala."

The Bishop slowly looked at him.

"You wouldn't dare, Don Ramón?" he said.

"Yes. It is what I shall do."

There was dead silence. The Bishop was gazing with black, blank eyes at Ramón, his face expressionless, almost childish. Then he put his fist on his breast.

"Such words break the heart in my breast," he said.

"It must be," said Don Ramón.

There was silence for some time. Then the Bishop exclaimed energetically:

"No! It must not be! It cannot be. We won't allow it."

Don Ramón slowly shook his head, and Cipriano smiled.

"Yes, it must be," said Don Ramón.

Then the Bishop rose in anger.

"And who says so?" he demanded. "Who are you, Don Ramón Carrasco, to utter such a monstrous assertion? You, you would burn the image of Our Lord and the Santísima Maria and the saints, all of them, no doubt –"

"All of them," answered Don Ramón gravely.

"By God, it shall never happen."

"Yes, it shall happen," said Ramón.

The Bishop stood for a time at the window. Then he turned to the room again.

"Burn Our Lord and Our Lady, and desecrate the altar –"

"No," said Ramón. "We will desecrate nothing. The altar is the altar to the Most High God. But Jesus, and Mary, and the saints, these must go."

"Man, you are mad. All the demons in your body. You will see what fate will overtake you – yes, and all Mexico –"

"I am not afraid. But I wished to prepare you. If you are wise, you will be with us –"

"With whom?"

"Myself. General Viedma. And Mexico."

"You, Don Ramón, are a madman. General Viedma is one more Mexican general. I need add nothing to that. Mexico has had generals enough. And as for Mexico, which I notice you place last, Mexico is not yet yours for the taking, Señores."

"Nevertheless, Bishop, if you are a wise man you will wait and see the issue, before you take sides too actively. I would like to make the Church in Mexico the Church of Mexico, instead of the Church of Rome. And the mediators between us and the Most High shall be none but our own gods, Quetzalcoatl and the re-born gods of our race. The altar is the altar of the Most High God. The Church is the Church of the invisible God. But the chapels are the chapels of Quetzalcoatl and Tlaloc and Coatlicue; the manifestations of the High God are Indian manifestations. It shall be so."

Again the Bishop seemed confused, as if numbed.

"It is all impossible," he answered.

"Nevertheless it will be so. General Viedma and I are of one mind. With me are the people of the place. General Viedma has the soldiers. Wait and see how the change goes, Bishop."

"It can lead to nothing but more disaster," said the Bishop, in chagrin.

"Wait and see."

And so the second interview was over.

Cipriano smiled when the Bishop had gone.

"He fears the loss of his office, no more," he said.

"If he will be our friend at the right moment," said Ramón, "that will be of great assistance."

"Ah, as for such friends – !"

"They are symbols in the eyes of the people."

"Ramón," said Cipriano, "this removing of the figures from the church means a very great deal to you, doesn't it?"

"It is the great crisis of my life, of my soul."

Cipriano shook his head.

"It is curious," he said. "You almost tremble when you think of it."

"I actually tremble."

"Curious! You are a strange man. I should enjoy making a bonfire of all the crucifixes and the detestable, long-faced pietistic figures. How can you feel disturbed about it?"

"I do. It is the crisis of my life, and the life of my soul."

"Strange you are. But I will help you. Yes, I will. If you feel like that there is reason for your feeling. Don't think I question you. But you are beyond me. Those ridiculous wooden images! Frankly, I like putting the Judas dolls in their place. But to you it is much more serious. I recognise that. I recognise something beyond me. You are the living Quetzalcoatl, Ramón."

"God be with me," said Ramón, smiling enigmatically.

"The people think you're something superhuman."

"Your soldiers think the same of you."

"Ah, me! That's because I know how to command them. As a pair of gods, we are an amusing couple, don't you think? Although –" and Cipriano straightened his dark, black-bearded, ironic face sternly: "although," he repeated, "you are more godly than anything else I know in the world. Ramón, I kiss your hand."

And quickly, before the other had realised, the general in his uniform had lifted the hand of the silent, abstracted Ramón and had kissed the fingers with a passionate reverence.

Ramón looked up into the eyes of his friend, but did not speak. Then the two men rose, and silently embraced, breast to breast.

Kate noticed more soldiers about the village. When she went to the post office, she saw the men in their cotton uniforms lying about the wide doorway of the barracks. There must have been fifty or more. Yet they were very rarely seen in the streets. They seemed to be kept in reserve. After dark there were patrols of horse-soldiers through the village. The inhabitants were requested to be indoors by ten o'clock.

Altogether there was an air of excitement and mystery, as if another revolution were brewing. The church, she knew, was closed. The old priest had preached against the hymns and worked himself into a great rage. Now his life was threatened. Continually men were sending word by the old woman who served the priest in the house by the church, that the next time his reverence opened his mouth, church or not church, they would shoot him. So he closed the church, and there was no mass on Sunday. This put the village into a great state, chiefly of rage. Practically all the people who came over the lake on

Sundays went in to mass in Chapala church. The great door stood open all day. The men, as they went to and fro from the lake to the market, lifted their great hats passing the front of the church. All day long people were kneeling there in the aisle or among the benches, the men kneeling erect, their big hats down by their knees, their curious tall-shaped heads with thick black hair slightly bent; the women hooded in their dark rebozos spreading their elbows on the bench as they kneeled with clasped hands. At the early mass the church was packed with a solid throng of peasants, there was music of violins and cellos, and a choir of men's voices, solid, powerful, moving, in the gallery behind.

The people had need of worship. And yet it was hardly worship, as they kneeled there. It was a kind of numbness in the house of God. A sort of arrest. And as men and women streamed out from church, there was a curious numbed look on their faces. They had need of worship. They had need of the church. They had need of something to kneel before, something stately in their lives. Coming from their little reed hovels, living in the animal-like little squalor of their days, there was something relieving and soothing about the big, lofty church, its silence, its images, its strange, dead dignity.

But it was a dead interior. The church was pleasant enough, all whitewashed, and decorated with grey scroll-work decorations. Very plain, a trifle vulgar with the grey stencilling and whitewash everywhere. The windows were high, and many, the place was full of light. Something like a school room. But its proportions were none the less dignified, and there was a sense of dead, whitewashed nobility in the lofty arches and the rounded vaults of the roof.

Curious, the sense of deadness inside nearly all Mexican churches; much more so than in the churches of Italy. Whether overloaded with decoration, or only whitewashed and stencilled like the clean, airy church of Chapala, there was a sense of barrenness about them all. As if the spirit of God had never descended upon them. Which was curious, when the kneeling congregation seemed so dumb and humble before the mysteries. But it was true, as Don Ramón said, there was a gulf between the god of Christianity and these people. They worshipped dumbly, in a numb fashion. Worship they must. Yet the feeling did not flow. They were pagans forever nipped in the bud.

The month of Maria had gone by, the blue and white ribbons were all taken down, the palm-trees in pots were removed from the aisle, tiny little girls in white dresses and little crowns of flowers no longer came with a handful of flowers, at evening. The month of Maria was ended, the day of Corpus Christi was gone. There had been the high mass of this great day, and the church full to the doors with kneeling peons, from dawn till midday. There had been the feeble little procession of children within the church, because the government no longer allowed religious processions out of doors. For the Church was nothing if not political in its activities. And then, the doors had been closed.

Not to open again, even on Sunday. The consternation was great. As it happened, it was a big market. Much fruit and stuff had come over the lake, from the south, from even as far as Colima. There were piles of fruit, and men with lacas, wooden bowls, and women with glazed pottery. And at the same time, there were men crouching in guard over twenty centavos' worth of chilis and tropical plums, piled in tiny pyramids, two centavos' worth, and five centavos' worth, on the roadway. The much and the little.

It was a big market, with the much and the little of the Indians. And everybody in a state of consternation. The church doors were shut and locked. The people could neither hear mass nor go to confess. It was as if they could not change their dirty clothes of the week for the snow-white which they put on on Sundays. It was as if they could not escape the dirt of the week of work behind. They must go on with the old dirt upon them. No mass, and no confession.

Everyone was talking, but in low tones. Every man was glancing nervously over his shoulders. The vendors squatting on the causeway crouched tight, as if making themselves low and small, squatting on their haunches with their knees up to their shoulders, like the old Aztec figures. Soldiers in twos and threes were standing everywhere.

At about eleven o'clock a group of men appeared in the plaza wearing white sarapes, poncho-fashion, their heads through the hole in the middle. White sarapes with brilliantly coloured borders and fringe, and little flame-like flowers on the shoulders. They moved in a little throng across the plaza and down the short road to the space before the church, their white blankets with the gaudy fringe swinging to their soft tread, their white cotton trousers bound at the ankle above coloured [guaraches]. And at the centre of the group, tall, stately, in a big hat and a sarape of white with blue and black at the neck, was Don Ramón. On either side of the group went six soldiers.

Instantly, and in silence, the whole plaza was on its feet, the people in a great silent body were flooding down towards the lake, towards the church. The men in white sarapes passed through the broken iron gates into the open space of the church-front, the soldiers mounted guard at the two gateways. There was only a low wall around the church precincts. Outside this stood the mass of people, under the trees, by the tall palm-trunks, crowding round the standing motor-cars that had brought people from the city for Sunday, crowding round the cantina where drinks were sold, crowding the open-air food place, a mass of big hats and black rebozos in the spangled shadow. Behind them, the pallor of the lake through the fronds of pepper-trees.

Within the enclosure, in front of the big church-door, the men in white sarapes opened and formed a half moon. They had all taken off their hats. At the centre, Don Ramón. And in front of him, in a straight black cassock, the young assistant priest: the one black blotch in the fair, strange figures of the men. The crescent of black heads and dark faces remained unmoved.

A guitar began to strum quietly. The young priest, with his dark, wooden, stupid-looking face, took a step forward, and in the high, unnatural voice the people knew so well from church, he began to intone:

> *Despedida! Despedida!*
>
> Farewell! Farewell! The last of my days in Mexico has come.
>
> Farewell! Farewell! my people. It is the God Almighty calls me home.
>
> Back to my Father's house, back to my home in heaven, as fire goes up to its home in the sky, I go.
>
> I am Jesus, going home. And my mother, the most pure Mary, with me goes too.
>
> And my saints, the saints of heaven, will follow me, follow me home. Saint Francis and Saint Anthony, Saint Joaquin and Saint Anna, all my faithful ones. With me, Jesus of the Heart, Jesus of Nazareth, Jesus of Succour, and the Purísima, they go home.
>
> We go home to my Father, Almighty God, who is lonely, waiting for us.
>
> Because he has sent his Son, the God Quetzalcoatl, to be God in Mexico.
>
> And the wife and the cousins of Quetzalcoatl have started out on the long

Long way between heaven and Mexico,

To be gods in Mexico.

Farewell! Farewell! I take your sorrows to my Father, Almighty God,

All your tears and your failure I take to lay before God in heaven.

Now Quetzalcoatl is come, with one hand reaching to heaven, and one hand reaching to hell, to speak to the Mexicans.

The priest was silent, standing with bent head, a small, straight, black figure. Behind him the immovable semi-circle of dark-faced men in white and brilliant-edged sarapes.

Some women in the crowd began to cry the lamentation – "Ay-ee! Ay-ee!"

Two men stepped from the edges of the semi-circle, with guitars, and went forward and stood in the gateway between the soldiers, facing the multitude. In the multitude, the men were now all bare-headed. Then the two men lifted their naked arms, and began to play.

Do you hear the words of Jesus, *Despedida! Despedida!*

Do you hear the words of Jesus, bidding you farewell?

These again are the words of Jesus, we sing them over again to you:

Despedida! Despedida! –

And they repeated the chant the priest had sung.

These men were trained singers whom Don Ramón had found in low-class dives in Mexico City, men with magnificent voices, reduced to poverty during the troubled times, and with no way of earning a living save by singing in low-class drinking saloons. They sang the priest's chant in ringing, trumpet voices, every word ringing out to stamp an indelible impression on the soul.

The peons in front of the crowd outside kneeled down. In a moment the whole throng was kneeling in silence.

Then the young priest in his black cassock kneeled in front of Don Ramón, and gave him the great key of the church. Don Ramón silently unlocked the doors, and threw them wide. It was like opening a cavern. The church was quite dark, save for the small, dusky glimmering of little groups of candles, away back in the darkness.

The crowd kneeling outside murmured, clasped their hands and crossed themselves. The soldiers mounted guard. Don Ramón entered the church, followed by the priest and the men wearing white, brilliant-fringed sarapes.

There was a deathly silence. Then an approach of candles in the dark.

The priest emerged bearing aloft a crucifix, with a blood-stained image of Christ. Followed Don Ramón, naked to the waist, his sarape over one shoulder, carrying one end of the famous bier whereon lies the dead Christ of Holy Week. The other end of the bier was carried by a tall, dark man, naked to the waist. The crowd murmured as if in fear and doubt, crossed themselves, and some flung their arms apart, and so remained, arms extended.

After the bier of the Dead Christ, a slow procession of men naked to the waist carrying litter after litter. On the first, the wooden image of the Saviour of the Heart with outstretched hands, the well-known figure from the side altar. Then the second image of the Saviour, Jesus of Nazareth with crown of thorns. Then the Virgin in her blue mantle and golden crown. Then the brown Saint Anthony with a child in his arms. Then Saint Francis looking strangely at a cross in his hand. Then Saint Anna. And lastly Saint Joaquin.

The brown-skinned men emerged in the sunlight. The bell was slowly tolling. Soldiers had made a way through the crowd. The images glittered in the sun, the glass case of the bier of the dead Christ, a life-size, life-like figure, flashed ahead from the shoulders of the two powerful men. The strange procession made its silent way through the kneeling, moaning crowd. Some women cried aloud, crying: "*Purísima, Purísima,* don't leave us!", and the men murmured and murmured: "*Señor! Señor!*", in a kind of anguish.

After the images came the last of the men of Quetzalcoatl, carrying the musical instruments, the guitars, the violins, the curious old harp.

The procession went slowly down the sand to the water's edge, where soldiers stood guarding the boats. The naked shoulders of men shone soft and brown in the sun, the coloured fringe of the folded sarapes swung behind as the men walked, the images rocked and fluttered, the great glass case went steadily. Jesus in a red silk robe, Jesus in a white, Mary in blue and white satin fluttered in a little wind. But the Saints were painted.

The priest, a slim black figure staggering with a heavy crucifix, slowly lowered his cross into the first boat, climbed in, then sat down and raised the crucifix again. The Crucified Jesus, all caked with gore, turned towards the land. Two men pushed off the boat, and the crucifix was slowly rowing away on the pale, smooth, sun-blenched lake.

Don Ramón came down to the water's edge, with the great bier of the dead Christ. He and his fellow-bearer waded slowly out to a black canoe, a big, native boat. Men in the black canoe took the ends of the bier. The glass case was glittering rather tawdrily within the boat. With long poles the boatmen pushed off from the shore. Don Ramón slipped on his sarape and put on his hat, sitting in the bow. The black canoe was rowing swiftly across the blenched water.

One after another, swiftly, the images were placed in boats, the boats pushed off, and the slow, irregular procession continued in file across the surface of the lake, yet rowing swiftly. They were steering towards the Island of Scorpions, a little islet with a few trees and bushes plainly visible not far away in the lake, at a distance of an hour's row. The tall crucifix led the way on the smooth water, heaving like a mast to the pull of the oars. Followed the black canoe with the glass case. Then the boats with the other images, the well-known, beloved images of the village, standing erect and small as the boats diminished on the surface of the water.

The great mass of the people had flooded down the shore to the water's edge. There they stood, the soldiers on guard preventing any from wading out to the boats anchored at a little distance from the shore. Soldiers embarked in two motor-boats, and making a wide detour, took up guard away on the right and on the left of the slow convoy of the procession, as they steered for the Isle of the Alacrans.

While on the shore stood the men of the lake, watching with a fixed, Indian look as the boats got smaller and smaller, sometimes shaking their heads and speaking in low tones together, then again fixing their eyes on the dots of the boats. The boats grew rapidly smaller. The people, with a dumb kind of patience, sat down on the sands, waiting. The bell tolled slowly all the time. Soldiers guarded the closed door of the church. And people again began to buy ice slush from the ice-cream man, and water-melons from the great pile of huge, dark-green globes. In silence a woman bought a melon, returned to her place, smashed the melon open on a stone, and broke it into pieces for her children. In silence the men sprinkled salt on the thick slices of cucumber sold by the woman under the tree. They were all watching, and murmuring among themselves.

The boats were no longer visible, they must have landed. The crowd on the shore watched intently. There was an exclamation as a thin thread of smoke mounted in the air. The bells of the church suddenly clashed. And from the low end of the island out in the lake rose a ragged, orange-reddish flame, with a fringe of bluish invisibility and of smoke. The people were all on their feet again, the men crying in blind, strange voices *Señor! Señor!* the women throwing their hands to heaven and murmuring, moaning *Santísima! Santísima! Santísima!*

It was noon, and a hot day. The flame and the smoke melted as if by miracle in the hot air. The opposite side of the lake, through the filmy air, looked brown and changeless. A cloud was rising from the south-west, from behind the dry mountains beyond the lake, like a vast white tail, like the great white fleecy tail of some squirrel that had just dived behind the mountains. This tail was fleecing up towards the sun in the zenith, straight towards the sun. And before the fire had yet burned out, a delicate film of shadow was over the earth-white lake. Low on the stony end of the Isle of Scorpions fire still made a reddish mark on the air, and smoke filmed up. But it was getting less and less, less and less.

Jesus, and his mother, and the saints were gone, and Chapala was empty of God. Lost, and deprived of speech, the people drifted away to their mid-day meal.

XII

THE AFTERNOONS WHEN RAIN DID NOT COME were very hot. Kate took an old Ford car and went out to Las Yemas. She wanted to see Don Ramón and tell him she was in sympathy.

Arrived at the house, which looked shut up, she asked for Doña Carlota. Two men, mozos, were there in the silent courtyard. The patrona was away: she had returned to Mexico with the boys. Don Ramón, however, was at home. Kate thought he too must be preparing to leave, as everything seemed so shut and so silent, lower windows all shuttered, doors closed. Only two upper windows open.

The mozo looked at her strangely, as if wondering why she had come. The chauffeur of her car, who had been speaking with the other mozo in the courtyard of the hacienda, came edging towards her at the same moment as Don Ramón opened the door and appeared on the threshold. He wore peon's dress, but of fine white linen, and a heavy cartridge belt.

"Ah, Mrs. Burns! This is a very great pleasure!"

Kate thought, however, he wasn't very cordial. He seemed abstracted.

"*Patrón! Patrón!*" said the low voice of the chauffeur, as he edged nearer.

"What do you want?" asked Don Ramón, turning to him quickly.

"Am I to stay?" asked the man, in a low voice.

"Yes."

"*Patrón,* I am not armed. *Patrón!*"

"Good! Go to the village and get your arms, then come back."

"I will go, *Patrón.*"

The man saluted and turned away. In another minute the sound of a Ford's engine rattled the air. In contrast the hacienda seemed very still. The wind-mill that was spinning in the wind, drawing up water, made no sound. The peons had not yet come in from the fields, where they were planting maize, three grains in each little hole. The two mozos, who both, she noticed, wore cartridge belts, were at the gateway peering down the road after the departing automobile.

"Why does he want arms?" asked Kate.

"Oh, they're afraid of bandits again. It is an epidemic."

"But *are* there bandits?"

"They say so. – It is just rogues and scoundrels who get into gangs and take any opportunity to way-lay a man if they think he has money, or capture him if they think a ransom will be paid."

"But where do they live? In the hills?"

"In the hills? No! What would they eat and drink in the hills? They live in the villages, Ajijic, San Pedro, like other people."

"It seems horrid."

She went as usual through to the inner patio, where was a basin with a few blue water-lilies. She noticed the big doors to the lake were shut. That was strange. They had always been open before, giving a lovely glimpse through a wide tunnel-archway of the mango-grove and the lake. Now the patio was shut in. Don Ramón closed the great door to the entrance courtyard, by which they had entered, and the two climbed the wide brick steps to the terrace. There Don Ramón offered her a chair, and clapped his hands for a maid. Kate sat down, and saw between the thick mango-trees the ruffled, pale-brown lake, the dark mountains of the opposite shore, above which lay a heavy but distant black cloud, in which lightning flapped suddenly and uneasily. The wind was strong and cool. No servant appeared.

"I am sorry Doña Carlota isn't here," said Kate. "When did she leave?"

"A week – ten days ago."

"And are you leaving too?"

"Not immediately."

"Excuse my coming uninvited. I did so want to tell you how wonderful I thought it was, Sunday. That seemed to me real heroism." – She seemed almost apologetic to him.

"Heroism?" he smiled – "I don't think there was much danger."

"No, not that kind of heroism. No –" she said earnestly. "I don't mean the heroism that faces death. I mean the heroism of – of *men* –"

When she thought of the scene at the church, she was very much moved, moved with an emotion that she found almost irksome. She felt reverence for Don Ramón, and the men in white sarapes.

Don Ramón glanced at her keenly.

"The man who stands between us and danger," he said, "is General Viedma. It is he who assumes the greatest responsibility."

"Perhaps," said Kate, slowly. Then she added, looking up at him with a hesitating glance: "But I think it is a wonderful thing that men should be doing this. – I call it heroism." Her voice was small and abashed.

Don Ramón, sitting very still, looked at her steadily and inscrutably.

"Will you join us?" he asked.

Kate looked down at her hands. She was afraid, and troubled. Then she lifted her eyes to the dark, immovable face of the man looming opposite her.

"I will if I am not afraid," she said, again looking down at her hands.

"We are all a little afraid," he said, smiling slightly. "But fear is smaller than the other feelings."

Looking at his eyes, she saw his eyes were not afraid. They were dark, and proud, there was a depth in them that went deeper than fear. As he sat, he put the tips of his slim brown fingers together, holding his hands in front of him, as if completing some circuit. She had noticed the gesture before.

"What should I do," she said, "if I joined you? I mean, how can I join you?" Again he turned to look at her. And this time she was sure that between his brows was anger. Anger like the blow of a hammer between his brows. And his body slack, inert. Only the curious touching of his finger-tips.

He seemed, also, to be listening to something else. His body so inert.

"What would you do?" he replied. "For my part, I should only ask you to come to church, next Sunday, at eight o'clock in the morning."

"Will the church be opened then?"

Don Ramón nodded. He was listening.

"But," faltered Kate, "what will be happening? I thought the church was closed for ever, now that the images –"

Before she could answer Don Ramón had sprung up like a great cat and slammed to a large iron door at the top of the staircase leading from the patio, shooting two heavy iron bars.

"Please go into that room!" he said to her, pointing to a dark doorway with one hand while the other hand was at his hip drawing a steel revolver.

Kate now heard the shot of a pistol from the entrance courtyard, and a man shrieking in hysterics: "*Patrón! Patrón! Patrón!*" Then two more shots and a bubble of silence. Ramón had gone to the end of the terrace and with long, cat-like leaps was springing up the narrow stairs that led to the roof. Kate, from the doorway where she stood, heard an explosion and a loud hiss. She saw something swish up past the dark mango trees. A rocket burst in the afternoon, cloudy sky, exploding in the air with noise of shots, and with bits of flame and puffs of smoke after each detonation in the heavens.

"*Holá!* Friends!" She heard the angry, ironic voice of Don Ramón from the roof above. Such anger that it was almost laughing.

A subdued menace of voices came from the invisible courtyard, and shots.

Kate did not know what to do. Again, the casual sound of shots in the afternoon, but this time from above; and again a muffled shout from the outer courtyard. Kate wanted to run far, far away. But she could not. She could not enter the dark room he had indicated. So, trembling, she hurriedly climbed the narrow steps up to the roof, the azotea. All seemed quiet there.

The roof was flat, but irregular. It had a low wall round it, and at each corner a small tower. Trembling, hesitating, she went forward. She had just come into sight of the open gates of the entrance courtyard, and the black huts on the slope just outside, where all seemed quiet, the country all quiet, when something gave a slight smack and bits of plaster flew into her face and hair. Speechless with terror she ran back to the top of the steps, where there was a little tower place, and a stone seat, and a high iron gate that stood open. She sank trembling on to the seat. Looking down the narrow brick stairway, where only one person could come at a time, everything seemed quiet. She thought she would wait till the trouble passed.

The roof was peaceful in sunlight. Trembling in her retreat like a rabbit in her hole, she could look across the roof and see the figure [of] Don Ramón in one of the towers, aiming carefully through a loop-hole. She could not see his face, but his figure stood perfectly motion-less, one arm bent, apparently pointing the revolver at the slit of the loop-hole. He had thrown off his white blouse, so that the white should not show through the embrasure, and stood there in the shadow of the turret, dusky in his brown skin, his cartridge belt heavy above his white, loose pants, his dark head looking intently down-wards.

The sun was shining yellow, the clouds had shifted. Kate saw the mountains peaceful in the afternoon light, the fleece of young green faint and beautiful, now that the rains had started. Don Ramón, she knew, had a good position. He commanded the great door of the house, and also the wide doors which led through from the entrance courtyard to the garden in front of the house, towards the lake. Kate knew these doors were shut: they had been all closed when she arrived. And she knew the big doors leading to the lake were fast. She only wondered what had become of the two mozos, and if the one whose shriek she had heard was dead. She wanted to know. That was why she had been advancing towards the parapet.

Occasionally there was a spatter of lead and the mild sound of shots. Occasionally Don Ramón fired from his vantage place. He stood perfectly still. Kate could not see his face, only part of his back: the splendid brown shoulders with brown, soft, fine skin, the beautiful black head with thick hair, the slant of the cartridge belt above his loins, and the wide, floppy cotton trousers. He had not seen her. Evidently he did not know she was there. That made her feel lonely, but she was also glad. She didn't want him to be aware of her.

She felt it wasn't a very serious business. The afternoon was so still. The house was well barricaded. And soldiers would come from the village. She need only wait a little while. But she started as Don Ramón fired again. Every time he fired she started, it seemed so near.

Suddenly she gave a piercing shriek and in one leap was out of her retreat. She had seen a black head at the bottom of the stairs. Before she knew where she was she was out on the roof, and Don Ramón was jumping past her like a great cat. At the same moment the man sprang from the stairs on to the roof, crash into Don Ramón. A revolver went off, two men were on the floor. But even falling Don Ramón had dropped his revolver and seized the clothing of the other fellow, bringing him down with a crash. His hands seemed to run up the other fellow's body, to the wrist that still held a revolver. This revolver also went off, but Don Ramón had got the wrist. A redness of blood appeared on the white cotton clothing as the two men sprawled on the floor, writhing and struggling.

Don Ramón shouted something in Spanish. Kate, in perfect horror, was oblivious, watching. Ramón had the other, smaller man by the wrist and by the hair. The bandit had his teeth in Ramón's naked arm, and was struggling, flourishing his loose arm, to draw his knife. His ghastly eyes, with his teeth fixed in the other man's arm, were too horrible. Kate was afraid the loose arm might get the revolver on the floor. In horror she ran and picked up the weapon. As she did so her heart stood still, for the bandit had succeeded, with devilish cunning, in wrenching Ramón's own knife out of its sheath. The man seemed like a devil to her. He could not get any play with his left arm, but he gave a feeble blow with the knife, sideways, into Ramón's naked back.

Kate ran forward to prevent it. As she did so she saw another head emerge in the stairway. The hand that held the revolver was tense. She fired straight in front of her, twice. A black, hairy head came pitching at her. She recoiled in horror. There was red among the hair. The man fell, and twitched horribly, face down, his buttocks humped up. Kate looked at Don Ramón and saw him, with an absolutely blank face, striking the other man in the throat with the dagger, once, twice, thrice, while blood spurted and there was a noise something like a soda syphon. Then Ramón, who still held his enemy by the hair, watched him, watched the livid, distorted face with the ghastly eyes in which the ferocity seemed to freeze.

Then, without letting go of the man's hair, he cautiously looked up. To see the second man, his black hair matted with blood, and blood running into his dazed eyes, slowly rising to his knees. It was the strangest face in the world: the high sloping head with the thick hair all bloody, blood trickling down the narrow, corrugated dark brow and running along the eye-brows above the dazed, black, numbed eyes, in which ferocity seemed to have merged into a black, numb wonder, which in turn was merging into cunning again, on the way back to ferocity. It was a long, thin, handsome face, with a sparse black moustache under which showed longish teeth, and the absolute living night of those numbed, wide eyes staring.

And instantly Ramón had let go the hair of his victim, whose head dropped sideways with a ghastly, gaping red throat, and had risen to a crouching position. The second man had already drawn his knife. So the two crouched for a moment, the one on his knees, Ramón squatting. The wounded man reared up a little. And instantly, Ramón's knife flashed in the air as he threw it. It went deep in the man's abdomen. The wounded young bandit stood kneeling a moment as if in prayer. Then slowly he doubled up and went on his face again. Ramón, his face still perfectly abstract, his black eyes glittering with acute, almost supernatural attention, rose slowly to his feet. Blood was running down his left arm, down his back, and his side. His white drawers were red with blood below the belt, and there was a red stain all down. But he paid no attention. He stepped quickly across, coolly took the fallen man's knife from his hand, lifted the chin, and plunged the knife into the throat. There was another convulsion.

But Ramón only wiped the knife on the man's back, on the grey workman's blouse, and put it into his own sheath. Then he stepped quickly across the blood on the azotea, and picked up his revolver, examined it, and re-loaded it, standing as he did so at the top of the stairs. When he had finished he glanced round at Kate.

She still stood petrified beside the central chimney-flue, holding the revolver, and turning aside her face so as not to see the occasional hideous bunched-up twitch of the second man, or the ghastly sprawling of the first man with his evil face fixed and his awful throat still running blood into the dark sea of blood in which his head lay. Occasionally a faint rattling, bubbling sound still came from the second man, a mechanical, shocking noise.

She felt Don Ramón's keen eyes on her face, and looked back at him. But she could not bear the keen, black, inhuman look. Don Ramón's face seemed roundish, and empty of any feeling at all.

"Is he dead?" she asked, pointing to the second man.

"Oh yes. He is dead."

The voice came thin and strange, and, Kate felt, cruel.

"It is fortunate," said Don Ramón, in the same thin, toneless voice, "that you were here. The god of battles sent you. You hit your man, but you only grazed him and stunned him. That was enough, however."

"No, it's horrible," said Kate with sudden passion. "I shall never feel clean again. I shall never be the same again."

"Never again. No, never again. You have shot your man. – Go and put your finger in his blood, and hold up your finger to the sun, and say: *Take this life to thy life!* Go! Do it!"

"Why?" said Kate, amazed and horrified.

"It is the sacrament. Do it. It is the communion with God who is angry. They wanted to kill us for the sake of money. Offer up this blood. Only dip your finger and lift it to the sun. It is blood shed by you. Offer it to the god of anger. Do it. Do it and belong to us."

"No," said Kate, shivering.

"Isn't it good that such men are dead?"

Kate met the black eyes again, with their awful point of light. She quailed. But then her heart hardened. Ramón was right. But it was so ghastly! Must one live to this?

"You must do this to belong to us," he said, in his thin, curious voice, so strangely imperious.

And almost hypnotically she went and with her forefinger touched the bloody hair of her dead man, who lay all in a heap. Her finger-tip was red with blood. She turned to the sun, that was sinking to the edge of the cloud of the west, beyond the mountains, and lifted up her finger. The light seemed to come straight at her.

"*Take this life to thy life!*" said Don Ramón.

"*Take this life to thy life!*" she repeated, in a low, rhapsodic voice.

Because the dark soul in her, deeper and sterner than pity, knew that it should be so.

"That is good," said Don Ramón, always watching the stairs.

"Are you much hurt?" said she.

"Not much."

He was listening to the sound of a motor-car that was approaching on the uneven road.

"Go carefully," he said, "and look from that corner place, at the automobile."

She stooped and ran across the roof. The courtyard was empty, save for the dead peon who lay against a wall. A motor-car heaved in sight. It was full of soldiers. Immediately behind was a cloud of dust, of soldiers galloping. The car drove straight into the courtyard. There was no sign.

"The cowards," said Don Ramón, "sent up these two so that they could all escape from the courtyard. But how did these two get in?"

He pushed over the second dead man with his foot, and looked at the long, handsome face, staring wide-eyed in death. Then he turned to Kate and said: "Stay here while I go down and unbar the door for the soldiers. I will fasten the door at the foot of these stairs, so no one can come up."

She watched him, all bloody as he was, with his revolver ready, go slowly down the stairs.

The soldiers had dismounted in the yard, the officer was banging on the door with the butt of his pistol, and calling *Don Ramón! Don Ramón! Are you there?* The horse-soldiers rode through the gate in a cloud of golden dust.

"He is coming to open the door!" cried Kate, in a high voice. She hated having to shout. The officer cupped his ear with his hand, and she had to shout louder. And as she shouted Don Ramón stepped out of the big doorway. The men saluted him, the Captain shook his hand. But Don Ramón was creamy pale, and when he turned his back, there was blood from his shoulder to his heels, his cotton pants red and stuck to his loins. The soldiers in their rather shoddy-looking cotton uniforms were dismounting from their horses, and wiping their brows and thick hair with coloured cotton handkerchiefs. They looked mostly quite young men, short in stature, with sun-blackened faces and devil-may-care bearing, real sons of Satan, though not ill-humoured. Some of them, with a sergeant, had turned over the body of the dead peon that lay by the wall, and Kate saw the legs of the dead man suddenly twitch. Perhaps he was not dead. She looked round with horror at the dead bodies close behind her. Supposing they were not dead! – But in the yellowing light they lay sprawled in heaps, in the blackening blood. One, her man, wore a workman's grey blouse and blue cotton trousers. He was surely dead: such a heap. He had been handsome, when he was alive, tall and full of native vigour. Now he was a heap, his black eyes glassily staring, and the thin line of black beard that framed his handsome face looking artificial. He was no longer a man, no longer handsome: just dead, and a heap. Carrion! Human carrion!

"While some become flesh that they may die and fertilise the earth."

This sentence from she knew not where came to her mind and made her heart sink almost to extinction. Had he been born and grown and become handsome, so that he might die and serve as a fertiliser? A fertiliser for other life? The handsomeness of these dark natives became repugnant to her. Even handsomeness like Don Ramón's. A heavy repugnance filled her sunken heart. And for a pure moment she wished for men who were not handsome, women who were not beautiful. People who were neither ugly nor beautiful, but really themselves. People who were not carrion when they were dead. Her husband had not been carrion. No. He looked like a man who had made a fatal mistake, and who was returning home sadder and wiser. So he looked when he was dead. Taking home with him into death a sad, heavy secret of failure, but a treasure all the same.

She sat in the corner of one of the towers and again wept bitterly.

There was no help for it, only bitter tears. Neither the gold of evening nor the red of darkening blood mattered to her any more. At this moment neither Mexico nor Ireland existed. Only bitter tears which blotted out the world and the reality of men.

She was aroused by the appearance of the Captain, followed by a woman servant and four soldiers. She hid her tears hastily, and tried to look bright. The Captain saluted. The woman-servant, hardly noticing the dead bodies, came to her and stroked her hand.

"Do you feel ill, Señora? Don Ramón says won't you come down?"

Kate rose to follow the woman. She didn't want her hand stroked. She did not want to be touched.

Don Ramón sat in a leather garden-chair in the courtyard, still in his blood and half-nakedness. He lifted his eyes as Kate came down, black eyes in which the soul had retreated very remote. And he rose from his seat, stretching out his hand that was streaked with dried blood.

"Thank you for saving my life," he said, "and forgive me for letting you stay – for not sending you back at once in your car."

It was evident he made the speech with effort, because he had it on his mind, prepared.

"But you didn't know," she said, "that this would happen."

"Yes, we knew. I was ready. The servants had run out to hide. But we had expected this attack before, and I despise false alarms. And perhaps I wanted your help. So now I must thank you very much."

His face was creamy brown, his eyes black and remote, he seemed to make the words from his lips as he stood before her.

"Wouldn't it have been better if you had soldiers to defend you?" she asked.

"I wished to try without soldiers. With your help."

"Won't you go to bed and have a doctor?" she said.

"Yes. But it is nothing. It is when the soul feels stabbed –" And he looked at her with a strange dumb pathos.

She knew that feeling too: as if her soul were stabbed. The tears that darkened the world rose to her eyes again, and she was aware of nothing for a moment.

The soldiers were carrying out the dead bodies of the men from the roof. They laid them beside the dead peon. Kate now realised that most of the horse-soldiers had ridden away. Only half a dozen remained. The courtyard was littered with horse-dung, and smelt of horse-dung and sweaty soldiers. The grey motor-car stood in the middle, by the well. Peons had come in from the fields in their soiled white garments and great floppy trousers and big hats. They came carrying hoes and mattocks, their old sarapes over one shoulder. Then a string of donkeys came trotting through the gateway, although it was not yet sunset.

The peons gathered round the dead men. Don Ramón joined them. They knew the dead men. One was a boat-man from Chapala, the other was a muleteer from Ajijic. Don Ramón took the names and all particulars, and the Captain did the same. Then the peons carried out the ghastly bodies.

"I am sure," said Don Ramón to Kate, "that you would like to go home now. The car will take you home."

"Can't I do anything for you?"

But she could see he wanted her to be gone, so she stepped into the motor-car. Outside the gates, by the white barn place under the trees, the officer in the car stopped to talk with two picketed soldiers. A bullock wagon with solid wheels, drawn by six bullocks, came slowly to a standstill beside the car, and a peon on a delicate pepper-and-salt horse skirted by under the pepper-trees. Inside the black huts it was already quite dark, for the slope was in shadow, and out of the caves of the window-holes faces peered. But children were again running around, and a woman was coming with a brand of blazing wood, to kindle a fire outside her house for the evening meal. Several fires were flapping in the breeze, under the pepper-trees and in the open earth-trodden yards round the ugly huts, which, built of big bricks of sun-dried, grey-black mud, looked almost gruesome. Little sandy pigs with short, frizzled hair came sniffing at the tires of the car. Knots of peons in their white floppy clothes stood talking casually. They had all come in from the fields. An overseer and his assistant, heavily armed, trotted the length of the lane between the huts. A man went to a hut with a wide opening in the black wall, and an old grey man standing inside. It was a sort of shop. The peon bought a drink for one centavo, and a piece of rope for three centavos.

It was evening, the same as all other evenings. The car started, and in half an hour Kate was home, to find Felipa sitting on the road by the gate in the evening light, resting, and voluble with an account of the egg-woman who wanted six centavos for an egg.

"And I said to her – I said to her, we buy them at five centavos –"

XIII

TWO DAYS LATER Viedma came to see Kate. He called at an unfortunate moment, when Kate was feeling sore. She had noticed that lately there seemed a conspiracy to get money out of her. Felipa, whom she had thought at first so honest, now came almost every day, saying: "Niña, how dear everything is here! Oranges are ten centavos each. The woman wanted twelve centavos, but I said etc. etc." Now Kate didn't care about the few centavos. But she did resent having even one centavo bullied out of her.

She realised she had made a sad mistake. In buying new boots for Felipa, and having a doctor to attend to her sore feet: in making new frocks for the girls, and giving a dress of her own to Felipa: in providing them all with money for feast days, she had spoilt them. They now only thought of what they were going to get next. Appetite was awakened, and they were quiet, heavy leeches. That was how she felt them: quiet, heavy leeches on her.

Then the lack of honour. She knew that Felipa entered into a conspiracy with her acquaintances in the village, to get a higher price than the just price out of the Niña. The ordinary townspeople, boot-makers and carters and shop-keepers, were all conveniently bolshevistic, or communistic in creed. And being bolshevistic or communistic means that you hinge your whole life on acquiring, by force, the possessions of your richer neighbour. The naked, hideous, hyaena-like struggle and tussle over possessions.

Now Kate had thought out this possessions problem long ago. She was born into the possessing class, though she was never rich. She had married an idealist whose one idea was liberty and happiness for the poor of his native land. "Give all thou hast to the poor."

She had realised that this command was specific: it was a command given to just one man. Probably he *needed* to give all he had to the poor. But she herself, who was too honestly struggling with her soul, to make life more living, was she to give her little income to these

Indians, for them to waste it in rubbish, and so reduce herself to their squalid level? No. She had to exert the upward pull, as hard as she could. It was really a passion with her, that life should *not* sink and become lower, meaner, more squalid. Truly in her heart of hearts she didn't care about money or possessing. And of one thing she was certain: she hated communism, bolshevism, because it reduced all human relationship to the sordid hyaena-tussle for the world's money. It left room for nothing else. It wasn't a question of "Give all thou hast to the poor." No. It was plain and stark: "Take all he has from the rich man." An ugly spirit. A base proposition.

Gladly she would have shared all with the poor, if they would have shared all again with her again in the same spirit. But well she knew, if she were left penniless in Chapala, she would be treated as brutally as the tree-toads which the men stoned so evilly in the trees. They would just torture her to death.

So much for the poor, once the hyaena spirit has taken possession of them.

She didn't want life to sink below a certain level. And she had realised the fallacy of theory. "Give all thou hast to the poor" is a theory, and just as much a theory is: "Take all he has from the rich man." She couldn't solve the problem of the whole of humanity. She couldn't theorise herself, because she didn't believe in it. But she could try always to lift the life around her to a little higher level.

So she had given Felipa clean dresses and aprons, had bought her proper-fitting shoes and had her sore feet attended to. She had bought cotton material, and the little girls had sewn dresses for themselves with her, had read their school-books with her, and sung songs to her.

And in return, Juana belched loudly in her face, out of a sort of self-consciousness and a curious desire to demonstrate the animal basis of life. Kate had no intention of denying the animal basis of life. But neither had she any intention of denying the passion and power of growth in the Tree of Life, its sending out great branches and boughs, unfolding leaves and blossoms, and shaping manifold fruits. Agreed, it all rose from the animal basis. But it rose.

In return, Pedra was always waiting to see what would be given to her next.

In return, Felipa was always hinting that Kate should give Juana a rebozo, or Rafael a sarape, or Pedra an excursion on the lake.

Worst of all, began this conspiracy with the woman who sold eggs and chickens, the vegetable woman, everybody, to extort a little more and a little more. Kate realised that the people didn't respect her, because she didn't fight for every centavo. They just did not respect her.

But she refused to fight for every centavo. If life was no more than a fight for centavos, better be dead. "Became flesh so that they should die and fertilise the earth." This seemed to her the last truth about these people. When Juana belched in her face, she smelt the human animal destined to become manure. These people should die, and fertilise the earth for a higher race, with greater souls.

So she felt, in the terrible reaction after the fight at Don Ramón's house. She felt she had been stabbed in her soul. The so-called bandits that had attacked the house were only a gang of ne'er-do-wells from Chapala and the neighbouring villages, egged on by the priests. Don Ramón had been warned. His peons had got wind of the intending attack. Yet nobody moved to protect him or help him. None of his servants. Nobody. He could have had soldiers for the asking. He preferred to try alone.

The emptiness of the people. They had no souls. There was no answer in them.

Again her heart fell dead in her breast, her soul felt as if it were bleeding inside her. And a great, grievous bitterness and a slow, burning desire for revenge was at the bottom of her soul.

"Felipa," she said, "have you brought my sandals from the shoe-maker?"

"No, Niña. I will go and ask him how much they are."

"Better take the money and pay for them."

Felipa took two pesos, and set off. It was a sunny morning after rain, the birds were lively. Kate was beginning to feel restored. She wanted the life of the morning, the green of the tropical leaves, the white of the perfumed oleander in the garden, the red balls of the double hibiscus hanging from the bush, the scarlet-headed birds dashing at the tub of rain-water, to drink, and the big grey humming-bird hanging before the flowers.

But no. Back came Felipa creeping, followed by a fellow holding the sandals.

"Niña! Niña!" How Kate had come to hate the sneaking call. – "Ah! Here is the man with the sandals! Look how well he has done them."

The morning went black for Kate.

"How much?" she said abruptly.

"Two pesos," replied the lout: exactly the money Felipa had taken.

Now the work was worth at most one peso. Felipa herself would have paid, probably three-quarters of a peso.

"Look!" said Kate, suddenly trembling again with anger, as she had trembled after the affair of the bandits. "This work is not worth more than one peso!"

"Oh, Señora!" said the man impudently. "The leather cost me ninety cents."

Kate knew this was a lie.

"No," she said. "That is not true."

"Everything is very dear at Chapala – everything!" – chanted Felipa.

"Ninety centavos!" repeated the man. "You must pay two pesos."

Kate gave him a peso and a half.

"Take that. It is enough. And go," she said.

"No, Señora! No, Señora! One-fifty I can't take –"

She threw him another twenty cents, and went away into her bedroom.

She knew she ought to have said to Felipa, in the beginning: "Ask the man how much he will charge to mend these sandals, and come and tell me." That was what she ought to have done. But it is hard to keep one's soul screwed down to these miserable details. The treachery was Felipa's. She should have asked without being commanded. But Felipa was in league with the fellow. And once the sandals were mended, they were not going to abate their price.

It was the second day of the month. Kate went to her table, wrote out a cheque for her month's rent, and a letter to the landlord saying she would leave the house at the end of the month. This done, she sent Felipa with the note at once. Then she sat rocking in her rocking-chair. She had at least done something final. She would clear out in three weeks' time, and leave these people to stew in their own un-pleasant gravy. Ah God, it was enough.

She sat rocking in the rocking-chair in her sala, and the day outside was black for her. "It is my own fault," she repeated to herself. "It is my own fault. I treated them as if they were on my own level, instead of defending my own level against them. I have let them swarm over me, and now I feel degraded. It is my own fault. I ought never to have let them come near. I should have kept them back, down, in their own place. I have betrayed myself."

As she sat thus musing, she saw General Viedma, in uniform, pass the window. She sprang up to escape, for she was in a common, cotton house-dress, bare-footed, wearing Indian sandals. There was, however, no escape, because he had glanced through the big open window as she sprang up startled, and, slightly startled himself, saluted her in passing. She twitched at her dress and felt her hair. She knew she looked her worst, because her eyes hurt her: the sun or the hot wind had got them. But there was no escape. He was there in the open doorway on the verandah. She recovered herself and went forward to him.

"This is the first moment I could come to see you," he said. "I went to Ramón last night."

"How is he?" she replied. "Do sit down."

He bowed, and sat in the other big looped rocking-chair, opposite her. He sat quite still, and she tried to prevent herself falling again into the uneasy rhythm of her rocker. Cipriano's face was motionless, expressionless. His mouth was closed firm under the clipped black beard, his thick hair brushed sideways over his forehead. He slowly turned his military cap on his knee.

"Ramón is well," he replied, "or almost well. He was hurt very little. We have to thank you for saving his life." The General was grave.

"I don't know," she said. "My part of it did itself by accident."

She had again started to rock in the unhappy rhythm of the chair. The sun had caught her face, it looked scorched, her eyelids looked burnt. She felt she was awful. Cipriano looked at her with his full, strange black eyes, less human than Don Ramón's. The eyes of a soldier who sees beyond human lives, counts human lives as nothing, having some further, dangerous purpose.

"You saved Ramón's life," he repeated gravely, his great, black, sombre eyes still on Kate's face, so that she felt the powerful, inhuman quality of his will. "And saving that, you saved more than my life for me."

"Why?" she asked bluntly. She wished he would cease looking at her in that inhuman way, overpowering her.

"Why? Because Ramón means more than my life to me. He creates hope for me. He gives me something at last to do. But for Ramón there would be no light in my sky, and my heart would be dead."

Kate quailed before the stress of this utterance. And she felt a tiny twinge of jealousy.

"I want you to understand this," he added, heavily.

"Why do you want me to understand it?" she replied, rocking quicker in her chair and feeling rather like a victim.

"Because you belong to us now."

"Don't I have any choice?" she laughed. She was frightened of his heavy face and his black, fixed, heavy eyes. She wanted him to laugh too.

But his soul was heavy, he didn't laugh. And the attempt died on her face.

"As I see it, you have no choice," he replied.

"But don't be so solemn about it," she laughed, her soul recoiling from his heavy black stress, "or I shall run."

But not a muscle flickered in his set face, his black eyes changed not the slightest in their black intensity.

"I don't wish to laugh," he said, with a certain dignity; looking away to the verandah where Felipa had just appeared.

"Niña!" cried Felipa. "Niña! Don Antonio says he is coming to see you."

"When?" said Kate.

"Now. He says he is coming at once."

"Go and tell him I will see him this afternoon at five o'clock."

"Ah! You won't see him now? He will be on the way. Look! He is here!"

Kate saw the stout figure of her landlord on the walk outside the window, taking off his hat and bowing low to her. She looked at him as if he were not there. Then she turned to Felipa.

"Tell him," she said coldly. And she sat rigid in her chair.

"Ah!" exclaimed Felipa, gasping. And she scuttled round to the pathway by the gate, where her low volubility could be heard, rather plaintive, to Don Antonio. To this fat landlord she was all humble. He was much more important to her than her Niña.

Don Antonio raised his cap – he wore a cloth cap, of all things, in this land of huge hats – and again bowed low from the pathway beyond the window. Kate nodded coldly. Then Felipa scuttled into the doorway again.

"He says he will come at five. – Shall I bring anything?"

"Will you drink anything, General Viedma?" asked Kate.

"Nothing," he said.

"Nothing," repeated Kate to Felipa. "And don't trouble me again."

"Very good!" retorted Felipa, drawing her black rebozo about her.

This time Viedma smiled a little, meeting Kate's angry eyes.

"Who is Don Antonio?" he asked.

She told him, adding in the same breath:

"He wants to see me because I have sent a note to tell him that I am leaving this house at the end of the month."

"You have decided to leave?"

"Yes, I want to go."

"Where will you go?"

"To New York – then to England."

"At the end of the month?"

"Before then. In three weeks' time. I must go in three weeks."

"Why *must*?"

"Oh, I have had enough. I have had enough. It is like being in a black bog, and sinking in, all the time sinking in. I must go in three weeks."

"What is like a black bog? Mexico?"

"Yes. These people. The servants. Everybody. All the people that Don Ramón is trying to do something for. Like a black bog. They are like the bottomless pit. Everything just sinks into nothingness in them. It seems to me they could swallow the universe and leave nothing to show. Ah no, I want to go, I want to go. They have nearly swallowed me already."

She now had lifted her scorched face like a mask, the laughter gone away from her. She was rocking fatally, automatically in her chair.

"That is just what we must prevent," he said.

"You can't prevent it," she cried. "I knew it when I first saw Mexico from the train – all the ruins of the things the Spaniards had put up. It is a bog, and everything sinks and at last collapses. If the United States took over Mexico, Mexico would swallow up the United States in her bottomless pit. These people are a bog, a bottomless bog, that slowly swallows everything up. – Oh, I feel there is nothing on this continent but negation, negation, negation, and evil negative gods, that swallow life back. There is nothing else. And I can't bear it."

"There is Ramón. Is he a bog?"

"I don't know."

"I know he is not a bog. And to me, Europe seemed like a white bog when I was there. It is true there are many bad people in Mexico, and many who are, as you say, like the bottomless pit. But then white people, who are so greedy and mechanical, are they any less empty and bottomless?"

"Yes, they are not so bad as these people," said Kate. "These people have absolutely no honour. They've got no centre at all. They're like a bog. – And you need not say the Spaniards and foreigners all came for money, and gave nothing in return. It seems to me they poured endless energy into the country. And the Mexicans turned it all into nothing. Look at all the Spaniards did, all the energy they put into this place. And what do the Indians do? They just negate it all again. Whatever you try to do here in this country, they will turn it into everlasting negation. And that is why I want to go. And that is why it seems to me no good trying as Don Ramón tries. It isn't any good."

There was a silence. Cipriano's face remained fixed and resistant.

"And it isn't true that these people are religious!" Kate went on, in her bitter voice of disillusion. "They are superstitious. They have to have a God because of their own hollowness, and they'd believe any foolish superstitious tale, rather than accept the responsibility for their own deeds and their own decent living. It isn't religion. It's because they have no pride as men and women that they go crawling on their knees down a church aisle, or holding up their arms for hours. They have no pride and no honour, so they like to invent gods and saints who enjoy tricks and perversions. – And whatever God Don Ramón gives them, they will turn it into superstition and a degraded sort of devilment. They only worship a vulgar sort of devil all the while, never a god."

Cipriano was silent for some time. It was evident his fear was something like Kate's own. His fear was that his own experience led to the same conclusion.

"That is all true," he said. "And for a long time it seemed to me that it was the only truth. And that was like a prison to me. But Ramón broke a hole in the wall of the prison for me, so I shall never go back. And though it is true that most of the people remain inside the prison of what you say, yet there is a way out. They may not come out. They

may die in the bog of themselves, or in the prison, whichever way you
like to put it. But since I know Ramón I know that there is a solid
pathway out of the bog, and a hole in the wall of the prison. Since I
know Ramón I know this, and I will never again change from knowing it."

"It may be," she said, rocking violently. "But I don't see it myself."

"I see," he said, "that Ramón is not a bog, in the first place. He is a
man that will never collapse, and can never collapse."

"What if the bandits had killed him?" blurted Kate.

"They did *not* kill him – You were there," replied Cipriano.

"They *nearly* did."

"They could never kill him."

"But if they did?"

"Then let me die too, and let the bottomless pit swallow Mexico
and all the Mexicans. – But those are words. No one could kill him, he
is beyond it."

"A bullet will kill him as easily as it will kill me," said Kate. "Think
if I had not happened to be there on that roof! Think of that horrible
peon who ran up those stairs. Ah, how can I forget it! There seems to
be evil at the back of one all the time, evil at the back of one. All the
mass of evil there is at the back of Don Ramón: and him with his naked
back that any mean knife or bullet can cut into. No, it's horrible."

"We will always guard him from behind," said Cipriano.

"How can we!" Her face changed suddenly. "How did those two
men get upstairs?" she asked, with sudden interest.

He smiled a slight, sardonic smile.

"There are mango trees growing near the east end of the house,
are there not, towards the lake?"

"Yes," said Kate. "I remember."

"And the balcony-room at the end of the upstairs terrace has a
lattice window which opens towards these mango trees."

"That I have not noticed."

"Yes, it has. So! If the lattice-window is open, a man who can give
a long leap can leap from a bough of the mango tree on to that
window-sill. But it is dangerous, because if he falls he falls on to those
rocks that are made into rough steps, sloping down towards the lake."

"Why was the lattice-window open?"

"Because one of the mozos opened it, some days before the attack,
and no-one noticed. The same mozo told one man. Whoever killed

Don Ramón was to get a large reward. The mozo was to share this reward. – So, the man from Ajijic, who was the mozo's brother-in-law, jumped first. Then the boatman, who had been running round to look for a way into the house, jumped too. After which the mozo himself jumped, but missed, and fell on to the rocks, breaking his leg very badly and injuring himself inside. Then apparently the soldiers came. One of the soldiers found the mozo, who thought himself dying. When the motor-car returned with the doctor and the priest, the mozo insisted on confessing there and then – and Don Ramón and the doctor both heard the confession."

"A traitor as usual," said Kate bitterly. "Have they cut the bough down?"

"They have cut the bough down."

"And did he die?"

"No, he is getting better."

"Then I hope he will be hanged."

"Yes, we shall hang him."

"How I *loathe* a traitor! But somebody would *always* be a traitor in this country."

"We will try to exterminate the creatures," said Cipriano.

"I don't *like* Don Ramón, that he has a Judas," said Kate, rocking angrily. "I *loathe* Judases, and I loathe men who are betrayed by them."

"This one will betray no more," said Cipriano.

He glanced round at the clock.

"I must go," he said. "I am going to the end of the lake, in a motor-boat. I don't know if it would please you to come too – your woman could go with you."

Kate was not in much mood for outings. Yet rather than sit and rock and do nothing, she consented. Felipa of course was in a seventh heaven, dumb with bliss.

It was a fairly large boat, with a boatman and two armed soldiers. Cipriano had his revolvers at his side. Felipa sat in the front seat. The wind was fresh, the boat rose to meet the little waves with a smack. On the right, the high, dry, mountains, just coming green, rose precipitous from the low strip of shore, that was sometimes green and fleecy with willows, then again bare. Sometimes a white church tower among trees. Sometimes natives on donkeys. Sometimes bits of ploughed fields with stone walls.

Jocotepec was hot as a lava oven. The little black houses of dry-mud bricks, with tile roofs, lined the broken, long, dilapidated streets. Sometimes a collapsed house. Blazing sun, brick pavements all worn and smashed and sun-wasted, little black walls of houses, a dog leading a blind man hither and thither over the unevenness, a bit of ruin, a trail of goats, a man on a dainty arab horse, gun behind. So, dazed, to the plaza, the great square with lousy palms and a sun-decayed church, space, sun, dilapidation, and a kind of dreariness unspeakable, in the flat-faced buildings and the broken, cobbled pavement and in the very sun itself. Men in big hats, on horse-back, trotting daintily side by side! Curious how dainty and exquisite they looked in that desert of life.

"What am I doing here?" thought Kate. "What does this place exist for, anyhow?"

But she toiled along beside a silent Cipriano, up a street of hovels that ended blind on a wild hill. A man went in front, and knocked at big doors. She was stepping into dark, grateful shade.

In the inner courtyard, or back yard, was a whole weaver's establishment. A fat one-eyed man came bowing, sending little boys to fetch little chairs. But Kate was too much attracted to sit down. There was a great heap of silky white wool, and in the black shed of the inner courtyard, all kinds of work. Two youths with flat square boards were carding the white wool into thin films, which they took off the board in filmy rolls like fine lint, and laid beside the two girls at the end of the shed. These girls stood by their wheels spinning, standing beside the running wheel, which they set going with one hand, while with the other hand they kept a long, miraculous thread of white yarn dancing at the very tip of the rapidly-revolving spool-needle, the filmy rolls of carded wool just touching the spool point and at once running out into a long, pure thread of white, which at once wound itself on the spool and another film ran in. At the other end of the shed, in the shadow of the black mud walls, two men were weaving at wooden looms, treadling one foot and then the other. They were weaving white sarapes, and one had magnificent zig-zag stripes of black, blue, and scarlet running length-wise. It was wonderful to see the man, with small bobbins of fine yarn, quickly threading in the colour of the stripes with his fingers, then weaving the white up to it. Every stitch he threaded in with his hands. Yet the work went quickly. The other man was weaving plain white, throwing the spool of yarn from side to side, between the long harp-strings of the warp, and pressing down each thread of this woof with the wooden bar, then treadling to change the long, fine threads of the warp.

They were weaving the sarapes for Don Ramón. In the shadow of the mud, the white wool looked like something mystical, especially rayed with scarlet and blue. And the work went on without ceasing, the carding, the spinning, the weaving, while the soldiers stood in the dark doorway, and the one-eyed man was showing Cipriano two finished sarapes, one all white with a fine centre of blue and black diamonds, the other white with red and blue bars. They reminded Kate of beautiful striped synagogue robes. And they were finely, beautifully woven, of delicate wool, for the one-eyed man was a master.

"White and blue and black are the colours of Quetzalcoatl," said Cipriano to Kate. "This with the colour at the middle is for the day of petition."

"And what is the one with red and blue bars for?" she asked, wondering.

"For the messengers of Huitzilopochtli," he replied.

She ate in a little fonda, while Cipriano attended to business in the barracks. The eternal hot soup, and rice cooked in grease, scraps of dead boiled meat, and a mess of little squash vegetables: always the same. And the hostess, a nice woman, running every minute with one or two more tortillas, hot from the fire. Ah it was so hot! And nothing but bottled beer to drink, because the water smelled slightly.

It was one of those bad periods when the rains seem strangled, and the air is thick with thunder, silent, ponderous thunder in the air from day to day, mixed with thick, strong sunshine. Kate often felt that between the volcanic violence under the earth, and the electric violence of the air above, it was no wonder that men were dark and incalculable. One walked a narrow level between two spheres of violent force, an upper and a nether mill-stone. The west wind seemed fresh, but it was a running mass of electricity that burned her face and her eyes and hurt the roots of her hair. She simply felt she could not live. And she looked at the dark natives with resentment. Like salamanders they seemed, full of sulphur and dormant, diabolic electricity. They did not suffer from these days. Only they seemed wicked, demonish.

It was some distance from the plaza to the shore, down the black, shattered, sun-ruined street trailing blindly. But Cipriano had got a donkey for her, with a sort of chair side-saddle, and a horse for himself, and a donkey for Felipa. As he sat there on the light, beautiful arab horse, moving with it like one flesh, and looking down at her with dark eyes, she suddenly saw how different his blood was from hers, darker, foreign as the blood of an animal or a lizard. She could almost feel the powerful yet stealthy surge of his blood, a sort of dark river softly lapping, and full of sulphur and electricity, corrosive. She shrank away from this blood-presence, which seemed almost likely to envelop her.

For the first time she felt definitely the terrible difference between his blood and her own. And he wanted their two blood-streams to meet and mingle. That was what he was after. She knew it. Pursuing her as if she were some prey that was cool and thirst-quenching to him, as cats with their sulphureous blood are fascinated by cool, watery fish. She remembered the story that he had serpent's poison in his blood, and that his bite was venomous. She felt it might easily be so. He looked down at her as he rode, with centuries of dark waiting in his eyes, and centuries of slow pertinacity. And her breast seemed to wilt. She felt that never, never could she give her blood to contact with him. As if, were she to do so, a stream of dark, corrosive effluence would enter her from him, and hurt her so much she would be destroyed. – No, the thing she had to do was to preserve her own integrity and purity. She understood why half-breeds were usually all half souled and half unnatural.

They reached the silent shore of the lake end, where the delicate fishing-nets were hung in long lines and blowing in the wind, loop after loop after loop striding above the stones and blowing delicately in the wind. The flat land was cultivated, with half-grown maize waving its flags, and some scattered willow trees soft and fleecy green coming down to the wide flat shingle where the lake gave out. A group of white-clad fishermen were holding a conclave in a dug-out hollow by a tree. They saluted and lifted their hats. And as their black eyes looked up, she saw how they were one blood with Cipriano, but how they were the death of her.

The lake stretched pale and unreal, far, far away into the invisible, with dimmed mountains on either side rising bare and abstract. Away on the shallows near at hand rode [the] white motor-boat, and three anchored sailing-boats, with their black, stiff contours. A woman was coming across the shingle with a jar of water on her shoulder, and black birds were bobbing on the pallid luminous lake. Otherwise it was just lonely.

Cipriano held up the nets while she rode under. The soldiers and the donkey driver were crossing diagonally to the water's edge. It was silent, abstract afternoon; with the wind running fresh yet electric heavy. She got down on the sands. The boatman, a tall fellow who reminded her of her dead bandit, came to carry her out to the boat. Because for some distance the lake was less than knee-deep.

"No, no!" she cried, sitting down on the sands and unlacing her white shoes. "I would rather walk."

A queer smile was on the boatman's face as he backed away.

"Ride your donkey to the boat," suggested Cipriano.

She looked across the pallid, dim-shining distance to where the white boat rode like something unreal. Then she shook her head.

"No, I'd rather walk."

So she took off her shoes and stockings, gathered her skirts above her knees, and set off blindly. The water was almost hot. The boatman was carrying the black-skirted black-scarfed Felipa on his shoulder just ahead. Behind her came the rustle of the nervous stepping of Cipriano's horse. She went blindly forward, her head dropped. And Cipriano, riding slowly behind, watched her forward-stooping figure that was as if bowed under the heavy light, and the lifting of her well-modelled white legs that shone wet, while water splashed from her feet. And it was true he wanted her. But with no blind desire. The centuries of unfulfilment and suffering behind him had given him a sort of second sight, and an eternal sort of patience. It was true he wanted her. But with no momentaneous desire. It was as if he looked through the mother-of-pearl of her flesh to her lonely, unmated, wincing soul. And it was that he wanted. Haste was no good, and violence was no good. The darkest, oldest manhood in him realised this. No rash contact would serve. His old, frustrated race-soul had learnt the bitterest lesson, of steady, doom-like patience.

He knew there must be a call and an answer. The call was in his own soul. The answer was not in hers. Violence would not help. And persuasion would not help. The answer must come from her, not at his suggestion. He must not suggest an answer. The call in him must be steady and enduring. Until such time as the answer came from her.

It might never come. That he knew. Then some-one after him would have to take up the call. For himself and his life, he called now. If there was no answer, well, he must go to the shades unanswered, as generation after generation of his people had gone. Anyhow he was a soldier.

His horse had found that it liked the water, and had started, in the oddest manner, pawing the lake rapidly as an impatient horse paws the ground, making the water fly up and splash gratefully over its legs and belly. But this splashed Cipriano too, so he lifted the reins and touched the animal with his spurs. It jumped and went half stumbling, half dancing though the water. Kate, who had reached the boat, looked round excited. But Cipriano had got his horse down to a slow walk again, it was wading uneasily through the shallows of the vast lake.

Then again it stood still, and with a rapid beating of the fore paw was sending the water splashing against its own legs and belly, till its black belly glistened wet like a crow's back. And again Cipriano lifted its head and touched it with the spurs, so that the delicate creature danced in a churn of water.

"Oh it looks so pretty! It looks so pretty when it paws the water!" cried Kate. "What does it do it for?"

"To make itself wet, I suppose," said Cipriano laughing.

A soldier came running to take the horse's bridle, and Cipriano dismounted neatly on to the side of the boat, dropping on to the seat beside Kate, who was just pulling on her shoes. The boatman deposited Felipa. The two soldiers, followed by the donkey-man, came riding through the water on the two donkeys, laughing at the joke. The soldier from Jocotepec was leading back the mare to the shore, and she kept pulling at the bridle to stand still and paw the water and splash herself, while the soldier shouted at her.

"Look! Look!" cried Felipa. "Oh I think it's so pretty."

The soldier sprang bare-foot into the saddle, and rode the horse out towards where an old woman, hardly noticeable before, was sitting in the water with brown bare shoulders emerging, ladling water from a half-gourd-shell over her matted grey head. That was the Indian manner of bathing: to sit in shallow water and ladle water over one's head with a calabash saucer. The horse splashed and danced, the old woman rose, with her rag of a chemise clinging to her – they always bathed in a chemise – and scolded in a quiet voice, while the horse again joyfully pawed the warm water. It was splashing all the handsome leather harness, but the man would make His Excellency responsible for that.

The lake end, the desert of shingle, the blowing, gauzy nets beyond, and beyond them, the black land with green maize standing, and further fleecy green trees, the broken lane leading into the trees. There was a ranch, too, a long, low black building and a cluster of black huts with red tiles, empty gardens with reed fences, clumps of banana and willow trees. All in the changeless heavy light of the afternoon, the long lake reaching into invisibility, between its mountains.

"I think the lake is beautiful here," said Kate. "One could almost live here."

"Do you know what is Ramón's idea?" he replied, looking at her with curious subtle eyes. "Later on we shall make all the land for some distance, five miles, ten miles round this little town, belong to the commune. And some the commune will divide out among the families. And some the commune will keep, and will work with hired labour of young men. And we shall establish a system something like the old Indian village system, with a war chief, and a cacique, and a peace chief. But also a chieftainess, and a woman cacique who will suffer with the women. Then the women will weave again in their houses, and spin for themselves. And the woman of peace will be chieftainess of them all. And the peace chief of the men will divide the land and be chief judge and the living Quetzalcoatl."

"You can't have a living Quetzalcoatl," she said.

"Why not? In China there is the living Buddha, when they celebrate their great man. The living Quetzalcoatl in every pueblo will be the peace chief, in whom the God lives most. Ramón is the living Quetzalcoatl of Mexico."

"And what are you?"

"I am the living Huitzilopochtli."

He looked into her eyes as he spoke, and the strange dark fluid power seemed to flow from his eyes. He neither smiled nor deprecated his words. It was evident that he felt in himself the presence of a god-power.

"Ramón is the living Quetzalcoatl," he repeated. "He is only a man, and he knows it. He has all the weaknesses of a man, and he knows that too. But the deepest root of his soul goes down to God, and he rises from God, and he is the living Quetzalcoatl."

Kate did not answer for some time.

"I am rather mistrustful of men being like gods," she said.

"Not *like* gods. In so far as our deepest soul goes down to God, and takes its source in God, we *are* gods. I am the living Huitzilopochtli, the god of war. The old Huitzilopochtli was monstrous. I am a man, so I shall not be monstrous. I am only a man. And at the same time I am the living Huitzilopochtli."

He watched her with subtle eyes, frank, and yet frightening. Her heart quailed before the profound, dark male in him.

"And you," he said, "are you not rooted in God also? Does not your soul go deep down, as deep as God? Does not the tree of your body have its roots in God?"

"But I am only a woman."

"Does not your body and your being rise like a tree that is rooted in God? You will not dare to deny it."

"That does not make me a goddess."

"Yes. That makes you the living Malinchi, the white goddess, mother of rain. You are the living Malinchi, and nowhere wants you as Mexico wants you. And no man wants you as I want you. Because it is the living Malinchi I want, not this Kate the Irishwoman who carries a British pass-port."

"You see," said Kate, "it's no use your making a living Malinchi and a goddess of me, if I don't feel a goddess or a living Malinchi. I don't feel like a white volcano goddess, no I don't. I'm just a woman, just myself."

"What does that mean?" he laughed. "Just a woman! Just yourself! If you are just yourself, and not a human theory, then your soul comes to you from the Godhead, and your soul's best blood is godly. So, in the best blood of your body you are a goddess. And you are a goddess and mother of gentle rain, which Mexico needs, not our heavy, breaking Tlaloc rain. You are Malinchi of cool water from above, for which our souls are thirsty. And I, who am the living Huitzilopochtli, shedding blood, I need you as a volcano needs snow."

Kate thought of the white-topped Peak of Orizaba, under which he had been born, and under which he had spent his boyhood.

"But you don't love me?" she said, almost scientifically, looking at him with cool and scrutinising eyes.

"To tell you the truth," he said, "I have never been able to understand that word love. I have known desire. And the white woman who adopted me for a time was a wonder-woman to me, yes, like a sort of goddess. But I knew no god in myself then. I never knew the god in myself till Ramón taught me. And now I am no longer a man desiring a woman. I am a god-man asking for the god-woman who belongs to his destiny."

"But for all that," said Kate, "there is a good deal of ordinary male desire in it, apart from high words."

His eyes looked angry, fixed on hers.

"That is true," he replied. "I am an ordinary male. But if it were no more than the ordinary male in me desiring you, I would forget you. I have my moments of desire for women, when the girl has dark eyes with far, yielding distances in them. – But I put these desires away, and forget the girl utterly."

"Perhaps you shouldn't," said Kate.

"What?"

"Forget the girl so utterly, if she attracts you."

His face turned away from her, and became remote again.

"I too used to think that. But Ramón taught me the god in me, and the god in me has its own deep, unchanging desires. So I have decided to give up the little changing desires of the man in me, to be true to the long, enduring desire of the god in me. I am learning how not to forget the god in me, and how to forget the man in me. I am the living Huitzilopochtli, and I am Cipriano Viedma. But the most of me is the living Huitzilopochtli."

"It's a hard name to remember, anyhow," said Kate.

He laughed quickly.

"Cipriano Viedma is much easier?" he asked. "I don't see why. It is just as long. You think it would be better for some brown-skinned girl to be Señora Viedma, than for you to be the wife of Huitzilopochtli? – No!" he shook his head. "I am the living Huitzilopochtli. Ramón is the living Quetzalcoatl. My destiny lies that way."

The motor-boat, with the waves behind, was running quickly along the pale water, that looked like brownish milk of fishes, as Owen said. Felipa, in the front seat, had the glazed, stupefied mask-face of the people when they are sleepy. She would soon give up, and curl on the seat. The two soldiers behind were already asleep in the bottom of the boat, two little heaps lying in contact. Human men! But so near the animal. She could understand Cipriano's insistence on his own godliness. The boatman, a tall handsome fellow, sat erect in the stern by the pulsing motor, gazing ahead under the shadow of his great hat, whose chin-ribbon fell black against his cheek. He was almost as still as an image. There was something god-like about him too, but the strange empty godliness of a pre-human being, rather than the godliness of the super-human.

Cipriano, in a white uniform and high black riding-boots, sat on the seat facing her, spreading his arms along the back of the seat, and relaxing to the motion of the boat. For an Indian, he was rather thin, his cartridge-belt sagged on his hips. His cap lay on the seat beside him, and the wind blew his thick black hair across his forehead. He was screwing up his eyes a little, because of the light that came back from the lake, and gazing at the shore without seeing anything. The white awning flapped overhead, and he lifted his hand unconsciously, holding down one of the side-flaps.

Seated thus, quite still and given to the motion of the boat, he looked good-humoured and debonair, like any other man, except for his black beard, which was unusual among his people. Yet even in repose his face had some of that demon-like resolution which frightened Kate. And she had learned to see, in the amiable Indian contours, the stealthy flow of a powerful, masterful dark blood, that was waiting darkly for the moment when it could re-gain mastery. The repose, the self-restraint, and the waiting, stealthy, devilish masterfulness.

It seemed to her that though he could communicate with her in words, in language, in ideas, this currency of all mankind, there was absolutely no communication between his blood and hers. She mistrusted and feared that dark, stealthy, tyrannous blood in him, in spite of all his words. It seemed to her he wanted to obliterate her.

And yet – if she should accept her own god-being? If she should accept herself as a goddess, in so far as her nature was rooted in God and flowering from God! If she could accept the god-woman in herself, accept herself as god-woman, and live as a god-woman, be as a god-woman! If she could dare to undertake the life of the living Malinchi, as he put it, wouldn't she dare to meet him then? Wouldn't she dare risk the terrible ordeal of blood-contact, meet the man in him with the woman in her, blood to blood?

But her soul shrank away from the thought. Oh, she wanted to be left alone, to remain alone, apart, just true to her solitary self, for the rest of her days. She had been through the great experience of womanhood, wife-hood, mother-hood. Now, at her age, she could be still for the rest of her days. Her soul could not rouse and answer any more calls. Especially the great soul-effort she would have to make, to answer this man in his overbearing demand for the god-woman in her. No no, she wanted peace.

But she could see now, at last, the possibilities. Himself, the living Huitzilopochtli. Herself, the living Malinchi. A union of the god-man in him with the god-woman in her. Whether the union took place or not, he would go forward as the god-man, the living Huitzilopochtli. He had such an immense belief in Ramón Carrasco. The living Quetzalcoatl. In spite of herself, she could not think of Ramón as the living Quetzalcoatl without being impressed. Cipriano, sitting there with his arms spread out and his white uniform crumpling up on his chest, he was a little bit absurd as the living Huitzilopochtli. Just a bit ridiculous. Until you met his eyes, as she just happened to, with the dark, unchanging resolute power in them. And then you felt another atmosphere deepen around you, in which the silent, resolute Huitzilopochtli was more real than General Viedma in his uniform.

"And does the living Quetzalcoatl find no goddess for himself?" she asked, half mocking, half earnest.

"Who knows!" he answered.

"Because Doña Carlota will never be guilty of such impiety."

He smiled slowly and shook his head, tightening his eyes.

"Who knows!" he said again. "It would be good if Ramón too found a real woman. I think it would. But we can do nothing till she appears."

"No. – I prefer your gods for that, anyhow, that they are not intended to be womanless," she said.

"No, they are not intended to be womanless," he replied smiling. "But perhaps the living Quetzalcoatl will be womanless now. Perhaps he has passed into a certain loneliness. The woman belonged to the man. Perhaps the returned Quetzalcoatl has no woman. Who knows?"

The breeze had been gradually dying. Suddenly the motor stopped dead, the waves lurched the boat. Everybody looked up, Felipa awoke.

"What is it?" asked Cipriano.

"I think we want more gasoline, Excellency," said the wide-eyed boatman, who was standing over the engine, abandoning the tiller.

The boat swung and drifted, veering round. They were towards the shore, not far from where the white tower of San Antonio rose from the trees in the near distance. And the waves drifted them and spun the boat slowly round.

"Is the water coming?" asked Cipriano.

"I believe it is, Excellency."

"The rain?" said Kate, who never quite got used to the word *water* as meaning rain.

"I think so," said Cipriano.

"Yes! Yes!" said Felipa. "The water is coming. Look!"

She pointed to a place where the black clouds were rushing up like smoke from behind the mountains, and another place farther off where great banks were rising with strange suddenness. The air seemed to be knitting together overhead. Lightning flashed in several places, and thunder muttered. Still the boat drifted, as the man pottered with the machinery. Then at last he got the motor going again, only to stop it after a minute. He rolled up his trousers and to Kate's amazement stepped over the side of the boat. Though they were quite far, comparatively, from the shore, the water was not up to his knees. So shallow was the lake. And the water always filmy, you could never look into it. He walked slowly in the water, pushing the boat before him, towards the deeper places.

"How deep is the lake further in?" asked Kate.

"There, Señora, where you see the birds with the white breasts swimming, it is eight and a half metres," said the man, pointing as he walked.

"We must make haste," said Cipriano, "if the water is coming."

"Yes, Excellency!" – And the man stepped on board, with a stride of his long, brown, handsome legs. The motor was sputtering again, the boat was travelling before the waves. A new, more chilly wind was springing up. But away ahead they could see the sprinkled white buildings of Chapala among the trees of the fore-shore, and the two white towers of the church like candles, and the small white boats laid up at the water's edge like a long row of white pigs sleeping. On the left, just inside a flat promontory, was Las Yemas rising from its dark mango-trees, the pale, primrose-yellow of the upper storey looking like sulphur above the black-green trees. The gates of the house at the end of the mango-avenue were open, you could get a glimpse of flowers and the two palm-trees rising up, and white door-arches.

Then only the black huts of the peons above the mango-trees and the bananas: peon women washing in the lake, kneeling on the stones in front of the bright green willow trees, where a small stream ran in.

"Didn't you want to land at Las Yemas?" asked Kate.

"I must go to Chapala first."

It was a race between the boat and the rain. A cool wind was spinning round in the heavens. Black clouds were piling up. But the first villas of the pueblo were already abreast.

The rain had just begun when Felipa and Kate ran through the gateway under the cuenta tree. It was about four in the afternoon. The wind hissed in the leaves, and suddenly the rain was streaming down in a white smoke of power. The water-spout from the verandah poured a great jet. Pedra, like a little demon in a pink rag of a frock, was scooting out and putting a pail under the jet. Up it splashed into her face. Juana was crouching on the ground holding a big red water-jar under a thin stream, and Carmen, the bride, was skipping excitedly back and forth along the edge of the downpour, holding her skirts back from her bare brown legs, dabbling her bare feet, and skipping away again, self-conscious still from her bridal self-consciousness. What a queer, stiff way they all had, ungraceful, yet not ugly! Their backbones too hard, too insentient, Kate thought.

In a minute Felipa had got out of her black skirt and her boots, and was splashing in the rain in her under-skirt, collecting water. Kate had to do the same. She slipped on a plain cotton frock and ran out with an umbrella, barefoot, bare-legged, into the solid white smoke of the downpour. It almost smashed her umbrella in above her head. She had to run back. Water, cool water was dancing up madly from the earth, and rushing with a smoke of speed down from heaven.

XIV

T HE BIG WINDOW of Kate's bedroom opened on to the street – or lane, for it was a dishevelled, grass-grown, rubbish-cumbered road with a ploughed field on one hand and the high wall of an orange and banana orchard on the other. The window was the west window, the one that admitted the fresh west wind. But it had to be shut at night, much to her chagrin. The nights still had their terrors, and it needed all Rafael's pistol outside her door to reassure her.

Usually, at dawn she got up and opened the big window to look out. Already silent women were going down to the lake with red, pumpkin-smooth water jars, silent little girls in their raggy rebozos were going barefoot, with smaller jars, the aguador was trotting barefoot, his two cans hanging from a pole, a man on horseback was walking behind four silent cows, and two ragged boys were distantly following a brown goat, two towsled black sheep, a hairy frizzy brown pig with three little ones. And down the damp road they all trailed silent and inconsequent, with the unspeakable dumbness of the night and the country upon them. If she did not open her window she heard no sound, save perhaps the shuffle and rustle of sheep's footsteps, or the subdued little grunt of a pig, or perhaps the low voices of two little girls resting their water-jars on her window-sill, which came down low almost to the road.

For, Kate had realised, it was the fashion in Mexico to have windows opening straight on to the pavement and reaching almost to the ground; which windows, especially on holidays when you have put flowers on the table and arranged everything like a display, you leave wide open so that the lucky passers-by can stay and feast their eyes. To stand staring in at a big open window is not rude, but almost an essential act of politeness.

Kate, however, continually thwarted Felipa's longings for a display by keeping the sala window closed and shuttered. Her bedroom window she could not keep shut.

She opened it at dawn, and looked down to the lake. The sun had come, and queer blotty shadows were on the mountains across the lake. Way down at the water's edge a woman was pouring water from a calabash bowl over a statuesque pig, dipping rapidly and assiduously: the little group seen in silhouette against the pale dun lake.

But she could not stand at her window. As if by magic appeared an old woman with a wooden dish of green chopped-up nopales, the tender leaves of the big cactus chopped up small for a vegetable, thrusting the dish at Kate, who stood there in her nightdress. And Kate bought three centavos worth, on a plate from the sala. Instantly a little girl appeared, unfolding three eggs from the corner of her ragged rebozo, and thrust them imploringly towards Kate. At five centavos! Kate bought them. She saw an old man hobbling for all he was worth, just as the sunshine flooded into the road, and she turned to flee, knowing he had a sad story for her.

At the same instant she realised the sun was on all the orange trees beyond the wall opposite, deep gold, and her heart started to a sound which is strange, frightening, and at the same time familiar from past ages in the blood of all men: the rapid, savage beating of drums, the vibration of tom-toms. She knew the sound rising in the tropical dusk at nightfall from the temples in Ceylon. She knew it pulsing from the roofs of the big houses of the pueblo Indians in Arizona, in the desert. Now, most frightening of all, she heard the rapid, summoning noise in the Mexican sunrise. A violent throbbing of two drums pulsing unevenly against one another, then slowing down, then falling into one slow, continual, monotonous note, thrum! – thrum! – thrum! – thrum! – thrum! – thrum! – like great drops of sound distilling dark and falling plumb out of the dawn on to the inner consciousness. She always felt that tom-toms resounded straight upon her solar plexus.

The sound came from the church. Beyond the orange garden directly facing her window rose three tall, handsome, shaggy palm-trees, side by side. And from the very top of each outer palm-tree, like a crest, she had looked at it often, rose the two Latin crosses that finished the church-towers. The towers themselves were not visible. The trees were exactly in front of them. And exactly from the summits of the green, huge palms, rose the two crosses. And now she saw that these crosses were enclosed in a golden ring. The original shapely iron crosses of openwork metal, dark within a glittering gold ring, in the heavy morning light.

The two drums suddenly were beating against one another once more, making the whole air of the morning throb with a summons that sounded almost sinister. Kate felt her hands flutter on her wrists, with fear.

"Niña! Niña!" cried Felipa's voice outside on the verandah. "Listen! Listen to what they are doing in the church, Niña."

She was frightened. Rafael, who lay later on his mattress outside Kate's door, on Sundays, was speaking in his deep, half-broken voice, hitching his loose pants around him. Kate went to the door and looked into Felipa's black eyes. Usually she forgot that Felipa was dark. For days she would not realise that the woman was different from herself. Till she met the black, void-black eyes with the glint of light on them. And then Kate was always startled. She realised the great blood-difference between the two of them.

Sometimes, when she caught Felipa's black, reptilian eyes unexpectedly, Kate asked herself whether it was hate she saw. Did Felipa hate her? Or was it only the difference, the unspeakable difference in blood? The formless, extraordinary blackness of Felipa's slow eyes might mean anything. Certainly there was fear, primeval fear in the black orbs that seemed not to have sight in them, yet which saw so quickly. Fear, and a certain cringing, and a certain slow, savage nonchalance, defiance. And all the time, the hopelessness that was yet not quite daunted. Not quite daunted. That was the last word.

"Eyes like the sun," said Pedra, of Kate's quick-changing, grey-gold eyes. But to Kate, Felipa's eyes were darker and more primeval than any night, black and yet living as the eyes of an unyielding reptile.

"Listen, Niña! The drums! They don't ring the bells any more for mass! Listen then!" – The drums were shuddering rapidly again. In Felipa's eyes was fear, excitement, and a lurking triumph also.

"Come and look!" said Kate, going across the room.

"Look! Look!" murmured Felipa in a hushed voice, standing in front of the window and seeming rather small, as if her soul were sinking earthwards. "The crosses inside the sun! Look! There are no more pure crosses!"

Queer her voice was! She seemed like a heap of darkness rather low at Kate's side. And the strange, reptilian quality seemed to come out of her stronger than ever.

Suddenly she turned with a brusque movement, gauche, and pattered out of the room, calling: "Look! Look Pedra! Look Juana!"

Kate went to close the window. As she did so a man in an

earth-dark sarape with blue and white stripes thrust a note at her suddenly, silently. She started back, then took the note. She was in her night-dress. The man stood plumb before the low, big window-space, static. She realised he was waiting for her to read the note.

"Will you come to the church at seven o'clock, when you hear the big drum begin to beat? R. C."

That was all. She looked at the man in the street. His black eyes were fixed on her, under the shade of his huge hat.

"Say that I will come," she answered.

He lifted his hat in silent response, and moved a few paces aside. Kate closed the street window, and began to get dressed. The tom-tom was beating a slow drop of sound in the air, unnoticeable unless you noticed it, and then, once you had heard it, occurring in your very blood. Felipa and the family were in the street, speaking a few brief, untrustful words to some man, who answered in monosyllables. Evidently this man in the striped sarape was waiting. That brief, laconic question and answer across a distance was characteristic of the people, when speaking with a stranger.

Kate put on a white dress and a yellow hat, and a long string of yellow topaz. She heard the swish of Felipa's sweeping the verandah. Then she went out into the patio. The earth was all damp with rain, the leaves were fresh and tropical thick. Felipa saw her mistress dressed.

"Ah! You are going out! Aren't you taking coffee! Wait, wait!"

There was a running of the children with cup and plate. They had got clean frocks on. Kate was just sipping her coffee when Rafael stalked into the patio with his head erect and eyes glittering. A hubbub of voices at the farther end of the house. And then a soft, slack thud in the air, seeming to leave a gap behind it, a dark gap. Thud! Thud! Thud! It was the big drum.

Kate rose at once from the coffee.

"Felipa!" she cried, "I am going to the church!"

"Ah! You are going! One moment, I am coming."

She trotted back and reappeared in a moment, wrapping her black rebozo round her, and running with short, quick steps.

Two men in earth-coloured sarapes with blue and white stripes were waiting by the gate. They followed silently behind Kate and Felipa.

"Look!" said Felipa in a hushed voice. "They are accompanying us. They are not from here. They are those of Quetzalcoatl. Look at the sarapes!"

Kate looked, though she had seen before. The men had dark sarapes with blue and white stripes across the end, and a blue and white square at the neck. They were the colours of Quetzalcoatl. The men of the district wore either black sarapes with pink and white and blue flowers, very gay: or else the big scarlet blankets with black borders.

It was Sunday morning, the sailing boats lined the water's edge. But the beach was empty: absolutely empty. All the people were in front of the church. The big drum was slowly thudding, the little drums shuddering rapidly and excitingly. Kate had her heart in her mouth as she approached the church.

There was a great throng of natives in white, with their red and their dark, flowered sarapes, and their dark heads: very few wore their hats: also many women in dark rebozos: and all silent, no hustling or shouting, waiting silent in a mass before the church. The church-yard space was almost empty. Inside, the low wall was lined with a row of men in the earth-dark sarapes with the blue and white decorations, each man of this guard holding a gun with a fixed bayonet. Two groups of the dark guard of Quetzalcoatl stood outside the gate entrance, and three lanes of guard held open way through the crowd, one lane towards the lake, one straight forward from the gateway, one towards the plaza.

"Pass!" said the soldiers of the guard at the end of the lane through the crowd, as Kate approached.

"You, no!" they said, barring the way to Felipa.

Kate walked slow and self-conscious between the dark-eyed men in their big hats and dark sarapes. She was aware of their eyes, and the gleam of the bayonets as she passed. She looked down at her feet, and stumbled. It seemed an eternal distance to the church-gate, and she felt she was going to execution.

Inside the church-gate a brilliant striped figure came to meet her. It was Cipriano, in a big hat stitched with gold, and a fine-woven sarape of stripes of white, black, scarlet, green, white, yellow, black: stripes running lengthwise. The curious stiff Indian poise and the balance of the great hat saved him from any suggestion of ridicule. A small group of men in black sarapes, with red and white and yellow stripes at the ends, stood in the centre of the church-front, with bayonets, as a sort of guard for Cipriano.

"Stand here with me a moment," said Cipriano to Kate, taking his place on the right hand side of his guard.

Kate stood there in her white dress, holding her yellow parasol, feeling afraid, feeling she had been trapped, feeling that this was death for her: a sort of death. She dropped her head and made marks on the earth with her parasol. The drums were going furiously overhead.

"If you would rather go away, go now," said Cipriano in her ear.

She looked up. The great mass of dark faces under dark hair, beneath the trees. The dark sarapes of the guard. She could not walk through it all again.

She looked towards the church. The great doors were shut. But by the doors stood two groups of men in white sarapes with the blue and black-brown borders.

Everybody was waiting. The drums overhead suddenly dropped silent, only one tom-tom kept up a slow, stressed rhythm: *dumm*-dumm! *dumm*-dumm! *dumm*-dumm! And the men in the white sarapes suddenly began to chant, in deep voices:

"Hie! Hie! Hie! Oye!! Oye!! Oye!!"

"Hie! Hie! Hie! Oye!! Oye!! Oye!!"

As they chanted the wicket-door opened in the great church-door, and a tall priest in a black cassock stepped out, carrying a black rod. The chanting suddenly stopped, only the one tom-tom continued from above its slow, thudding rhythm.

"God is One God," chanted the priest, in a high, ecclesiastical voice. And after a long pause:

"God is One God," chanted the men in the white sarapes.

The tom-tom kept on beating with insistent monotony: *thud*-thud! *thud*-thud!

Many people in the crowd began to kneel down. There was a pause. Then the high voice of the priest arose.

God is One God.
No man can see Him.
No man can speak to Him.
No man knows His Name.
He remains beyond.

The slow, slack hollowness of the great drum shattered in the air, once, twice, thrice. The kneeling people lifted wonder-struck faces. And then the men in white sarapes answered the chant:

> God is One God.
> No man can see Him.
> No man can speak to Him.
> No man knows His Name.
> He remains beyond.

And again the deep slack explosion of the great drum. After which the soldiers of the guard repeated the same words:

> God is One God.
> No man can see Him.
> No man can speak to Him.
> No man knows His Name.
> He remains beyond.

It was a loud, hoarse resonance of many men's voices, led by Cipriano.

The great drum gave one more stroke. Then there was dead silence.

The doors of the church opened, and there was a sound of music, violins, guitars, violas, and in the doorway stood Ramón, bare-headed, in his beautiful soft white sarape with the deep borders of blue and brown-black at the ends, white and blue and black diamonds intricately woven on the shoulders, the creamy fringe hanging in front of his white trousers, bound at the ankle. His bare feet were thrust into dark blue guaraches.

He lifted his naked arm, and the music stopped. Only two tom-toms had started, softly, it seemed a great way off. Ramón's face was creamy pale, almost unearthly. His wide black eyes seemed to have no expression. He seemed to be hardly a man, who would open his mouth and speak. His soul had gone deep, deeper than death, as he stood there in naked, sacred responsibility. Nothing in him moved or trembled. The black eyes seemed fixed for all time.

Then he began to sing, in song, not in chant, and in the queer, naïve, blind way of the people. But without the native plaintiveness. A full, manly, *naked* voice, so simple that it was almost anguish.

> I am Quetzalcoatl, Son of Almighty God.
> I am Quetzalcoatl, Lord of Mexico.
> Sent by Almighty God
> To be Lord of Mexico.
> I am Quetzalcoatl.

The tom-toms kept up their steady, monotonous pulse. Then the voice of the man rose again, a little harder than before.

> I am Quetzalcoatl, betrayed once in Mexico.
> I am Quetzalcoatl, from the bosom of Almighty God.
> I am not twice betrayed.
> I am the Mexican Lord.
> Hear me, Mexicans.

He waited again for the tom-toms.

> In my Father's house are many mansions.
> Out of the gates of death go many roads.
> But the Mexican road is my road.
> And the Father has given to me
> The key of the Mexican house.

He turned and went again into the dim church. The men in white sarapes followed him. The tom-toms dropped into the one slow beat.

Then came the sudden voice of Cipriano, facing the throng.

"Hear me, people. You may enter the church. The women may kneel in the benches. The men shall stand. The new God will have no men kneel."

Cipriano went with Kate to the church-door, while the soldiers of the guard of Quetzalcoatl formed a lane from the gate-way to the church-door. Kate, fascinated, looked in to the church. It was all different. The roof was dark blue with gold stars, all the vaulting and arching was blue, coming down to the white walls. Then, breast-high from the floor, the lower wall was all painted in perpendicular stripes of red and black and green and yellow. The pillars were dark green, rising to the blue roof. Two little blocks of naked wooden benches occupied the floor of the church, with a narrow lane between. But on either side, between the striped wall and the benches was a wide space of floor, for the men to stand in.

Cipriano led Kate down the church to the very front, on the left, and gave her a chair to kneel to, whilst he stood behind her. The white high altar of the church still occupied the usual place, but it had been lifted higher, and a low wooden chair, or throne, stood at the very foot of the altar itself. The rails had been taken away, and the raised space in front of the chair was clear. One tiny light hung suspended above the altar.

But in front of the niche on the right, where the Saviour had stood in his white silk robe, a low stone pillar had been erected, and on this pillar stood a great statue of dark, raw wood: a flat, archaic statue of a man with legs together and arm raised just above his brow, while from the upraised wrist, a spread eagle, much simplified, was reaching darkly into the air; and in the left hand, which was down near his thigh, the god held a serpent whose length was coiled round his leg.

This great dark statue loomed stiff like a pillar, obtruding into the space of the apse, where stood the uplifted altar.

The priest in the black cassock mounted the pulpit. The musicians in the gallery over the entrance door began to play slow, monotonous music, and suddenly the people were admitted. The church was dimmer than before the change. The throng involuntarily hesitated on the threshold, in wonder, and a strange murmur came from them.

"Men to the right and to the left. Women to the benches. Leave the centre way open," commanded the priest from the pulpit.

The men in their white clothes, with folded sarape slung over one shoulder, hesitatingly drifted to right and to left, then, scattered, went down on their knees, crossing themselves.

"Men, stand up! Men, stand up! So!" and the priest, standing erect in the pulpit, faced the image of Quetzalcoatl and lifted his right arm high, the palm of the hand flat towards heaven. It was something the attitude of the god-image, save that from the wrist of Quetzalcoatl rose the archaic eagle.

But the men in the congregation were too dense or stupefied to understand. So the men in white sarapes went among them, pulling them from their knees and pushing up the right arm. So that gradually the bulk of the men were erect, more erect still because of the strong upthrust of the hand. And for example they had on either side of the altar-space three splendid men in white sarapes, facing the Quetzal-coatl image with naked arm uplifted, revealing the naked side and the dark-blue sash round the living waist. They stood still as statues, erect and splendid in a noble gesture, faces slightly uplifted.

Kate looked at the tall forests of men with white-sleeved arms upstretched and dark hands like leaves, tall forests beside the low dark shrubs of the kneeling women, whose heads were veiled in the black [rebozos]. And her heart quivered, seeing how the new religion was to arise from the splendid animal virility of the people, instead of from humility.

The church was full of silent people. The monotonous music continued. The strange branches of the uplifted arms of the thicket of men rose against the pearly whiteness of the wall. High up, the iron-barred windows were all open, letting light into the blue vaulting of the roof. And down below, between the green pillars, crouched the black women, like low shrubs. A solid churchful of people.

The priest in the pulpit lifted his hand. The music stopped. The men in white sarapes dropped their arms suddenly. And the arms of the men in the congregation wavered.

"Lower your arms!" said the priest.

And the white sleeves of the men rustled down, the forest of dark-headed men seemed shorter. The church was still and all dim down below, the light remaining overhead, over the nave. Above the high white altar hung one spot of ruddy light.

"This is the house of God," began the priest. "That little light is the light of the presence of the Everlasting God. He is the God of all people, in all the world. All people in all the world shall cover their eyes and be silent, before the light of the Everlasting God."

A little drum was struck twice. The men in the white sarapes swung full facing the altar, lifted their faces to the Holy Light, and covered their eyes with both hands.

"Cover your faces and be silent, before the Everlasting God," said the priest, turning towards the altar and shading his eyes as he spoke.

The soldiers in earth-dark sarapes, among the congregation of men, were heard muttering commands. And gradually all the men had lifted their dark heads and covered their eyes with their hands. The kneeling women did the same. There was dead silence, only the rustling sound of the breathing of many people. Then the drum again sounded twice.

"Look up!" said the priest in the pulpit.

The people looked, and saw six tall green candles burning with a greenish light before the lofty, impressive dark image of the god Quetzalcoatl. The music of the gallery began softly to play, and in slow procession entered Don Ramón, naked except for a white breech-cloth, followed by six men in white sarapes with blue and brown-black bars. Ramón slowly went up the altar steps to the foot of the altar, turned, and faced the people, his arm uplifted in the salute of Quetzal-coatl. His six guards, three on either side of the altar, stood erect and flashed up their arms. The men in white below the altar steps, and the priest in black in the pulpit, with Cipriano and all the soldiers present in the congregation simultaneously flashed with the same movement, the salute of Quetzalcoatl. And the dazed men in the congregation, as if hypnotically, did the same. Ramón, naked save for the white breech-clout, stood there before the altar, facing the people in the grand salute, motionless, remote, the living Quetzalcoatl.

The silence of wonder was broken by a low moan, rising into a high, hysterical cry. A woman in a black dress, letting her black scarf fall back from her head, came creeping on her knees down the narrow central aisle between the women, moaning, her hands clasped in supplication before her face, working forward on her knees and moaning and crying aloud:

"Lord! Lord Jesus! Forgive him! Lord! Lord Jesus! Lord Jesus! He knows not what he is doing! Forgive Lord! Forgive! Lord! Lord Jesus of the Heart!"

It was Doña Carlota, in a religious ecstasy. There on her knees, with supplicating hands and thin white face uplifted, she worked her way, a crawling woman in black, along the brick pavement towards the altar steps. The church seemed suddenly to become dark and tense with a conflict of agony. Kate, kneeling at her chair near the altar steps, half rose to her feet. But Cipriano's hand pressed her down. The kneeling, creeping black figure emerged from the aisle and reached the foot of the altar steps. There it threw the clasped white hands aloft:

"Jesus! Saviour! Christ Jesus!" came the strange ecstatic cry of Doña Carlota. "Jesus! Jesus! Jesus! Jesus! Jesus! Jesus! Jesus! Jesus!"

Her thin black body convulsed, the cry came in a strange, convulsive, strangled sound, different each time, freezing Kate's bowels with horror. And all the time, naked before the altar, with naked arm uplifted in salute, stood Don Ramón, the living Quetzalcoatl, looking down without change or motion, his black eyes wide and inalterable, watching the woman.

Terrible convulsions took possession of the body of Doña Carlota. Then came her voice in the mysterious rhapsody of prayer, seeming to sound inside the soul of her listeners:

"Lord! Lord! This blasphemy! Forgive!

"Jesus! Jesus! God of Love! Look down! Forgive him, he knows not what he does. Forgive him! Forgive him! He knows not.

"Lord! Lord Jesus! End it now! Take him, Saviour, take him now, before he sins further, before sin takes root. Have mercy on him, and take him to Paradise, Father, Almighty God.

"Almighty God, take his life from him, and save his soul."

Her voice had gathered strength, till at the end it rang out like bronze, on the great invocation that was almost a summons:

"Almighty God, take his life from him and save his soul."

She remained with her white clasped hands upraised, and her white arms and her white face showing mystical, like white onyx, from her thin black dress. She was absolutely tense in an ecstasy of prayer. Don Ramón, naked, with upraised arm, further back, looked down at her all the time abstractedly, his black eyes changelessly watching.

A strong convulsion seized her body. She became tense again. Then another convulsion seized her. Still she recovered, and thrust up her clenched hands more intensely. A third convulsion seized her as if from below, and she fell with a moan in a little heap on the altar steps.

Without knowing, Kate had risen and run to her. Ramón dropped his arm and stood with both hands stiffly by his thighs, his impassive face watching. There was a darkness between his brows, his head dropped a little, his mouth was set in an old pain. Only his wide, dark, proud eyes watched without any change, as if from some changeless distance.

There was a little froth on Doña Carlota's discoloured mouth. Kate wiped it gently and lifted the black-garbed figure in her arms. It was all heavy and inert, the hazel eyes were staring glassily.

"We must take her out," said Kate, looking round to Cipriano.

He nodded, stepped forward and looked down at the unconscious woman. Then he slipped off his sarape, and putting it over the dreadful, pitiful figure, lifted Doña Carlota, wrapping round her the brilliant sarape, as if to hold her together. With this strange bundle in his arms, he went down the narrow aisle of the church between the kneeling women, followed by Kate. The wicket door was opened, a shaft of sunlight fell on the colours of the wasp-striped wrap, that was yellow and black and white and red and green, in equal stripes of colours that seemed almost like sounding strings.

"I am the living Quetzalcoatl!" came the low, distinct voice of Ramón.

Kate glanced round. A drum had begun rapidly, shudderingly to beat. She saw Ramón with one foot stepping forward, his right arm again uplifted. And she felt that Doña Carlota had died from fear of him.

"I am the living Quetzalcoatl!"

This, and the shudder of the drum, was the last sound she heard from the church as she stepped into the great and unreal light of the morning. It was only afterwards she heard of the rest of the ritual.

Naked I come from my Father.
Naked I come from out of the deep, having taken the far way round, from
    heaven where the angels are, and the sons of God.

With the eagle of my right hand down the farthermost sky.
With the serpent of my left hand I travelled the under-earth.
The sky is mine, in my right hand, the earth is mine, in my left.
But my heart is the heart my Father gave me, more than the heart of a
    man.

I am Quetzalcoatl, Lord of Life between earth and sky.
All things that rise from earth towards sky in the lift of living are mine.
But the heart is my Father's.

The roots are mine, down the dark, moist paths of the snake.
And the branches are mine, in the paths of the sky and the bird.
But the heart invisible belongs to my Father, the Everlasting God.

The feet of men and women are mine,
The feet and the legs and the loins, and the bowels of strength and of seed
    are mine.
The serpent of my left-hand darkness shall kiss your feet with his mouth,
And put his strength round your ankles, his fire in your legs and your
    loins, his circle of rest in your belly.
For I am Quetzalcoatl, the serpent of the earth's caress.

And I am the eagle of the sky, filling your faces with daylight
And fanning your breasts with my breath
And building my nest of peace in your bosom.
Quetzalcoatl.

This was afterwards Kate's favorite hymn among the hymns of
Quetzalcoatl. Don Ramón made it when Cipriano carried away his
wife from the church.

They carried Doña Carlota across to the hotel, and Cipriano laid
her on a bed. Then he unwrapped his sarape from round her, and
slung it over his shoulder, and returned to the church, in time to see
Ramón being invested with the sacred sarape of three colours, with a
white fringe. It was earth-coloured: and from the earth-colour rose
the blue, and beyond that the white. And the fringe was white. Then
he stepped into the wide white drawers, and two of the priests of
Quetzalcoatl bound his ankles with the cord of earth-coloured wool
mingled with gold, and tied with tassels of silver: which was for the
serpent-strength of the earth. And round his waist they put the sash of

the dark-green earth. So he sat in the chair of the altar, the clothed god.

Every year, at the coming of the rains, they would celebrate the return of Quetzalcoatl.

The priests of the earth and sky then celebrated the first brief mass of Quetzalcoatl, before the altar, and before the dark statue with its green candles of life, and before the living Quetzalcoatl.

Then they sang the song of the Welcome of Quetzalcoatl, dancing in a slow, measured step in front of the altar, teaching the people the dance-step of Quetzalcoatl. And Ramón also danced.

> We are not godless, we are not alone:
> *Quetzalcoatl has come!*
> We are not weeping, our complaint is finished:
> *Quetzalcoatl has come!*

> Deep from the earth glides out the black and golden
> Quetzalcoatl snake.
> Coiling round our ankles strong for dancing,
> Spitting earth-fire from volcanoes in our loins,
> Putting sleep as black as beauty in the secret of our bellies.

> Ask me not why my face is shining:
> *Quetzalcoatl has come!*
> Hovering round my head his sunny eagle.

> We are like trees, the tall and rustling
> Mexican men.
> *Quetzalcoatl has come!*

> We have our feet upon the dark earth.
> We have blue daylight in our hair.
> We have hearts god-given in our bosoms.
> *Quetzalcoatl has come!*

When the ceremony was over, and the drums were beating in the towers, and the people were all streaming out of the church, then on the flat roof of the church men's voices again took up the strong, manly chant of the Welcome of Quetzalcoatl. Kate heard it from the room where she sat with Doña Carlota, and even there it was impossible not to feel the exultation, the new manly strength and the joy in strength.

Inside the room, the white, unconscious face, the upturned eyes, the pitiful, horrible figure in the bed. And outside, the strong, exultant singing of men's voices, thrilling with an immense dark joy. It was as if a stone had been rolled off the lives of these dark-eyed men, and now, for the first time they came from their prison into a wide day. Never till now had Kate heard the Indians sing with a full, complete voice. Before, there had always been a suppression, or a strain. It was one of the worst things in Mexico, this sense of silence, an inward suppression that turned into devilishness. And their singing was always half held back, as if they were attempting to make it inaudible.

But now the stone was rolled away. She went to the window, from which, through the trees, she could catch a glimpse of the church-roof, of big hats and shoulders in white or in dark sarapes. And just as the old tension and pain would be coming over her heart, the Song started again:

> We are not godless, we are not alone:
> *Quetzalcoatl has come!*
> We are not weeping, our complaint is finished:
> *Quetzalcoatl has come!*

A strong, deep sound, full of joy and complete with courage. Kate stood in the window and wept with relief. The deep, magnificent male courage, the complete life-daring. It seemed as if she had been waiting all her life to hear it, and had prepared to die without ever hearing it. Now the sound was there like a strong, rich darkness in the air, the strength of the god-accepting courage of men, like an eagle slowly fanning into flight.

What did it matter that the woman lay unconscious there on the bed? What did it matter? What did it matter that she must die? Let her die! What did it matter if she made small, moaning, horrible noises, and her turned up, full eyes were ghastly? Outside, the slow, strong chant, with its undertone of joy and exultation, fanned like a dark eagle of life in the air.

They kept it up all day: either the drums, or the music, or the chanting. Sometimes it would be only the slow *thud! thud!* of a single tom-tom. Sometimes it would be a rapid, complicated rhythm of several drums. Cipriano had brought Indian drummers from the north. Then it would be the music, music of queer, savage tropical instruments, playing the same music of the Welcome to Quetzalcoatl from the church-roof. And then, suddenly, the massive chant would start again.

Any men who wished were allowed to go up on to the roof. So that by evening the whole azotea was crowded, and men were crowding in the towers, where the bells still hung, and men had even climbed up in all the trees in front of the church, to get nearer the fascinating sound. So that little by little the obstructions of silence broke down, and man after man, after singing softly, half ironically to himself, suddenly, as the chant arose again, broke into a full, released singing, exulting within himself. At nightfall the chant was heard everywhere, like a sort of laughter, out of the darkness. Fires were lit on the beach, the plaza was thronged. Motor-cars came and went. The drums throbbed and went quiet. And all the time, first here, then there, without interval rose the solid singing of men who exulted as they sang.

The lake had come to life.

And through it all, Doña Carlota lay unconscious. The doctor came, and tried remedies. The old priest came, and a little boy, with the viaticum. Don Ramón came and looked down at her silently. But nobody could tell what he felt. After a few moments he closed his eyes, turned aside, and went away.

Through it all, she remained unconscious. Two more doctors came, there was a consultation. But it had no effect. She died in the morning, before her boys could arrive from Mexico, at dawn, just as the ship-load of travellers pushed off to catch the dawn-breeze from the east, and the Chant of the Welcome of Quetzalcoatl rose again, unexpectedly, from the water.

XV

K ATE WAS USED TO GO every morning to the shore, to sit by the lake in the early light. Between the rains, the mornings came wonderfully clear, she could see every wrinkle in the great hills opposite, which were already covered with a green sheen. And the pass where the river came through to Tizapán was so plain, she felt she had walked through it. The frogs too were whirring in the morning, and the red birds looked as if they had been newly dipped in colour.

But now there was a difference. Continually, from the church towers, came the rolling of drums or tom-toms, a sound which never failed to darken the air and startle her heart. She would never have believed it possible to miss the harsh jangle of the bells, but she did miss it. Between the rapid thudding of the drums the air had a softer, more velvety silence, unshattered by metal.

They took Doña Carlota to Guadalajara to be buried, and on that day the drums were silent. Don Ramón, in conventional black, and his boys attended the funeral, and Cipriano was there in uniform.

"This is my last concession to the world," he said to Cipriano when the ceremony was over, and he sat in the General's quarters in the Palace.

He sent for the boys, who had accompanied him to Cipriano's place. They looked odd little shoots in their black suits. They were both round-faced, and creamy brown in complexion, and both had a touch of fairness. The elder, a lad of fourteen with bare knees under his short black breeches, resembled his father more than his mother. But his hair was softer, finer, more fluffy than his father's, with a hint of brown, and his dark eyes had not the inky Indian blackness. He was now sulky and awkward, and kept his head ducked.

The younger boy had the fluffy, upstanding brown hair of his mother, and her innocent hazel eyes. He was evidently prepared to accept somebody's guidance all his life: probably that of Francisco, his elder brother.

Don Ramón sat in a deep arm-chair, with his hands clenched on his knees. The boys stood by Cipriano's writing-table, side by side.

"What do you want to do, my sons?" he asked them. "You know your mother left all her fortune in trust for you, under my charge. What do you want to do? Will you go back to Mexico to school, and live with your Aunt Margarita? Or would you like to come with me to Las Yemas?"

The elder boy, with pale angry lips, looking at his father's shirt-front and not at his face, his hair seeming to fluff up with indignation, asked:

"Papa! Is it true that you want to found a new religion?"

"Yes, my boy."

"Is it true you call yourself the living Quetzalcoatl?"

"That is true."

There was a dead silence. The boy was white with rage, and the little lad was looking up to him sympathetically.

"It is very ridiculous," said Francisco. "I don't know how I can live under such a ridicule."

"You can change your name if you find it too difficult. You can leave out the Carrasco, and call yourself only Gutierrez de Lara. That will please your mother's family."

"You killed our mother," blurted the boy.

"How?" said Don Ramón.

But there came no answer, and he did not insist.

The younger boy, Pedro, was looking up at the elder as if to get his cue. His eyes were already swimming with tears. But Francisco's face was set with anger.

"Yes, Papa," said Pedro. "They say that you killed our mother. They say that you are in mortal sin. They say you are Satan, and that you have demons round you."

The little boy urged all these things in a blind, naïve, complaining way.

"It isn't true, my child," replied Ramón gently.

"Isn't it true," burst out Francisco, "that you stood naked at the altar of Chapala Church, pretending you were Quetzalcoatl?"

"That is true," said Ramón.

"You want to kill me with shame, as you killed our mother with your eyes," said the boy, looking now at his father with male hatred.

"I don't think you will so easily die of shame, Francisco. And I did not kill your mother."

"Yes Papa," reasoned the little boy hastily. "They say she came up the church on her knees, and you looked at her till she died. Because you have given yourself to Satan, and you can kill us with looking at us, if you want to. – Isn't it true, Francisco?" he added, backing round his brother nervously.

"It isn't true, my child," said Don Ramón gravely. "Do you think so much evil of your father?"

"Yes Papa, because Mama said you were in mortal sin, and now she has gone to Paradise because you killed her," retorted the child, sheltering behind his brother.

"No, it's not true. None of that is true," said Ramón gently.

"Yes! Yes! At Las Yemas thou usedst to go about with no shirt and a sarape. Yes! Thou usedst to sing with those men, and teach them Satan songs. Yes! And Mama used to cry. And so you have killed her. Yes! It is so."

"You are only little. You can't know these things, child," said Don Ramón.

"He is little, but he is right," said Francisco, with the black, atavistic hate of a boy. "You have killed our mother, and I hate you. You have killed our mother, and one day I shall kill you."

It was out now, the thing he had on his soul. He became dead silent.

"Say no such thing," replied Don Ramón, with quiet sternness. "Say no such thing." The boy looked up at him with proud, malevolent defiance. "Because," said the father, meeting his son's eyes, "if ever thou shouldst try to kill me, I shall kill thee first."

The two stared into each other's eyes for a moment, then the boy dropped his gaze. He was cowed. Don Ramón looked at him steadily.

"Forget all this foolish talk," he said. "Thou shouldst be too much of a man to listen to the things that servant-women and priests will tell thee against me. Where is thy loyalty to thy father?"

"I am loyal to my mother, who is in Paradise," replied the boy, with another flash of hatred and defiance.

"Surely, surely, be true to thy mother in Paradise. But dost thou think thy mother would wish thee to say the things thou hast said, her soul in Paradise?"

"Yes! I think she would!" said the boy, with finality.

"Good. Then think it if thou must. But thou wrongest the soul of thy mother. – And remember this. Whoever tries to kill me, I kill him first."

"Yes, he would kill thee," said Pedro naïvely, taking his brother's hand and looking up at his face.

"Come here," said Ramón to the little boy.

The child shrank behind his elder brother.

"Come," said Ramón, holding out his hand.

"No, you would kill me," said Pedro.

"Little coward!" smiled Don Ramón. Then he sat erect.

"Good!" he said, in a changed voice. "So it is! You will go back to Mexico with your Aunt Margarita. It will be best if you use your mother's name, and be both of you Gutierrez de Lara. You are neither of you Carrasco any more. If ever you want to see me again, you must send me word: *Papa, I was foolish, forgive me.* Otherwise, remain with your mother's people, and think no more of me."

"And the money?" blurted Francisco defiantly.

"That will be paid to your guardians, little bourgeois. Now go!"

The two boys pattered to the door, the little one holding by the jacket of the elder. Don Ramón watched them go. Pedro peeped round the door as he was disappearing, to look at the bogey of his father. The father laughed to himself at the odd little sight. He loved his little boy. He loved both the boys. But what was the good of love, if they were hostile in faith? – He sat by the window and watched them go out into the Plaza of the city, attended by a man-servant. What a pathetic sight the poor, self-conscious Francisco looked in his boy's new suit of black, that left bare knees, a new and expensively tailored suit, and the absurd little black felt hat. Yet it was correct, and so the lad felt haughty and superior. As they walked across the Plaza, conceitedly, followed by the man-servant, Ramón felt they were walking ridiculously out of his life.

"How ridiculous they look! How ridiculous they look! Poor Carlota, why was she such an obstinate narrow fool! To think they are my children! That pair of little jackanapes! The little fools! The little fools!"

And he thought to himself, passionately:

"If ever they as much as lift a finger against me, I will shoot them. There shall be no traitors in my life."

Cipriano came back, and the two men sat talking. The Quetzalcoatl movement was spreading like electricity through the country. But there seemed, perhaps, to be more zest in burning the old images and slighting the old faith, than in accepting the new. Quetzalcoatl was a name, and a magic name in the mouth of the people, but it was a name they took all too lightly. And this was the danger. They had learned, during the last twenty years, to treat every name lightly. To respect nothing but the man with a revolver, and to reverence nothing at all. The danger was, that the new movement would lead to more chaos.

"It is no use, Cipriano," said Ramón. "You will have to come in as Huitzilopochtli, and put fear into the people, or they will break the spell and become just insurrectionists again."

Cipriano thought about it. He was a general in the government service, and he did not wish to betray the government. By the sheer magic of his will, he had an immense influence over his soldiers. But could he trust his officers? Also the Knights of Columbus, one of the extravagant half-secret societies of America, which included the bulk of the frightened Mexican property-owners and which swore death and destruction to anything anti-Catholic, were working hard in politics to bring the downfall of Viedma, when they would at once use fire and brimstone to destroy every trace of the Quetzalcoatl movement. There was a fairly large party of priests within the Church, however, who, strangely enough, looked on the Quetzalcoatl movement as not strictly anti-Catholic, and who secretly aspired to a Mexican Church with a Mexican God-symbol and a Mexican ritual.

Ramón and Cipriano spent many hours thinking and discussing, they had endless interviews, endless, with the clergy, with heads of business houses, with the leaders of Worker's Federations, with the governor of the State, with military men. Ramón had a fair success with the clergy. It was curious, but most of the priests seemed ready to abandon Christianity as such, if only the Church would continue.

"The Church shall and must continue," said Ramón. "The people shall and must have a religion. What is more, they shall have a true faith. And that needs a new symbol. God is always God. But men need a new approach. Especially in America the old Christian approach is ineffectual, rationalised to death."

"I am no enemy of the One Church," he said to the priests. "I am no enemy of the Church of the One Everlasting God. But men are human and diverse, and they must have different ways of coming to God. Different Saviours, according to their different needs. God is One Great God forever. But Mexico needs a different Saviour. Otherwise the Church will collapse altogether, as a church, here in America.

It will become a political institution. And at last, in the final frenzy of political hate, it will be destroyed altogether. You know it is so. You know there is no help for it. You know you are doomed."

Another time he said to them, the chief clergy of the state:

"I am a Catholic of Catholics. I believe in the One Church for all the world. I have no hatred of Rome, as the Metropolitan City. Only now the Church must prepare to modify her forms, or she will collapse. We, who are men capable of grasping an abstraction, we know that God is One God, One Source for us all. But from the God-Source come many divers channels, to us men. And unless we find the true channel, we die. Buddha would be useless to us here. So would Brahma, or Mahommet. Our souls are not keyed to their call, to their vibration. We need our own god, with a name that is answered in our own blood. We need Quetzalcoatl, and Huitzilopochtli, and Malintzi.

"Let there be one Catholic Church in the world. Let there be one esoteric priesthood over all the earth. But different countries must have different Saviours, different Gods, different ritual. It must be so, or we are killing the imaginative souls of the people.

"And why should not the great Mother Church be the first to realise this? Why should she not wish her children of different nations now to have religions of their own, with their own native gods, and their own vivid Saviours, and their own honest, passionate priests? But a priesthood initiated by degrees into the central mystery of the One Everlasting God, and united in concentric circles in the One Church of the Earth, centreing if you will in Old Rome, the same."

The more intelligent priests listened, and some were filled with joy at the bigness and the splendour of the new conception. A delegate set off for Italy, feeling a new hope and a new strength in his heart, confident, as was Don Ramón himself, that the true religious honesty of spirit still existed in the Church of Rome, more, perhaps, than in any Protestant body. If the time had come for a great change, the great Church would not be unready.

Don Ramón had against him, of course, the idealists, those who believed in Liberty and in Education. He himself had once believed in Liberty and in Education, so he knew most of the people who honestly entertained the same belief, and who were not just greedy or obstinate politicians. And these men too he met.

"You can't believe any more in the rule of the people," he said.

"There is no such thing. The people are, in the most democratic of democracies, only fooled into believing that they rule. As for Russia, after all, what keeps her bolshevism solid *is* the pressure of the capitalist world outside. Russia unites in one feeling of hatred for the capitalist world. But supposing there *were* no capitalist world? What would unite Russia then? – Why nothing. She would be a mob. No denying it.

"You *can't* educate the people. Beyond a certain point, it is impossible. You can teach them to add up figures and brush their teeth. But you can't give them insight or imagination, if they haven't got these things. And insight and imagination are what make a man educated. But only a comparatively few people have these qualities. And even then, in differing degrees.

"So all that remains to do is to unite the people of insight and imagination. Because, after all, these are the only people who can be depended on. They are the only ones who are pure in spirit. They are the only ones who understand that any form of exploitation is just a negation of living.

"It means a new aristocracy. An aristocracy of the soul, not of birth or money. An esoteric, united aristocracy of the world. Chosen in the honest religious spirit, and no other. Self-elected, because of honest righteousness. And electing others for the same.

"So let us begin. But we must begin at home. And we must begin with a religion. We must derive our strength and our inspiration from the religious root, from the God-source. Religious belief is the only permanent source of strength and inspiration. But also we must use our intelligence every moment, keep our intelligence alert and fighting, every moment."

It was Cipriano who went to the secret meeting of the Caballeros de Colon, the Knights of Columbus: those stout and propertied gentlemen who swear such bloody oaths against everything heretical, but who are thinking all the time of their property and of communistic outrages.

"Don Ramón is not really antagonistic to the Church," he explained. "He only wants a new adjustment, a new, more native form. In fact, a national Church of Mexico. Though there need be no actual split with Rome."

"And his greatest idea," he continued, "is to draw away the minds and the energies of the peons and the workmen from politics and from all this communist stuff. He sees, quite rightly, that you can only drive out a bad passion by arousing a good passion. He considers, as I do myself, that this morbid political frenzy for taking everything away from the people who are considered rich, and for pulling down everything which looks like authority, is in itself a bad passion, the worst passion that could possibly get hold of mankind. It is the most ghastly of all vices. And you see yourselves how it is spreading. And you know yourselves, that even if you do succeed in working the Church interest, and in getting together a Fascist reaction, you are only staving off the evil day. Fascism won't hold against the lust for anarchy which is at the bottom of the Fascisti themselves. The Fascisti only live because they think they can bully society. It is a great bully movement, just as communism is a bully movement. But communism is a more vital feeling, because of the big grudge that burns in a communist's belly. And in the end, that grudge will burn holes through all Fascism, and down you'll come again, and the Church with you, in a big smash.

"Now Don Ramón doesn't want this. He wants a people really stable. And the only thing to keep them stable, you know yourselves, is a religious faith. But all these agitators have destroyed the bulk of the old faith. The bulk of the people no longer believe in the Church. You know it yourselves. So, without smashing the churches or hurting anybody except a name and a wooden image or two, Don Ramón wants to introduce a new faith, to draw away the attention of the people from all this political agitation, into another channel, a peaceful, fruitful, religious channel.

"If you are wise men, you will sit tight and let Don Ramón go ahead. You will encourage your peons to sing the hymns of Quetzalcoatl. While they are singing those they won't be listening to these bolshevist agitators. And once they get the taste for these hymns, they'll have no more use for politics.

"You should encourage them to sing the hymns of Quetzalcoatl. You should sing them along with your people. After all God is One God, and as like as not your priest will have nothing to say against it."

"But doesn't Don Ramón want to end up with communism?"

"Communism? No. He has no idea of dividing up the big estates. He doesn't believe in your millions of little farmers idea. He knows that little farmers simply won't stand the life for two seasons.

"No, he wants to go back more to the old-fashioned hacienda

system, much more patriarchal. A humane, religious system. But at the base, patriarchal. His chief idea is the sacredness of authority, as against the communist idea that authority is in itself a blasphemy. Even if the land were communal, belonged to the nation, still he believes that the working of the land and the control of labour should be in the charge of the best men in the community, acting very much like the decent hacendados did in the old days, with unquestioned authority, but like fathers, fond of their people, and looking after them well."

The Knights of Columbus went away unconvinced, but also shaken. It might be just as well to wait and see.

Many of the business men were also Knights. But to those who lived pure business, Cipriano said, in addition to the above:

"Don Ramón makes no attack on property. As a matter of fact, if you would give him your private support, I think he would guarantee to keep things quiet, to maintain a steady supply of labour, and to keep the wage question absolutely in abeyance. What he wants is a religious revival, and a quiet country with sufficient property to make it possible."

So the sly Cipriano schemed for secret funds: and got the promise of them.

He had still the workmen's federations to meet. And these were the devil. Particularly the railway-men, many of whom were now earning monstrous huge wages. To these he said:

"No one believes more than Don Ramón that an industry exists solely for the sake of the workers of that industry, and for the people who need the products of that industry. He is dead against the capitalist.

"But, he says, you will never change Mexico till you change the religion. And I think you'll agree with him. You know who your own enemies are. Now he won't interfere with you in the least. You go ahead your way, politically. And he, trying to change the religion of the people, will go ahead his own way. And I think you'll see that a Mexican Church of Quetzalcoatl, instead of blocking your way, as the Catholic Church does, would most likely open the road to you entirely. It is a means to an end. And I think, privately, that you and Don Ramón have both the same end in view."

In spite of this, it was Federated Labour which entertained the deepest hostility to the new religious movement, and which started the first persecution.

Last of all remained his officers and his soldiers.

"In the first place, we are men," he said, "and we're not going to see the people of this country turned into so many machine-slaves, like the gringos.

"We are men, we have valour, and we've got to live up to our valour.

"We've got to keep the white gringuitos back. By God we have. We wish them no harm, so long as they don't try to put it over us. But they do try to put it over us.

"And, men, where we are ten they are a hundred. We send up one aeroplane, and they come down on us with a cloud of a thousand aeroplanes. We send one big gun to the frontier, and we see the snouts of fifty Berthas, all bigger than our one, facing us across the border.

"Men, it won't do. War we can't have. It means Mexico lost.

"Peace we can't have. It means Mexico swallowed by the white gringuitos who are after our oil, our silver, our copper, our sugar, our cotton, our timber, our corn, our land, our labour.

"What can we do?

"We'll turn to one another. And we'll turn to our own God. We'll take back Quetzalcoatl, and as sure as the old Mexican blood is in my veins, we'll be the best men of America again, as we were before the gringos ever came.

"We're the best blood in America, the blood of Montezuma. We've gone against our own blood, serving the gringos' gods, and kneeling down on our knees.

"We'll kneel no more. Quetzalcoatl hates the sight of a kneeling man.

"My knees are made to hold me straight. My hand is made to hail my native God, or to shoot the devil who tries to prevent me.

"After all, we are men, we are not lackeys or machines.

"I am a man like you are, naked inside my clothes like you are. And there's many a man among you is bigger than I am. There's many a one of my own men who could break me if he grappled with me naked, being bigger and stronger than I am. But it's the heart that matters. And there's a god and a devil as well inside my heart, and nobody is going to put me down.

"Oh, I'm a man and I'm a Mexican, and you are my men, and Mexicans. While we are together, while this god and this devil are in my heart, we are the only men in America.

"For I feel the God Huitzilopochtli inside me, like the volcano of Colima, the Mexican God of War come back to me.

"Are you my children? Are you the children of Huitzilopochtli?"

When Cipriano was really worked up, and his black eyes blazed, and he opened his mouth and his white teeth flashed, something seemed to be starting out of him, as if some strange, invisible, dark-feathered demon were leaping with wings out of his breast and shoulders. His black aura seemed to bristle with wings, and his men, in a kind of second-sight, actually saw a bristling savage god. And involuntarily they gave short, barking cries of acclamation:

"Hie! Hie! Cipriano! Cipriano! Hie! Hie!"

The whole strength of the movement was in the response of the peons and the soldiers. Cipriano had not very much belief in his officers, the higher officers at least. It was the younger men who stood for him, and the common soldiers themselves. They called themselves Ciprianistos, and addressed one another as such. "How are you, Ciprianisto? Well, son of Cipriano! – Pass me that knife, Ciprianisto! Olà! Ciprianisto, don't you touch me again." And their catch-word all the time was *Cipriano!*

When their general announced to them that the God Huitzilopochtli was inside him, they took it with great good-humour. The word amused them. They would say to one another, à propos of nothing: *Huitzilopochtli!*, with explosive vigour. And this was for some reason a rich joke. From this gradually they invented themselves a new nick-name: *Pochtlotes.* But about this name they were touchy, not allowing any outsider to use it. In common use, they were Ciprianistos. Only in private, on odd occasions, did they come out with *Pochtlote,* as if this name had a significance they were not altogether easy about.

The curse of the Mexican army, Cipriano said, was that most of their time the men were lying about like pigs, with nothing to do. They were not rigorously drilled, not by any means. They were by no means spick and span. A shirt, an old cotton tunic and breeches, cotton leggings, and bare feet never washed since their beginning, thrust into flat sandals held on by leather strings. There was a soldier: plus cartridges, revolver, knife and gun. He slept in his clothes on the floor, anywhere: pushed tortillas down his throat at meal-times: and for the rest lay about like a dog, or strolled in gangs on a kind of patrol.

Cipriano was determined to put more discipline into his men, and he did it. But the God Huitzilopochtli himself would not have got much order into the devils. The General did not intend to try. He knew his men were best left fairly loose and reckless. *We are men!* was their great assertion. Or else: *Don't you believe that we are valorous!* To tell the truth they were more like savages than men, and often like untamed dogs. But cowed they were not. And valorous, in their own way, they were. Valorous as demons the moment they were roused. And he wished to keep them so.

Taking a leaf from Ramón's book, he bought them guitars and encouraged them to sing. He had little gatherings of the musicians among the soldiers, and they learned the songs of the country. Then he introduced the tom-toms. He got Indians from the north to join with their savage drums and their unintelligible wild songs, he got them to dance their savage dances round the drum. He himself sometimes joined in these savage dances, naked to the waist, dancing for hours, sweating and singing the chant in the unintelligible Indian dialect. He found it exhilarated him and strengthened him. These dances round the drum seemed to generate a new sort of energy inside him, that lasted over the following days, and seemed to smile exultantly inside him. Because it was not the mere old dance of the northern Indians. It was the dance of his determination to make a change in life for all the people of his blood; a great change, not back to the old gods, but, in an ascending spiral, overtaking the old gods in a movement to the new. A new epoch for Mexico. Eventually, a new American epoch.

He knew what he was doing. Ramón had made it very plain.

"What is the good of waiting for inspiration pure and simple," said Ramón to him. "We are men, Cipriano. We've got to act as men, not as would-be angels. Belief in us is a matter of hard determination and shrewd intelligence. And at the bottom, pure belief in the life-sources. Pure belief that we are opening new valves to the life-flow, to manhood. We know what we're doing, Cipriano. We are men, and we've got to put this thing through, without any of the arguing and snivelling of white people."

They were not going back to savagedom. They were opening the old well-springs of life in their souls, that Christianity had bricked over.

"I don't want human sacrifices and hearts pulled out," said Ramón. "But neither do I want penitentes whipping themselves, or celibate priests, or nuns, or nations of people crawling on their knees and snivelling to a dead Jesus with a crown of thorns. I want men again, I want new men. Manhood! My priests will be men, entire, and not eunuchs. And they'll be like pagan Roman priests, men active in civilian life, who only perform the ritual and study the mysteries as part of their life-work. We'll have no more of your set-apart clergy and priesthood. You are a general. And you are the chief priest of Huitzilopochtli. And you are the living Huitzilopochtli. But all the time you are General Cipriano Viedma, commander-in-chief of the army in the west.

"Don't you think, Cipriano, we are strong enough now? Don't you think you can be invested in your proper divinity?"

"You know, Ramón," said Cipriano laughing, "I still feel a bit shy of stepping into history as a divine, or semi-divine character. It's all right for you: there is something special about you. But me! Isn't it enough if I keep command of the army and act under your orders?"

Ramón was silent, and the dark, remote look slowly settled on his face. He had gone back again into his deepest self, to think from his deepest soul.

After a while he rose, with the remote, inevitable look on his face, of which even Cipriano stood a little in awe. He went behind the other man's chair, and quietly put his two hands over Cipriano's eyes, pressing them shut. Cipriano, startled, braced himself to resist. Then again he relaxed to the soft, firm pressure of the hands that darkened him. But his back was straight and erect.

"Cipriano!" came the quiet, deep voice of Ramón.

"Yes?"

"It is dark in your eyes. Is it dark and still in your heart?"

"Wait a bit," said Cipriano; and he let the darkness sink from the hands that closed his eyes, slowly down over his heart. His heart was dark.

"Yes," he said, half conscious.

"Is it dark and still in your belly as well?" came the quiet, deep voice from behind him.

"No," faltered Cipriano. And making another effort of faith in the dark hands that covered his eyes, he struggled to let the warm, soft darkness sink deeper into him, over the resistant pulse he felt beneath his navel. And gradually, without his knowing, the darkness softly, peacefully invaded him in his depths, and his consciousness was only like a speck of light reflected on the dark surface of him.

"Yes," he said, his own voice seeming far away.

Ramón pressed one hand over both Cipriano's eyes, and pressed the middle finger of the other hand over a certain awake place at the base of Cipriano's spine.

"And here?"

Cipriano felt he no longer heard with his ears, but, as in a dream, with all of his darkened self. His soul seemed to tremble, and he longed to leap away from that one place of pressure in all his consciousness, at the bottom of his back. He was unconscious now of Ramón, aware only of that one spot of resistance which was himself. He wanted to leap away, to maintain the resistance. His heart gave a little wrench in the darkness. But then his last-remaining consciousness roused itself strangely to a new act of abnegation, like a bird that opens its breast to die, above an infinite darkness.

And like something dissolving out, he felt himself going in a warm death. He was passing into death, into all complete darkness: but it was warm, and infinitely grateful. Slowly, slowly he passed away into the inner darkness. He had no consciousness any more, was just a darkness within the dark, that was warm, and infinitely satisfying. At last.

How long he was dark he did not know: moments, minutes, eternities were all the same. He was aroused by becoming aware of Ramón's slow breathing behind him, then by the slow withdrawal of Ramón's hands, then by the slow necessity of opening his eyes.

Never had the daylight, and the hard look of the objects in the room seemed so cruel and undesirable to him. He closed his eyes and covered his face with his arm. But he could feel his coat-sleeve, it was not the perfect warm death it had been to him before. He would have to come back.

He opened his eyes. Ramón was standing before him in silence. The eyes of the two men met, and again Cipriano found the perfect warm, everlasting dark.

"Well, what are you?" asked Ramón, smiling slightly.

Cipriano considered the answer. "I am a man." But that was inadequate. "I am myself." But that didn't have any meaning.

"Yes, the depths of me is God," he said, convinced.

"Never go back on it," said Ramón.

Cipriano had now to square himself to this new conception of himself. It was his innermost secret. It slept at the depths of him when he was inspecting his soldiers, when he was having a discussion with the President of the Republic, or when he sat at a military council, or when he was at dinner with his officers. Sometimes the rage and vexation of the political intrigue in which he was involved, and the strange dry activity of the world that surrounded him and impinged on him, would make his secret seem absolute nonsense, his own godliness a thing of ridicule. A mocking look would come over his face, and he would lose the magic out of himself, and become common. Then he noticed small insults and impertinences.

But he had chosen within himself, to remember. He had pledged himself to his own soul. So when he felt himself lapsing into the commonness and vulgarity of the rest of people, he would try to remember and get back to the darkness where he had found such a different flow. And it was not always possible. Particularly the political scheming against him, with all its lies and its busy cleverness and its plausibility, would sometimes swing him back into his old lust, the lust for getting power in Mexico, to make himself President, dictator, tyrant, so as to have revenge and power.

"Revenge is for the gods," he would say to himself cynically, "and I am one of 'em." Because he burned for revenge, having such burning contempt for his enemies.

But he realised that the revenge he was hankering after was personal, not divine. He was tangled again in his personal existence, and how he hated it. How he hated being dragged down to his own personality. He wanted to be his divine, dark self.

So then he would go to Ramón again. Ramón's soul was steadier than his own.

"Put your hand over my eyes, Ramón. I am all General Viedma, Huitzilopochtli has gone out of me; and I want him to come back."

Then Ramón would laugh, and the very sight of Ramón's fascinating, gentle, almost wicked-seeming laugh would make the ugly world of men rip in two, and set the dark warmth flowing again like blood in Cipriano's soul.

After which, remembering his lapse into barrenness, he would say:

"Even as a god, Ramón, I am a god of revenge. Invest me in my godhead, I accept it. Make me the living Huitzilopochtli, I'll be it, in the face and in the teeth of everybody."

For Cipriano, who had such a strong sense of the world, and the world of people, it was a serious decision. He had to cut himself off, essentially, from the world in which he held his commission, he had to turn subtly and completely against this world. And at the same time he had to conquer it. He knew that only his force and his army saved Ramón and the whole new movement from extinction. He, Cipriano, *had* to reckon with the world, far more than Ramón did. He *had* to live with it and deal with it. He had to conquer it. He knew this. And therefore it cost him some effort to come out before the world as the living Huitzilopochtli. It cost him an effort to make it publicly evident that his god-self was more important in every way than his human-social self. That he looked upon himself as a god, not as a mere man in the service of mankind, this was by no means easy for him to announce. For above all things he was a man of common sense.

He decided, however, it must be done. He would come out and take his stand. He would be the living Huitzilopochtli, first and foremost, and General of the Mexican army afterwards. He would be the god first, and the man afterwards. That was the final decision.

He was to be invested on Thursday: Thursday was his day in the new calendar. The ceremony was to take place in the night, in the church. Like Ramón, he was to come naked before the altar, and be invested in his colours of red and black and white and green and yellow. The big, hard-sounding war-drums would beat inside the church, and they would dance the war-dance.

Inside his heart of hearts, all the time, was a steady spark burning for revenge, for vengeance. But he was glad that it was no longer the corrosive personal desire. That had gone. And in its place, a steady, almost laughing spark of everlasting vengeance, that would kindle in its own hour and could wait for that hour for ever. There was no hurry. The hour would come, as all hours come, from the unknown. And he would be ready for the hour. And meanwhile the spark was an eternal fire in his heart and his belly, nourishing his manhood and leaving him free to laugh and to love. He was the keeper of the Lord's vengeance, the living Huitzilopochtli. He had many men with him, and power over them. He wanted his race to live, his breed to continue.

He called a third time to see Kate at her house. It was the afternoon before his investiture, when the hard war-drums were rattling from the church-towers, and the war-rattles were scattering sound like gravel.

"Listen," he said, "to my music. I become a god tonight."

"Doesn't it feel queer?" she cried.

"No, not once you have made up your mind to it," he answered.

"I should think it felt awfully queer."

She looked at him. His smallish figure was very still, but his eyes were all life, smiling their Huitzilopochtli smile, as Ramón called it. A slight, dangerous quiver, like light along the edge of a sharp blade, and at the same time a full, warm, good-humoured flow. Like a warrior abstractedly and good-humouredly playing with his knife.

"As a god," he said, "I want a goddess more badly than as a man. As General Viedma I feel no imperious necessity to take a wife. Rather the contrary. But as Huitzilopochtli I feel badly in need of a mate. Perhaps I am lonely or unfinished in my godhood. I want a Malintzi to share my strange condition with. Won't you be married to me?"

Kate looked at him: so isolated, so much a thing by himself, and yet, needing her. It seemed hardly possible that he should need her. But what he said, was true. He needed her, he knew it, he said it to her. She thought him very lovely.

And then, like a demon, came back the memory of the past. Or like a strange white mist rolling over the present and making everything in it unreal.

"I almost might, at this minute," she said. "If –"

"If – ?" he echoed.

"If I hadn't had my life. I've had my life."

"So have I had my life. Several. This, you will admit," he said, smiling a dangerous smile that showed his teeth, "is the entry into immortality. I want somebody to be with me in my immortality. My *life* I can easily live alone."

She was thinking again, of her dead husband, and the life she had lived with him, and the self that was pledged to him. Somehow it didn't seem to involve the thing that Cipriano wanted of her. She felt that by accepting Cipriano she would be able to soothe and reassure her dead husband like a sleeping child. Her dead husband was like a sleeping child to her, by whose side she watched and watched in a perpetual grief for him. If she married Cipriano she need have no more grief for the dead one, and he could sleep his sleep in death complete and at peace.

But she could not marry Cipriano. Just physically she couldn't. She didn't understand his way of love. He didn't love her. He just wanted her for his life, as he had said to her before. And she was used to being loved, not merely wanted for a man's life.

To be sure, to be wanted by a man for his life was better than being loved. She knew it. But oh, a woman can't change so easily! She had been a woman who was loved, and she had loved her husband again. All her body and soul was built that way. How could she change and become the wife of a man who wanted her for his life, not for herself? She had always wished to be wanted for herself. That and that only. And that she had had.

How could she go back on it by giving in to a man who just wanted her for his life? It meant going back on all she had ever been.

What he said about wanting her for his immortality she inter-preted as wanting her for his real, inner life. The life that he could easily live alone was his social life. This too she knew. But even that a man should just want her for the fulfilling of his inward life seemed a little bit arrogant to her.

"You see you don't consider *my* life," she said.

"Your immortality," he replied with a smile, his eyes watching her closely to see how she softened, and how she hardened again.

"Ah, my immortality will look after itself," she said casually. "But my life is my own. You don't consider that. You don't consider my life, do you?"

"Your life," he said, "will be made good by my life."

"You take it easily for granted," she laughed. "Don't I have any say?"

"Ah you!" he replied. "You say your says out of perverseness. If I want you for my life, it is because your own life is nothing apart from mine. The gods make it so. Apart from my life, you have no life. You have only your own ego. You may keep your ego. But that is not life, it will never be life."

"How do you know?"

"I know."

"And your life? Will that be a life apart from mine?"

"Not a complete life. I have told you that. But a life nevertheless. I am still the living Huitzilopochtli."

"And you have Don Ramón."

"I have Don Ramón. He is very much my life to me."

"So anything else is only a trifle to you."

"Ah no, don't believe that." His voice was suddenly so simple and earnest, she was terrified for her defences. "There is something missing forever from my life and my immortality, unless you will come into it. – But you must come of your own free will." – He added the last words mournfully, as if regretting sincerely that the admission must be made.

"I should think so," she laughed. "If you think about your life, I must think about mine, you know."

"Think about your immortality, Malintzi, and you will see it unites you to me," he said, half mocking.

"Oh, as for my immortality! A woman prefers to be very mortal on these occasions."

"On which occasions, *Señora mia?*"

"Oh! Why, marriage and so forth."

"Then be very mortal, and accept this marriage and so forth."

"No! No!" she cried. "I'm not ready. Don't try to force me. You always try to overpower me. I feel it all the time. And that will *never* make me give in. I have lived too long and fought too hard to be *forced* to yield."

"*Qué Amazona!*" he replied satirically.

"Yes, an Amazon," she retorted, flushing, "when anyone tries to overpower me."

They had the Huitzilopochtli ceremony at night, in the wide yard-space in front of the church, with two lines of men in striped sarapes, like wasps or tigers, red, black, yellow, the stripes lengthwise, holding blazing torches of ocote wood, stretching from door to gate, a bonfire built between them, half way, but unkindled, the hard drums and rattles going like Pandemonium. Cipriano, naked with a black loin-cloth, came running out of the church between his guards, holding a torch. He kindled the central bonfire, waited till it blazed, then seizing a blazing faggot from the rush of flame, tossed it over the heads of the guard to a naked man. He tossed four brands to four men, in the four directions. They ran in the four directions, and kindled four more bonfires of ocote wood, built like little hollow towers, while Cipriano flung brand after brand at the heavens, and the guard dodged as they fell, singing all the time in a monotone, and dancing the war-step. The only word intelligible in the chant was the continually recurring: *Huitzilopochtli.* Two naked attendants threw over Cipriano's head first a yellow silk cloak, as he danced the war-dance, and a tall yellow flame rose from the fire. Then they threw a red silk cloak over the [yellow] one, as the yellow flame died. And in a moment a fountain of red flame rose slowly, with a strange, slow, phallic ebbing, higher and higher in the air, till the whole place was lurid red, all the dark faces were red-dark, it was like a scene of demons. Then attendants threw over Cipriano's head a black sarape with a red and yellow fringe. The fire slowly died. There was nothing but embers. Cipriano ran among these, and stamped them underfoot.

Then a voice, not his own, began to sing:

I am Huitzilopochtli.
I am the red of the blood of men.
I am the yellow in the fire of the blood of men.
I am the whiteness of living bone, within the red of the flesh of men.

I am Huitzilopochtli, out of the blackness of night.
I am the angry manhood of men.

I am Huitzilopochtli, waiting in the dark.
Waiting for the enemy,
Waiting for the traitor,
Waiting for the coward,
Waiting for the weak.

I am Huitzilopochtli, out of the blackness of night,
The angry manhood of men.

I am Huitzilopochtli, with a blade of green grass between my teeth.

In the stillness of my night, the grass grows.
Far below the roots of the trees, my fire is below like dawn.
At the centre of the earth my light is yellower than the sun.

I am the hidden star.
I am the invisible sun.
I am the middle of all.
I am the angry manhood of men:
Huitzilopochtli.

The fires had all died down, the torches only were burning. At the back, in front of the solid white church-wall, a platform had been built. A man went hanging six oil torches against the wall above this platform. The guard all withdrew to the low outer walls of the yard, their backs to the crowd. The drums were gradually going quiet: only a single, slow beat, at last.

Cipriano had folded his black sarape inwards till it hung in front and behind in one long bar. The folded red sarape was red outside that. The yellow flowed loose. He looked like a dark stroke rising from the earth, from which fluttered red and yellow, like flame. In his hand he held a bunch of black strips of palm-leaf.

He went and pushed open the doors of the church, then turned, and slowly mounted the platform. Behind him came a procession of two and two: a guard of Huitzilopochtli, in black and red and yellow stripes, leading a peon in floppy white work-clothes, the peon blindfolded with a black cloth. They mounted to the scaffold, six blindfolded peons, six guards, and stood facing the great dim crowd outside, under the torches.

Last came a seventh peon, limping, with a black cross painted on the breast and the back of his white cotton jacket. Cipriano went to the front of the platform, and called in a loud voice:

"Men! Listen! These are six of the bandits who tried to murder Don Ramón, who is the living Quetzalcoatl.

"The one with the black cross is the peon who betrayed the way from the mango tree into the house.

"He is a traitor.

"Every traitor dies.

"The bandits are cowards. They only attack unarmed people or people much fewer than they are.

"In my law, traitorous cowards die too.

"But because the grass is green, and it likes to grow, and because sometimes men are deceived into playing the coward: we will put one green blade among the five black blades.

"But five must die, out of these six."

He held up the bunch of black blades. Then he gave it to one of the guards. The prisoners in their white work-clothes had the black bandages removed from their eyes. The guard went and offered the bunch of black blades to the first.

"Draw one," he said.

"They are all black," said the man.

"One is green at the lower end," said the guard.

The prisoner drew a long leaf. It was all black. He looked again.

"Black," said the guard.

The man threw away the strip with fatal indifference.

"Kill me," he said.

The second man drew a leaf.

"Black," said the guard.

The man made no sound, but stood looking at the leaf.

The third man touched the leaves and drew back his hands as if they were red hot.

"There isn't one! There isn't one! There isn't a green one!" he yelled in a sudden frenzy of terror.

"Give him a black leaf, he is a coward," said Cipriano.

The guard glanced at the under-side of the leaves, drew one out, and handed it to the man. But the man put his free hand behind him.

"I won't take it," he said. "You can shoot me."

The guard pushed it into the breast of the man's jacket.

The fourth man silently drew, and looked at his leaf in silence. The guard looked too.

"It is green," he said. "You can go."

The guard who held the prisoner by a rope fastened to the man's right wrist unloosed the rope and took it off. Then he gave him a little push.

"Go!" he said.

"Where can I go?" asked the peon.

"Where you like."

"What are you called, you?" asked Cipriano.

"Julian Gonsalvez, Señor."

"Have you got the green leaf?"

"Yes, Señor."

"Do you know you ought to die?"

"Yes, Señor."

"Good. Keep the green leaf, because green is life. But remember one end of it is black, and black means death."

"*Sí*, Señor."

"Now go."

"Where can I go, Señor?"

"Where you like."

The man walked quickly down the scaffold steps, across the yard in front of the gate. The guard made way for him. He was gone into the crowd.

The guard with the remaining leaves showed them to the two remaining prisoners. They nodded.

The limping peon was brought forward and stood facing the crowd, his kerchief taken from his eyes.

"You know you are a traitor?" said Cipriano to him.

But there was no answer.

A guard, naked to the waist, suddenly stepped behind the peon, a knife flashed in a great stroke, the guard lifted the severed head quickly in the air, and quick as lightning, before the decapitated body could move, put it back on the neck again. There was a great murmur of applause from the crowd. This was one of the time-honored feats of these people. Then the body was caught and carried into the church. The great drum on the roof was reverberating in slow, slack thuds.

The wrists of the five prisoners were released, their feet bound. They were given the black cloths, to blindfold themselves if they wished. Two men quickly tied up their own eyes, and stood waiting. One man, only one, begged for a priest, to confess. The priest came, the man kneeled down and made a short, earnest confession. And after that, without anything more said, the five were shot. Their bodies fell upon the platform, and one by one were carried into the dim church, lit by oil torches and candles.

Black was hung round the green pillars of the church, and on the high altar was a black cloth. Facing the statue of Quetzalcoatl was the new statue of Huitzilopochtli, in black lava-stone: a short, heavy, seated statue with a bunch of black and green palm-strips in one hand. And the six bodies were laid in front of this image, beneath the candles.

Ramón sat in his chair below the altar, wearing his white and blue and earth-colours. On his right hand sat Cipriano. Six of the white guards were on the right hand, six of the striped guards of Huitzilopochtli on the left. Music was playing slowly and monotonously from the gallery. Incense was steaming up from in front of the altar of Huitzilopochtli.

Then the throng was admitted, men crowding thick to right and left, erect, and then standing among the benches. Women were not admitted. The black priest was in the pulpit. The drums sounded the salute of Quetzalcoatl, and all the guard and the soldiers saluted, then the people, lifting the hand on high. The drums of Quetzalcoatl were still, the hands fell. Then the hard war-drums of Huitzilopochtli filled the place with sound, and the guards of Huitzilopochtli struck one fist, a clenched red fist high in the air. It was the salute of Huitzilopochtli, to strike the air with a clenched fist, a fist dyed red by the striped guard.

Cipriano rose and stepped forward. Ramón rose, stood a little further back.

"Are we men?" cried Cipriano, in a loud, strong, soldier's voice.

"We are men," responded the guard, striking the air in salute.

"Why are our hands red?"

"With the blood of traitors and of cowards."

"Shall they be always red?"

"No, we will wash them in the stream."

"What stream?"

"The clean water of Malintzi."

Two guards in white and grey and pink brought in a big basin of silver, another brought a large silver ewer. They poured water over the hands of Cipriano. He washed his hands, threw the drops of water towards the congregation of men, and turned to Ramón with hand uplifted in the Quetzalcoatl salute.

"Quetzalcoatl, is it well?"

"It is well."

The bodies of the five dead men were carried across to the foot of the Quetzalcoatl statue, and covered with a white and blue and earth-[coloured] cloth.

"What are we doing?" cried the six guards of Huitzilopochtli.

"You are giving us the souls of the dead," replied the white guard of Quetzalcoatl.

Then the guards of Cipriano brought him a black cloth.

"Put the traitor in the everlasting dark," they said.

And he went and covered the dead body of the treacherous peon with the black cloth.

The music began to play quietly and gently. Then the guard of Huitzilopochtli sang, magnificently:

Scarlet Huitzilopochtli
Keeps the day and the night apart.

Golden Huitzilopochtli
Stands on guard between death and life.

No grey dogs of cowards pass him.
No spotted traitors crawl by.
The false weak ones cannot slip through.

Gold-red Huitzilopochtli burns them in his flame as they come,
Only brave men have peace at nightfall.

Only true men dare look at the dawn.
Only men in their manhood walk free in the blueness of day.

Scarlet Huitzilopochtli
Is the purifier.

Golden Huitzilopochtli
Is the liberator.

Black Huitzilopochtli
Closes the everlasting end.

White Huitzilopochtli
Is the clean forgetting.

Green Huitzilopochtli
Is a leaf of grass.

At the beginning of each verse the men of Huitzilopochtli struck the air with their fist, and the drums gave a great crash. When the song was ended the drums gradually died down, like subsiding thunder, leaving the hearts of the men re-echoing.

The black priest mounted the pulpit, and covered his eyes with his hands, crying:

"Remember Almighty God, whom men will never see."

The men of the congregation lifted their faces and covered their eyes with their hands. Stillness slowly spread.

"More silent than silence is Almighty God," intoned the priest, and the people held their breath to bring the perfect stillness.

"Beyond the white of whiteness, and beyond the darkness of black, in the silence, waits the Almighty God forever," intoned the priest.

There were two minutes of absolute stillness, all the people standing with covered eyes, hardly breathing. Then came the faint, clear note of a silver bell, struck once. And immediately, from outside, the heavy reverberation of the biggest drum.

"Look!" said the priest.

The church was dark save for the one small light over the altar, the light of the Everlasting God.

"God is One God," said the priest.

"God is One God," replied the people.

"Light the green candles of Quetzalcoatl, like trees in flower," cried Ramón.

"Light the red torches of Huitzilopochtli," commanded Cipriano. And as the flames gradually came again, the priest said:

Huitzilopochtli is the son of God, the brother of Quetzalcoatl. He followed our Quetzalcoatl from heaven to Mexico, carrying a torch of red fire in one hand, and the black leaves of death mingled with the green leaves of life renewed, in the other.

The torches of Huitzilopochtli discover the traitors and the cowards. Though they hide under heaps of earth, or in caves of the mountains, or in secret houses, the torches of Huitzilopochtli will shine on them, and Huitzilopochtli will give them the black leaf of death.

To traitors and cowards he will give the black leaf.

And traitors will sink in the blackness. There will never be any end to their sinking in blackness.

But the dead cowards Huitzilopochtli will give to Quetzalcoatl. And Quetzalcoatl will bury them in the dark brown earth, where the ants are, and the snakes. And their flesh, and their bones, their eyes and their mouths will fade into brown earth.

Then the blue air of Quetzalcoatl will lean down and softly blow over the earth, and the water of Malintzi will fall, and green blades will rise from the earth, from the dead, from those that are dead, green life and trees will rise.

And in the white sky they will flower, hoping again towards Almighty God.

But many rains will come, and many years will pass, and Quetzalcoatl will speak many times with the Father, before Almighty God will give them again the hearts of men.

Men with the hearts of men are neither cowards nor traitors. They are proud with the pride of Huitzilopochtli, and in their hearts is the red seed of his fire, which is the anger of men in their manhood. The men of Mexico are Huitzilopochtli's men.

But they are the children of Quetzalcoatl, who makes the brown earth sweet for them, and the blue air good in their nostrils. Who brings the flowers out around them, and waves the tassels of the maize in a light wind. Who puts young children between the knees of the father, looking up at him with shining eyes.

Quetzalcoatl from the whiteness of God, who will never forsake the Mexicans.

Quetzalcoatl, the faithful, the patient, who has come back to us.

Quetzalcoatl who laughs without fear, beloved of Huitzilo-pochtli.

Two brothers, who hold each other's hands, and love with the love of all time:

Huitzilopochtli and Quetzalcoatl.

XVI

D ON RAMÓN DID A THING which surprised Kate. Quite soon after the death of Doña Carlota he married again. She knew nothing about it: there was only a quiet civil marriage, and no festivity at all: until she had a note from Ramón saying: I have married a wife, may I bring her to see you?

She was a shy, gentle creature, about twenty-five years old, called Teresa. She had known Don Ramón since she was a child, he and her father having been friends since boyhood. All her life she had lived on the tequila hacienda of Opatlan, behind the mountains from Las Yemas, with her father and two ne'er-do-well brothers. Last year her father had died, after having made a will appointing her as administrator of the estate. But the brothers had installed themselves in the hacienda and ran the place by sheer brute force. Don Ramón was one of Teresa's guardians. He found the brothers obdurate: they intended to administer the estate. And a law-suit would have been a miserable business. So he arranged a modest dowry for his ward, and married her, and brought her to Las Yemas.

She was rather small, and pale, with a lot of loose black hair and wide, gentle black eyes. Yet in her quiet bearing and well-closed mouth you could see that she was used to authority. She had been her father's right hand on the hacienda, and she was profoundly indignant with her brothers for having usurped her place as administrador of the hacienda, by sheer brute force. Against brute force she could do nothing. She had shed many tears, which were still evident in a certain wanness round her eyes. But they had been tears of anger and helpless indignation. That was evident from the closed pressure of her mouth.

She was very shy and distant with Kate. Evidently she was not used to her new position, and she did not quite know where she was. Don Ramón's Quetzalcoatl activities were completely bewildering to her. All she could do was to make her mind a blank in that direction. Which she did easily, after all. Because the image of the man himself filled her consciousness, and if he said he was the living Quetzalcoatl, what was that to her, when he was her own god.

When she sat in Kate's sala, in a simple white dress with a black gauze rebozo, her brown hands motionless in her lap, her dark neck erect, her dark, slender, well-shaped cheek averted, Kate thought her rather like a little sempstress. And from time to time the black eyes of Teresa glanced swiftly, searchingly at Kate, and glanced away again as quickly. While from her well-closed mouth a muted word came now and then: or she smiled a constrained smile. She did not even look at her husband, but kept her cheek averted from him all the time. Only when he said to her, laughing:

"How much do you charge per word, *Chica?*" – she turned and gave him a quick, flashing look and a little smile, while a warmth crept under her dark skin. Then she settled herself again immobile, with her hands in her lap.

It was evident to Kate that she was hopelessly in love with Ramón, that he was her great pasha, and that she was his harem. She could give such looks with her black, silent eyes, she could assume such a proud, blank reserve towards the other woman.

"She despises me," thought Kate, in some confusion.

For all the talk was going on between Ramón and Kate. Ramón, in white cotton clothes and a small white cotton jacket, was in the best of humours. It evidently suited him to be the great pasha. He talked and jested about small things, making rather small jokes, not at all brilliant. And then, in his slow, handsome way he set about mixing a cocktail, of gin and vermouth and orange-juice and lime, Teresa watching him from a corner of her eye.

Kate had risen to get him a spoon, at the same moment as he stepped back from his little table, where he was stooping mixing the drink. So they brushed against one another. And she noticed, as she had noticed often with the Indians, how subtle his contact was, how he seemed to slide aside, merely brushing her, without any jolt. The soft, unmuscular movement of the dark-skinned people, their fine, unmuscular flesh, nothing braced or taut or hard, but a sort of liquid softness of texture in the skin and the flesh. So different from the muscular, jolting white people.

At the same time she shrank a little from it. That kind of liquid physical voluptuousness was somewhat repugnant to her. She preferred the dry, hard, virile contact of a white man. The blood of these people was different from her own. And they seemed to be all blood, without sinew or nerve. Silky, soft blood-flesh. Her hand where she had touched him was startled and a little shocked. That was the man of flesh he was! And a slight revulsion came over her again.

Teresa was watching with a black, seeing look. She watched Kate's starting away, her quick flush under the fair skin, the startled golden light in her eyes. She saw Ramón's subtle swerving aside, and his hasty apology. She saw the moment of race-hostility between the two people of different blood, different nerve. And she rose and came at once to Don Ramón's side, looking in the tumblers, bending over them and asking, in that curious conscious childishness of dark women,

"What do you put in them?"

"Look!" said Ramón. And with the same conscious, male child-ishness of dark men he was explaining to her gin, and vermouth, and letting her smell the bottles, and putting a little gin in a spoon for her to taste.

"It is an impure tequila," she said naïvely.

"Eight pesos a bottle," he said, laughing.

"Really!"

She looked up at him with a long, exposed dark look, and he looked down at her, his dark face seeming warmer. So she got back her blood-intimacy with him, and he was captured into that foolish-seeming softness of dark men, as if something were melting in him.

"They are all full of harem-tricks, these women," said Kate to herself.

She was a little impatient, really, seeing the big and portentous Ramón in the toils of this little woman. He who had taken such a grand attitude to marriage, when Doña Carlota was alive. And now he was as soft as warm dough in the hands of this little prostitute dress-maker. Kate resented being made so conscious of his physical presence, his full dark body inside the thin cotton clothes, his straight, strong, yet soft shoulders, and his full, splendid thighs. And the little woman drawing him hither and thither with her black eyes.

What a will the little creature had! What a powerful female will in her little dark body! She wanted to make him big and splendid. And by making him big and splendid, to hold him in her spell. The bigger and more splendid he was, the more she held him. Just his physical bigness, and the richness of his soft, dark flesh. While she herself seemed to become a small, inconspicuous thing. Only her big black eyes full of power, full of a tiger's will.

Like a revelation Kate saw it happen, saw the secret of these women. She saw why Don Ramón had wanted another wife, and another wife of his own sort, of his own blood. This new little wife of his had an almost uncanny power over him, to make him rich and gorgeous in the flesh, while she herself became inconspicuous, almost, as it were, *invisible,* save for her great black eyes. And when he was most physically gorgeous, then, by using all the power in her tense little dark body, she held him most completely.

Kate realised that once Ramón met Teresa's eyes, she, Kate, with all her understanding and her fair play, disappeared from his ken completely. He was just this big, fluid male, magnetised by the tense little dark female who was his wife. All the rest he cared nothing about. Kate was a mere extraneous presence.

And this was the only way of love Ramón would ever know, or ever want to know. It seemed a little repulsive. The big, fluid male, dark and gleaming, was slightly repulsive to her. And the little, tense female with the pallor under her dark face, and her big black eyes rather wan underneath, and opened so very wide, all her female being tense in a great effort to control the man and have him entirely, by giving him a mindless, glistening, animal preponderance, this, for a moment, enraged Kate. She couldn't bear the mindless smile on Ramón's dark face, nor the curious gleam in his eyes as he met the black, exposed eyes of his wife. But most of all she wondered over the erect, tense little figure of the dark woman, who looked so insignificant, and had such a power.

It was not fair to call her a prostitute, or to call her way of power, prostitute tricks. Teresa would be absolutely blank towards any other man except Ramón. The whole of her female soul was involved in her husband. For all other men she was a negative, silent presence, a complete evasion. As for her way of rousing and keeping Ramón, Kate hated it because it was the way of another race, and she herself couldn't do it. She called it underhand, and low, and humiliating for a woman. But in her calmer moments she was forced to ask herself, was it low and underhand?

She knew that Teresa regarded her white woman's direct approach to a man as something fake, ugly, distasteful. All the dark woman's flesh winced from the outspoken free-and-easiness of the white woman. It was true, the flappers and young women of the so-called upper classes in Mexico had started to imitate American women in ways of freedom and boldness. A distressing spectacle they were, too. Shrill, noisy, shrieking, aggressive and impudent, without any of the reckless man-to-man daring which gives a certain charm and pathos to the white flapper. Her dare-devil courage and "sporting" recklessness makes the white flapper still a bit of a heroine, even if of a misguided sort. But when the Mexican miss takes to flapping she adds even a touch of cowardliness, most often, to her aggression. She has not inherited that white ideal of being "sporting." She has inherited the dark ideal of being hidden and secret in her womanhood. And this underlies all her flaunting.

So that although the Mexico with money is becoming rapidly Americanised in every way, even in the way of its women, there is still the bulk of the population which understands only the old approach between men and women, male and female. There are still a good many women who know only the ancient mystery of female power, through glorifying the blood-male. And there are still a good many men to whom the free and easy, "equality" approach of the white woman is repugnant, something unwomanly and hostile to life.

Now Kate had all her life despised what she called the "slave" approach in a woman. Teresa, to her mind, made a slave of herself before Don Ramón. She grovelled before him, like a slave or an odalisk. She wanted nothing but the sex in him. Like a sort of prostitute.

Stay though! Was this true? Was Teresa just prostituting herself to her man? Or was she fighting all the time to keep him blood-faithful to her?

Not mind-faithful or nerve-faithful. Not merely faithful in sympathy or companionship. But blood-faithful. She was fighting to keep the man faithful to her from his blood: as, truly, he wanted to be kept.

Kate suddenly realised that this is the great fight which woman has to keep up through all the eternity of woman. This is the root and base of all human life, the blood-relation between a man and his woman. An honorable woman fights all her life to keep one man's blood faithful to her, and her triumph is her greatest honour. The man has no say in the matter. He will be kept if the woman can keep him.

Now in her previous life, Kate had kept her husband. But it had been the faithfulness of mind and nerve and sympathy, not the heavy blood-faithfulness she saw in some of the proud, dark Indian men. These men beat their wives to keep them also faithful. That too was true. But so long as the beating was simply passionate and human, the woman did not mind. Because, in the deepest soul, a proud man desires to be kept blood-faithful, and a decent woman desires the same: even at the expense of a beating.

In human relationship, the deepest desire is the desire in a man and in a woman, that they shall both be kept blood-faithful to one another. And this means a life-long fight for each other. But the fight is love, not hate, profoundly constructive, not destructive.

Kate realised, here among these people, that Desmond Burns had kept her mind-faithful, nerve-faithful, and faithful in sympathy. But he had not quite kept her blood-faithful. They had loved one another and the love had been an accepted thing to both of them, and to *this* they had remained both of them faithful.

It wasn't like Teresa and Ramón, though. She had never kept Desmond blood-faithful and blood-glamorous, as Teresa was keeping Ramón. If she had, he would not have died.

This came to her definitely as she was looking in her trunk for a book she had offered to lend Ramón. She had gone away and left him and Teresa alone in the sala, because the sight of Ramón in love had been so strange, and suddenly revealing to her. The mindless smile on his face, the black gleam of his eyes, his heavy, dark blood-presence leaning by a curious gravitation towards the little dark-faced woman, as he offered her a little gin to taste, in a spoon, and she made a blank, childish sipping-face: this had been too much for Kate, she had gone into her bedroom. The alien race. The atavistic way of love. The dark atavism of him.

This was what he was, underneath all his striving: a dark savage with the impossible fluid flesh of savages, and that way of dissolving into an awful black mass of desire. With the male conceit of savages swelling his blood and making him seem endless. While his eyes glistened in their blackness, as if the man were dissolving into a black, thick liquid.

No, she could never have physical contact with such people. Her pride of race came up strong.

And yet – this came back to her like a funeral bell clanging: if she had made Desmond a man of the blood, like this man, he would never have died. He would never have died. For it seemed to her woman's fancy that men of the powerful blood-freedom could not die. Ramón could not die. Especially with this little woman.

And Desmond would not have died.

Her heart stood still as she piled the books around her, kneeling on her knees. Desmond – ! But it wouldn't have been Desmond! Desmond! the eager, clever, fierce, sensitive Irishman, who could look into her soul, and laugh into her soul, and who had died under her eyes. Desmond, the father of her two children.

If ever he could have been the dark, mindless blood-presence that Don Ramón was now, he would not have died, and the children would have been different.

But he couldn't have been. That was the end of it. She wouldn't have wanted him to be. It meant stepping over into another race. Best stick to one's own race. Best live and die true to one's own race.

Teresa came stepping timidly into the bedroom.

"May I come?" she said, looking round excitedly at everything.

"Do," said Kate, rising from her knees and leaving little piles of books all round the trunk. There was not a book-shelf in the house.

The bedroom was fairly large, with doors opening on to the patio and showing the wet garden, the smooth mango-trunks rising like elephants' trunks out of the earth, the wet grass, the chickens beyond the sprawl of banana leaves. It had rained heavily in the night, the sky was still low with clouds. A scarlet bird dashed and sprang about a bath of water, opening and shutting brown wings from a body of pure, lovely scarlet.

But Teresa was looking with interest round the room, at the algerian curtain hung behind the bed, at the coloured bed-cover, the navajo rugs on the red tile floor, the dresses hung against the wall, the litter of books, jewellery and cigarettes.

"How nice!" she said, fingering the bed-cover.

"A friend made it me in England," said Kate.

Don Ramón's wife was fascinated by the unusual fabrics and the unusual patterns. She wanted to touch everything, especially the tangle of inexpensive jewellery that Kate left carelessly on her dressing-table. But she was careful not to admire anything aloud, lest Kate should feel constrained to give it her.

And Kate, looking at her brown neck bending down absorbed in examining the Italian toilet-cover, at the loosely-folded masses of black hair held by tortoise-shell pins, at the thin shoulders with their soft brown skin, thought to herself: this is the woman that holds Don Ramón in a spell! This little, humble, insignificant dark thing! Who would have believed it?

But Kate could not deceive herself. Teresa was not really humble or insignificant. And underneath the soft brown skin, that stooping female spine was hard and powerful, with an old, powerful female will which could call up the blood in a man and glorify it, and by glorifying hold it to herself. A new mystery.

On the sewing-table was a piece of fine India muslin, pine-apple colour, which Kate had bought in India, and which she had been cogitating over. It really was too young for her. She didn't quite know what to do with it. Teresa touched it, looking at the thread of gold along the edge.

"It isn't organdie?" she asked.

"No, it is muslin – the hand-made India muslin they used to wear so much. Won't you take it? It doesn't quite suit me, and I'm sure it will be perfect for you. Look!"

She held the muslin against Teresa's dark neck, and pointed to the mirror. Teresa saw her own eyes, then the warm-yellow, fine fabric. She said nothing, but her face glowed.

"Do take it," said Kate.

"Oh, thank you, no!"

"Yes. It doesn't suit me. I shall be glad to give it away to someone whom it becomes."

Kate was imperious too, upon occasion. Teresa took the muslin and went soft-foot, like a child, to Don Ramón in the next room.

"Look!" she said shyly; "what the señora has given me."

"Doesn't it suit her!" cried Kate, entering the sala from her bedroom. "It was made in India for someone as dark as she is. Doesn't it suit her!"

"Yes," said Don Ramón. "Very pretty."

And Teresa was covered with confusion and pleasure.

Don Ramón asked Kate to come and spend a few days with his wife at Las Yemas.

"Would you like me to?" asked Kate of Teresa.

"*Mucho! Mucho!*" came the answer, and the black eyes in the sober little face shone again with anticipation.

"She needs women-friends," said Ramón. "She has nobody."

"No," she said, turning to him. "I don't *need* anybody. But if the Señora Catarina will come, that will be *much* pleasure, *much* pleasure."

Kate went, and before the two women knew where they were, they were busy dress-making, cutting up the muslin for Teresa. Poor Teresa, for a bride her stock of clothing was scanty. She had never learned to make dresses for herself, and there had never been much ready money at her father's hacienda. She had a few poor things made by a village dress-maker, and a few old-fashioned jewels and some lace, from her mother. No-one had ever thought of dressing her up.

So Kate pinned the muslin over the brown shoulders, wondering again at the strange, uncanny softness of the dark skin, and the stiffness of the straight dark back. She draped the muslin over Teresa's slim arms. Teresa insisted on long sleeves.

"No! No!" said Kate. "It's so much prettier with short sleeves."

"But my arms are so thin!" murmured Teresa, hiding her slender brown arms with shame. They were not at all thin, only naturally slender, to suit her build. "Ah, if they were beautiful arms like yours."

Kate, as was becoming to a woman of forty, well-built and strong, was well-rounded, with full white limbs. She was afraid of getting fatter – wished she could get thinner.

"No," she said. "Your arms aren't thin. They are so pretty! Just right."

"Ah no!" said Teresa with regret. "They are thin. If they were only like yours. The men don't like little thin women, here." She spoke quite sadly.

"But Don Ramón likes *you!*" cried Kate. "I don't know what you want."

"Ah yes! Yes!" replied the other, with quiet pride. – "But I would like to be fatter. The men like it."

She was quite definite and quite determined about it.

Kate had promised to stay a few days at Las Yemas. There was a good library of books, there was a horse to ride, a boat to row, and all the fascinating life of the hacienda. Teresa was the one most interested in the hacienda. She and Kate rode out across the fields, to inspect the cactus for the tequila, or to look at the growing maize. Teresa examined the long rows of bee-hives under the trees, because the bees were not thriving. She visited the peons in their huts, encouraging the women to spin and weave. Don Ramón had introduced light looms for cotton-weaving for the women. Then tequila was being made, the whole place was full of the sweetish scent of the distilling liquor, stronger still when the sort of bark waste was spread along the road for a sort of road-mending.

Don Ramón saw his administrador every morning, but did not devote much of his time to the hacienda. He was a great deal alone, pondering the next moves, studying, thinking. Then he had to teach the hymns, the doctrine, the ritual to the minstrels and wandering priests. For this he was a great deal in Chapala. Then he had continual private interviews. As soon as the dawn came he was busy, and he continued all day. Yet in the day he never seemed tired. He seemed to put no effort into his activities. But by night-fall he was silent and ready for sleep. He always retired about nine o'clock.

Kate too usually retired early. But on the second evening of her stay, she remained up reading after Don Ramón and Teresa had gone to bed. She was agitated. She could not quite adjust herself to this marriage. It seemed to her so earthly. It seemed to make everything Ramón and Cipriano did seem a little bit cheap.

It was a very dark night, with lightning beating about on the horizons, but as yet no thunder. The rain would come in the middle of the night.

Kate went slowly and silently along the upper terrace towards the look-out. Everything dark, save the intermittent pallor of the lightning. When she came out on to the end terrace she was a little startled to see, in a gleam of lightning, Teresa crouching with her back to the wall and Ramón lying on the floor with his head against her knee, while she was slowly ruffling his thick black hair. The pair were as silent as the night.

Kate wished so much she had never come down the terrace.

"Oh!" she stammered. "I am so sorry to disturb you."

She was withdrawing in confusion. But Ramón rose slowly from the floor, and pulled forward a leather garden-chair.

"Stay for a little while," he said quickly.

Then he put a chair for Teresa, who sat down demurely. He remained standing.

"How dark it is!" said Kate. "But for the lightning I should never have seen you."

"Do you regret having seen us?" he laughed.

"Of course I didn't want to disturb you. And it *is* a surprise," she said in English. "I never thought of you except as the living Quetzal-coatl, so naturally –"

There was a moment's pause, in the black night. He stood in front of the two women – hardly discernibly white. Then the distant, bluish lightning hovered ghostly again.

"Before anything else, Señora," came his deep, insidious voice, "man is a column of blood."

He spoke in Spanish, so that both women understood.

"Is what?" said Kate.

"Man is a column of blood."

"Not only," said Kate.

"Before anything else."

The voice was so quiet in the utter darkness, so like the blood itself speaking, Kate could have screamed. There sounded something sardonic in the invisible man.

"And woman?" she asked ironically.

"Also. She is a valley of blood."

"I am more than that," said Kate, in a hard voice.

"Surely. But in the first place, a valley of darkness."

"No, I am a woman. I am myself," persisted Kate.

"Of course. But before anything else, the dark valley of blood. And man is a column of blood. Before anything else, he is that."

"I thought you were the living Quetzalcoatl."

"Quetzalcoatl is a column of blood, in the first place."

Kate was silent. All her womanly nature resisted this reducing back. She felt she had been brought to Las Yemas to be imprisoned and destroyed.

Then she felt a cool, soft, snake-like little hand seeking her own firm hands, and caressing her wrists with soft, subtle fingers.

"La Señora Catarina is alone," came Teresa's pitying, protecting voice.

Kate laughed a hard little laugh.

"I am not *less* because I am alone," she said.

"Ah yes! Ah yes!" came the soft, gentle, protective refrain from Teresa, while the delicate soft fingers, like soft-caressing little snakes curled round Kate's wrist.

"You think a woman is nothing if she is alone?" said Kate, derisive.

"She is not much. She is not much. A woman cannot remain alone and remain a woman," replied the soft voice, infinitely caressing and tenderly condescending.

Kate's very soul bristled. That little brown object of a Teresa was tenderness itself condescending to her. She withdrew her hands from contact, brusquely.

"I think I am myself, and perhaps a good deal more myself, and more of a woman, when I am alone, than when I am submitting to some man," she said.

"No, no, my dear!" crooned the soft voice of Teresa. "It isn't that you submit. I don't submit to Ramón. I don't understand it. It is that I like him very, very much, with my soul. I don't understand about submitting."

"But you think your life would be nothing without him."

"Yes, I think it. But I should live if I didn't have him. Listen. If the bandits had killed him on this roof, when you saved him – for which I like you very, very much, always. If they had killed him, I should never have married him. And I should have been at Opatlan, looking after the hacienda. Or I should have married some other man. And then I should have talked like you: *am I any less myself because I am alone?* But yes! yes! It is not that I love Ramón. I love him, yes. But perhaps I could have loved another man: you know, *love!*" – she spoke the word rather deprecatingly. "It really isn't that I love Ramón," she repeated, in her distinct, lucid, childish way. "It is that he takes charge of my soul."

"Wouldn't you rather take charge of your own?" said Kate.

"No, my dear. I can't. When I have to take charge of my own soul, I am nothing. Only when a man comes who can take my soul from me, I am something."

"And what about his soul?"

"I take it."

"Where?"

"Here!" she placed her hand on her side. "If he gives me children, the children leave me again. But I keep his soul here, always" – and she pressed her side again. "And it is this that makes me something. A woman can't be something by herself. It is like the seed in a man. It is nothing till he gives it to a woman. And a woman's soul is nothing till she gives it to a man."

"And he betrays her," said Kate.

"No no, my dear, no no!" said Teresa, shaking her finger in front of Kate's face in the dark. "He won't betray me. I have his soul in my womb, and if he betrays me I will kill his soul. He knows it. He won't betray me. And I look him in the eyes. If he begins to betray me, I see it in his eyes, and I say to him 'Look! Thou dost not betray me!' Of course I say it. But Ramón does not betray."

She ended with a certain fierce complacency. A fierce little body, full of odd conviction and savage little determination. And, in her fierce little way, very condescending to Kate.

"Still I think," said Kate, "it is better for everybody to look after their own soul."

"No no! No no! You can't. Your soul is a seed you have to give to somebody else, before it will grow. I give mine to Ramón, and he keeps it – I don't know where he keeps it. – Where do you keep my soul, Ramón?" she asked suddenly.

"I don't know," he said out of the dark. "In my heart."

"I believe it would be in his heart," said Teresa. "But I keep his soul in my inside: in my womb. And if he gives me children, they will be inside his soul, in my womb, and they will be children of his soul. Yes. Indeed I believe it. – Isn't it true, Ramón?"

"Yes, I well believe it."

"You hear! He believes it! The Señora Carlota was not like that. She loved him. She loved him very much, poor thing. But she wanted to keep her soul to herself, to give it to the Lord. – You can't do it. If you marry a good man, you must give your soul to him, and pray to the Lord for yourself and him. It is no good praying to the Lord for yourself alone, after you marry a good man."

"But I have been married – to a good man," said Kate.

"Yes. But you didn't give him your soul."

"He didn't want it. He believed I should keep a soul of my own."

"Look now! There are many men like that. They are afraid. But Ramón is not afraid. Nor am I either. I say to Ramón: 'Look! Thou'st got my soul – I don't know where. And I've got thine inside me. Don't make any mistake.' – But I always look him in the eyes. I look in his eyes. Always. I am afraid to do it, but I look in his eyes, even if one day he kills me. – However he won't kill me."

"Come! Come!" he said. "Thou'st talked enough. The Señora Catarina will have a head-ache."

"I don't think it," said Teresa. "She doesn't like it that thou sit'st on the ground and I play with thy hair. She thinks thou'rt only Quetzalcoatl, as thou sayst. And thou sayst thou'rt a column of blood. It's the same to me. Thou art Quetzalcoatl and thou art a column of blood. Very good. It is true. But I keep thy soul in my inside, and thou hast not got two souls, however many names thou hast, Quetzalcoatl or Column."

"Also Ramón," said he, in a laughing voice.

"Also! Don't I know it. Thou art great among men. If thou sayst thou art a god, then it is true. I well believe thou art a god. But I have thy soul in my inside, and I hope to have thy children there too, Don Ramón, or Quetzalcoatl, or Monsignor Column, as you like. It is already much. If thou art not a god, there are no gods. And if thou wishest me to be a goddess, I will be it. Always at your service. Since thou hast my soul – I don't know where. And I have thine, I know where."

"Come! Come! Enough, thou art wound up," said he, drawing her from the chair.

"Yes, I am wound up. Because the Señora Catarina thinks thou shouldst not have a Teresita for a wife. But I say, yes. The Señora Catarina is ashamed for thee. But she saved thy life, and therefore I will tell her. Yes, yes, I would not tell these things to my father confessor, nor to the soul of my mother. I would not tell them to thee. But she saved thy life, and she is ashamed for thee, because I have thy soul. So I tell her. If thou dost not want to hear, thou shouldst go away."

"Ah, *Teresita mia,* come, thou hast had thy say. Come."

"Yes, I have had my say. Good-night, Señora Catarina. You understand me."

"Good-night, Señora Teresa. Yes, I understand you."

"Good-night, Señora Kate. Las Yemas is a hacienda of words."

"Good-night, Don Ramón. It is well to understand."

Kate went to her room considerably impressed by the little viper of a Teresa. What a fierce little savage she was! And how she had thought things out, in her logical, half-Latin way. She was not afraid: she was not cowed. Always Kate came back to the same admiration for the unbroken courage which surged up volcanic. The strange fiery courage of life, such as she had never met before. Always she had known the courage of sacrifice and suffering and death. But there was no thought of sacrifice in Teresa's mind. She would give a lesser thing for a greater, or an old, unliving thing for something new and living. And that was the extent of her sacrifice.

The next day Teresa seemed more blithe. She had walked before under a certain repression, her big, dark eyes had had a faint veil of resentment. She knew Kate looked on her as in some way an inferior. And she was not prepared to accept this. Kate was a tall, blooming, handsome woman, a woman of the world, a woman used to associate with clever men, men of the world. A woman with all the education of the white people. Whereas she, Teresa, was small and brown and ignorant and poor. But after all, Ramón had never wanted to marry Kate: that was obvious. And he had truly married herself, Teresa. Why didn't he want Kate? And why did he want Teresa?

Teresa had answered these questions in her own way, and taken her stand. And she had fathomed her secret dislike of the white woman, the same dislike she felt for all foreign white women. They were so assured, and they kept their souls so fast for themselves. They never gave their souls to their husbands.

Before she married, Teresa had thought they were right, the white women, to keep their souls for themselves. She had thought they were right, in being assured and in full possession of themselves.

Now, since she had given her soul to Ramón, and taken his soul, she suddenly felt contempt for these assured, foreign white women who talked to men like men. They roused in her a certain disgust: the disgust that foreign white men had always inspired in her. They seemed to her unnatural and ugly in soul: ugh, so ugly! As white foreign men were almost invariably ugly, physically unclean, in spite of all their washing. Unclean *under* their skin.

But Kate had saved Ramón's life. And Kate was undeniably beautiful. And *somewhere* Kate had a true tenderness, like Teresa's own tenderness, which was also cautious and reasoning as well as deep. And Ramón wanted Kate to marry Cipriano, because Cipriano wanted it.

So, for all these reasons, Teresa did the last thing expected, and told all her private, passionate woman's thinkings, told them all out before Kate and Ramón. Ramón loved her no less. She had known he would not love her less. He loved her more, because of her fiery, passionate courage. She knew he would love her more. The passionate courage he held sacred.

But would Kate now leave off treating her as an inferior? That was the point. For, undeniably, Kate, in a very subtle and indefinable way had treated Teresa as an inferior. Had *felt* her an inferior: slightly.

Teresa had known this always from white foreigners. She saw that white foreigners, all of them, in their heart of hearts looked on all Mexicans as inferiors. At the worst, they showed contempt. At the best, they were cautious, showing a certain false deference. She had seen plenty of white people show this false deference to Ramón. To her, however, to the insignificant Teresa they had only too often let the contempt come forth into sight. And all her life she had more or less allowed it. Not that she felt inferior. On the contrary, she felt as a rule that the white foreigners were actually, in their being, the inferiors. But they seemed to have the money of the world in their hands, the sway of the world's dominion. Therefore one had to let them assume this superiority. One had to allow them to imply to one a certain inferiority. It was almost a habit.

Since she had married Ramón, however, Teresa was determined not to accept this implication of inferiority. She had been to school with American girls, and her brothers had always brought foreigners to Opatlan. Now, since she had married Ramón she had determined to know no more foreigners. So the first woman Ramón had presented her to, was, of course, the foreign Kate. And Kate, quite subtly, but quite unmistakably showed that she looked on Teresa as an inferior. Nay more, Kate didn't want to look on Teresa as an inferior. She did it against her wanting.

And Teresa was determined not to have it. So she came down to breakfast next morning with a new *insouciance* and a sort of silent blitheness.

"How did you sleep?" she said to Kate courteously, as she would have said it to a Mexican.

As a matter of fact Kate had slept very badly. The night had been black, black dark, a blackness thick enough to contain anything. This sense of black, *active* darkness was, in Kate's mind, peculiar to Mexico. In all other countries darkness seemed immobile. But here it seemed alive and rather horrifying. And then, just as she had dozed off, bang came the thunder and down came the rain, smashing down with a weight and a ferocity unnatural to water. This in thick darkness, with occasional watery gleams of lightning. And a drumming crash of falling water kept up for hours. Add to this Kate's thoughts: her conning over and over again Teresa's declaration and challenge. For of course it was a challenge to Kate's womanhood, flung right in her face. Teresa's gentle, subtle, serpentine condescension, with its poisonous tang of contempt. Teresa's delicately unveiled contempt for Kate's womanhood, for Kate's way of wifehood.

"Does she expect me, then, to behave to Cipriano Viedma as she behaves to Ramón?" Kate asked herself indignantly. And of course had to answer herself, that they all *did* expect it, Cipriano no less than the others.

"Am I going to give my soul to Cipriano Viedma, and live around his soul in my womb?" she asked herself indignantly. "Be, in short, his slave-woman, only living to carry his soul in my womb, with no soul of my own? Am I going to do that? Am I going to be slave-woman to one of these Mexicans? I am *not!* Insidious little viper of a Teresa, she knew what she was doing. She wanted to bring me down to her slave level of life and love. But I'll show her. – That's what they've got me here for. Don Ramón the same. Sly, sly, sly, all the time trying to bring one down to that level. – We'll see!"

And she lit a cigarette in the dark and smoked furiously.

"That miserable old trick of a woman living like a slave, just for the sake of a man. Only living to carry his precious soul in her womb. And his equally precious children! I, at my time of life, and after all I've lived through! I should think so."

Kate was indignant, but she could not quite make her indignation thorough. Somewhere she was playing the traitor to herself. Somewhere she was envying, oh, so slightly, Teresa her dark skin, her subtle, serpent-delicate fingers, her big dark eyes with their savage assurance, and above all, the man's soul in her womb. She *looked* as if she had got a man's soul in her womb, and that was what gave her her secret, savage pride. Her conceit. Her darkie's conceit! Her straight little back.

All very well if you'd been *born* dark, born that way: nearer to the slave. But if you'd been born white, and if you disbelieved even in voluntary slavery, then you had nothing to do but remain true to your own colours and colour.

"Not very well," said Kate. "The rain kept me awake."

"You look as if you had not slept very well," said Teresa. "Under your eyes."

Kate smoothed the skin under her eyes with her finger.

"One gets that look in Mexico," she said. "It's not an easy country to keep one's youth in. But you are looking awfully well, after your fierceness last night."

"Yes, I feel very well."

Teresa's face was not so wan, and her dark eyes had a laugh in them, her brown skin was recovering its delicate, fruit-like bloom. Yes, she had the bearing of a little Aztec princess, in her soft, silent pride and distant assurance.

"Ramón has gone away again," she said. "He says he hopes I can entertain you, but I told him I hadn't much hope. But we can bathe, or ride, or row in the boat. I'm afraid the sun won't come out just yet."

They were taking coffee on the upper terrace. The sky was low with cloud, the frogs were singing frantically. Across the lake the mountains were deep blue-black, and little pieces of white fluffy vapour wandered low and horizontal. The tops of the mountains were in cloud. The cloud made a level sky-line of whitish softness the whole length of the black mountains. Across the dove-brown water one sail was blowing.

"It is like Europe – like the lakes in Germany and Austria, in the Tyrol where it rains so much," said Kate.

"Do you like Europe very much?" asked Teresa.

"Yes, I love it."

"Do you feel you must go back to it?"

"Soon. If only to look at it."

"Do they want you very much in Europe?"

"Yes," said Kate. "My mother, and my children." – Then she considered a while, and a sense of truth made her add: "But not *very* much, really. They don't want me very badly. I don't fit in with their lives."

"Ah, they don't want you very much!"

"Yes, they do. In a way. Only –"

"But here they want you very much."

"Who?" said Kate, taken by surprise.

"We do. I know Ramón wants you very much to stay."

"Because of General Viedma?" said Kate, making the plunge.

"Yes. Also. But apart from General Viedma, he wants it."

"Why?" said Kate abruptly.

"Who knows! I also don't want you to go away. I want you to stay here always."

"But why?"

"Who knows! Only I want it. I don't want you to go back over there."

"Yet it is my home."

"Yes. Hernan Cortés' home was in Spain, but he made it here in Mexico."

"And what good did it do?"

"I believe, much. I believe that Mexico wants a few good people from over there. But the good people don't come, only those that want money. You don't want money from Mexico. You don't want anything. You want only to live here."

"I must go to Europe first."

"But why?"

"I must."

Teresa looked at her with big, contemplative black eyes.

"You are a woman of will," she said.

"And you?" laughed Kate.

"Yes. But different."

XVII

I T HAD RAINED VERY HEAVILY in the night. Kate went to the roof, to look at the world. The morning was sunny, with many silky white clouds in the sky, piling and rolling along the tops of the low hill-mountains opposite, and casting dapples of shadow on the green, distant slopes, and the grey scores of rock. Near at hand, the shore was all fleecy and pale green with the round, drooping willows that Kate liked so much. The mango-trees stood solid, dropping their hard green fruit like the testes of bulls. The red-roofed, mud-black cabins of the peons stood among the greenness of trees on either side of the road, a wagon with solid wheels was being hauled by eight bullocks, while another wagon with four long-eared mules was going down to the shore for sand. She saw the mules jumping and floundering in the sand as if they were swimming, pulling out the heavy wagon on its high wheels, while the tall peon in white flourished the lasso-reins. Scattered on the slopes and in the flat fields by the lake were white peons, dotted in twos and threes like white sea-gulls. Among the spikey tequila plants a long line of peons were busy upon the steep slope rising to the mountains. The mountains beyond rose bare and empty, the empty abstraction of Mexico.

Cattle were wandering round the hacienda and straying on the shingle beach, cropping the new-coming grass among the acacia thorns and stones. There were many donkeys, and mother-donkeys with little foals all legs and long, long ears pricking up in delightful anticipation of existence, flicking themselves suddenly into a staccato gallop and going to the she-ass for a drink. There were calves careering with uplifted tails, frisky, and two bull-calves having an earnest fight. A black ram was persistently tormenting the young sows, sniffing at their rear and butting them, while they ran squealing away. Till one sow turned with a grab and a fierce rush, and the black ram with flat horns went off helter-skelter, his thick tail flopping between his legs.

All the animals seemed to be entire. There was not the rage for castration that there is in Europe. And they had quite a different rhythm from that of European animals. Kate used to say that all the animals in Mexico seemed cowed. But as she watched them she decided it was not so. They only had their own heavier, more silent way of life. The donkeys all the time were nipping one another and kicking out, then running towards one another in the weirdest way possible, necks stretched out, to bray. And the peon was throwing stones at them.

Always throwing stones. The peons were always throwing stones: at the cattle, at the pigs, at the birds, at one another. The girls threw stones at the boys, the boys threw stones at one another. If a mother was angry with her daughter, she immediately stooped to pick up a stone to throw at her. Whizz! she threw so viciously. But always so as just to miss. And that was how they were. They threw so viciously, aiming just wide of the mark. The same with the men throwing at the cattle. They wanted the stone to go just *over* the animal's back: not quite to hit. And the cow or the donkey knew perfectly. It always amused Kate to see a woman taking her pig on a string down to the lake to drink: the pig so often escaping: and the woman viciously throwing stones at it all the way, to drive it home. And the pig skipping quite aware of the woman's intentions.

Always this *appearance* of violence and sullen ferocity, without much damage done. Although, to tell the truth, somebody was always killing somebody. The ferocity was real enough. But also was real a long, passive tolerance, and a certain static fidelity. A basic faithfulness, where faith was possible and where faith was understood.

Kate could not say of the country: This is my country. But then she could say that of no country. There was no charm of Europe here, none of the delicacy and the winsomeness and exquisiteness. This was heavy, and of the earth. There was no delightful appeal. This heavy-footed *à terre* spirit was sometimes hateful to her. This slow, indomitable kind of waiting, waiting, enduring: he lives longest who lives last. Spreading the will over slow, dark centuries, and counting the individual existence a trifle. A faithfulness that could be the same, slow, dark, age-long. And a sudden ferocity that could take life suddenly, for a mere trifle, and suffer the death-penalty without caring a straw.

A different *tempo* of life, darker, heavier, more resistant and more enduring. These people could forget so quickly, and care so little. And yet they never changed. They were not faithful to the moment. They were faithful to something darker and slower, within themselves. Careless, callous, ferocious, brutal. And at the same time capable of dark, powerful affection and a heavy, lasting, impersonal gentleness. It was hard for Kate to get the clue to the impersonal brutality and the impersonal gentleness of the people, their capacity for dark, callous fidelity, which ignored the accidents and the ruffling of the personal surface. In European life, every personal ripple is of perfect importance. These people had a certain brutal indifference to the personal ripples. They would play at personal tricks. But either satirically, for fun; or sardonically, jeering. Underneath, a black indifference to the personal world and the personal values.

The familiarity of the servants and the peons also was a burden to her. It was as if they were silently, darkly insisting, all the time: *Blood is one blood. We are all of one blood.* They were deferential. They were ready to serve. But out of their dark eyes all the time came the heavy, overbearing assertion: *The blood is one blood.* They silently, unconsciously claimed a blood equality. In blood, in sex we are all equal.

Kate was of good family. She had been brought up to believe that her blood was special, finer than the blood of the common working people. She was to be reverenced for her fine blood.

And therefore she resented deeply, darkly the blood-familiarity of these peons. They looked on her as a blood-equal. She saw it in the eyes of the men, she heard it in the words of the women. The men would not at all have thought it an unspeakable honour to possess her. Their blood was as good as hers. Which she could never allow.

At the same time they did honour her as a higher being. But for her own individual spirit, her greater consciousness and her greater range of understanding. So long as it was basic blood-knowledge. As soon as she used her mere learning, they jeered at her. As soon as she used ready-made opinions and judgments, they made a mock of her. Everything must come straight from the blood, and the blood was one blood.

But the man or woman who rose beyond them, in understanding, in courage, in prowess, this man or this woman was higher than they, and tinged with divinity. Courage was the great god-quality. And the courage of living understanding was the highest courage, the highest godliness.

She realised how clever Don Ramón really was. In wearing the sarape and the linen drawers, and in having the guaraches on his bare feet, he was as they were, a blood-being. He was naked as they were naked. He made no pretence otherwise.

But in the fineness of his sarape and the speciality of the colouring, he claimed a distinction which belonged to him alone. This they accepted at once, gladly. They were glad, overjoyed to salute their superior, and to give service. But not a superior who imagined himself above them in blood. And not a superior of mere cunning and circumstance. Least of all a money superior. Money-superiority brought out the very worst in them, that brutal cynicism which is death to living manhood.

Kate understood, now, Don Ramón's position. She understood the confident familiarity of the peons and the men who served him, the singers, the guard of Quetzalcoatl, the ordinary peons. They spoke to him as if he were one among them. And he allowed it: did not seem at all perturbed. Which, at first, had outraged Kate. But now, as she saw these men at Las Yemas, as she saw them coming and going about the business of Quetzalcoatl, she realised that they had given to Ramón, finally and forever, a beautiful easy fealty that cared nothing about straining gnats or swallowing camels. Ramón was a man as they were men. At the same time, rising from the same roots of manhood as they rose themselves, being a man of the pulsing blood, as they were, he rose higher than they, the pulse of his blood was more subtle, his being was beyond them. And therefore he was the Chief, he had something godly in him, which they were overjoyed to serve. Because he was so intensely a man, with a beating heart and secret loins and lips closed on the same secret of manhood, because he was so intensely a man, more intensely a man than they were, therefore he was a god to them. He was their god. And they worshipped his supremacy in the mystery of being a man. That was all they cared.

They gave him a splendid fealty, easy and natural. They would swallow none of his camels. But they would strain none of his gnats. They knew him.

And this, Kate realised, was the secret of American democracy, had always been the secret, would always remain the secret. The man of the greatest manhood, he was the chief among men, he represented God. Not the man of the idea, not the man of any special emotion or capacity. The man of complete, male manhood.

Primarily, man was a column of blood, said Don Ramón. But a column of individual blood. Nakedly individual. None of the father to son fallacy. The father in his manhood is one column of blood. The son in his manhood is another, absolutely different. Manhood is not a family affair.

It was no wonder Ramón succeeded. It was no wonder the mass of men were with him. They were with him naturally, even without excitement or enthusiasm. There was more enthusiasm for Cipriano than for Ramón. But then Cipriano was a man of action and personal leadership, Ramón's was the leadership of the manhood of understanding.

"If Don Ramón is Quetzalcoatl and a god," Kate said to Teresa, "don't you want to be the same? Don't you want to be a goddess, as much as he is a god?"

"No," said Teresa. "I don't want it. The same Ramón doesn't want it. But he thinks it is his duty as a man."

"Do you mean Don Ramón doesn't want to be the living Quetzalcoatl?"

"No. No. He doesn't want it. He *is* it, you understand. I believe it. Ramón is a god as well as a man. It is easy to see. No other man is like him. But he doesn't like to be there before all the people. As a man, he is not like that. He is shy, and very private. He suffers, yes, he suffers at having to show himself. But he says the man in him must suffer at times for the sake of the god in him, and the god in the people. And I – yes! Yes, if it was necessary I would go before the people to represent the goddess, because I am Ramón's wife, and I am so much of a goddess. But I *don't* want to. I would do it for Ramón's sake. And he says no, not unless I do it for my own sake. No, I can't do it for my own sake. I don't understand enough. And Ramón has got all my soul. If they want a woman who gave her soul to her husband, and carried his soul always inside her, so that she never cared about anything else, they can put a wooden image of me sitting with my hands in my lap. But not me myself. Because I am Ramón's all the time, I don't belong to all the other people. I belong to only one man, not to all the men of the world. I say to Ramón they can put an image of a woman with her head bent down and her hair hiding her face, sitting still with her hands in her lap, always like that, if they want the wife of Quetzalcoatl. But she would never look up. – However, that is only for me. You are different. You are different."

"How am I different?" said Kate, rather jealous.

"Yes, you are different. You are woman for all the people in the world, as Ramón is Quetzalcoatl for all the men in the world. I, no."

"You don't think I'm the perfect wife?" said Kate, chagrined.

"You, no! You, no! You are more. You ought to be a wife, yes. But you are a woman of all the people in the world. So you are."

"You think I ought to be a goddess?" said Kate ironically.

"Yes! Yes! Also Ramón thinks so. He says that you are the universal woman."

"No more than you are the universal wife."

"It is different. A wife is only a wife. But a woman is woman to all the men and all the people in the world. So you are."

"You don't think I could ever be the perfect wife?" Kate repeated the question.

"No! No!" replied Teresa, with a melancholy sing-song.

"Then I'd better not try being a wife any more."

"Yes! Yes! There are men who don't want a wife like me. Ramón wants it so. But there are men who don't want it so. There are men who want a universal woman for their wife. Men who don't understand everything, everything, like Ramón, they want a wife who knows a great deal, knows the world and all the things that matter. I, no. I don't know. I don't know. But Ramón knows."

"And you think Cipriano Viedma doesn't know so much?"

"He knows already very much. But not as Ramón knows. It is different. It is different. He is very good, very good, Don Cipriano. Ramón loves him very much, he loves him very much."

"And he thinks I ought to marry him?"

"Yes. He says it would be good for Don Cipriano if you married him. Because Don Cipriano wants it very much, very much he wants it."

"And what do you say?"

"I say yes. I say yes. You would be a very good wife for Don Cipriano, he likes you very much. But you don't like him?"

"Yes, I like him."

"But not much? Not enough to marry him?"

"Perhaps. But I'm not sure. I don't believe that people should marry when their race is so different as mine is different from General Viedma's."

"But I have got Spanish blood and native blood," said Teresa. "I am the daughter of different races. And who knows if Don Cipriano is not the same."

"He *feels* so different from me."

"It is true. But at times one must do something that is different from everything else. The priest told me I should probably lose my soul if I married Ramón. He said if I believed that Ramón was anything more than an ordinary man, not divine at all, I should certainly be damned. But I married Ramón and I believe he is more a god than other men. I believe he is more of God than the priest or the bishop. I believe that Ramón can save my soul. So I don't confess any more, and I don't take the sacrament. And that is really a big change. If you have to make a change by not marrying a man of your own colour, who knows, perhaps it is the will of the Lord."

"It may not be my own will."

"Ah, that is different. – But if you want Don Cipriano to come here, I will send him a word. If not, he won't come."

Kate sat for some time with narrowed eyes, cogitating. Then she said:

"Yes, tell him to come, so that I can know him better. But only for that reason, so that I can know him better. But I don't know how I shall feel when I do know him better."

"Very good. I will write a note to Ramón, and he can telephone from Chapala."

XVIII

T HIS BROUGHT CIPRIANO in the evening, along with Ramón. And in Cipriano's eyes the suppressed gleam of desire, and the darkness of his intense, heavy *will,* which always made Kate withdraw on her defences.

They talked the affairs of Quetzalcoatl, and there was a good deal to say. The Archbishop of Mexico had excommunicated Ramón and Cipriano, and had preached death to all their followers. Having succeeded in rousing considerable blind enthusiasm, he had marched out of the cathedral and headed a procession to the church of San Juan Batisto, the church of the Black Saviour, which had become the metropolitan church of the Sons of Quetzalcoatl. The government, who knew that they would have to fight the Archbishop sooner or later, had sent soldiers, arrested the Archbishop for conducting a procession through the streets, which was an illegal proceeding, and after some bloodshed scattered the procession. San Juan, the church of Quetzalcoatl in the capital, was defended by a host of the guards of Quetzalcoatl, and the mob were threatening to attack. The Knights of Columbus had brought out their secret stores of arms, and were arming the people in the name of the Church. Some priests had gone over to Quetzalcoatl, some were haranguing the people in the churches, preaching death and extermination to Quetzalcoatl. The government had ordered the cathedral and all churches to be closed. The streets of the capital were full of people, some streets all white with a sudden out-flow of white sarapes with the blue and earth-brown decorations, other streets full of men armed by the Knights of Columbus. At any moment General Narciso Beltran might declare a rebellion in the name of the Church and the army. In which case Cipriano would call up his men in the west. And the government would either have to take a stand between the two, or declare for Quetzalcoatl. For the government could not possibly unite with the Church. In all probability it would depend on General Gallardo and the socialist interest.

Ramón had not been anxious to have the government declare for Quetzalcoatl. He wanted as long as possible to avoid the political taint. But it is never possible for long, particularly in a country like Mexico.

The government refused to liberate the Archbishop, because the Archbishop refused to pledge himself to compel peace as far as possible, and to obey the conditions of the law which established freedom of worship in Mexico. The Archbishop flatly refused to pledge himself to abstain from any form of attack, in church or elsewhere, upon any other form of religion. He declared that Quetzalcoatl was not a religion, but a blasphemy. So he was kept in prison. While the Knights of Columbus raged, and more priests were arrested, and General Narcissus was expected to pronounce at any moment, from the city of Puebla. But Puebla is not yet Mexico.

"The Archbishop will bring us once more into civil war," said Cipriano. "It is the usual act of Christian charity."

"It still may be possible to prevent a break with the Church," said Ramón. "If the Church will accept Quetzalcoatl, the people may still confess and obey the priests, the priests may still celebrate the mass, at certain seasons."

"Isn't that a curious compromise?" said Kate.

"The Christian Religion is the religion of the soul's redemption – mine is the religion of the redeemed Adam, in whom dwells the Holy Spirit, the Holy Ghost. I will kneel to the old mass of Redemption, if they will lift up their hands with me, as the Risen Adam, Redeemed with Blood. I will still kneel at Easter."

"I don't understand," said Kate.

"Don't you know the mysteries? In all religions the dead body of Adam, or the unredeemed Adam, was buried at the foot of the cross, and the blood of the Redeemer showered down on him. So he rose again, as before the Fall. Mine is the religion of the Redeemed Adam, guided from within by the Holy Ghost. But I will still kneel, at Easter, to the great mass of the Sacrifice. I will take from the priest the sacrament of the Crucified Redeemer. I will do it at Easter, in re-membrance. But my ritual will be the ritual of the Redeemed Adam, and the cross is again enclosed in the circle of the Unity. And the foot of the cross is in the House of Life, not in the grave. It is the Lower Root from which everything proceeds, and has proceeded, in genesis. The risen Adam. And at the head of the cross is the Ram with the

Golden Horns. The passion of the Lamb is consummated, the blood of Sacrifice has done its work and ceased to flow. At the summit of the cross is the Ram with the horns of power, and thunder is in his forehead, when the earth once more marries the heavens."

"I don't understand," said Kate.

"You would, if you studied the Old Mysteries. The day of the naked cross is over, the soul is whole again over and above her divisions. The rose is exalted around the cross. And the four winds of heaven blow from the four quarters of the sky, and the soul sways, like a rose on a stem, but bleeds no more, like the plucked rose. The lance that separates those things which proceed from genesis and from below, from those things that proceed from above, is no longer a weapon inflicting two wounds, whence the water and the blood flow together. The lance passes and makes no wound, through the side of the Redeemed Adam, because in him the cross is accomplished, and the soul recovers her wholeness. Whole beyond even the Tau and the Life-Loop. The soul resumes her wholeness; it is the Redeemed Adam, it is the rosy cross. The rose of life assumes ascendance over the cross of sacrifice."

Kate watched him with wondering eyes.

"It is only the language of the old symbols," he said, smiling. "I can tell it no plainer. If you do not understand, that is because you have not chosen to understand." He was still teasing her.

"Do *you* understand?" said Kate to Cipriano.

"Ramón taught me," he said, carelessly.

"I don't think I want to understand," said she. "I never cared for mysticism and New Jerusalems and Rosy Crosses and Ankhs and Heavenly Brides. They always seemed to me a bit feeble."

"Very good! Very good!" laughed Ramón. "It is only the semi-barbaric method of thinking in images: image-thinking, I believe they call it. It was once supposed to be the finest and purest form of thinking. It still has a charm for me. The mysteries become so real. The mysteries become so real, and governments, presidents, popes, proletariat, all become so unreal. The life of the soul." His dark eyes seemed to dance, and his face to glow.

"But the soul which flies off without a body."

"Yes. Yes. I know it. It isn't good. But sometimes it is Lethe, the Chalice."

"I didn't think you wanted Lethe, and forgetting."

"Sometimes. Sometimes. Sometimes. Sometimes I must drink from the old chalice. Listen! Listen Señora! The Little Creation, of the Logos, is consummated again. The Æon of the Little Bear is ended. The earth has passed Polaris. Listen! Listen! The Rose has fallen over the Cross again. Or rather, the Cross has fallen into the Rose. The Return is over. You white people are the people of the Soul's Return to the Creator, the reverse direction, the soul's regeneration. You are the people of the Little Creation, the creation of the Logos. And your travel is finished. Drink with me, Señora. Drink with me. Cipriano has drunk already, and Teresa is always in the cup. You drink with me. Let it be intoxication, and then Lethe. Drink with me."

He poured the red Spanish wine into her glass.

"Look!" he said. "It is red. The Catholic Church wouldn't let you drink the blood. The blood of the Tree. The blood from the neck of the Bull. The blood from the severed head. But this is the blood of the Thigh, and you may drink with me. Poor Persephone. You can be queen in hell, with us. Cipriano will drink with us."

He filled Cipriano's glass too. Kate watched him fascinated. Her knees were trembling with strange excitement and with fear. She felt her heart would die. Ramón fascinated her. He seemed so big and demon-like, and his strange exultation made her tremble all through her body.

"I don't know what I am drinking to," she stammered, fingering the stem of her glass. Cipriano never looked at her. He sat beside her with his head sunk, and a dark, secret look on his face, as if gloating.

"Drink! Drink!" said Ramón. "You will never know till you have drunk. The Æon of the Little Creation of the Logos is closing. The Little Cosmos of Polaris is done. We've come to the end of the Via Crucis, we've finished the road of the Cross, the road of Return, the road of Redemption. The sun is dark again, and the moon is blood. Listen!

"When the Great Creation set forth, the human soul climbed down the seven heavens, into Matter, seeking, seeking, seeking. Tell me what she was seeking? She was seeking her husband. The soul was striving through Chaos and through all the spheres, and gradually, like a pearl, accomplishing herself in the flesh. Stride by stride, with great effort, she became flesh, the naked bride of the soul, the intact virgin. What did she want? She wanted a husband to cover her nakedness. She wanted a body to consummate her. She was the slow pearl slowly forming. The soul.

"And sphere by sphere she climbed eagerly into Matter. And each time she entered a new sphere, came the great intoxication of her delight, as in one more degree she became flesh. It was her great creative marriage, the soul wooing Matter and becoming flesh. Each time it was the bride when the bridegroom cometh. And each time again, Lethe! Lethe! Lethe! Lethe! Don't forget the forgetting. Each time the soul in delight became more perfectly herself in flesh, she forgot the star she was before, she forgot the nebula that ante-dated the star she had become. Wedding after wedding, till the soul was incarnate. Beautiful, incarnate soul, with a mouth and breasts and belly and thighs. Such as we have.

"And then the Great Journey of creation was consummated, the Great Cosmos was created, the seven heavens were substantiated. When the soul passed the sphere of the Sun, fire filled her, she was clothed in the Sun. But when she entered the sphere of the Moon, blood leapt into all her veins, and she knew the perfect rapture of incarnation, that was the intoxication. Ah, that was the day. And after that day, ah, such a forgetting. Such a perfect forgetting. Only we for whom the moon in her heaven once has turned to blood can know the rapture of such a forgetting. From the sphere of the moon's forgetting, with blood in her veins and perfect forgetfulness of all the trembling journey of her previous bodilessness, the soul that was clothed in the moon of blood stepped into the next sphere, partook of the next cup of intoxication, entered the realm of earth, and became flesh, with strong bones within her like the branches of a tree.

"And then the souls of man and woman danced on earth, in the perfect rapture of their consummation, the glory of their incarnation into flesh. Many days they sang, in the manner of birds, and many days they danced. Till the sleep of the intoxication overtook them, the Lethe of perfect forgetfulness. After which the soul awoke in complete forgetfulness of the tremulous, staggering, bodiless journey down the ladder of stars, she thought she had always walked in the pride of her flesh, the accomplished pearl. This was the perfect Adam, and the perfect Eve.

"But the Lord God had planted the Tree of Memory, the Tree

of the Knowledge of Return, in the middle of the Garden. And at the foot of the Tree was the ever-unsatisfied serpent.

"Now let me tell you the tragedy of the serpent, that great dragon. As his soul climbed slowly down the stair of stars, through the seven spheres, towards the great accomplishment of incarnation, he failed in one of the stages. He slipped, as it were, on one of the stars, before his incarnation in that star was accomplished. Perhaps it was in the sphere of the sun that he quailed. He quailed, and the sun never clothed him perfectly. The perfect intoxication of the sun never overtook him, and never the perfect sleep. Never the perfect forgetting. He put his mouth to that cup, and trembled, and the drink was spilled. He never was perfectly clothed in the sun, he never was gathered into Lethe. He never was able to forget.

"He never was perfected. And he never was able to forget. And this is the serpent's tooth. His imperfection rankling, and rankling his inability to forget. He could be neither in one blessedness, nor the other. Neither [be] perfect in his flesh, like a pearl of the greatest price, nor perfect in his spirit that knew no flesh. Neither one nor the other. He had desired flesh, and quailed. Now, from his unperfected flesh, he desired again the state of pure spirit, before flesh had divided him off from the all.

"Cowardice had made him fail. His failure made him wish that all should fail. He saw Adam and Eve in the Garden, accomplished and perfect in the flesh, perfect in incarnation like pearls of the greatest price, and perfect in forgetting, like gods of the flesh. And envy filled him: envy, envy, envy, which is the stem, as cowardice is the root of evil. Fear is natural to all souls. But cowardice is failure to accept the consummation granted.

"The serpent envied Adam and Eve the beauty and the wholeness of their incarnate being, two souls perfectly fulfilled, like pearls, in tender flesh. And he said: 'How shall I spoil the beauty of their completeness?'

"Therefore he encouraged Eve to eat of the Tree of Memory. And Eve ate, and was amazed. Then she said to Adam: 'You eat.' And he ate, and was amazed.

"For immediately they had eaten of the Tree of Knowledge, vague memory filled them, of the Æons when they were not flesh, but spirit, of the Æons even before the sun, when Chaos was not entered, and they were souls immobile and changeless, in the changeless bright lake of souls, which is the Father. Vague memory of all the Æons, of all their successive stages of incarnation, of all their strange, painful journey down the stair of stars, into the present being in flesh, vague and confused came the memory of all this upon them, causing the first great woe in the heart, the first startled rebellion in the mind.

"The serpent had done his work. The heel of Eve was as a bruise, the heel of her flesh which must forever kiss the earth, the heel of her earthly flesh. She had forgotten utterly the bright glad quest of her own incarnation, the bright glad triumph of her being in flesh. And Adam even more so. He rebelled against the earth and the bone of his own body. He rebelled against the moon of his blood. He looked at the sun, and wanted to go back, to take the backward track, back, to be clothed in the sun, back to the great moveless, changeless lake of bright souls, which was God.

"It was done: the serpent's poison of discontent was in his blood. 'Good!' said the Lord Almighty. 'Good! If it be so, go forth, and find your own way back. There is a way. Climb back into bodilessness, as you climbed down.'

"So the first thing was sacrifice and the shedding of blood. The shedding of the blood of sacrifice.

"First, they made the body a thing unclean, the woven tissue of this flesh they wanted to strike away. Then, when the flesh with its primal needs and appetites was struck down, laid low, when the mind had conquered the flesh, then it was the greater conquest, the conquest of the blood, the conquest of the moon, the conquest of woman, the conquest of sex. All the time the mind, which is in living man the same as spirit in the heavens, was struggling back, back up the spheres, off the sphere of earth, to the sphere of the moon and the blood. Beyond the sphere of moon and blood, back to the sphere of fire, to be clothed in the sun. And beyond the sphere of the sun, past Gemini and Taurus and Aries, to the New Jerusalem.

"They killed the passion of the body and the bowels and the heart, and ruled all this with the mind. They killed the passion of the loins and the breast, and governed sex and the love of men and women with the mind. They killed the mystery of the thighs and their manhood and the soft thighs of womanhood, full of the strength of their going. They killed the mystery of the shoulders and hands and all the busy magic of making. They killed the kneeling Hercules of the first strength of uprightness, they killed Taurus of the neck where the bull's blood is at its most perfect. Men neither eat nor drink any more, save with the mind. No woman nurses her child any more at the soft breast of the happy pearl, fulfilled of Lethe and forgetfulness. But with the mind she nurses her child, and her mind dwells on the child that is starting in her womb, so that from the first day of the Conception it knows no intoxication and no forgetting. No man seeks his woman, but his mind runs before him and possesses her, and afterwards remembers his knowing. The mind drinks the intoxication before the body reaches the cup, the wine is spilled, Lethe drains away and there is no forgetting, neither for man nor for woman. They lie there and remember, remember, remember, till remembrance is like a wheel. No man has a friend, except his mind has analysed that friend and scattered his parts like a dead Osiris, torn him with the first great wound of friendship in the thigh, and then gashed up his sides. No more man holds the life of his servants as he holds his horse, between the power of the thighs of his manhood. No man kneels to his God any more, but he asks himself: What am I kneeling to? No man sings or speaks in his throat, making language and utterance, but he says: Do I hear myself? Mind, art thou master of this? No man lifts his hands without saying: Do I lift my hand with my mind? You walk no more on your feet, but go in machines. You weave no more, and spin no more, you sow and you reap no more: always with your minds you guide great machines.

"It is the triumph. It is the triumph of the spirit. It is the triumph of Mind over Matter. Your machines and your education are your triumph. You have cast off the flesh, you [have] achieved the disembodied spirit. And your bones are wilting inside you. Wait! Wait! Your day is over.

"It is the end of the Return. It is the close of the Little Creation. It is the last day of the Little Creation of the Logos, the reversed creation, of the spirit seeking its own bodilessness. You have triumphed, you Galileans. The emptiness of your ears of corn covers all the world. But the harvest will be short. The Lord of harvest will not reap these fields of empty, upstanding white wheat-ears. He will sow fire in the corn-fields, and in a day the world will be black. He will put a light to the fields of growing chaff, and in a rustle of flame the harvest of empty corn will be over. Wait! Wait! The earth is pointing beyond the Little Bear, she has already forsaken the Pole-star. The earth has turned away from her pole, she is about to enter a new house. The little Cosmos of the poles of the north is finished, it has had its day. Quickly it will cease to be. The little creation of the Logos.

"But I and my people, we stand at the gates of the sun. And as the souls of the world fly back, back out of creation, back in the great reversal, the great undoing of the reversed creation: as you fly back through the sun, and unclothe yourself of the sun. As you fly naked and invisible away, like the ghosts of dead moths leaving a candle, departing into the night. As the sun falls away from you, ceases to clothe you, leaving you free and invisible:

"It is we who step into the sun. It is we who clothe ourselves with fire. It is we who are clothed in the sun.

"We have waited long, long, long at the gates of the sun, for your flying souls to fly past, like ghosts of moths streaming back into the deepening night. You are flying back to the dark whence all men came. But we are going on, through the glory of the gates of the sun, along the strange, sweet canals of the moon, full of white water-lilies, till we step on to earth as lords of the earth, as men of the world, as the Dark Pearl.

"We are the Dark Pearl of the new flesh. We are the masters of the new gates. We are the axle of the turning of the Æon. We are the feet upon the mountain, the mountain of the sun. We are the sons of the morning, now your twilight is ebbing into the invisible.

"Therefore I say to you, drink! Therefore I say to you, the wheat is in green ear, the maize is man-high, in Mexico. The bull is lowing again, and treading down the empty wheat. The bull is hungry again, he is trampling the priests, he has thrown over the altar of sacrifice. The throat of the Volcano is yellow as the sun, and the serpent has slid into the cup. The mixing-bowl of the moon is brimming with blood, and the eagle is bathing therein. The serpent is in the chalice of fire, and the eagle has flown into the moon of blood. The wheel of the Æon has turned, and Quetzalcoatl is snatching the Dark Pearl from the mouth of the dragon. The world has shifted her pole, and Huitzilopochtli jumps down from the sun, to deliver the maiden thrown to the snakes. The rider on the white [horse] has passed by down the road of tombs, and the rider on the black horse is knocking with thunder at the gate. 'Lift up your heads, O ye gates!'

"The grail of the sun is in the hands of Quetzalcoatl, and he puts it to Mexican lips. Drink then, and let the initiation begin."

Suddenly he ignored anything and everything, lifted his glass with two hands and swaying it for a moment or two, drank it off. Kate watched his throat move to the drink. With wide eyes, she looked at Cipriano. He too had lifted the glass with two hands, and was swaying it as if it were a game. Then he put his mouth to drink, and that she could hardly bear to see. Her whole body was finely quivering, and her heart was echoing all the time: I dare not! I dare not! She picked up her glass, and it spilled over her fingers. Ramón had put down his glass, and with his hands spread on the table, was looking at her with black eyes of judgment. Hastily she put her glass to her lips, spilling the wine down her, and in eagerness and in fear she drank, looking over the rim of her glass with her golden, frightened eyes, at Ramón. But she was able only to swallow three mouthfuls. Then she put down her glass, saying panting, as if she had drunk a great draught:

"I can't drink any more."

"It's enough," said Ramón, keeping his eyes on her, and smiling. She was terrified, feeling the two men were going to do something to her. She dared not look at Cipriano. His face had looked so black, and his mouth so terrible, as he drank. He seemed like a doom to her, not like a lover or a deliverer. Like a demon who was her doom. "Woman wailing for her demon lover." It wasn't true. When the demon actually came, she was agonised with terror. Perhaps the snake felt like that, in the sphere of the sun. In the ordeal of fire. When its psyche was being clothed with the sun. For the first time a great understanding and a great sympathy with the snake entered her heart.

"You have pledged yourself," said Don Ramón, watching her.

"What to?" she asked, terrified. She was afraid they would say she had to marry Cipriano straight away, and that would have killed her.

"To us," said Don Ramón, keeping his black eyes on her.

"I'm very frightened," she said.

"But you are stronger than your fear," he said.

"I'm not so sure," she replied.

He smiled teasingly.

"What do you want me to do?" she asked, in her nervousness holding the bowl of her glass – it was a large glass on a stem, that the Mexicans call a *Copa,* a Cup – and swaying the wine mesmerically. The glass was half full. Don Ramón watched the dark red wine rocking and slowly forming into a vortex.

"Drink just a little more, now," he said gently.

And perhaps for the first time in her life she obeyed as a child obeys, implicitly, and drank a little wine at once. And almost immediately she doubted herself, and looked back at him with eyes like a roused snake.

It wasn't her nature to obey. All her life, if asked to do anything, she instinctively paused, waited, and in that moment's pause, refused. But then, in the next instant, reconsidered, and if her reconsideration decided her to accede, she complied. This moment's negation, moment's consideration, and moment of compliance usually took only a second or two. But it made all the difference in the world between implicit acceptance, implicit response, and a considered response, a considered acquiescence. Long as she had known her husband, well as she trusted him, she had never, not once in all her life implicitly obeyed him. By taking a round-about method, he could trick her into spontaneous compliance. But if he said to her simply: Hand me my pencil! she instantly, instinctively hesitated before complying. And usually she would remind him: *Please!*

Her instinct, in fact, was not to comply.

If he said: "Will you please pass me my pencil," she passed it at once, almost eagerly. But she insisted on this bridge of politeness. She was like the Lady of Shalott, always in a castle surrounded by a moat, spinning the web of her own particular life. She would let down the drawbridge instantly, upon request. But after the petitioner had passed, she drew it instantly up again.

And all the Launcelots in the world might have crossed her mirror, he would have had to doff his hat and give at least a pleading look before she would go to the window. She always waited for that look of capitulation, or that word of capitulation from the other party, before she left her fortress.

Now she realised that Don Ramón had caught her for one second disarmed of her will. She had obeyed him like a child. And instantly her soul was up in arms again, she was looking at him with roused yellow eyes.

"Why did you want me to drink more?" she asked, adding at the back of her mind: to bully me?

He saw her aggression and smiled quietly.

"Because you had created the vortex," he said.

Instantly she was all puzzled.

"What vortex?" she asked, in doubt and wonder.

He pointed to the wine, which was still slightly rocking.

"In your wine. Don't you know that in the mysteries you must drink from the vortex?"

She pondered that. She had spun the wine and created a vortex. And she had drunk from that. – In spite of herself the words and the act had magic for her: the magic of the ancient blood, before men had learned to think in words, and thought in images and in acts.

The vortex! She had created a vortex, and drunk from it. What mysteries lay behind! What mysteries did Don Ramón know? What was she entering upon? She was full of doubt, and at the same time deeply drawn. Something in her nature responded to this symbolic language. It was a great rest from the endless strain of reason. It was like the blood flowing released, instead of knotted back in thought.

"What vortex did I drink of?" she asked.

"Oh insatiable Eve!" laughed Ramón.

"What vortex?"

"The vortex of the Dragon in the Cup."

"What cup?"

"Which you like. The Grail! The Cup of Dionysus. The cup of Liber."

"And what Dragon?"

"The Serpent in the Wilderness."

"You just put me off with words."

"You know Moses' Serpent in the Wilderness."

She was silent, puzzled, vexed, yet in a way fascinated and dominated.

Suddenly Cipriano gave a loud laugh, and reached his hand to her glass, looking across into her eyes.

"Do you know what it all means, Señora?" he said in a curious mocking-sounding voice. And he lifted her glass, which was still half full of wine. "This is your blood." – He filled his own glass half full, and lifted it. "This is my blood. In this glass is the dragon. Do you want to know what the dragon is? It is desire. Always desire is the

dragon. Good desire is the Serpent in the Wilderness, all gold. You
have only to look at it and you are strong. That is the serpent in this
glass: the serpent of my desire in the cup of my blood. Then the Lord
Almighty looses the flood. See!" And swiftly he poured the wine from
Kate's glass into his own. "And that creates the vortex. Look!" He
rocked the wine subtly with both his cupped, brown hands. "Look!
And the vortex is the mingling and the wheeling of creation in the cup,
with the Lord Almighty in the middle of the Red Sea, dividing the
waters of the Red Sea, look, in the hollow of the cup, so that the soul
can pass from the Egypt, which is the unblest flesh of me on the other
side of the Red Sea of this cup, to Canaan, which is my blest soul after
its consummation in this cup. Look! The vortex of my blood with
your blood, and the Lord Almighty dividing the flood for the consummated soul to pass on to a Canaan of tomorrow. Look! Look!
That is why I must make a vortex. That is why I must drink of the
vortex. Look!" and he caught the spinning wine with his lips, and
drank slowly, deeply, leaving only a little wine at the bottom of the
glass. This he spun round vigorously. "There!" he said. "Take it, and
drink. It's my blood. Drink it! You have my explanation. It is exact.
Ramón's covers the whole cosmos. What is that to me! The two
explanations are one and the same, but his is the macrocosm, and I am
the microcosm. I am the little cosmos. There's my blood in the glass,
with the serpent of fire. And the Lord Almighty poured down the
flood of your blood into mine, and created the vortex of the Red Sea,
in the middle of which He stands making a way for your soul and
mine, his little Israel, to pass into the promised land, out of the
bondage of that old Egypt of unconsummated flesh. There you have it
all. Drink, drink while the vortex lasts. Drink! What is Eleusis to me!
This is Mexico, and I am Huitzilopochtli, and I know the mysteries. I
am the man with the sword. You are the woman bound. There, take
the cup and drink. Take it!"

Kate took the glass. This was becoming more than she could bear.

"I will drink it," she said gravely, the tears not far away. She felt
the men like two demons pressing on her. If her tears came, and they
would come soon, she would be helpless before them for ever. So she
must go away at once. "I will drink it," she said, "but then you must let
me go away at once to my room, because I am tired."

"Drink!" said he, still holding the glass out to her between his two
cupped hands and rocking it swiftly, subtly, while all the time he kept

his black, bright, strange eyes on her face, in a strange smile that seemed to hypnotise her, like a serpent gradually insinuating its folds round her.

"If I drink," she faltered, "you must let me go at once."

"Yes," said Ramón quietly. "You shall go."

She looked to him, because of her great fear of Cipriano. And the look of Ramón's silent, impassive face steadied her. She turned again and looked at the glass, not at Cipriano, and at the two black, sun-blackened hands that wreathed it. She held out her hand.

Cipriano put the glass into her hand carefully, but still she did not look at him. She looked only at the dark, spinning wine. Then she lifted it to her lips and drank as in an ordeal. And at the same moment came his voice:

"Is it not my blood? Is it not my warm blood with the dragon of fire in it? Is it not the sacred vortex?"

She shuddered, putting down the glass and wiping her mouth with her hand. For the wine was heavy, and hot-warm like blood, and seemed to smell of blood: his dark blood. And there was a fire in it like a dragon. And it seemed to coil round her throat and her heart, and in another moment she would cease to care, she would cease to care, and she would never, never care again any more, not through all eternity. She knew it.

She rose with a sudden jerk, as if something in her thighs had twitched her to her feet. Her chair fell over, but she stood motionless. The two men had risen too. Don Ramón opened the door, and she went out swiftly and stiffly, feeling her thighs hard and insentient like iron. Though she did not look round, she felt Cipriano's black eyes watching her go, black, gleaming, and taunting, gazing at her shoulders.

Once in her room, with the door locked, she stood motionless. She had brought in with her the night-light that had been burning outside her door. She blew it out. The night was black dark, so dark that the clouds of the sky were not visible in the one blackness. The lake seemed suddenly to start to sound. Frogs were rattling and an owl was hooting softly, flying so that the hoot came now loud, now low.

"I can't!" said Kate, standing rigid before the window. "I can't! I can't! I can't!"

She felt something had turned to iron inside her, and it would never soften again. This iron resistance inside her would prevent her living. When she had drunk the blood something had fixed into iron inside her, and she could not release it. Now she would go in misery. The incantation, or the initiation, whatever they liked to call it, had failed, and she was fastened on to this hard rock inside her, a miserable prisoner with all the appearance of freedom. Now she would know nothing but a hard, fast misery. Her emotions could not flow any more. Her emotions were fastened with iron to a hard rock at the middle of her. Lucky those men, who could sit mixing mysteries in their wine. For her there was no mystery. She was set into a hard rock, like the rock before Moses smote it and released the flow.

But it was night, and she slept till morning. When she awoke it was already day. She got up to push wide the window doors of her little terrace looking to the lake.

It was day, but the sun was not yet on the lake. The morning, for once, in the middle of the rainy season, had come blue and cloudless. The mountains opposite had the sun, and were magically clear, as if some magic light were focussed directly on them. She saw all the green furrows of the mountain sides as if it were her own hand. Two white gulls were flying down the lake. They too caught the sun, and glittered. She thought of the sea. It was not very far away, the Pacific, yet the sea seemed almost to have retreated entirely out of her consciousness.

Cipriano was going to bathe. She saw him throw his wrap on the jetty and go wading through the shallow, pale-dun water, naked save for a scrap of black at his loins. How dark he was! How dark he looked against the pale water. Nearly black like a negro. It was curious that his body was as dark as his face. And nervous and active-looking. He waded along slowly in the shallow lake, which still was only up to his knees, a dark brown figure in the pale water. Then he dropped in, and swam as best he could in the ever-shallow lake-side.

When he rose again the water was shallower than ever, though he was far out. But he rose in the sun, and he was red as fire. The sun was not red, it was too high. The light was golden with morning. But as it flooded along the surface of the lake it caught the small figure of Cipriano and he was as red as fire, or as red as a painted red buoy floating in the sunlight out on the lake. She had noticed before, how the natives shone pure red when the morning or evening sun caught them. And now she saw Cipriano. A red Indian.

Clothed with the sun. Clothed with fire. He really looked like it. The sons of the morning.

No, it was not really that she was afraid. She was afraid of nothing that would be true to her own being. But would it be true for her to marry that red man out there in the water? She could not feel it. She admired him. She liked him too. But she must remain true to her own innermost self. And her own innermost self had no communion with him. How then could she force herself to be his wife? It would only make a false marriage. There was a gulf between him and her, the gulf of race, of colour, of different æons of time. He wanted to force a way across the gulf. But that would only mean a mutual destruction. No no! She knew it was braver not to accede to any union, until her soul should agree to it. It was no good forcing herself. And no good his trying to force her. Unless she could give herself from her soul, it would be cowardice to give herself at all. It would be cheating him as much as herself.

She felt she was on the brink of her own being. But she did not want to be pushed over a precipice. If she went over a precipice with him she would only be helping to break him, not to make him. Better die alone than help to break the new thing in the men.

She knew what she wanted. She wanted to go home, before deciding anything. And from the distance look across, and choose. She wanted to see her children and her mother. Perhaps after all she could win her children over to a heroic way of life. She had loved them when they were little, so much. How could she go back on it? And her mother! She was fond of her mother. And she was an old woman now, tolerant and so sensible in her old age. She understood her daughter Kate, too, for she herself was of a wilful, downright nature. But Lady Fitzpatrick had always loved the framework of society, as a setting. She loved it still. It was always a kind of game to her, to be Lady Fitzpatrick and have generals and lords for her friends. She always kept staunch men-friends, did Lady Fitzpatrick, but no-one had ever thought scandal. Sir Anthony, her husband, Kate's father, had been rather scandalous. But the Baronet was dead these ten years, and the title went to Kate's boy, Frederick.

Kate thought of her home in Devon, the old stone house, and the wild park, the sea invisible but only four miles away. Kate had loved Uthway, as the house was called. She thought of it now: her mother with her lovely white hair, like thistle-down, sitting erect and handsome, rather stout, in her black silk or her black net or her white dresses, with a bit of fine lace carelessly put on, and probably a spot or two *somewhere* on the dress. For Lady Fitzpatrick was really a rough-handed woman. Kate had hated her mother's heavy hand, as a child, and her mother's rough, caustic, humorous nature. She had loved the subtle, untrustworthy Sir Anthony.

"Ah Anthony! Anthony!" her mother would say of him. "He is the saint to pray to, if you want to find a lost reputation."

So the rough-handed, rather selfish mother maintained all her life the most delightful romantic friendships with paladins of the old school, General Mornington, Lord Eppingway, and Lord Neagh. General Mornington painted her portrait: he was an amateur. Lord Eppingway sent her interesting things and long letters from Egypt and Abyssinia: he too was an amateur. And Neagh had once proposed to Sir Anthony: "I think it would be a good thing if Lady Fitzpatrick went away with me. I haven't spoken to her yet, as I thought you and I had better arrange the difficult matters." Sir Anthony had immediately darted into his study for a pair of pistols, and Neagh had said: "Ah, if you take it like that, why, of course, consider it unsaid." So Sir Anthony had considered it unsaid, and had departed to Ireland to shoot and make a few more debts. Which Lady Fitzpatrick haggled over, and paid when she had haggled to the lowest figure.

But Anthony was dead, and Neagh was dead, and Eppingway was dead. But still Mornington was faithful. He was still painting, though a martyr to his kidneys. And he still called every day. And Lady Fitzpatrick still received him in the little drawing-room. And she would still bridle like a girl who was receiving her beau. And he would peer at her through his pince-nez, and say to her:

"Is the lace of your collar torn?"

"Torn? – Where?" And she would crane her neck. "I don't think so."

"Look here!" – He would lift up the torn place.

"Ah that! That is nothing!" she would reply, patting it down with her heavy white hand. "That is nothing. You always were a governess."

"I can hardly walk today," he would say, putting his hand to his back.

"Oh dear! Oh dear! Does it hurt you again?" she would cry, as if in fear. She still called him General, and he still called her Lady Fitzpatrick, after forty years.

And a maid-servant outside would be pursuing the young master,

calling in an adoring voice: "Sir Frederick! Sir Frederick!", to which
Frederick would gallantly reply:

"Clear out! I am studying Tchekov's technique."

Whereupon the young man would turn his back on the servant,
stare at the book in his hand – Tchekov's Plays, open at *The Cherry
Orchard* – and stride once more across the lawn. He was playing the
whole play all by himself, in silence, with the lawn for a stage. Because
he was "interested in drama." But his interests would be interrupted
by the arrival of Cathy and two girl-friends, all with canvases under
their arms.

"Show us your sketch, Cathy!"

Cathy calmly showing, and the youth looking critical.

"Not bad. Not at all bad. I'm inclined to agree with General
Mornington, that you've got a touch of genius. Don't know why
you're so fond of pink, though."

"I love pink. And I love green. Though most people say they hate
them."

"No need to hate them. They *needn't* be lobster salad."

"They're never lobster salad, if you can see a tree as a tree."

The young lady was tall and thin, stalky, but she had talent, and
Freddy was awfully proud of her.

Kate could see it all. The carelessness of the life. And at the same
time, the tightness. But she loved her children, and she loved her
mother. How Freddy would *loathe* Don Ramón and his God stunt, or
his Quetzalcoatl stunt: as the boy would call it.

"Doesn't the fellow know his own limitations?" she could hear
her son asking.

And how Cathy would hate the thought of her mother's intimacy
with such people. "Little darky people!" she would say. Cathy had
always despised her mother's friends. "I don't like your little sort of
people, Mother," the child had said at the advanced age of ten. "Why
don't you have friends like General Mornington, only not so old? Why
don't you be friends with Basil Slaney?"

"He bores me."

"I'd rather be bored by nice sort of people, than by the other sort."

Kate had laughed. Basil Slaney was, as Cathy put it, quite nice.
But even Lady Fitzpatrick called him stupid. Lady Fitzpatrick had
really loved Desmond, Kate's husband, quite well. "If he'd only rest
from his labours," she had said rather sarcastically. She disliked Social-

ism and Labour, because they were unattractive. They spoilt all the charm of things. Desmond was a charming man. Why waste his life in these unpleasant democratic pursuits? She herself, she said, was perfectly democratic. Which was true. She talked just as simply, was just as much herself with a casual farmer as with Mornington. When she was sixty, she had sat chatting on a bench at Porthcothan, with an elderly, good-looking fisherman. He was a widower, she was a widow.

"I've got no ties in the world, and seemingly you haven't," he had said to her in the end. "Why don't you and me make a match of it?"

"Nay! Nay!" she laughed. "I shall never marry again."

"Come! You're young yet. Think it over. Why you and me are just built for one another. I never liked the cut of a woman better."

She had really been rather pleased. She told the story to Mornington the moment she saw him. And he had answered, in his correct way:

"Well, I suppose it is a tribute to you."

"Why it's the best feather I shall ever put in my cap," she replied.

The atmosphere of home came over Kate, and she knew she would have to go. For the relief. As a relief to herself. Her soul was strained, straining away so far.

The drums were sounding outside. In the open clearing of the mango-trees, men were dancing in a ring, and in two long lines, a stiff, stately, rapid-treading dance, threading curiously in and out. They were naked to the waist, and carried gourd rattles. They danced in a rhythm of five, shaking the rattles at every fifth, while the drums kept up a subtle, rippling rhythm, which she could not quite unravel.

But her eyes were full of Uthway, the little breakfast-table on the lawn, her mother's bedroom-window, next the little drawing-room, wide open, and the children standing outside on the path shouting to their grandmother, who was taking her breakfast in bed.

"Grandmother! You're having kidneys for breakfast! You know the doctor says they are bad for your heart."

"Now all the world has its eyes on my forkful of devilled kidney!" came the exasperated voice of the grandmother, from her bed.

Kate would not go to look. – She could see plainly enough, in her mind's eye, her handsome mother with fine white hair hastily but attractively caught up, sitting in bed wearing a little cotton jacket scalloped all round with blue, which she had scalloped and made for herself, greedily eating devilled kidneys from a large white-and-gold plate. And Frederick climbing through the open window.

"I shall not allow you to eat all that, grandmother."

"Yes! Yes! Ah, am I to be bullied by these men all my life —"

"Yes, you are, till you know what's good for you."

The young baronet came to the window and handed the plate to Cathy.

"Call Lupin!" he said.

"Lupin! Lupin!"

A black dog bolting from round a corner, bolting the kidney as if his haste were unspeakable, then slowly, carefully licking the plate, accurately. While the grandmother's voice came from her room:

"No! The ugly dog. He shan't come in the house. Dogs in the house I will *not* have."

"Lupin! Was it good, Lupin!"

But Kate was sitting at a little table on the terrace at Las Yemas, with Teresa, listening with bitter unwillingness to Spanish, eating rolls and honey and eggs and smelling the hateful smell of mangoes and pineapple and guavas, in a big wooden bowl on a chair. It was the time of cherries and the first strawberries, at home.

Cipriano came to table too. He wore the little white cotton blouse of the peons.

"What is your news?" she asked him.

"The Archbishop is deported, ordered into exile: was put on a ship, a German ship leaving for Spain and Hamburg, yesterday evening. Gallardo is still quiet. The government has declared it will protect the churches of Quetzalcoatl with troops. And I must go back to Guadalajara in an hour."

To Kate it all seemed so unreal. All except the Archbishop sailing for Europe. That was all she heard: someone sailing for Europe.

"Won't you take this ring, now, as a pledge?" he said, pulling from his finger a worn old gold ring, a flat serpent with scales faintly outlined in black, and a flat green stone in its head.

She picked it up and looked at it abstractedly.

"What a queer old ring!" she said. "Is it Aztec?"

"It may be. Will you accept it?"

"No," she said, putting it down on a plate on the table. "I must go home. I must go home to England before I decide anything. Perhaps once I have been home I shall be able to choose. But now I can't choose. I must go home. I must go home now."

"Home to what?"

"Home to my children. And home to my mother, who is getting old now. She is over seventy."

"And you must go now, just now?"

"Yes, I must go now," she replied, sighing. "It is all such a strain on me here. I can't bear it any longer. I must go home. I said I would go at the end of the month, and I must stick to it. I can't bear to stay any longer."

She knew there was a great resistance and a great rebellion in him. But she could not think about him any more. Her soul ignored him. Fleetingly, she remembered him, the red man glowing like a bit of red, heated iron, in the light on the lake. Clothed in the sun. Then her soul turned aside its face. She could not think of him, she could not even be aware of him.

The sky had clouded over and rain was falling on the mountains opposite, brushed down like grey hair. It would be raining at Uthway. It would be raining, and she would be going out in a waterproof, and a sailor's waterproof hat, to walk in the garden in the summer rain, and smell the roses. The big, wide damask roses. And the velvety dark-red ones. And the Glory up the side of the stable. And pinks would be out, beds of white pink, and then those big old pinks with a dark red spot, the sort that so often broke their calyx. She would give her whole soul to smell pinks and roses in the rain, and the lime tree in flower by the little summer-house. To sit in the little rustic summer-house, and see the honeysuckle, almost day-scentless, drip with rain round the door, and the garden with roses and a privet screen, and the plain stone houses beyond. Or to ride in the rain down to the sea, and sit in the rocks watching the big waves break, grey, with a great mass of fern, in the rain.

"Will you bring your children here?" he was asking her.

The thought almost made her smile.

"Perhaps," she said.

"If you wish to have a house like this, to bring your children here," he was saying.

A house like this! With Mexican servants around her all the time. And the alien, intolerable pressure. Bring her children here! How they would hate her for it, after the first two months. Ugh, how they would hate it! More even than she hated it. And yet she said:

"Perhaps! Perhaps! I shall have to see, when I get to England."

"Why must you go now? At once?"

"This is too much for me. I can't bear it. – It is too far from me. You ask too much from me. This is too far. The change is too great. I can't make it. I can't change my race. And I can't betray my blood. I can't. Even if I married you, I shouldn't really change. It would only be betraying my race, and my blood, and my own nature. No. And we could neither of us be happy. That kind of suicide."

"It would be suicide?" he said.

"Yes. For you too. You would know, after a while. And you'd wish you had married one of your own people. If I were free to choose, in the same way that I am free to choose my hat or my dress, I would stay. Yes, I would. But I am not free. My race is part of me, it doesn't leave me free. My blood *is* me, and that doesn't let me become Mexican. I *can't* choose to belong to you, and to [stay] here, because it isn't in me to choose."

"But you can stay here for a *time* – as you have stayed."

"Yes, I can stay for a time. Knowing I am going back. If I stayed, like Mrs. Norris, all my life, I should always in my soul be going back in the end, going home to die. Because I belong to my own people, to my mother and my children and my husband."

"Could you not stay with me here for a time?" he asked. "For three months. For one month, even. Live with me for one month."

"No, I am not like that. Either at the end of the month I should not be able to go away. Or if I went, I should feel I had betrayed myself for ever."

He was silent for some time.

"Am I wrong, then," he said slowly, "in wanting you?"

"I think you are," she said, also slowly. "If you realised *me:* my feelings, my blood, my race, my colour, the whole loyal part of me, you would know I *can't, really,* become the wife of a dark, Indian Mexican, I can't give myself to Mexico, and let Mexico be my country for ever. I can't. If I could, I would. If I *could,* I would stay and do as you wish. I don't hate you for wanting me. But I think, in part at least, you are mistaken, and arrogant. It is rather arrogant in you to assume a certain right over me. And it is arrogant that you insist on asking from me something which it is not in my nature to give. That is arrogant. Perhaps it is your dark nature to be unknowing and arrogant, when you want a thing. But when anyone tries to *force* me, I only hate them."

He sat motionless, staring at the water dripping past the terrace.

It was raining heavily again, the drums were silent, they two seemed shut in in the veils of tropical rain.

"Perhaps I would rather you should hate me," he said, "than that you should be gone from me altogether."

This made her heart stand with fear, for a moment.

"Surely you have Don Ramón, and your Huitzilopochtli, and your army, and your country. Surely having me and hating me would only spoil it all for you."

"Who knows," he said darkly.

"I know," she replied.

But she didn't. She was afraid of him. Perhaps the devil in him would like having her and hating her, once he was thwarted. So for a moment, fearing him, she did hate him. And she longed, longed to be gone out of Mexico.

"I must go," he said, rising.

"Won't you take your ring?" And she held out the plate to him, on which it lay.

He looked at her once more.

"Will you not keep it in remembrance of me?" he said.

She met his eyes, and glanced away.

"I should like to, if you won't look on it as a pledge."

He smiled at her darkly.

"I shall look on it as nothing," he said.

She took up the ring. But when he had gone, she put it down on the table again. And she went to the azotea to see him ride away. In uniform, the dark-grey uniform, on a red, silky, delicate horse. He belonged to his horse more than to any woman, she thought, watching him in secret. Like a subtler sort of centaur, he rode.

The rider on the red horse.

She went down and walked a few moments by the shore, beyond the low break-water wall. Suddenly before her she saw a long dark soft rope, lying over a pale boulder. And instantly, the dark soul in her was alert. It was a snake, with a subtle pattern along its soft dark back, lying there over a big round stone, its head sunk to earth. It felt her presence, too, for suddenly, with incredible soft quickness, it contracted down the stone and she saw it entering a little gap in the stone wall. The hole was not very big, and as it entered it looked quickly back, with its small, dark, wicked-pointed head, and flickered a dark tongue. Then it eased its dark length into the hole. The hole could not have been very large, because when it had all gone in, Kate could see the last fold still, and the flat little head resting on this fold, like the devil with his chin on his arms looking out of a loop-hole in hell. There was the little head looking out at her from that hole in the wall, with the wicked spark of an eye. Making itself invisible. Watching out of its own invisibility. Coiled wickedly on its own disappointment. It was disappointed at its failure to rise higher in creation, and its disappointment was poisonous. Kate went away, unable to forget it.

XIX

K ATE WENT HOME THAT DAY. She didn't want to stay longer at Las Yemas. She felt a certain tenderness for Cipriano, but she almost hated Ramón. Teresa too. But particularly Ramón. Those mystical, life-destroying men, with their hateful abstraction and imagery. Posing so large, too. And looking at her so calmly and dispassionately. He need not pretend so much calm and dispassion, for she believed he hated her, at the depths of him. His excessive maleness hated her because she was a woman, and not humble. He wanted her to be humble, like Teresa. He wanted to humble her, before his uninspired maleness. He would not succeed. And of course he was jealous of Cipriano's feeling for her.

So she was rowed back to Chapala. She was forced to admit the lake had a real beauty, now the rains had moistened the hills and soothed the air. The wind came fresh and healing, sunlight lay in bright gleams on the mountains of the shore, and shadow deep and velvety. The folds and the slopes were all green, save where the ploughed earth was reddish. But the ridges of rock were grey still, through a sprinkle of bushes. Red and bright green and pale green and dark green and whitish and grey lay the splashes of sun, the villages were white specks here and there. Dark, dark green, paling to blue-green and deepening to indigo spread the subtly-varying shadows. The lake had come alive with the rains, the air had come to life, the sky was silver and white and grey, with distant blue. There was something soothing and, curiously enough, paradisal about it, even the pale, dove-brown water. She could not remember any longer the dry rigid pallor of the heat, like memory gone dry and sterile, hellish. A boat was coming over with its sail hollowing out like a shell, pearly white, and its sharp black canoe-beak slipping past the water. It looked like the boat of Dionysos crossing the seas and bringing the sprouting of the vine.

When she had landed and was going home, she saw such an

amusing group perched in silhouette on the low breakwater wall –
not much more than a foot high – against the dove-pale background
of the lake. It was a black boat with her tall mast and red-painted roof,
pulled stern-up almost to the wall, aground, and from the wall broad
new planks for a gangway. Men in white with big hats standing
loosely grouped on this gangway, looking down into the dark belly of
the boat, under its low, red-painted roof. Then on the wall, four-
square in silhouette against the lake, a black-and-white cow, with a
man in dove-brown tights and dove-brown little jacket, and huge,
silver-embroidered hat, standing at her head: the perfect old tall,
slim-legged, high-hatted Mexican silhouette. With him, loosely, two
more peons, whose wide white pants flapped like skirts in the wind.
One had his red sarape over his shoulder.

Behind the block of a cow, three white peons, and two on the
ground, looking up at a huge black-and-white bull, a colossus of a bull
standing perched motionless on the wall, broadside, a passive monster
spangled with black, low-aloft. Just behind him, one white peon with
a red sash determinedly tied.

Kate of course had to stand and watch. The group of men broke
into motion. The gangway was ready. Two peons began to shove the
cow from behind. She pawed the new broad planks of the bridge
tentatively, then, unwilling, lumbered on to them. They edged her
down. She peered into the dark cavity of the boat, and dropped neatly
in. It was the turn of the massive, immobile bull.

The farmer in tights gently took the ring in the monster's nose,
gently lifted the short, wedge head, so that the great soft throat was
uplifted. The peon behind put his head down and with all his might
shoved the living flanks of the bull, as if he were shoving a truck. The
bull delicately stepped, with unutterable calm and weighty poise,
along the wall to the gangway. There he stopped. And everything
stopped for a few moments, as the white figures of men re-arranged
themselves.

Then two peons loosely passed a rope across the haunches of the
bull. The farmer took the nose-ring once more, very gently. The bull
lifted its head, but held back. It struck the planks with an unwilling
foot. The farmer pulled again, carefully, two peons at the back, their
heads down, shoved with all their strength in the soft flanks of the
mighty creature, sticking out their white, red-sashed loins flexibly.
The bull stepped slowly, imperturbably, but with ill grace, on to the

loose planks, and very slowly, pushed from behind, moved to the end, above the low cavern of the boat.

There he stood, huge, silvery and dappled like the sky, with snake-dapples down his haunches, looming massive way above the red hatches of the roof of the canoe. How would such a great beast pass that low red roof and drop into that hole? It seemed impossible.

He lowered his head and looked into the cavern. It seemed not to trouble him at all. The men behind shoved in his living flanks. He seemed to take no heed. Then he lowered his head and looked again. The men behind pushed once more. Slowly, carefully, he crouched, making himself small, and with a quick, massive little movement dropped down into the cavern of the boat with his fore-feet, leaving his huge hind-quarters heaping up behind. There was a shuffle and a little stagger down below, then the soft thud as his hind feet leaped down. He had gone. The massive, sky-like animal had gone down into the bowels of the boat. There was another loose pause. Then the peons moved again to a different arrangement.

The planks were taken away. A peon had run out to unfasten the rope from the stones on the shore. There was a slight thudding of strange feet in the dark belly of the boat. Men were pushing at her stern, to push her off. They were pulling away stones from under her, to make her float a little. Slowly, casually, they flung the stones aside, into the shallow water. And the flat-bottomed boat moved, edged out to the water, slowly, she was afloat. Slowly the peons poled her away from the shore, running silently, barefoot along her deck, pressing on their poles, till they reached the stern. And with her hidden cargo of silver-spangled mighty life she slid slowly out, till it was far enough, and they could hoist the sail. The wide white sail thrusting up her one horn and curving to a whorl in the wind like a shell. She was already getting small on the surface of the water.

Kate turned away home. It all happened so quietly, no noise save the thud of hoofs at one moment; so softly and unviolently, with the loose pauses and the casual, soft-balanced rearrangements at every pause. And now the boat was softly on the water, with her white sail in a whorl like the boat of Dionysos, going across the lake. There seemed a certain mystery in it. When she thought of the great dappled bull upon the waters, it seemed mystical to her.

A man was stripping palm-stalks, squatting in silence in his white cotton pants under a tree, his black head bent forward. Then he went to wet his long strips in the lake, returning with them dangling. Then silently, deftly, with the dark childish absorption of the people, he was threading his strips of palm and mending a chair-seat. – A roan horse, speckled with white, was racing prancing along the shore, and neighing frantically. His mane flowed in the wind, his feet struck the pebbles as he ran, opening his nose and neighing anxiously. Away up the shore he ran. What had he lost? – A peon had driven a high-wheeled wagon drawn by four mules, into the lake. It was deep in the lake above the axle, up to the bed of the cart, so that it looked like a dark square boat drawn by four soft, dark sea-horses, with long ears, while the white peon with his big hat stood erect. The mules buried in the water stepped gently, curving towards the shore.

It was spring on the lake. New white-and-yellow calves, white and silky, were skipping, butting up their rear ends, lifting their tails, and trotting side by side to the water to drink. A mother-ass was tethered to a tree, and in the shadow lay her foal, a little thing as black as ink, curled up, with fluffy head erect and great black ears reaching up, for all the world like some jet-black hare of witchcraft pricking its abnormal ears. A little black spot with a big head and high, startling leaves of black ears. Kate was delighted. She waited and waited, but it did not get up.

"How many days?" she called to the peon who was passing to one of the straw huts.

"Last night!" he called in answer.

"Oh! So new! He won't get up. Can't he get up?"

The peon went back, put his arm round the foal, and lifted it to its feet. There it straddled in amaze on its high, bent hair-pins of black legs.

"Oh! Oh! How nice!" cried Kate in delight, and the peon laughed back at her, passing on to his straw hut in silence.

The ass-foal, black as ink, didn't understand in the least what standing up meant. It rocked on its four loose legs, and helplessly wondered. Then it hobbled a few steps forward, to smell at some growing green maize. It smelled and smelled and smelled, as if all the æons of green juice of memory were striving to awake. Then it turned round, looked straight towards Kate with its bushy-velvet face, and put out a pink tongue at her. She broke into a laugh. It stood wondering, lost in wonder. Then it put out its tongue at her again. And she laughed again, delighted. It gave an awkward little new skip, and was so surprised and rickety, having done so. It ventured forward a few steps, and unexpectedly exploded into another little skip, itself most surprised of all by the event.

"Already!" said Kate. "Already it skips, and only came last night into the world." After bethinking itself for some time, it walked uncertainly forward, to its mother, and straight to her udder. It was drinking. The mother, a well-liking grey-and-brown ass with not a hint of black, stood with a rather smug self-satisfaction, Kate rather envious of her, deciding it was time to go home. As she went in, she noticed what long green shoots the roses had put forth, with new leaves, and how many opening buds there were. The dark green oranges also were growing big.

But she had come home to pack. As she changed into her house-dress, one of the scarlet little birds, more scarlet than a flower, came flying with its brilliant breast and head to her open window, from the wall of the orange-garden opposite. Then it settled on her window-sill, closing its brown wings like a little brown cape over so much pure scarlet-rosy red. Only its head still flamed. It stayed a while, looking round. "Paying me a visit," said Kate. Then it was gone again. She looked up and saw the golden circles round the dark Greek crosses of the church-towers, above the new green of the big palms.

"I am going back to Europe," she said.

And suddenly Europe seemed very pale to her, pale, almost ghostly. The life seemed thin and unreal, as if you could see through the people, as you see through ghosts. Nevertheless, she went to the box-room, and began packing the household trunk, that held the linen and towels and table-cloths she had brought.

"Ah Niña!" cried Felipa. "You are packing the trunks! Are you going?"

"Yes, I must go to my children and my mother."

"Ah no! No! Don't you go! – If you take me, I will work. You needn't give me any money, only my food and clothes, and I will work for you. I like to work. Me, I work like a donkey. I will work for you over there."

Kate had one glimpse of Felipa in an English country house.

"It is so far, Felipa. So very far."

"Very far, yes," echoed Felipa. "But I want to see the world. – Is it true that you go like *that* – ?" and she curved her hand round swiftly, to describe the motion of sailing round the globe.

"Yes," said Kate. "But it always *seems* flat."

"Ah, it is true!" And Felipa burst into a wild little laugh. "Look!" she said, turning to Juana and Pedra, who stood there. "When you go to the Niña's country you go like *that!*" And again she swiftly delineated with her hand, the side of a ball.

They watched every rag Kate packed, with fathomless curiosity. But the greatest object of wonder was a brilliant modern-art tea-cosey. It was some time before they grasped what it was. Pedra had to fetch the tea-pot. Then all three went into shrieks of wonder-struck laughter, over the tea-pot's mantle. Rafael, who had come home for mid-day food, was summoned from the back premises. Felipa held up the brilliantly decked tea-pot as if it were some magic grail, and off they all went into peals of wonder-struck laughter.

Under these trying circumstances Kate tried to get on with her packing.

TEXTUAL COMMENTARY

The text of this edition is based on two sources: the manuscript in Lawrence's own hand, partially revised, now in the Harry Ransom Humanities Research Center of the University of Texas at Austin; and the typescript in the Houghton Library of Harvard University, made from this manuscript, incorporating its revisions, and adding minor revisions and corrections. The present text represents a collation of these two sources, with primary reliance upon the manuscript. The text, with few exceptions, preserves Lawrence's punctuation. Spelling has been normalized, except for a few places where Lawrence seems to be using dialectal variants: "earthern," "girdle cakes," "snirt."

Lawrence's knowledge of Spanish was rudimentary, picked up in Mexico from conversation and reading. His spelling of Spanish words is often phonetic, as in the spelling of "oyocitas" for "ollicitas," perhaps a local variant for "ollitas" (little pots). Spelling of Spanish words for the most part has been normalized, allowing for Mexican usage, as for instance, Lawrence's "guaraches," a Mexican variant for "huaraches" (sandals), and his spelling "sarape," the correct Mexican usage. Lawrence sometimes underlines Spanish words, but much more often he does not, apparently preferring to allow the Spanish words to blend in with the English. The text therefore does not italicize Spanish words, except when they are unusual or when they occur in conversation.

The novel developed in three stages: (1) the original writing done at Lake Chapala in May and June of 1923, writing that can in most places easily be read underneath the lines of deletion drawn by Lawrence; (2) the partial revision of this draft; and (3) the total recension done in Oaxaca from November 1924 to February 1925, representing the version that Lawrence published in 1926. Extensive revision of the Chapala manuscript occurs mainly in chapters III through VII (pages 73 to 177 of the manuscript), where the equivalent of thirty pages is completely re-written, while hundreds of smaller revisions occur. When did Lawrence perform this revision? It is astonishing enough to realize that he could write the original manuscript of 479 pages in this brief period of two months. Yet the typescript leaves no doubt that the revision of chapters III and IV was in fact performed at Chapala. The first 81 pages of the typescript, including these two chapters, and incorporating all of Lawrence's revisions, were done by an expert typist with large type and identical paper throughout; the remainder is done in élite type, on different kinds of paper, by a less skillful typist who commits many overstrikes and cancellations. We know that the first 81 pages with their identical typing and paper must have been typed in Chapala because of a letter that Lawrence wrote from Chapala to Middleton Murry on 26 May 1923, saying that he was "having the first slight scene of my novel – the beginning of a bull-fight in Mexico City – typed now" (*Letters,* IV, 447).

On page 108 of the manuscript either Lawrence or the typist has drawn a line after the portion that has been typed in Chapala, where the name Chapala remains as it has been typed throughout the preceding pages. But in the lower half of the page Lawrence has three times changed the name to "Sayula," the actual name of a much smaller lake in the region, and he continues to make this change (with two slips) throughout chapters V, VI, and VII of the manuscript. At the beginning of chapter V he has also written in a title, both in the manuscript and in the typescript: "Kate Moves to Sayula." And on the covering page of the manuscript he has written what appears to be a direction for the second typist: "Change the word Chapala to Sayula." Throughout chapters V, VI, and VII he has also changed the names of the housekeeper and her family from their actual names, which he had used in the original writing, to fictitious names: Felipa for Isabel, Juana for Carmen, Pedra for Maria, Carmen for Pedra, and Rafael for Daniele; and he has noted these changes on the covering page of the manuscript. (For the actual names, see *Letters,* IV, 453.) But after chapter VII, where the extensive revision ends, Lawrence has left the original names intact, apparently trusting the second typist to follow his directions. One or both of two motives may have caused Lawrence thus to break off his thorough revision. He wanted to give his manuscript to his publisher for typing before he left New York City; he may simply have run out of time for further revision. But, as L. D. Clark has suggested in a letter, a deeper cause may also be involved: "Lawrence's realization that he must transform the work by delving much

deeper into the Mexican national and mythical consciousness –
as well as that of New Mexico – probably came on by degrees as he
pondered in the process of revising as far as he went. He saw that he
was not going to achieve a Quetzalcoatl rebirth with the fiddle and
guitar ceremonies and with the Ramón and Cipriano so far created. . . . The culminating conviction of the impossibility of merely
revising *Quetzalcoatl* throughout did not come to him fully, it seems
to me, until he reviewed the typescript in Oaxaca and rejected it for a
new start."

However this may be, something has happened to make the first
typing break off after it had gone four pages into chapter V. Presumably the cause was Lawrence's harried departure from Chapala, to
make the journey to New York by train, and from there to find a quiet
retreat for a month in the hills of northern New Jersey, in a cottage
provided by his current publisher, Thomas Seltzer. During his stay
there Lawrence was busy with correcting proofs for three books, but
in letters from Chapala in June he had told both Thomas and Adele
Seltzer that he hoped, in addition to correcting proofs, to "go through
my novel" (*Letters,* IV, 454, 456). The proof-reading went rapidly,
and it would appear that he could have had a week or ten days in which
to perform further revision before handing over the manuscript to
Seltzer for typing, as he did before he left New York in August, 1923.
On the other hand, he may have done all the revision before he left
Chapala.

No problem of inconsistency arises from accepting the fictitious
names for Isabel and her family, since Lawrence had earlier given
fictitious names for other characters based on actual people: Mrs.
Norris (Zelia Nuttall), Owen (Witter Bynner), and Villiers (Willard
Johnson). In any case, without special information, readers would
never know whether the names for the family were real or fictitious.
But serious problems arise with changing the name Chapala to Sayula,
for his revision is incomplete: Lawrence clearly plans to develop the
work further in a direction toward the creation of a mythic realm,
since he says in many subsequent letters that the work is not finished.

A crucial issue thus arises in editing *Quetzalcoatl,* for with his
revision unfinished, Lawrence has left intact the actual place-names
for all the other villages around Lake Chapala, as in the opening of
chapter X:

On Saturday afternoons the big black canoes with their large square
sails came slowly approaching out of the thin haze across the lake, from
the west from Jocotepec with hats and pots, from Ocotlán and Jamay and
La Palma with mats and timber and charcoal and oranges, from Tuxcueco and Tizapán and San Luis with boat-loads of dark-green globes of
watermelons, and tomatoes, boat-loads of bricks and tiles, and then more
charcoal, more wood, from the wild dry hills across the lake.

In *The Plumed Serpent* (229) all but one of these names are fictional-
ized to read: Tlapaltepec, Ixtlahuacan, Jaramay, Las Yemas, Cux-
cueco, Tuliapán. San Luis is here changed to San Cristóbal, an actual
name. Further problems arise when on two occasions Kate looks
across the lake from Chapala to Tizapán, an actual place (changed to
Tuliapán in *PS*); or when in chapter XIII Kate makes her trip down the
lake with Cipriano to Jocotepec, an actual place (changed to Jaramay
in *PS*); then, on the return, Kate sees the place "where the white tower
of San Antonio rose from the trees in the near distance" (changed to
San Pablo in *PS*); and a little later in the trip back "they could see the
sprinkled white buildings of Chapala among the trees of the fore-
shore, and the two white towers of the church like candles, and the
small white boats laid up at the water's edge like a long row of white
pigs sleeping." The name Sayula thus forms an anomaly in the geo-
graphical context, and for this reason alone an editor might consider
keeping the name Chapala as it appears throughout Lawrence's original draft. But there is a much weightier reason for keeping to the name
Chapala.

The change to Sayula does not accord with the original impulse of
the draft written in Chapala, which remains close to the local scene
and shows the religion of Quetzalcoatl arising gradually from the
actual landscape and native life, accompanied by the native music of
guitars and violins (as several passages cited in the Introduction
demonstrate). The early version is thus a novel based upon Lawrence's
conception of "the spirit of place," as set forth in the first version of his
essay by that title in 1918. This essay, drastically revised, forms the
opening chapter in the American edition of his *Studies in Classic
American Literature* (1923), for which he was correcting proofs during his stay in Chapala. This conception of "place" was therefore very
close to the center of his mind as he was composing *Quetzalcoatl*. This
early version breathes the very spirit of place: the people and the
landscape express the emergence of the new consciousness that Law-

rence longed to feel arising in the New World. "For every great locality has its own pure daimon," says Lawrence in this essay, "and is conveyed at last into perfected life."

> Every great locality expresses itself perfectly, in its own flowers, its own birds and beasts, lastly its own men, with their perfected works. Mountains convey themselves in unutterable expressed perfection in the blue gentian flower and in the edelweiss flower, so soft, yet shaped like snow-crystals. The very strata of the earth come to a point of perfect, unutterable concentration in the inherent sapphires and emeralds. It is so with all worlds and all places of the world. We may take it as a law.

"So now," he concludes, "we wait for the fulfillment of the law in the west, the inception of a new era of living. . . . We wait for the miracle, for the new soft wind, . . . we can expect our iron ships to put forth vine and tendril and bunches of grapes, like the ship of Dionysos in full sail upon the ocean."[1]

This is also the ship that emerges in the final chapter of *Quetzal-coatl,* inseparable from the landscape. Since the spirit of an actual place, Chapala, inspires the novel, the authentic names of the locale have been retained.[2] The creation of the mythic realm of Sayula in *The Plumed Serpent* had to await realization for the full development of Lawrence's prophetic vision.[3]

NOTES

1. Lawrence, *The Symbolic Meaning: The Uncollected Versions of Studies in Classic American Literature,* ed. Armin Arnold (New York: The Viking Press, 1964), 30.

2. For consistency we have omitted the heading for chapter V and have changed to "Chapala" two occurrences of "Sayula" that appear in passages added by Lawrence in his partial revision. Lawrence provided titles only for the first seven chapters.

3. For a more detailed account of the textual problems and further comparisons between the early and final versions, see the essay in *D. H. Lawrence Review,* 22, (1990), 286–98.

GLOSSARY

acobardado: cowed, lacking courage

aguador: water-carrier

alameda: public walk, avenue

amueblada: furnished

arriero: mule-driver

azotea: flat roof

barca: small boat

bonita: pretty thing

bueno: good, excellent

calabacita: little squash or gourd

calzones: trousers

camion (properly *camión*): bus, in Mexican usage (Lawrence anglicises
   the word)

camote: sweet potato

campesino: peasant

canoe (properly *canoa,* as in *PS*): a large wooden sailing boat (Lawrence uses English spelling in *Q*)

cargador: porter, load-carrier

charales: tiny fish abundant in Lake Chapala

chica: small; affectionate term addressed to women: "dear little girl"

chiquita: diminutive of *chico, chica:* small

cosita: little thing (affectionate term)

cuna: foundling hospital

despedida: farewell

feo: ugly

florecita: little flower

fonda: inn

gringuito, gringuita: diminutive of *gringo;* a friendly term (Lawrence
   writes *gringito, gringita*)

guaraches: Mexican spelling of *huaraches;* leather sandals

hacienda: farm, ranch, large estate

hacendado: owner of a *hacienda* (usually referring to owner of a large
   estate)

lacas: lacquered wooden bowls (Lawrence writes *lacques*)

maguey: large cactus

mameyes: fruit of the mamey tree (Lawrence writes *mameas*)

mozo: male servant

muy: very, greatly

niña: literally, child, young girl; in Mexican usage, a term of respect
  for a superior or an employer

nopale: prickly pear

ollicitas: very small ceramic pots; apparently a local variant for *ollitas*
  (PS); (Lawrence writes *oyocitas*)

patrón: master, owner

patrona: owner, proprietress

pitahaya: fruit of a variety of cactus (Lawrence writes *pitayas*)

sarape: Mexican spelling of *serape:* a heavy shawl or small blanket

planta: plant (power plant in *Q*)

pronunciamiento: official pronouncement

pulque: fermented juice of the maguey (cactus)

pulquería: place where pulque is sold

rebozo: long narrow shawl (Lawrence usually writes *reboso*)

real: once an actual coin, but in the 20th century simply a term for
  one-eighth of a peso: twelve and a half centavos

sala: living room

sinverguenza: scoundrel

tepache: beverage made of pulque, water, pineapple, and cloves

zapote: fruit of the sapodilla tree

zócalo: public square, plaza

Readers will be puzzled by the one occurrence of the strange
word "glotzing" in chapter VIII. This is a Germanism, probably picked
up from Frieda; it means "staring," from German *glotzen,* "to gape or
stare."